FROM WEST, WITH REGRET

BRITTANY TAYLOR

Want to be notified of Brittany's upcoming releases?
Sign up for her newsletter here
https://www.brittanytaylorbooks.com/contact

DEDICATION

*To the ones who have every
reason to leave but choose to stay.
You are brave enough.
You are strong enough.*

CONTENT NOTE FROM AUTHOR

Hello dear reader!
I hope you enjoy this *spicy billionaire ex's brother* romance.
West and London's story is the second in the NYC Billionaire
Series. **Please be aware** this book is highly emotional and
contains scenes and topics which may be sensitive to some.
Topics include discussions of physical and emotional abuse,
descriptions of drug use, and attempted rape (described on
page).

I sincerely hope you enjoy reading West and London's journey!

Xoxo,
Brittany

ONE

LONDON

I was born with a broken heart, I'm certain of it.

Okay, maybe not a hundred percent certain. It's hard for someone like me to be sure of anything.

Fragments of my life come back to me in flashes. They don't make sense, and sometimes I try to capture them and shove them into a back corner of my brain to piece together later. My mind is full of tiny, little puzzle pieces waiting to be put together, waiting for me to connect the fractured parts of my life. If I spend too long forcing the pieces together, an overwhelming sense of suffocation smothers me. If I allow those thoughts to snowball, my entire body seizes, and the edges of my vision feather with darkness—a darkness that squeezes every bit of breath from my lungs. A darkness so ominous, I'm almost certain I'm dying.

That's all my life has ever been, shadowed by complete and utter emptiness. At least the first thirteen years. I may only be twenty-eight, but my life feels cut short, considering I only remember the last fifteen, as though I've been simply existing, only ever knowing half of myself the whole time.

So, like I said, I'm certain I was born with a broken heart.

I wish I could remember my birth parents. I wonder if they ever loved me at all. Were they born with broken hearts, too? If so, did the cracks of theirs widen the day they decided to give me up?

I quickly shove those thoughts aside, knowing there's no use asking questions I will never have the answers to.

Today, though, my heart doesn't feel quite as broken. More... numb.

I nervously click the end of the pen in my hand repeatedly as I tug on the large, wooden door into the bar only blocks away from the Hudson River, hoping the ceiling of dark-gray clouds hanging above don't decide to break before the funeral. The last thing I need is to show up looking like a swamp rat.

I have no idea how much longer the walk to the cemetery will be, but I'll take the gamble. Whether I'm late or show up dripping wet doesn't matter.

You can't start a funeral without the decedent's widow, right?

Widow.

That's what I am now.

I don't feel like a widow in my bones. I don't feel the expected immense sadness that comes with losing the love of your life. Because Heath *wasn't* the love of my life.

It's a secret I've kept buried deep in this broken heart of mine, along with any emotion I carry for losing him. Simply because I don't *have* emotions for him.

It's a horrific thing to say, coming from a wife who's lost her husband. It's a terrible notion for someone like me who has nothing to say about his death, but it's the truth.

Ever since the day I woke up in a hospital bed with nothing in my mind but those scattered puzzle pieces I can't keep in order, I've decided to live in my truth.

And the truth is death can set you free.

Is it horrible for me to not be heartbroken over my husband's death? Probably.

Society tells me I should be inconsolable, but I remember what it was like to be married to a man who had immense wealth and absolutely no soul.

Heath's funeral is being held in the center of a cemetery along the Hudson River, giving him a perfect view of the city for the rest of eternity... or as long as his body remains buried beneath the cold, dark earth. All it would take is another filthy-rich billionaire making an offer the city can't refuse and building another fucking skyscraper in its place.

Heath buried under a sixty-story building. Seems appropriate.

Up until the attorney read Heath's will to me the day after his death, I never knew my husband had held such adoration for the city he always pushed away. Not enough adoration to commit his body to it for the rest of eternity, anyway.

Finally, warm air wraps around me when I step inside the bar that feels as though I've fallen down a rabbit hole and into a dream world, so different from the bustling city on the other side of the large, wooden door I just walked through. The walls of the interior are painted a rich, dark forest green. Brass lights hang above each black-stained table. Soft piano music fills the air, as if it's purposely trying to lull you to sleep. It isn't until I slip into the first open barstool at the end of the counter that I realize I didn't even pay attention to what bar I was walking into. I just needed to escape the mounting pressure growing with every step I took closer to the cemetery. I survey the space, hoping to find the name of it displayed somewhere.

I glance down at the other side of the wooden bar top, where a small, black caddy holding cocktail straws and napkins rests on the edge, looking for anyone who works here, but there's no one. Aside from five people seated at two tables in the back of the dining area, and the middle-aged businessman sitting at the opposite end, downing his cocktail, the bar is empty. I tap my finger on the counter before leaning forward to steal a napkin from the caddy, then sit back down to stare at the words printed on the bottom: **The Veiled Door**

Clicking my pen, I scribble the first thing that comes to my mind.

Reasons I'll miss him:

My mind draws a blank as I tap the tip of my pen against the white paper, and ink bleeds into it. Needing a distraction, I flip the napkin over and start drawing the first thing that comes to mind in place of the lack of sorrow I have for Heath.

I've almost finished my drawing when emotion swells in my throat, though I know it isn't for Heath. It's for something else. Something I feel I've lost. Another puzzle piece to lock away for later.

I close my eyes and dig for any feeling I have toward losing my husband of six months, only to come up empty.

My shoulders drop with a sigh, and I open my eyes.

The man standing behind the bar catches my attention. He's at the end of it, in front of the swinging door that leads to the back. His black button-down shirt is rolled up his arms, revealing dozens of intricately drawn tattoos on his skin. The first few buttons of his shirt are undone, revealing the top of his sculpted chest. A thick beard covers his jaw, and his intense blue eyes flash in my direction.

Searing heat spreads across my face. I clear my throat and dart my eyes away from his unrelenting gaze.

I finish the last line across the bottom of my drawing and flip the napkin back over, forcing myself to think of one good thing to say about Heath.

Still nothing.

"Can I help you?"

I look up and find the man with blue eyes now standing in front of me. His long fingers grip the edge of the bar, the muscles beneath the inked skin of his arms straining against the sleeves of his shirt.

"Um." I tuck my bottom lip under my teeth, unsure if I should even bother grabbing a drink. I flash my eyes toward the front of the bar before swinging them back to the man. "No, I think I'm good."

"So," he says, glancing down at my napkin. "You come into a bar, draw all over my napkins, but you don't intend on ordering anything?"

I narrow my eyes. "Do you have a rule saying I need to buy something to sit here?"

His lips part as he scratches at his chin. "No, though I do believe it's an unwritten rule." The corner of his mouth lifts. "When customers come into a bar and sit down, they usually order at least one drink."

"Fine." I deadpan, hardening my gaze. "I'll order a beer."

I focus back to the napkin, pretending I know what I'm going to write in spot number one.

"What kind of beer?"

I look up at the man again with a huff. A knowing grin lifts his too perfect lips into a smile.

I slide my eyes toward the row of taps to my right. "One of those drafts." I try to resume my task.

"Which one?"

Snapping my head up to the bartender, I press my lips together, swallowing under the heat of his searing gaze. I smirk but make sure to give him a pointed stare. "You pick."

"Okay." He pushes off the bar and grabs a frosty glass from the cooler below him, then fills it to the top with one of the draft beers, never taking his attention away from me. His stare burns into my skin, and I'm suddenly unable to focus on what I'm trying to write.

My mind draws a blank again, but this time it's due to the bartender staring at me.

He grabs a fresh napkin and sets the beer on top of it.

My mouth pulls into a small, closed-lip smile. "Thank you."

He gives me a slight nod in response, then lowers his gaze toward my napkin.

"Having trouble?"

"Oh." I drop my shoulders and sit back against the stool, my mouth turning down into a frown. "It's nothing."

"Nothing?" His eyebrows shoot up, revealing more of his cerulean blue eyes. "Doesn't look like it's nothing to me."

"Why do you say that?" I cock my head to the side, intrigued.

"The way your eyebrows pulled together, and the way you tucked your lip under your teeth. The way you were tapping your pen against the counter." He clears his throat, as though suddenly aware of what he's saying. "You were looking at that napkin as if your life depended on it."

Damn. He noticed that much within a few seconds of meeting me?

"Well." I sit forward and rest my elbow on the lacquered bar top, pressing my hand to my forehead, looking up at him with hesitation, and I breathe a little easier staring into his eyes. I can't explain it, but I feel like I can share my secrets with him, and he won't judge me for them. Besides, I don't ever plan on coming back to this bar, so what harm can it do? "My husband's funeral is today."

He clamps his mouth shut as he swallows. After clearing his throat, he grips the edge of the bar again and frowns. "I'm sorry for your loss."

I nod and give him a tight smile, forcing my confession down. I want to tell him the truth. That he, a stranger behind the bar, is sorrier for my loss than I am.

"Thanks."

"What are you writing?" He points to my napkin.

I stare at the paper, running the tip of my black painted nail across the number 'one'. "I'm supposed to speak at the funeral and give a eulogy."

"Looks like you're making a list more than a eulogy."

I lift one shoulder. "I figured it would be easier this way. Short and straight to the point."

"Why?" he asks, curiosity piquing his interest. "I'm sure the family will give you plenty of time to say whatever you want about him and your life together. You were his wife."

I avoid his gaze, looking back toward the front of the bar. "I've actually never met his family. Today will be the first time."

"Oh. So, were you not together very long?"

I turn back to him. "Not even a year. We were married for six months, together for a few months before then. He just never seemed to talk about them, and when I would ask, he'd shut me down."

He nods, glancing toward the front window himself. My attention falls to the silver chain wrapped around his neck. Whatever is dangling from the end of it is concealed by his black, button-down shirt. I fight the urge to ask him about it, wondering why, in the back of my mind, the sight of the metal causes my stomach to flutter.

He keeps his focus on the front of the bar. "Well, I'm sorry your marriage was cut short."

"You don't have to keep telling me that." I look down into my lap and eye the enormous ring on my fourth finger.

"Telling you what?"

I lift my gaze, and now he's staring at me again. My cheeks flush. "That you're sorry for my loss. I'm not."

Fuck, I'm being *too* honest with this stranger.

He keeps his mouth closed, but I feel like he's cut me open and unearthed my deepest, darkest secrets. Like he already knows how I truly felt about Heath.

"I-I'm sorry," I stutter.

"You don't have to tell me that." The corner of his mouth lifts into an unnerving smirk.

A small chuckle climbs up my throat, and I blink. "I shouldn't have said that."

"Honesty reveals itself faster than fabrication. You were just being honest."

"I think I'm just nervous. I don't know why considering..." I trail off.

"Considering what?"

I smooth my hands down the front of my black dress. *My funeral dress.* A short sleeve wrap, with ruffles that hit mid-thigh. I've considered burning it after the ceremony is over. It's a beautiful dress, but it's hard to love anything Heath gave me.

The silk feels like butter under my fingers, and a shiver breaks across my bare shoulders.

I close my eyes and remember the way Heath spat in my face, angry when I'd worn my forest green dress to his company party instead of this one.

Suddenly, I'm regretting my decision to wear it. Or maybe, deep down, my subconscious wanted me to wear this dress to spite him.

"Are you okay?" the bartender asks.

Kind eyes. He has kind eyes.

"I am now."

He's right. Honesty does reveal itself faster than a lie.

He straightens his back and keeps his gaze trained on me

before cutting it away. He grabs a small towel and starts wiping down the counter. I watch his hand move across the smooth surface, how his corded muscles stretch and flex.

"Have you ever done something, then regretted it when it was too late?"

He abruptly stops cleaning. I expect him to look up at me, but he doesn't. He keeps his eyes trained on the glossy wood for ten long seconds before resuming his work. "No." He clears his throat.

"Oh." I look down in my lap and play with my wedding ring. I slip it up to my knuckle, then back to its place at the base of my finger.

"But I have regretted *not* doing something once it was too late," he adds.

I snap my head back up to look at him, and my throat is suddenly dry. The necklace he's wearing glints under the golden lights above. I swallow the heat rising in my throat, allowing my confession to pour out of me. "I regret marrying my husband. Heath."

The bartender stops cleaning completely, dropping his towel back down behind the counter. He glances around the bar. Maybe I'm making him uncomfortable, but I can't help it. I'm never going to see this man again, and I've kept my secrets locked in a box for far too long. Freedom is now mine, and I have no one holding me back from speaking my truth.

"He was a horrible person." My confession easily slips through my lips. "At first, he was sweet. Said all the right things, did all the right things. He claimed to understand me and my hesitancy when it came to relationships." I keep the details of my accident to myself, because exposing that part of my life seems a step too far with this stranger. "He earned my trust, but it was almost as if he became a different person once we were married."

The bartender's shoulders tense, and his eyes harden. "Did he hurt you?"

"Physically, sometimes. Emotionally and mentally, always," I say, heat blooming in my cheeks. "He was an asshole. He'd get angry over the littlest things. He was possessive in a way that made me want to scream. He was controlling, and I felt trapped in a marriage with a man who promised everything but gave me nothing. He did it in a way that wasn't obvious, too. First, it was him asking me to put aside my art to make sure I was already home when he stepped through the door. Then it was the bank accounts, making sure I'd only spend a certain amount each day. Then it was what I wore and when. He gloated about his wealth. It became the spearhead for every aspect of his life, and he never made an effort to include me in it. Which leads me to today." I thumb the corner of my napkin.

"Where you're making a list as a eulogy."

"Yeah," I sigh. "You probably think I'm a terrible wife for not feeling sorry my husband is gone."

"Out of everything you just confessed, you think that's where my mind went?"

I shrug. "Whether he was a good person or not, a man is dead."

"How you choose to live your life matters. Even in death," he argues.

I blow out a heavy breath. "I guess you're right."

I'm staring at my napkin and the blank spaces, my mind just as blank. I'm not only talking about my lack of great things to say about Heath, either. In general, my mind is blank. There are nothing but black holes of emptiness begging to be filled with color, begging to be remembered.

My phone dings inside my purse, and I tug it free.

There's a text from my sister, Selene. I send her a quick message back, telling her I'll let her know when the funeral is over. After I hit send, I read the time in the top corner of the screen.

"Shit." I hiss, sliding out of my stool. My black ankle boots land on the marble flooring with a heavy thud.

"Everything okay?" the bartender asks, his eyes wide.

I sling my purse over my shoulder. "I have to go. I'm going to be late." I turn on my heel and take a few steps before screeching to a halt, then spin around and march back over to my stool. The beer I ordered still sits untouched. I fish inside my purse for my wallet. "How much do I owe you for the drink?"

"Don't worry about it. It's on me."

My heart hammers in my chest when my eyes lock on to his.

Kind eyes. He has kind eyes.

"Are you sure? Won't your boss get upset with you giving away a drink?"

"My boss can handle it."

I relax. "Thank you." Despite my need to get going, I don't want to leave. It's a strange feeling. Like there's an invisible string keeping me tethered to this place.

"No problem," he says on a breath, so quiet I almost think I didn't hear him.

I give him a smile, and when he doesn't give me one back, I try not to let him see how it affects me. I don't have time to decipher his sudden change in expression.

I turn to leave, and when I push through the door, I'm met with pelting rain. Sheets pour down on me, and I look up, squinting at the sky. Of course it would fucking rain.

Tucking my now-wet hair behind my ear, I march down the street toward the next block, knowing the inevitable is coming.

I'm about to meet my husband's family.

TWO

WEST

She steals the air from my lungs and takes it with her the moment the door shuts behind her.

She stands on the sidewalk for a few seconds, looking up at the sky. Rain pelts her face as her mouth falls open and her eyes squeeze shut. She's absolutely stunning. Her raven hair is quickly drenched, and before I can gather my thoughts, she swipes her hand across her forehead and marches on, soon disappearing out of view. Then it truly does feel as if every ounce of oxygen is gone, the raven-haired girl taking it without regard.

"Wow, it really just came out of nowhere, didn't it?" my bartender Lewis says. He moves to stand beside me, but I'm paralyzed, still trying to fucking breathe.

From the corner of my eye, Lewis plants his hands on his hips and stares out the window, shaking his head in disapproval. "I hate the rain."

I don't bother mentioning the fact it's been cloudy all morning and rain was inevitable. I'm still speechless, wondering how the fuck I'm going to go the rest of the day acting as if I didn't just see *and* talk to her.

When I don't respond, Lewis moves to the beer taps and starts wiping them down. They don't need to be cleaned, but I can tell he's nervous. He's always nervous when I show up. They all are.

"I didn't think you were coming in today," he adds, polishing the gold piping of the taps.

"I come once a month to check on the place. You know this."

My mind is still tangled up in London. An inexplicable pull urges me to follow her. I let her go one too many times before, and now, here I am, allowing her to slip through my fingers again. But how can I go after her when she just dropped back into my life out of the fucking blue? How can I follow her when I've been reduced to nothing but being a complete stranger to her?

"Yeah," Lewis continues. "But it usually isn't until the end of the month. And, well, I heard about your brother, so I figured..."

This time, Lewis's comment pulls my attention away from where London last stood.

"You had some ideas about how to better market this location," I cut him off, switching subjects. "I'm here to listen to you."

"Really?" Lewis's eyes widen, and his jaw drops. He's young —in his mid-twenties, at least—but I love his eagerness to pitch ideas on how to better some of the properties I've bought, from bars to restaurants, on the verge of collapse. Places such as this one. I've put in the work to revamp this old speakeasy, but I know there's still room for improvement. Lewis was hired by the bar manager, Piper, a couple months ago, and the few times I've met him, he's offered up his opinions. Ones I'm open to.

I raise my eyebrows, silently telling him I'm all ears, but I know I'm not being completely honest. My mind is still reeling from my conversation with London.

Lewis is right: I wasn't meant to be here today, and I wouldn't have been if it weren't for my need for a distraction. A distraction from the endless calls from my mother. Or the debate I've had in my mind ever since I found out about my brother's untimely, suspicious death.

My need to come up with any excuse to not go to my own brother's funeral led me straight to London.

London and her gray eyes, black as night hair, and perfect, pouty lips that I haven't stopped thinking about since the last time I saw her. Lips I haven't stopped thinking about since the last time we spoke to each other.

Before everything changed.

I'm still thinking about that perfect mouth of hers and the glinting silver ball pierced into the center of her tongue. Something she definitely didn't have the last time we spoke.

Lewis scratches his chin and looks around the dining room. I almost forgot we were in the middle of a conversation.

He points to the tables and then the walls. "I think the overall cohesiveness of this place is scattered. A singular message would work better. Maybe some new artwork or furniture that blends seamlessly together."

I'm looking around the dining room, studying the tables and chairs before scanning the walls. Most of them are blank, but the few pictures that are hanging are old photographs of the city. They're beautiful and artistic in a way, though I can see how they could be improved.

"You may have a point," I tell him. "I'll start thinking about it and let you know. Maybe we can talk about it in more detail another day."

"Wow." He gapes, practically bouncing on his feet as he takes a step back down the bar. "Thank you so much. I'm not an expert in design, and I can't draw for shit, but I'm studying advertising in grad school right now, so I can bring a vision to life. Charcoal sketches would be great in here. The contrast of the classic colors up against the rough black and white would bring warmth and comfort to a place like this."

I pause, digesting Lewis's suggestions. I don't disagree.

"Thank you, Lewis. And thank you for taking inventory of the bottles in the storage room for me before I head out."

"No problem." He nods. "I'm sorry you had to cover the bar. Anna was scheduled to come in an hour after me. I know you probably have a million other important things you could be doing."

"It's fine." I wave him off, biting back the sting of his assumption that I'm just another corporate douchebag too busy to pay attention to those who work for me on every level, even those in Lewis's position. "There's a reason I own bars across the city. I like serving customers, and I like getting away from the sterile environment of corporate America. It's important for me to keep life balanced."

I wasn't always this way. I didn't always have privilege and wealth, but no one in my life knows my past.

That reality hits me in the fucking stomach like a fucking wrecking ball.

A heavy weight bears down on my shoulders, and I can't explain the immense sadness and regret washing over me. I've lived a lifetime of regret for a series of decisions I've never been able to correct.

People often say they wish they could go back in time and change one thing. They believe a singular moment would have changed everything. But me? I have endless. A series of missed opportunities to regain what I've lost. The one person I promised I would never forget. But somehow, I was the one who ended up being forgotten.

I fight the urge to bend over and vomit all over the rubber

mat lining the floor. I clear my throat and run my fingers through my beard, needing to get out of here.

My driver Alden is still sitting at the end of the bar, sipping on his club soda with a slice of lime. He's been the only person there for the past hour.

Sensing my attention has shifted to him, he drops his glass on the bar top. "Are you ready to leave, sir?"

I open my mouth to answer him, but turn to my left when Lewis points to London's untouched beer.

"Is this someone's drink?" he asks. "I haven't seen anyone sit here." He grabs the glass and reaches for the napkin resting beside it.

Too quickly, I close the distance between us, and snatch the napkin from the bar top before Lewis has the chance to toss it in the trash.

I hadn't realized London left it.

I glance up at Lewis's worried expression. "They left. You can toss the beer."

He pours the beer into the sink while my gaze drops to the napkin in my hands.

There are a list of five numbers meant for London's dead husband.

A blank list with nothing but the name of my bar beneath it.

The napkin shakes in my nervous hands. I flip it over, and this time, I'm certain I can't breathe.

Sketched in black pen is a pointed clock tower beside a river. The distinctive hands on the face of the clock and the detailed architecture are unmistakable.

Big Ben.

Blood drains from my face.

"Sir?" Alden says behind me. "Are you alright?"

"He's as pale as a ghost. I've never seen him like this." Lewis says. "Are you okay, Mr. Knight?"

Swallowing the lump in my throat, I fold the napkin gently in half and shove it in my pocket. I begin to unroll my sleeves and walk around the bar, toward the exit, only to stop near the door and turn to face Alden as I'm buttoning my cuffs.

The shrill sound of the wooden barstool against the floor fills the silence when he stands quickly. "Are you ready to head over to your next bar?"

He's already closing the gap between us, ready to follow.

"Change of plans." I swallow thickly, knowing that, despite how I feel about today, I won't risk losing her again. Not when I've been given this chance.

London's drawing burns a hole in my pocket.

I button the top three buttons of my shirt, ensuring my necklace is tucked safely beneath it.

"Where to, Mr. Knight?" Alden lifts his chin, waiting for my direction.

I close the last button of my shirt and swipe my jacket from the back of the barstool. "My brother's funeral."

THREE

LONDON

The rain stops the second I step beside my husband's casket.

An entirely too large bouquet of black, purple, and white roses rests on the top of the lacquered walnut. The scent of rain mingles with the polyurethane, as though the funeral home insisted on adding another layer of protection to preserve my husband's body before lowering it into the ground.

My dress clings to my damp skin, and I cross my arms over my chest, afraid my peaked nipples will be noticed beneath the delicate fabric of my dress. My mother-in-law stands on the other side of Heath's casket, unable to take her eyes off her son's final resting place. She reaches under the toile shielding her face and dabs at the tears spilling through her lashes with her black handkerchief. When she briefly glances up at me, I squeeze my arms around myself, worrying she'll somehow be able to see my nipples through my dress. I may as well be naked as she sizes me up.

Does she know this was her son's favorite dress? Does she know he relentlessly begged me to wear it?

My mother-in-law and I haven't formally met before, only ever speaking over the phone, but I know she recognizes me, since Heath sent her pictures from our wedding day. Or so he told me.

The corners of her mouth twitch in acknowledgement before she moves on and settles in her seat in the first row.

I take a deep breath and do the same.

After sitting in the white, fold-out chair beside Glenna Hall, I hold my breath and keep my focus on the lone lectern placed in front of Heath's newly dug grave.

The seat is dry—they must have wiped them down as we were paying our respects to Heath—and my still-wet dress sticks to the plastic, pulling it farther up the back of my thigh when I shift in place.

"I'm sorry, Wyatt," Glenna says to the man moving to sit in the seat on the other side of her. "This seat is reserved for my other son. He should be here any minute. Seems he's running a little behind today."

"Oh." Wyatt frowns. "Of course." He glances between us before settling back on Glenna. "I'm sorry for your family's loss."

"Thank you. I appreciate that." She grabs his hand with her gloved one. "At least he's with his father now." Glenna nods to the elaborate headstone several feet away from where Heath is being buried.

I hadn't realized Heath's father was buried here as well. It must be why he requested to be here. To be with his father.

"Richard Hall was an exceptional man," Wyatt says to Glenna. "You and he contributed so much to this city. You've raised a wonderful family."

"Thank you, Wyatt." Glenna pats the corner of her eye and inhales deeply. "It's just the two of us now."

I chew on the inside of my cheek, knowing Glenna isn't talking about me. She doesn't consider me family anymore. How could she when she's never met me until today?

Glenna squeezes Wyatt's hand before letting it go. He leaves us, taking a seat in the row behind instead.

I force myself to keep my gaze trained on my husband's casket but can't help focusing on the opposite side of Glenna, to the empty seat. I didn't even know Heath had a brother.

"Heath would have hated that it rained today." Glenna leans into me, whispering. I turn my head and catch her sad eyes looking up at me. "He always loved it when the sun was shining."

Her lips are perfectly painted a deep shade of burgundy, her makeup flawless. The crow's feet at the corners of her blue eyes are barely noticeable, even if it weren't for the mesh fabric shielding her face. It's obvious she's had several sessions of Botox, at least, but she's still beautiful.

I give her a small smile, pretending to agree. I don't know what type of weather Heath preferred, much less whether he enjoyed the sunlight. We never discussed those types of things. But the grief and kindness is Glenna's expression makes me keep those thoughts to myself.

My mind wanders back to the bartender at The Veiled Door. My truths rest on the tip of my tongue, begging to be set free. I swallow them down. The bartender was right. The truth is easier to tell than a lie.

"He'll still get this beautiful view, though," I whisper back, nodding toward the river. It's the only bit of honesty I can offer.

It is a beautiful view. The still, heavy gray clouds float above the New York skyline. The chaotic sounds of the city seem so far away, even though we're just on the other side of the river. It's amazing how isolating it can appear from the outside. But it's a dream to be here for so many.

"He loved you, you know," Glenna whispers again.

I open my mouth and breathe in, her words hitting me. At one point, I did love Heath. I may not be broken hearted over his death now, but I don't believe it would have always been this way. I think back to when I married him and know what I felt for him at the time was love. But after the honeymoon period, my love for him quickly unraveled. Now, here I am.

The only sadness I feel is for Glenna—a mother who has lost her son.

"I'm sorry we didn't get to meet until today," I tell her.

"Oh, sweetheart." She waves me off and pats my knee, touching the silk fabric still clinging to my skin. "What's important is that you're here now."

I eye the empty lectern. "I just didn't want you thinking I didn't want to meet you. I asked Heath, but he never—"

"It's all right, London," she interrupts me, pinning her eyes on mine. "I'm sure Heath had his reasons. It's nothing to worry about now."

I swallow the lump in my throat and blink back at her comment. Her stare burns a hole in my ungrieving chest.

"Welcome, family and friends." The priest walks up to the lectern, finally taking the space behind it. He's dressed in a black robe with a deep purple sash draped over his shoulders. I didn't even know the Hall family was catholic.

"We're here to mourn and remember a life cut regrettably and tragically too short," the priest continues. "The life of Heath Preston Hall. A beloved son, brother, and husband." The priest scans the front row before landing on me.

"Before the ceremony continues, Heath wished for his wife to say a few words about him before the rest of his family." The priest lifts his arm and holds it out to me. "Mrs. Hall, please."

Feeling everyone's eyes on me, my cheeks heat against the sticky air. It clings to my damp skin, intensifying with every passing second. I swallow the lump that hasn't stopped swelling in my throat and run my hands down the front of my thighs. I can't tell if the moisture on my palms is from my dress or my nerves.

I clear my throat as Glenna lifts her hand and grabs onto my arm to give it a gentle squeeze of encouragement. I wish my sister was able to come. Her support would be more welcome than the one I'm receiving from the mother-in-law I haven't met until thirty minutes ago.

"Go on, sweetheart," she urges.

I nod and breathe through my nose, leaving my purse in my seat. When I stand, I adjust my dress, peeling it away from the backs of my thighs, and carefully walk up to the podium. My boots squelch into the soft, wet ground. The priest steps off to the side, and it isn't until I'm standing directly in front of the microphone that I realize how many people are at Heath's funeral. The crowd stretches far back past the ten rows of seating. When I first stepped up to Heath's casket to pay my respects, there were only a fraction of the people here now.

My gut twists, and I look down at the wood edge of the lectern. There's nothing but a Bible sitting there.

"Fuck," I mutter under my breath. I never wrote a speech. I couldn't even write five things I would miss about my husband. My mind drew a blank then, and it's drawing a blank now. I twist my fingers in front of me—twist them until my skin burns. Tears prick the corners of my eyes before I look down to Heath lying in front of me. To the lacquered coffin and mountain of black, purple, and white roses.

"Um." I clear my throat and speak into the microphone. "Heath was..."

I'm searching for the words while I search the crowd. A sea of strangers. Just like I was in Heath's world. A stranger. An outsider. Heath never let me in, yet somehow, he wanted me to speak first at his funeral. Perhaps he did this on purpose. He wants me to scramble to find the words to speak when it matters most. He's probably getting off on this from wherever he is, watching me sweat and squirm in public.

Blackness permeates the corners of my vision. I feel myself sifting through the puzzle pieces again, lost in the darkness of an unknown sea. I'm kicking and clawing to find a way out.

My attention comes to a stop at Glenna. She's staring at me blankly, but her wringing hands are unmistakable. She switches her crossed ankles before she shifts uncomfortably in her seat.

I clear my throat again and tuck my frizzy hair behind my ear. I run my fingers across the side of my face and lick my lips. "Heath was, um…"

Glenna's eyes slowly widen, her own panic taking over.

I think of the first time I met Heath, outside the bank in Boston, when I'd tripped on the curb. The black car barreling toward me as I laid on all fours, frozen on the asphalt. His arms wrapped around me, pulling me back.

He saved me.

I told him it wasn't the first time I'd been in an accident and then he played me, molding me into the wife he wanted me to become.

He took advantage of me.

"Heath was a good man," I whisper into the microphone. The lie tastes like bitter, sharp acid.

All eyes are glued to me, and they have no idea. They have no idea how many countless personalities Heath possessed and his ability to turn them on a dime.

I fell victim to the love he offered.

Glenna's eyes are now as wide as they will go. I can't tell from where I'm standing, but I'm certain her crow's feet will have completely disappeared.

My neck prickles with anxiety, and this time, I feel the tears coming. My boots are sinking into the ground, attempting to bury me right alongside Heath.

Panic starts to take over, when a pair of shiny, black shoes catch my attention.

I follow them as they move across the front row and stop beside Glenna. They glisten on the rain-soaked, manicured lawn, and my eyes move up the long legs of the man wearing them, taking in his black suit, before I'm staring back at a pair of familiar blue eyes.

Kind blue eyes.

A sharp jaw hidden by a well-kept beard.

Dark, slicked-back hair, revealing those eyes that warm me in places that have lied dormant for months.

His stare stops the ground from swallowing me whole.

The man beside my mother-in-law is the bartender I met at The Veiled Door.

Then it all clicks.

He's sitting beside Glenna. He's Heath's brother.

He must be. Right? Why else would he be sitting beside Glenna? She hasn't told him to leave like she did with Wyatt.

Memories of my conversation with the green-eyed stranger come flooding back to me like a torrential storm raging against the shore. The air is sucked from my lungs, and I grip the edge of the lectern to stop myself from fainting. The Bible in front of me begins to blur, the gold-etched lettering melding together.

The one time I was honest about Heath, the one time I told the truth about my husband, I said it to his brother.

My attention falls back to Heath's grave. Our secrets will no longer be buried with him. They're out in the open, living in the mind of his brother.

Fuck.

My nails cut into the wood, and my eyes roam over the crowd before finding Heath's brother again. With a watery gaze, I inhale a shaky, unsteady breath. The same erratic beat of my heart returns.

His dark eyebrows pinch together, and a look of concern washes over his gorgeous face. With his hand resting on his thigh, he closes his fist, tightening his fingers as if he's holding himself back. Back from what, I don't know.

But the worry etched in his expression is unmistakable. My stomach warms at the sight of him, mingling with the humiliation I feel. He's too familiar, but I know I've never met him before. The puzzle pieces are scattered even farther apart now, and the walls close in on me.

I'm suffocating. Again.

"I'm..." I'm certain I'm going to die right here beside Heath. And what a fucking shame that would be.

I shift to find Glenna staring at me. Her lips have disappeared as she presses her mouth firmly shut. A look of disapproval shielded by the mesh fabric draping over the front of her black hat.

"I'm sorry," I quickly whisper into the microphone, stifling my sob by covering my mouth before I leave the lectern as fast as my feet will carry me.

I swipe my purse from my empty chair, unable to look Glenna in the eye.

Then I run for the hills.

I let my feet carry me as fast as they can, considering the terrain. My boots land across a landmine of puddles and mud, the liquid splashing up past my ankles. Dots of water and mud spatter onto my bare legs, but I push through, putting as much distance between the funeral and me as possible.

I've nearly made it to the road winding through the cemetery when a hand latches onto my arm, pulling me to a stop.

"Hey," he softly says. "Wait, wait, wait."

I spin around, finding his blue eyes staring back at me. "I can't do this. I'm sorry." I shiver at his touch, the pulse of electricity shooting straight for my heart. "I need to go."

He frowns, his eyes soft. "You don't have to leave," he says, breathless from catching up to me.

"You said it yourself. The truth is easier than the lies. I can't stand up there and lie to hundreds of people."

He hasn't let go of my arm as he allows the silence to descend around us. I want to tell him all the reasons I shouldn't have come, but he already knows the truth. I want to tell him more. I want to tell him that the other reason I can't stay has nothing to do with my blank eulogy and everything to do with this feeling. The one taking over every nerve and muscle in my body.

Instead, the words lodge in my throat and my tears fall for a loss felt deep in my bones. One I can't place, but know it definitely has nothing to do with Heath.

"Don't leave," he pleads quietly on a heavy breath.

I sniff and stare into his eyes. "Was Heath your brother?"

His lack of response is enough for me to have my answer.

My body slumps, and he finally loosens his grip enough for me to back away, only for him to take a step closer.

"He was," I whisper for him, wiping the tears away from my face and nodding. "Heath never mentioned you."

"We—"

"And I told you everything," I cut in, clamping my hand over my mouth, cursing myself for opening up to him. I shake my head, tears welling in my eyes. "Oh, God." I lower my hand and press it to my chest. "I told you all those horrible things about him, and you're his *brother*."

"Yes." He grits his teeth. "And yes, I am his brother, but I think we've already established that."

I soften my gaze. As with Glenna, I feel sorry for his loss, not mine. "I'm sorry. I shouldn't have said those things to you. I don't know what I was thinking."

"You were being honest and spilling your secrets to a stranger you thought you'd never see again."

"Yeah." I scoff. "But now I've broken your mom's heart and humiliated your family in front of everyone."

"They will be fine, and so will my mother."

My mind doesn't have enough room in it to search for the deeper meaning to that statement, though. "I really shouldn't be here. I'm not family anymore, and I've hurt too many people trying to do the right thing. I thought it was what I needed to do, but I was wrong. This was a mistake."

I need to get out of here.

Then reality hits. I don't have a car, and I have no clue where I'm heading. Maybe I can head back toward the city, toward the direction of The Veiled Door, and ask Selene to pick me up somewhere down that street.

"That isn't why you're leaving," he says, his gaze falling to my mouth. He takes another step closer, and his scent surrounds me. Fresh rain and pine. I breathe him in when he steps closer, bringing his face inches in front of mine.

My attention falls to the chain around his neck once more. Whatever dangles at the end of it is still shielded by his buttoned black shirt, making it even more concealed than at the bar.

But he's right. I'm not leaving because of my failed eulogy.

I'm leaving because of him.

"I shouldn't be here." I back away. "I'm sorry for your and your family's loss."

"Wait." His hand flies to my arm again. This time, he starts at my bicep before slowly lowering his hand down the length of my arm, leaving a burning trail in its wake. His fingers feather against my skin before he rests them on my hand, which they delicately hold onto before he drops it and fishes in his pocket, pulling out a small, folded, white napkin. He unfolds it, then grabs my hands, turning it over. He lays the napkin in my palm, and suddenly I'm staring at the drawing I made earlier. A drawing of the same image that comes to mind every single day.

The tears I was shedding earlier had subsided only for a moment, but now they're back.

"Did you draw this?" he asks, his hand resting under mine holding the napkin.

"I did." I blink the tears away and look up at him. "But it's nothing."

"*Why* did you draw it?"

I shake my head. "I don't know. I can't explain it." Confused, I shake my head again and wipe at the tear sliding down my cheek. I look back down at the drawing of a clock tower. "I don't know why. Half of my life is covered in darkness. I don't even know if this has to do with it or not. It probably doesn't, but for some reason, when I close my eyes, it's the first thing I see."

"You see a clock tower? Big Ben?"

I shrug, uncertain where our conversation is going. "I think that's what it is, but it isn't necessarily the clock itself. I don't know, it's fuzzy. The image of the clock is fuzzy every time." I drop my shoulders. "Doesn't matter anyway. You probably think I'm crazy and not making any sense."

"I don't think that." He closes his mouth and looks down at the napkin. "You're very talented. Are you an artist?" He lifts his gaze again, and my heart stops.

"I am." My body hums with his touch and his breath and his voice. "But I'm not the best with pen. I usually go for charcoal or paint."

"I want to hire you."

My eyes shoot open, and my lips part. "What do you mean you want to hire me?"

"I don't know if you're still living in Boston or what your

plans were, but I need an artist to design pieces for my one of my bars."

"*One* of your bars?"

"Yeah, I own The Veiled Door."

"You own The Veiled Door?" I gape. Wow, this day just keeps getting better and better.

He nods, a small smile playing on his lips. "Yeah, and a few others scattered around the region."

"How many others?"

He scrunches his nose. "A few."

"How many is a few?"

"Twenty."

"*Twenty?*" I raise my eyebrows. "Twenty isn't a few."

"Technically, it was only a few until this past year."

I'm suddenly noticing everything about him. The white, gold-plated rings on two of his fingers. The silver chains on one wrist, and the chrome watch on his other. The silken fabric of his suit jacket. Fuck, he even smells of money. Despite these small details, though, there's still that warmth I felt radiating off him when we first met.

He didn't flaunt his wealth, never revealing his hand from behind that bar.

"You want to hire me based on a mindless drawing I did on one of your napkins?" I ask, shifting back to the original topic of conversation.

"Yes." He doesn't offer any further explanation.

I eye him skeptically, but the feelings stirring inside me are impossible to ignore.

His hand is still cradling mine, warming me in the most dormant of places deep inside me. The oddly comforting sound of his voice. His scent surrounding me. The familiarity of his touch even though we've never touched before.

This feeling is dangerous. A feeling I want to run away from yet stay rooted to. Right here where we're standing, with my hand in his.

I look past his shoulder to the funeral behind him. The ceremony has continued without either of us. No one cares that I left. Not even Glenna.

I slide my hand out from his and pass the napkin back to him. He takes it, worry etched in his expression.

"I don't think that's a good idea," I tell him.

"Why? Because I was technically your brother-in-law?"

"Yes," I choke out. "No." I shake my head and blink. "Maybe. I don't know." I inhale another shaky breath. "And technically, you're still my brother-in-law. My world is just kind of foggy and uncertain right now. I'm sorry. I really should go. I think I've been too honest for one day."

"Wait," he says quickly, digging into the inside pocket of his suit jacket. He pulls out a pen, grabs my arm again and presses the tip to my skin, at the midpoint between my wrist and elbow.

"This is my phone number," he says, flashing his hooded eyes up to mine as he stains my skin with the black ink before he looks back down to focus on my arm. His warm thumb presses into my flesh, and I can't stop staring at the point where we're connected. Like the ink of his pen isn't the only thing marking me, branding me.

When he's finished, he returns the pen to his pocket and keeps his gaze on my arm before looking back up. "Think about my offer. And when you make your decision, you'll know how to find me."

I briefly glance down at the numbers etched into my skin as he drags his thumb gently over them.

My mouth tugs into a small smile. "I could have just gone to The Veiled Door if I wanted. I know where to find you."

"I'm not always there. This way, you can reach me any time."

"Okay." I look down at my arm, my skin still searing from his touch.

I expect to find only the numbers inked into my flesh, but my gaze zeroes in on the name written above it.

West.

This stranger's name is West.

"Despite the reason we're both here, and what I said about Heath to you"—I clear my throat—"it was nice meeting you, West."

His smile wanes under the midday sun peeking through the clouds. "It was nice meeting you, too," he offers back.

"London," I say, pressing my hand to my chest, more to calm my beating heart than anything else. "My name is London. In case Heath didn't tell you."

"No, right." He blinks. "London."

The tweets of the birds nesting in the trees drown out our silence. Pressure builds in my chest like a taut thread, ready to snap. Unease settles in my gut, ready to snap the thread, and without another word, I spin on my heel and allow my feet to carry me out of the cemetery and away from the funeral. Away from West and the family I no longer consider mine. Not sure I ever truly did consider them mine at all.

Once I reach the outskirts of the cemetery, I tug my phone from my purse, desperate to call my sister. But even as I dial her number, I can't help thinking about West and how him leaving his name on the inside of my arm felt like more than just him giving me his phone number. It felt like he was marking me somehow.

For some reason, that thought brings a torrent of butterflies to my stomach, too.

One I welcome this time.

FOUR

WEST

She had the same glint in her eyes and the same dimples in her cheeks as she had the last time I'd seen her at thirteen years old.

The day I swore an oath that I failed to uphold.

The sun has finally peeked through the ceiling of gray clouds that have shadowed the city all morning. My feet are rooted to the ground where I watched London walk away. I haven't moved, replaying every second of every moment with her.

The same sense of dread I had watching her leave my bar earlier is no longer there. At least this time when I watched her walk away, I knew she had a way to reach me.

She also knows my name.

A name she clearly doesn't remember, not even when she repeated in out loud.

"What the fuck was that all about?"

Spinning around to the sound of her scolding voice, I find my mother stalking toward me. I roll my eyes and stuff my hands in my pockets, curling my fingers if only to give myself a distraction from the onslaught of a lecture Glenna Hall is sure to bring.

She lifts the veil covering her face, revealing her beauty underneath… and the scowl on her face. Fisting her black dress, she holds it above the ground, watching to make sure she isn't stepping into any of the deep puddles. Her bodyguard-assistant-secret lover walks several feet behind her. Henry was hired by my father nearly thirty years ago, and over time his job titles have shifted. First, he was my parents' bodyguard before I came along. Then, after my father's death, he quickly shifted to serving my mother's every need, even romantically. A fact she hasn't admitted out loud yet, but one I've gathered after observing them together over the past two years since my father's death.

"Answer me, Weston Knight," she demands, stomping toward me, using my full name to make an even sharper point. Her shoulders fall when she looks over mine in the direction London disappeared. "What was that all about?"

"Which part are you referring to, Mother?" I ask.

"All of it." She crosses her arms over her chest. "And you know I hate when you call me *Mother*."

I pinch the bridge of my nose and blow out a heavy breath. Patience. I need to give her more patience. "I'm sorry, Mom."

"That was your brother's wife, you know." She purses her lips as I lower my hand. "I never understood your brother's need to keep her a secret, and I felt sympathy for her. Remember how I told you his wife experienced an accident that caused her to suffer amnesia? Can you imagine forgetting half of your life? From what Heath said, it happened the day of her fourteenth birthday. A tragedy, honestly." My mother frowns.

I swallow the bile rising in my throat and clamp my mouth shut. I can't look her in the eye. Dragging the toe of my shoe through the mud, I flex my fingers and nod.

"Well," she continues, "I *felt* sorry for her, especially when I learned Heath had saved her from another incident when they first met that could have ended up with the same outcome or worse." She shakes her head in disapproval, then points behind her, toward Heath's resting place. "But that was unforgivable what she did back there."

"Give her a break. Her husband just died," I try to reason, but the admission sours my tongue. I don't need reminding that London married Heath. Even if I know the truth about their marriage and how he treated her behind closed doors.

"Right," my mother snaps. "So, would it have been difficult for her to say a few kind words about him? Anything? This family has welcomed her with open arms."

I frown. "I don't necessarily agree with that."

"What is that supposed to mean?" Glenna Hall has now transitioned into defense mode.

"You never even met London until today. Heath didn't invite anyone to his wedding. He never announced he was getting married. He kept her a secret from everyone," I say, despite knowing it won't be of any use. Glenna Hall will forever have a soft spot for her first born. "Heath didn't even give you the chance to open your arms to her."

"I'm sure he had his reasons for the choices he made."

I roll my eyes, and I can't help laughing cynically. "Heath didn't have reasons for shit. He was simply a dick, mother."

Fuck, I was right. Honesty is easier than falsehoods.

Tears well in my mother's eyes. My heart pinches with regret at what I've said. But she's delusional if she thinks she and Heath welcomed London into this family with open arms.

We both stand frozen in place, the weight of our conversation settling in the dewy air between us. When I see the pain in my mother's eyes, I know I've wounded her deeply. Guilt rests in my bones. I never intended to hurt her, especially on a day like today. But I guess the old saying still stands. The truth hurts.

Finally moving from her spot, she narrows the gap between us, still fisting her black dress. Disdain consumes her heated gaze, her ire aimed directly at me.

"Honestly, I wasn't certain you'd show up today, but since you did, you could have at least tried to show up on time," she practically hisses, as though one of the funeral goers from hundreds of feet away will overhear our conversation. "He is your brother, for God's sake, West. Whether you like it or not."

I purse my lips and shake my head, anger overtaking me. I can feel the veins in my neck bulging and stretching. My throat tightens as the oxygen burns its way through my lungs. I stare her directly in the eye. "He isn't my brother. He never was."

A tear spills over her lashes, dropping to the ground. She sizes me up, sneering in disgust as she takes me in. Her top lip curls, a look of revulsion washing over her whole expression. She clicks her tongue against the back of her teeth and narrows her gaze. "Well, I hope when the time comes for my funeral, you'll at least have the decency to show up on time." She takes a step back and begins to walk away. Keeping her pace, she glances over her shoulder quickly when she adds, "And maybe then you'll finally have shaved that fucking beard."

My nails slice into the palms of my clenched fists in my pockets, and I watch her rejoin the funeral.

Goddammit.

I remove one of my hands and run my fingers across my mouth.

Why can't I just shut my mouth for two fucking minutes?

Even if I hated my brother, a brother I'd only known for only a few short years, I hate talking bad about him to my mother. I've tried to keep my mouth shut over the years, but today I seem to be failing miserably.

Glenna Hall doesn't know the truth that, from the first day she adopted me, Heath despised me. He hated every fiber of my being. He saw me as a threat. Someone who would one day replace his coveted position and rank in the family.

Over time, our hatred became mutual, driving a wedge between a family who had once seemed perfect without me.

Now, when I think on it, maybe there's truth to why Heath felt threatened by me. I'm the only son left in the Hall family. Well, legally and on paper, but not in name.

Memories of half a dozen different foster homes, and the last one that nearly broke me, come barreling into my chest at full force, practically knocking me off my feet. I may have kept my birth father's last name, but it's the only evidence I have left of my old life.

I don't have London. I don't even have her memory.

The truth is, I lost her before the day she lost everything.

Part of me is thankful she doesn't remember, but it's difficult to reconcile the feeling when her memories of me have become collateral damage to everything else.

She's forgotten the pain.

But she's also forgotten me.

I close my eyes and try to breathe, forcing myself to think of only the good. The beauty in the darkness. It's difficult to shove down the scent of wet dirt, the feeling of it grating against my skin as I cradled London's face in my hands while she sobbed, gasping for breath, and willing the pain to go away. It's difficult to forget how my promise to her fell effortlessly from my mouth, swearing I would protect her at all costs.

Every day I live with the memory of the look in her soft, red-lined eyes as tears streaked her face, clinging onto my promise with every tight breath she brought in, believing every word I said.

Regret has owned me since failing to follow through on the one promise I made to her on the last day I ever saw that glint in her eye.

I'd sworn an oath to find her again, and now I have. I take one last look at my brother's casket in the distance as they begin lowering it into the ground, before I walk toward Alden, who is waiting at my car.

Once I slip into the back seat, I know there's no chance in hell I'm turning my back on the past.

Because my past is London, and fuck, I hope I don't lose her all over again.

FIVE

LONDON

I collapse in the middle of the floor, landing on my back with my hands over my stomach. The ceiling fan blades spin in a hypnotizing rhythm as I struggle to catch my breath.

Selene falls in a heap beside me, scooting closer until her arm is pressed against mine.

My entire body aches. My calves pulsate and my thighs burn. Not to mention my skin is covered in a thick layer of sweat, making the ends of my ponytail cling to my bare shoulder.

"I could have sworn you said spin class would help me clear my mind, but I'm beginning to think you may have invited me just to torture me." I roll my head against the hardwood, facing my sister, and crack a small smile.

Selene turns to look at me, giggling, and the sun catches her gorgeous eyes, sparkling with a happiness I don't see on her enough.

"You're my sister, London. I didn't bring you to torture you. I genuinely thought it would help clear your mind. It always does for me." She brushes her unruly blonde hair from her forehead and looks back up at the ceiling. A few stray pieces of her bangs stick to her forehead. Her face is makeup free, and her hair is in its natural state—a sight rarely seen when it comes to my sister.

"I guess after what happened at the funeral, I needed it." I sigh.

It's been one week since I walked away from my husband for the last time, but all I can think about is his brother West. I haven't been able to stop this unshakeable feeling I had that entire morning like I've met him before.

My lower stomach fluttered when he'd marked my arm with his name and phone number. I rest my hand on my stomach and think about the faded ink now. The intensity in the agonizing seconds as he scribbled on my skin a mere ghost of a memory now. Thankfully, I wrote his number down on one of Selene's notepads before it completely disappeared.

Fuck, what is wrong with me?

He's my dead husband's brother, and I only talked to him for a grand total of thirty minutes.

"I still can't believe what happened." Selene rolls onto her side, facing me fully as she rests her head in her hand after propping herself up on her elbow.

"What?"

"With Heath," she says in a hushed tone. "The way his helicopter suddenly went down like that. Did they even find out what happened?"

I close my eyes. I honestly haven't put much thought into the circumstances surrounding Heath's death. "Something about a mechanical failure."

"I feel sorry for the pilot in the helicopter with him. Must have been a shock to their family as well."

"Yeah," I agree, rolling back to face the ceiling. "I never met him, but I know him and Heath were fairly close."

A knot twists in my chest, remembering the last thing Heath

said to me before he walked out the door, on his way up to the roof, where his helicopter was waiting for him. I was on all fours, watching the blood spill from the palm of my hand as I tried to clean up the broken pieces of the ceramic dinner plate he'd smashed against the wall seconds earlier, narrowly missing my head.

"I wish I could have gone to the funeral with you." She confesses, her voice cracking. "At least you wouldn't have had to face Heath's family on your own."

"I know." I frown. "Glenna was insistent on it only being immediate family. Well, her definition of immediate family anyway."

Damn. The Hall family is confusing to say the least.

"Yeah." Selene allows her voice to drift off, accepting my explanation with reluctant acceptance.

I shift my gaze to the windows lining the front of my sister's small studio apartment. It's a modest home not far from Manhattan. The paint is peeling, and the toilet in her closet-sized bathroom doesn't flush properly half the time, but I know this place is just a steppingstone for Selene. It isn't her forever home but a means to an end when it comes to her dream.

"How's the book coming?" I ask, forcing the memory of my marriage out of my head.

"It's going," she says flatly.

"Doesn't sound like it from the tone of your voice. Usually, you're giddy when talking about it."

She frowns and stares off in to the distance. "I don't know. I want to pitch it to a traditional publisher, but it's not as straightforward as it used to be."

"So, publish it yourself. I heard the indie route is the way to go these days. You get full control and everything, right?"

"Yeah," she sighs, still not meeting my eye. "But you need money to make money... if I want to do it the correct way, anyway. Hiring everyone to design and edit the book isn't bad—I can save up for that—but diving into ads and marketing is what's terrifying. I would have to take on a lot of that myself or hire someone. It's not impossible, but it is a leap of faith for someone who is barely scraping by."

I roll to my side and reach for her hand. Half of my life may be a mystery, but I'm so thankful for Selene. She's been the one constant I can depend on, and I know if it wasn't for her, I can think of a million different scenarios that could have been worse. In all the darkness, she's my bit of light, and she has been ever since we lost our parents a few years ago in a situation neither of us have truly ever gotten over. Though I know Selene was affected the most, and it's taken years of therapy to get to where she is now.

"You have endless possibilities," I gush. "I know that whatever you decide, you'll make it happen."

"Thanks." She gives me a tight-lipped smile. "I love working for Charleigh at her flower shop, but I know it's not what I want to be doing forever. At least I know I have that as a stream of income for now."

"I love that she's kept you on her team."

"Yeah." She chuckles. "If I didn't already know I wanted to go into writing or publishing, I'd probably work there forever. She's the best boss and friend."

"Everyone's dream." I smile back, squeezing her hand.

We lie together in silence, which allows my mind to wander back to the faded numbers stained on my inner arm. My eyelids grow heavy despite what I know I need to do today. I lift myself up onto my elbow and search the tiny living room. "What time is it?"

Selene twists and grabs her phone from the floor behind her before she rolls back to face me and taps her screen. "It's nine."

"Okay." I lay back down, my arm burning. How is my arm

burning when we just spent the past hour in the spin class from hell? "My train leaves at two, so I still have time for a shower and to finish packing up before we see Grandma."

"You don't honestly still plan on staying in Boston, do you?" Selene asks. "There's nothing left there for you."

Her brutal honestly is like a small knife to the heart. She's right.

I don't have anyone or anything in Boston.

Our grandmother has been in a nursing home on Long Island for the past ten years, and contrary to the occasional visit I've managed here and there, Selene has made it her mission to visit as much as possible. Perhaps it's her way of making up for the ugliness we've endured in our lives. Being close to our grandmother reminds Selene of the past.

A past *she* remembers.

"Why are you going back?" she presses. "Aside from the fact your clothes and a few other things are back in that apartment you shared."

"I don't know. It's what I should do, right?"

"Why, because you were married to Heath?" she asks, stunned. "You weren't happy in your marriage."

I haven't told Selene the whole truth about my marriage to Heath. West knows more than she does, but that's only because I knew it would only give Selene more reasons to convince me to leave Heath. Skeptical from the start, she never liked him, and I couldn't blame her.

"I know." The truth is a hard pill to swallow.

"We've only been sisters half our lives, but sometimes it feels like it's been our whole lives. Call it what you want, intuition or whatever, but my gut always made me question his motives."

"What do you mean?"

"There were plenty of instances, but one of them was when you told me all about his stock trading." Her green eyes find mine again. "I can't say I know too much about Wall Street and stocks. Honestly, I think I'd rather eat cardboard than attempt to figure out how all that works. But the way he would brag about being able to manipulate the market with this stomach-turning money-hungry look in his eye. Like what he was doing was borderline illegal and he got off on it." She shivers. "Rubbed me the wrong way."

I process Selene's thoughts—the same thoughts I would have whenever Heath would come home late after what he would call 'a night out with the guys', even though I knew it wasn't as simple as that. He always counted on me not asking questions.

Selene is right to have had an unsettling feeling about Heath's stock trading. I've felt the same way. Especially when he started giving out stock advice to a number of his associates, as though he were an expert or something.

"Back to your situation." Selene cuts through my thoughts. "You may have your life in Boston, but you don't have me. Or Julianna and Charleigh. We'd be here for you... just in case you weren't aware."

"I am and I know the three of you would be there for me." I twist my mouth in thought, and stare up at the spinning blades as I feather my finger over the faded ink on my arm.

If I decide to leave Boston, I already have a job opportunity. West wanted to hire me based on nothing more than the drawing I sketched on a napkin. I still haven't wrapped my head around it, wondering why. Why me? Why is he so trusting of me to create pieces for his bars? How many pieces, and for how many bars?

The Halls are one of the richest families in the country. Heath never explicitly shared the depth of his family's wealth with me, but a simple internet search told me my husband was worth at least three hundred million.

Heat blooms across my chest when I think about me searching online for West the other night. I needed to know more and why he gave me this sense of familiarity, but I'd given up after nearly an hour of not finding a single profile or mention of a West Hall that matched the one with the kind blue eyes who brought heat between my thighs. Probably explains why I never knew Heath had a brother. He doesn't exist on social media.

I haven't told Selene about my interaction with West. That I was honest with him more than I've been honest with anyone in my life. I didn't tell her he'd given me butterflies and made me embarrassingly weak in the knees. I didn't tell her about how I'd humiliated myself when I'd caught him staring at me as I lied to the entire crowd about his brother when he'd known the truth.

Everything about West, I've kept to myself. Just like the darkness of my unknown past I carry with me.

My throat tightens, and I struggle to take a breath. The blades of the spinning fan blur, and I grow dizzy. Probably from the lack of oxygen going to my brain. I shoot straight up and move to stand, anxiously wrapping my hand around the back of my neck.

"I need to change out of this sports bra," I blurt out. "It's suffocating."

"Okay." Selene sits up, resting her arms on her bent knees, her brows pulled together. Her blonde hair shimmers in the sunlight. I don't want to leave, but there isn't a glaringly obvious sign telling me to leave the bit of life I have back in Boston.

Where would I stay? Here in this tiny New York apartment with my sister?

"Are you okay?" she asks, concern lacing her voice.

"Yeah. My body just hurts. My arms and legs feel like Jell-O. I'm going to shower."

"Okay." She rises to a stand, too. "Try not to take too long though because I need to shower as well, and the hot water only lasts so long. Or else we're waiting over an hour before I'll be able to take mine."

I nod. "I won't take long."

I leave my sister in her living room and walk the ten feet to her bedroom. I peel my workout clothes off my body and quickly step into the shower, not bothering to wait for the water to heat up, though it doesn't warm until I've already squeezed a dollop of shampoo into the palm of my hand. I'm careful not to get too much water on West's faded phone number, but when I catch a glimpse of it from the corner of my eye as I hastily smooth body wash down my legs, I know it doesn't matter if it disappears now. I already have it memorized.

How was West able to infiltrate my mind so easily after only a few hours of interaction?

As if he's turned himself into his own puzzle piece, I leave him with the rest I have yet to sort, and quickly rinse my body off before the hot water starts to dwindle.

Shivering, I step out and wrap a towel around myself, then squeeze the excess water from my long, black hair. I stare at my reflection in the mirror, deciding to go with a simple, relaxed look today. I brush a coat of mascara on my lashes and a bit of tinted moisturizer over my skin before stepping out into Selene's bedroom.

"All set, Selene!" I shout from the end of her bed.

"Great." She strides down the hall, making her way to the bathroom. "Just in time, too. The smell of my own sweat was getting to me."

I laugh as she scrunches her nose in disgust, curling her lip.

I'm slipping my shirt over my head when my phone rings

from my duffle bag that's sitting on top of Selene's dresser. After digging into my bag, I fish it out and read the Boston number on the screen.

"Hello?" I answer, bringing it to my still-damp skin. At least this time it's from the shower, not sweat.

"Hi, Mrs. Hall?" the woman on the other end asks.

"This is she. Who is this?"

"My name is Mercedes Rhodes, one of the lawyers from the firm that represented your husband Heath Hall."

"Oh." I blink, running my hand nervously down the front of my thigh before sitting on the edge of the bed.

"According to your husband and his family, I was instructed to give you this call in the event of the situation we are in."

Nervous, I look down at my lap and pick at a loose thread on Selene's blanket folded beside me. "Situation?"

"Yes. My partner, Eli? You spoke with him before about the funeral. He handles the wishes of our clients regarding the funeral service. I handle the financial side of things. Everything from estates to bank accounts to investments."

"Okay," I mutter, not knowing where she's going with this.

Mercedes pauses, no doubt waiting for me to ask a question. When I don't, she clears her throat and continues. "Your husband instructed us to turn over his apartment and bank accounts to his mother. He doesn't mention you in his will to receive any financial benefits from his death. We've also spoken with his insurance company, and there was no policy for you, either."

Tears sting the corners of my eyes. "I, um, I don't understand."

"I'm sorry." Her voice softens. "The only money and assets you keep are ones you had before your marriage to him. Ones you owned before him."

My eyes widen as they fill with tears. I take a mental inventory of everything I own that didn't involve my husband.

A bank account in my name, but not with nearly enough money in it to stay afloat on my own for long.

And my belongings in Heath's apartment.

"What about my clothes and some of my possessions?" I ask Mercedes, swiping the tears from my cheeks. "I had those things before I married him. Can I come get those?"

She hesitates. "I'm sorry. The instructions specifically state that upon his burial, you are no longer allowed access to his estate. Our firm will gather your belongings and send them to you. I will send you an email for you to list all the pieces and items that are yours. Is there an address you would like us to deliver them to?"

The air is sucked from my lungs. Is this even *legal*?

I think of everything I own inside that Boston high-rise apartment. Not much is valuable or sentimental, aside from a few items standing out to me, but the most important ones are my art supplies and a few pieces I've created in the makeshift studio Heath allowed me to have in our apartment.

Part of me wants to resist and fight back against Heath's wishes from beyond the grave, but the other doesn't. I have a separate bank account—one Heath never had access to—but I know there won't be enough money there. Not when if I want to take on the team of lawyers backing Heath. Even if I did have the money, I'm not certain I would bother, because putting in the effort would stop me from letting my tumultuous marriage with Heath go.

The memory of the cold tile beneath my hands and feet is more alive than ever.

A sea of broken glass surrounding me, and the grating echo of my husband's screams make it easier to let him go.

I shouldn't be surprised by this move.

It's typical of Heath. Ask for everything, leave me with nothing.

I straighten my back. "Sure. You can email it over."

"I'll do that once we end this call." Mercedes voice is filled with sympathy. "Again, Mrs. Hall, I'm so sorry, and I'm sorry for your loss."

The cynical chuckle of irony barely leaves my throat before Mercedes abruptly ends our call.

I drop my phone beside me and bury my face in my hands. No fresh tears come when I inhale three long and steady breaths. I squeeze my eyes shut, and the image of the clock tower plays in my mind, as it always does. I've researched it enough to recognize it as Big Ben, or by its other name, Elizabeth tower. In London.

The image playing in my mind now isn't the same as the photos taken or the one in real life, though. It's a small piece of metal, refracting in the sun. The sight of it warms my gut, filling me with a sense of comfort and peace.

I clench my fists, digging my black-painted nails into my palms. The sensation stings, pulling me out of what I assume to be a memory.

"Hey." Selene's soft voice causes my eyes to fly open. I snap my head to my left and look up at my sister. She's clutching the towel wrapped around her chest, and her blonde hair is draped across her shoulder, dripping wet. "Are you okay?"

"Yeah," I blow out, looking back down to my hands in my lap before my attention drifts to my arm and West's faded number. "I'm fine."

"Okay." Selene squeezes my shoulder before moving around the bed.

I twist at the waist and, over my shoulder, say, "One of Heath's lawyers just called."

"Really?" She's pulling on her pants, but she stops midthigh. "What did they say?"

"He's cut me off from everything." I stare off in to the distance, but I can still see the metal clock. I shove the memory back down.

"What do you mean, he's cut you off?"

A part of me hardens when looking back at my sister, the realization that returning to Boston was never a reality I wanted in the first place. Maybe Selene is right. Maybe my place is here, with her. With the only family I know.

"It's a lot to explain right now." I trace my finger along West's faded number.

"What a fucking dick." She scoffs in disbelief. "I know it's terrible talking ill of the dead, but shit..." She shakes her head. "Thank God you've created a following on social media to keep a steady stream of your artwork sales."

"Yeah, true." My sister is right. I nod, gnawing on the inside of my cheek. I've been selling copies of my artwork online since before I met Heath. I've only ever wanted to be my own wind beneath my wings. "But does the offer for me to stay here instead of returning to Boston still stand?"

Selene wraps her arms around me.

"Are you fucking kidding me, London?" She buries her face into my neck. "Of course it does."

I chuckle. The uncertainty of my future may be weighing on me, but I already know it's infinitely better than returning to Boston with nowhere and no one to turn to.

Selene keeps her arms wrapped around me as I eye the growing crack in her ceiling. "I don't know how long we'll last living in this apartment together, but I'll figure out something," I tell her.

"Stay as long as you need," she reassures me.

I return her a hug, knowing that, even if I wanted to stay forever, forever isn't a possibility. Even Selene will agree to that.

SIX

WEST

I haven't stopped thinking about London. I've carried her napkin drawing with me every day since she left, careful not to let it tear, folding it to where the clock tower is protected on the inside.

It's ridiculous, but the drawing is all I have to remind me that seeing and talking to London that day was real and not just another haunted dream of mine.

Regret settles in my bones. It's been three weeks since I've seen her. Touched her.

I down the last of my beer, overlooking the crowd in front of me, thinking about how I wrote my number on London's arm.

Why didn't I get *her* number?

Why didn't I say more?

Maybe she's worried about working with me because I'm Heath's brother. I should have explained my situation to her. I'm such a fucking idiot.

A small part of me has considered seeking her out in Boston. Despite not having talked to Heath these past few years, I still remember where he lived. Though the last thing I want to do is freak London out and push her away. From what my mother has told me, and the lack of communication I had with my brother, I've come to the conclusion that London and the rest of the Hall family aren't exactly close.

I've been trying to tell myself that waiting her out is the best way to handle this, to trust that she'll find me again on her terms, but it's difficult to hold onto that positivity when I've done nothing but let London slip through my fingers for the past fifteen years. And here I am, fucking doing it again. Three fucking weeks have passed, and every day that comes after it is another punch to the gut.

I've hung around The Veiled Door more than usual, all in the hopes of seeing her again. So much so, Lewis has started to think of me more as a friend than his boss's boss's boss— a situation I'm expecting will eventually come back around to bite me in the ass.

"So, what do you think?" The brewer I've been seeking out for the past three months stands in front of me with a mixed expression of fear and anticipation. His lips are pressed tightly together, and his nostrils are flared. He's about as young as Lewis, and has the same expression of hope, as though he still believes the world is a good place.

I swallow the last bit of amber liquid in my glass and nod as I drop it back on the tray the server standing beside me is holding. "Slightly more bitter than I was expecting."

"Oh." His shoulders fall, and his face relaxes, but his mouth still twitches with a smile. "That's our strongest IPA. We add a slightly larger number of hops to the batch. If you try our lighter IPA, you'll notice a bit more sweetness from the orange peel. It also smooths it out." He reaches for the full tasting glass next to my empty one on the tray.

I bring the glass to my mouth and take a small sip. The man's expression lands the same as it had a few seconds earlier. He's anxious again. I don't blame him.

This deal is huge for him... and me. I'm constantly searching the city for smaller breweries to add to my offerings at my beer garden and a few other bars.

When I'd called him a few weeks back to schedule a tasting and tour of his brewery, he'd invited me to come along to a nighttime tour he does once a month. I eye the groups of people surrounding the brewery, realizing why he invited me here. He wants to show me how popular his beers are.

The oversized crowd is enough to convince me to make a deal with Hopyard Breweries, and tonight is a simple formality. Despite my love for what I do, I hate that the pretentious nature of wealth plays into it. The more money you have, the more you're likely to succeed. Especially in New York City.

I swallow the smoother beer and nod. "I'll send you an email on Monday with an order and my team will draft up a contract for you."

"Really?" His eyebrows up, and he blows out a heavy breath as he slaps a hand to his chest. Man, he really does remind me of Lewis.

"Yeah." I nod, darting my eyes around the brewery. I'm excited about this deal with Hopyard, but I still can't stop thinking about London. It isn't until the owner of Hopyard is enthusiastically shaking my hand do I realize I've been searching the crowd for her all night. A foolish notion.

"Thank you, Mr. Knight." He beams.

"No, thank you," I tell him. "Your beer will make a great addition to some of my locations."

"Awesome." He runs a hand down his face. "I'll speak to you on Monday." With that, he walks away, sinking farther into the crowd, then stopping to talk to a group gathered on the other side of the room.

The brewery is in an industrial part of the city, with a view of the Hudson and the George Washington Bridge, making it beautifully picturesque, especially at night.

However, despite the crowd around me, a sense of loneliness and emptiness washes over me. I can't stop thinking about London, and even though I don't *want* to stop, I can't help being annoyed by the ache inside me. It's as if she's always within reach, but not quite.

My phone pings from my pocket, and I pull it out to find a text from my closest friend, Holt Capuleti.

Holt: Tossing the invite out there, even though I know you hate these types of things. Fundraiser at my estate in Brooklyn.

I look up from my phone, keeping my text thread open, and glance around the room at the endless sea of strangers.

"Fuck it," I whisper.

Grabbing a few drinks with a friend sounds infinitely better than standing here alone or going home to an empty apartment.

I type out a reply before the all too familiar feeling of regret stops me.

Me: Fuck it. Be there in thirty.

When Alden drops me outside Holt's building, I head straight for the roof, where I know Holt's fundraiser is being held. The elevators door slide open, and when I step out, I'm walking straight into another crowd. String lights stretch back and forth overhead, covering every inch of the massive, multi-tiered roof. The city glows in the distance, a mix of blue, white, and golden lights.

Sometimes I still wonder how the hell I ended up living this life.

I begin making my way through the crowd in search of Holt.

I don't have to look for him for long when I see him standing against the bar. The bartender behind the counter raises his arms in the air before rattling a metal shaker with expertise. He flings the mixer behind his arm. It spins in the air several times before he catches it. After popping the top part of the shaker, he pours the cloudy-yellow mixture into a martini glass, then slides it across the counter to Holt. Feels like I'm audience to a theatrical show rather than a guest at a party. Across from Holt stands Asher Owens; another rich fucker I've become friends with. Again, I'm not sure how this became my life, but here I am.

I meet Holt and Asher, and flag the bartender down for a beer. He quickly pops the bottlecap off one before sliding it over to me. I bring it to my mouth and down half of it in one gulp. The sharp, crisp bubbles burn down my throat, but I don't care. I can't help this feeling of helplessness. Dealing with myself is sometimes easier when I've taken the edge off.

"So, it's that kind of night." Holt laughs.

I give him a closed-lip smile and chuckle. "Yep."

"What's up?" Asher asks, leaning against the bar with his elbow. His brown hair is ruffled, a little messier than every other time I've seen him, and he's wearing a cashmere sweater, departing from his usual suit and tie.

"It's nothing." There's no fucking way I'm going into the complexities and ugly history I share with a woman who doesn't even recognize me.

What would I say? Well, actually, I fell in love with this girl I knew when we were kids who just so happens to have amnesia, oh, and there's the minor detail of her being my dead brother's widow. No big deal.

Instead, I settle on, "Just some personal shit going on."

"From the look on your face, you'll need another one of those ASAP." Holt points toward my beer before flagging down the bartender, signaling for him to grab me another beer.

I pull out my wallet and drop a one-hundred-dollar bill in front of him. His eyes go wide before he offers me a thank you and stuffs it into the tip jar sitting on the back shelf.

"What's this fundraiser for?" I ask Holt as I finish off the last of my first beer, then swap it out for the fresh one.

"My sister Julianna is raising money for underprivileged kids in the city. She runs a scholarship for those who've grown up in low-income households."

"Oh, wow." I raise my eyebrows, shocked to hear the type of fundraiser his sister is hosting, considering their upbringing. Children of the mayor of New York City have never experienced a life of uncertainty. At least not in the monetary sense.

"Surprising, right?" Asher says, laughing.

"Why is it surprising?" Holt asks him, his brows slanted.

"Nothing." Asher shakes his head, stifling his laughter. "I just wasn't expecting it, coming from your family."

"My father was the mayor, Asher. He always ran charity events and fundraisers." Holt chest puffs out defensively. "People always think we're assholes because we have money, but not all of us are. We try."

Asher's laughter is cut short. "I know. I wouldn't be friends with you if you were a complete asshole."

Holt cocks his head to the side. "So, you're saying I'm a *little* bit of an ass?"

"I think that's exactly what he's saying." I can't help cracking a smile. "If it's your sister's fundraiser, why are you holding it here?" I glance around at the party. The rooftop is large, and having been here a handful of times, I understand why it is great to host a party of this size, but it seems out of place for Holt.

Holt rolls his eyes. "I owe her."

"Owe her for what?"

"For ruining her birthday party a while back."

"Oh." Asher points at Holt, his face lighting up with recognition. "When you invited your family's enemy? What was his name again? Rome?"

"Yeah, him," Holt mutters, giving Asher a side glance as he lifts his drink to his mouth. Once he swallows the pastel liquid, he adds, "I'd rather not talk about it. The important thing now is she can't hang it over my head."

Asher laughs, tipping his head back. "Oh, she'll never let it go, but at least you're trying."

"I figured she would never completely let it go. Have you met my sister?" Holt mutters, his blue eyes scanning the crowd. "Where are the girls, anyway?"

"I'm not sure," Asher says. "Last Charleigh told me, she and Selene were gathering up a few of the bouquets they were donating for the auctions."

"Auctions?" I ask.

"Yeah." He points toward the other side of the roof to my right. "There's a silent auction over there. You should check them out."

"I will." I nod, taking another sip of my beer. Even if there isn't anything that piques my interest for the auction, I'll probably end up donating to Julianna's charity anyway.

I keep the secret of my understanding the recipients of Julianna's charity to myself and grab a fresh beer before leaving my friends to go check out the auction. I weave through the crowds, not recognizing a single person. Bouquets of black and white flowers are set in the center of each table, and I catch a glimpse of Selene, as well as Asher's fiancée Charleigh, adjusting a few flowers on top of one of the larger tables. I recognize both of them from Julianna's party months ago.

The one Holt said he owed his sister for ruining.

Though I remember that night for a different reason.

It was the first night I'd seen London in years. Raven hair, gold rings on each finger, the heart-shaped birthmark stamped on her hand. I was still getting over my shock of seeing her again when I recognized the man who'd wrapped his arms around her.

My brother Heath.

I swallow the memory of that night down with a swig of my beer, already on my third since I got here.

Walking toward the auction table, I read the clipboards laid out. Yachts and private jets are among a few of the prizes. I scoff under my breath, not understanding why rich assholes only feel the need to donate to charity unless they get something in return. Maybe it makes them feel righteous in their gluttony.

I shake my head at some of the bids already written down, when I catch a glimpse of black and blue coming from the lower portion of the roof. Behind the table is a metal and wired balcony overlooking the lower portion of Heath's rooftop property. Stairs to my left lead down to the large swimming pool. It's strange seeing a pool this size on top of a building in the center of Brooklyn, but considering its Holt, it doesn't surprise me. What sends the blood shooting down from my brain to my feet, though, is the woman floating in the middle. Her black hair is splayed out around her, floating on the surface. Her long arms are spread out beside her, and her feet are slowly kicking below the surface, keeping her in place. Her eyes are closed, mouth closed too, her ears beneath the surface.

I set my beer on the table and immediately make my way down the stairs, telling myself to move slowly, to take my time. She's here, and I don't want to startle her. She's clearly deep in thought, in her own world.

But like a moth drawn to a flame, I'm drawn to her faster than my feet can carry me. When I reach the bottom of the stairs, my pace slows, but my heart doesn't, and I swallow the nerves inside me. Shoving my hands inside the pockets of my slacks, I curl my fingers tightly around her drawing, clinging to it like a life raft.

London's long, dark blue dress clings to her skin while the backside floats freely in the water under her. The wet fabric highlights every full curve of her body. Heat expands in my lower belly noticing her perked nipples pointing directly at the starless New York sky. London's eyes crack open, and she keeps her gaze on the dark blanket above us, not noticing me standing just a few feet away from her.

Her mouth pulls into a ghost of a smile, and I doubt anyone farther than where I'm standing can see it. But I don't miss it. I can't. Not when the two dimples appear in her cheeks. Dimples impossible to forget.

I remember the sound of her laughter at thirteen, when I'd pointed them out to her at the kitchen table. When I'd reached out and touched her for the first time. She'd giggled, wrapped her hand around mine, and refused to let go for the rest of dinner.

I clear my throat and inhale a deep breath, glancing back up at the party, forcing the memory down.

No one seems to notice London here alone, floating in the pool.

No one except me. She's all I notice.

"Find one yet?"

London doesn't react to me interrupting her star gazing the way I expect her to.

Her chest stills, but she doesn't move from her position in the water, keeping her arms spread out and her legs like an angel's. She's fucking breathtaking, and I study her profile, forcing myself to breathe.

After rolling her head to the side, it takes her precisely three seconds to recognize me.

That's when she finally moves. She sits up as her feet sink beneath the clear blue water, and she pushes her hair away from her face, nervously glancing toward the party on the upper level. Her gray eyes swing back to me as a drop of water falls from her bottom lip. "Find what?"

I smile. I can't help it. I can't believe she's in front of me again. She's here, and not because we're both putting on a show for others like we were at my brother's funeral.

We're two ordinary people now.

"A star," I say.

Flicking her eyes upwards, she laughs under her breath. "No, I didn't."

"Impossible here in the city," I tell her, inching closer to the edge of the pool.

"Not much different from Boston, really."

"Right." I nod, swallowing my nerves. Over the years, I've thought of what I would say to her, but now I'm coming up empty. Just looking at her is enough, but I don't want to let this moment slip away.

"Do you come to these often?" I ask, nodding toward the party upstairs.

"No." She scoffs, shaking her head. She looks down at her hands skimming over the surface of the water. My gaze falls on her birthmark. "My sister and her friend's helped organize it. I just came along for the ride."

My eyebrows shoot up. "Sister?"

The corners of her mouth curl. I can tell this is a bright spot in her life, and the feeling it gives me seeing it on her face lights a part of me that's been lying dormant since I was fifteen.

"Selene Walker is my sister. She's friends with Julianna Capuleti, the one running the auction."

"You know Julianna?" I ask.

Wow. This truly is a small fucking world.

London nods, leaning back slightly in the water. Her face glows from the under lighting. "So," she says with a teasing glint to her eye. "Do you come to these often?"

I frown and shake my head. "No. I just came along for the ride." My mouth pulls to a grin, and my stomach flutters. "I'm friends with her brother."

She giggles lightly, but her smile falls fast. "Oh." She drags her bottom lip under her teeth.

God. Why am I imagining kissing her and sinking my fingers into her hair? Into the curves of her full, round ass and those perfect tits?

I walk along the edge of the pool, only a few feet away, staying close but eyeing her suspiciously, ignoring the twitch in my dick. "Oh, what?"

"Nothing." She smiles, shaking her head.

"No." I chuckle. "There was clearly something else beneath that *oh.*"

Her gray eyes can't stay still, looking everywhere but at me. I keep my hands in my pockets, my fingers wrapped around her napkin. I bend at the hip, forcing her to look at me.

Begrudgingly, she finally matches her eyes with mine. She sighs and leans back in the water, kicking back farther toward the center of the pool. "I just don't believe you."

"You don't believe me?"

"No, I don't believe you just come to these to appease others." She continues to dance her fingers along the surface of the water. "You're a Hall. You were raised on coming to events like these."

"Was I?" I ignore the punch to the gut. She's reminding me of who she thinks I am.

"Yeah. Heath always loved these types of events. Gave him an opportunity to show off."

"And you didn't enjoy going with him?"

"Nope. I don't think it's in my veins."

"Hence why you escaped to the pool?"

"I love the looks others give me." She tips her head to the upper level. "They look at me like I'm an alien from another planet."

The attendees gathered near the auction table eye us with suspicion before no doubt writing down their six figure bids. At least their money is going to a good cause.

"Sometimes I feel the same," I confess.

London scoffs as she rolls her eyes. "Yeah, okay."

"Ouch." I remove my hand from my pocket and place it against my chest. "I'm actually kind of hurt you don't believe me."

She frowns, and her eyes soften. "I'm sorry, I didn't mean to offend you. It's just..."

"No, it's fine. I understand." I remove my phone from my pocket, making sure I pull the napkin out with it. After tucking it neatly underneath my phone, I place it on one of the lounge chairs behind me and walk to the edge of the pool to, where I bend down, swing my feet out from under me, and sink into the surprisingly warm water.

London pushes away from me as soon as I'm chest deep.

Keeping my gaze locked on hers, I swim closer to her. Once I'm within two feet of her, I dip my head under the water. As soon as I emerge, I push my hair back and wipe my hands down the front of my face, clearing my vision.

London's gorgeous face is frozen with surprise. The closer I get to her, the more I find myself taking note of everything about her that reminds me of before. The angle of her nose, the way the gray in her eyes has a hint of blue from the reflection of the glowing water, and those goddamn dimples in her soft cheeks. I want to count her lashes and take inventory of everything I've missed over the years. Instead, I push down my thoughts and decide on another bit of honesty.

"You didn't offend me," I tell her. We move closer together. Her hands have disappeared beneath the water, and I fight the urge to search for them with my own. "Can I tell you a truth?"

Her black-lined eyes search my face. "All I ever want is the truth."

I anchor myself to the bottom of the pool, and my heart hammers like a beating drum in my chest. "I'm not a Hall. I never have been."

SEVEN

LONDON

Water drips from his bottom lip, disappearing into his thick beard. His hair is slicked back, revealing familiar eyes—ones that tug at my gut with a taut string, directing me to follow.

West's confession hangs in the air between us. There's hesitation mingled with a bit of fear in his expression, as though he's afraid I'm going to disappear.

"You're not a Hall?" I ask. "What do you mean?"

He looks down, then to his right, then up to the party. Anywhere but at me. But when his eyes finally swing back my way, I'm suddenly aware of everything. The way my dress tries to billow out under me, the fabric dancing around my thighs. The way the curves of my breasts rise above the surface of the water. The way West has inched his way closer to me.

Being this close to my ex-brother-in-law feels like it should be wrong, but the taut string tugging at my stomach tells me it isn't.

"My last name is Knight," he confesses.

My eyebrows pull together. "Wait. So, you aren't Heath's brother?"

He runs his hand down his face and leans to his left, and

within seconds, we're slowly spinning in a circle, never looking away from each other.

"On paper, I am. I was adopted at fifteen." He explains, the reflection of the pool a kaleidoscope of blue dancing across his body. "I never took their last name."

I can't pinpoint the sensation, but it feels as though a thousand needles are prickling under the surface of my skin. A vibration. A humming feeling I can't shake.

"West Knight." His name falls from my mouth on a whisper.

"My full name is actually Weston, but I go by West." He gives me a small smile, again looking at me as if he's imploring me to give him some deep response. But I don't have one. He studies me in silence.

"Oh." I nod, playing with my tongue piercing. I twist it in my mouth, clicking it against the back of my teeth while conflicted feelings brew inside me.

Even now, after learning West isn't related to Heath by blood, I still can't ignore the fact he's part of the family, and I was married to his brother, despite Heath never seeming to care to be involved with his family. At least not enough to add me to the mix.

I also can't deny the fluttering heat building in my stomach at West's proximity. The water is warm, but I know what I'm feeling isn't just from Holt's heated pool. The sensation I got from West the first time we met wasn't a fluke. My body reacts to him in a way that makes me feel delightfully dizzy. I want to reach out and press the tip of my finger to his. Our hands dance beneath the surface, and every few seconds, I feel the force of the water behind his hand touch mine.

I ache to touch him but know I shouldn't.

"So..." West sighs, his mouth curling to a satisfied smirk. "Now that I've told you a truth, it's your turn."

"My turn, huh?"

"Yes, your turn," West whispers, leaning closer but staying a foot away from me. We've stop spinning in a circle, planting our feet to the tiles beneath us. My toes grate against the rough surface.

"Every memory I had before my fourteenth birthday is gone."

West's expression is unmoving, but I can tell he's hanging on to every word—a stark contrast to his brother who always looked at me as if there were a million other people he'd rather have been with in any moment instead of his own wife. And though West doesn't ask me to elaborate. I feel compelled to, anyway.

"I don't have a memory of how it happened. I only know what the doctor's told me." I spin around, turning my back on West, my body humming as I sweep my soaking wet hair to the side, revealing the base of my neck to him, and glance over my shoulder as he inches closer. I point to the scar I know is hidden beneath my hair, near the back of my head. "My adoptive parents bought me a bike as a welcome home gift, and I immediately took it out for a ride, but I didn't see the car coming when I rounded the street corner. The person who hit me left the scene, and I laid there for almost an hour before a neighbor found me." I swallow the emotion thick in my throat. "But like I said, I don't remember any of it. That's the story the doctors told me."

Aware of every breath coming out of West's mouth, I spin back around to face him.

Sad.

Regretful.

His face is still, but his chest rises and falls with his weighted breaths.

"Sometimes," I say, bobbing up and down on my toes again, "sometimes I get these memories. At least what I think are memories. But when they pop into my head, I lock them inside a box and hope they'll come to me later. Sometimes I see them like puzzle pieces, waiting to be put together."

West closes his mouth and blinks for a few beats before asking, "Do you have any of them pieced together yet?"

"At times I think I have them put together," I confess. "But I never know what to believe. I never know if they're true memories or if they're just made up in my head. Memories I *think* I remember."

"The truth is always in front of us." His voice is soft, barely a whisper. "Sometimes you just have to dig a little deeper to find it." His hand moves closer to mine under the water.

"Maybe." But I'm not as easily convinced. It's been years, and the fear of my memory never coming back is a reality I hate facing.

"Did your parents not tell you about your life before they adopted you?" West asks. "I'm guessing they knew a little about your past."

I'm overwhelmed with sadness. It's not that I didn't love my adoptive parents—I did—but I haven't thought about the loss of them in a long time. I've been stuck between the desire to move on from my past, and the desire to be there for Selene, since her and our grandmother are the only family I have left.

Sometimes pain is easier to let go of when you have distractions.

"I never asked them," I tell West. "After my accident, they tried their best to give me the best life possible. I guess they wanted to move on and not dwell on it. I guess at some point I went along with it and accepted it. Then it just became habit."

"Couldn't you ask them now? Maybe it would help."

Tears sting the backs of my eyes. "I can't. They died a few years back."

"I'm sorry."

I think back to the first time we met, when West told me he

was sorry for my husband's death. Before he knew my husband had been his brother. I didn't want it then. I wasn't sorry for Heath's death.

But his condolence for my parents is one I welcome. Their death rocked Selene more than me. I was upset by their death, but seeing my sister distraught made me compare my emotions to hers. Then when Heath died, I was relieved in a way. Like I'd been set free. But thinking about Mom and Dad now, I don't think I ever took the time to acknowledge the trauma of losing the only parents I've ever known.

I continue to bounce in the water while staying close to West, drawn to him despite every alarm bell inside me warning me to stay away. Because of him, I don't feel like I'm the only one not heartbroken over Heath's death. There's history between the brothers. A reason why Heath kept his family away from me.

My fingers graze West's. Our breaths are heavy in the space between us, both of us clearly aware of the shift happening. We're standing dangerously close, closer than we should be, but West doesn't make a move to break this trance we've found ourselves in.

"Can I ask you something?" His eyes fall to my mouth.

"Yes," I breathe.

"Have you decided if you're going back to Boston?"

I open my mouth to answer him when I spot the light catch the sequins of my sister's black cocktail dress from the corner of my eye. She's walking down the length of the pool, toward where West and I are swimming in the middle. Behind her, Charleigh and Julianna follow.

"I've been looking for you everywhere, London," Selene says, crossing her arms over her chest once she reaches us. "I should have known I would find you here."

"Oh, come on. Can you blame her?" Charleigh says, tucking

a few strands of her brown hair behind her ear, which has been braided off to the side, revealing the newest flower she's had tattooed behind her ear. She asked Selene and me to go with her to the tattoo parlor yesterday. I was tempted to get one myself but decided against it. At least for now.

Julianna taps Charleigh's arm with the back of her hand. "Hey, what is that supposed to mean? Is my party boring?"

"I didn't say that," Charleigh argues, but I ignore her and Julianna's back and forth.

Selene's looking at me with pink cheeks. I've embarrassed her.

"I'm sorry, Selene." I never meant to embarrass her. I was caught up in my own thoughts, but I know she'll understand when we go back to her apartment later and explain.

Her eyes soften. She knows I've been through the wringer recently. "Julianna said there isn't much more for us to do here, so we can head out." Her eyes move over to West. She gives him a small, ghosted smile.

"Okay," I tell her, recapturing her attention.

"I'll meet you in the front lobby," she mutters, glancing between West and me before she walks away.

I watch her ascend the stairs and disappear into the crowd.

"I think the stress of finishing this book is getting to her," Charleigh says.

Julianna and I nod.

"I think so, too."

"Well, since you're here to stay, maybe we should set up weekly get togethers," Julianna suggests. "You know, like girls' night or something."

"I like that idea." I smile.

Charleigh and Julianna walk away arm in arm, promising to text the group chat later. I stare at the side of the pool for several seconds, wrapping my head around what has become my life.

Last month, I would have been surrounded by people like the ones upstairs, but now I'm here, with my sister and new friends. Not to mention that I'm swimming in a pool with my ridiculously handsome dead husband's brother.

"I guess that answers my question." West's deep voice slinks down my body like warm liquid. It slips between my thighs, vibrating against my skin.

I spin around to face him.

"So..." He smirks. "You decided to stay?"

"I was going to call you."

He tips his head back, laughing. The back of his brown head dips into the water, and when he looks at me again, his mouth quirks, and his eyes turn a brighter shade of blue. "Were you?"

"I was." My smiles fades. "It's just been a crazy time lately."

Realization settles in his expression. "Yeah. It has."

"Not because of him," I say, referring to Heath. "My life has just been a bit jumbled now I'm starting over on my own. But it's in a good way, and while I do need a job, I just felt like..."

"... it was weird since I'm Heath's brother?" he asks, lifting his brows.

I can't look at him. Admitting the feelings he's given me every single time I've seen him is a confession I shouldn't make out loud. Even if Heath was a horrible, mentally abusive husband.

"Yeah," I say instead. "I just didn't know if it was okay or if it was strange to reach out to you."

"It's okay. I get it. For the record, though, it isn't strange or weird. At least not on my end. Is it for you?"

"No, but it probably should be."

Just like I should have been more heartbroken when my husband died.

I get lost in West's kind eyes. Strangely, he's comforting. Like home.

My hands vibrate with the need to draw. I need to release the thoughts threatening to drag me into the darkness. The sudden urge to get out of the pool as fast as possible takes over.

"I should go." I turn and walk toward the set of stairs at the far end of the pool. The water resists and keeps me from putting distance between West and me as quickly as I want. The cool air pricks my wet skin the second my foot meets the first step and I begin emerging from the water. My dress clings to my breasts and abdomen, goosebumps prickling down the length of my arms. I've only made it to the third step when I'm pulled to a stop.

West's long fingers wrap around my wrist, his fingertips pressing to my pulse.

Can he feel how fast my heart is racing?

I look over my shoulder. He's standing waist deep in the pool with an immense look of worry on his all too gorgeous face. His, what I'm almost certain cost at least four-figures, suit clings to his skin. Every muscle is accentuated as water drips from his towering frame, the blue light below casting a glow on his glistening skin.

But it's the worry in West's eyes that causes my heart to race. He's looking at me as if I'm going to vanish if he so much as blinks.

"Wait," his voice strains. "I probably shouldn't be saying this..." He trails off.

"What is it?" I ask.

"I'm just not sure if I'm going to see you again, and... I want to. Fuck, I want to." He clears his throat as his gaze slips down to his hand on mine, and my skin grows cold the second he pulls it away.

"Ever since we met, we've been honest with each other," I say, rubbing the pad of my thumb across the birthmark on my left hand. "I meant what I said."

His brows pull together, and he takes a step back, but the worry in his eyes hasn't changed.

I give him a small smile. "I was going to call."

He blows out a heavy, relieved breath, and I can't understand his reactions. I can't shake this feeling that we've known each other a lot longer than since the day of Heath's funeral.

Can you possibly know someone without actually knowing them?

The brutal truth slams into my gut, jumpstarting my broken heart.

I want to see him again. I shouldn't, but I do.

"I could use the job," I confess. "If the offer still stands, of course." I swallow my nerves, worrying I sound desperate. But it's the truth. I need a job, and fast if I plan on staying in New York. I can't live with Selene forever, and I don't plan on adding to the statistic of a being starving artist in the city. "I mean, I understand if it doesn't—"

"No!" He cuts me off, his smile reaching his eyes. "It does. The job's still available."

I crack a smile of my own. "Good."

"Tomorrow. Meet me at The Veiled Door tomorrow. Nine a.m."

"Okay." I chuckle. "I'll see you then."

"Good night, London."

Warmth weaves its way to my heart. "Good night, Weston Knight."

I turn away from him and grab the bottom of my dress, pulling it up so I don't trip on my way out of the pool. Even as I push my way through the groups of people gathered at the auction, avoiding their confused stares, I can't get West's voice out of my head. Not the entire conversation, but the part where he said my name.

Like he's already said it a million times before.

EIGHT

LONDON

I stand at the foot of Selene's bed with my hands on my hips, not knowing what to take to The Veiled Door. Is this a job interview? Or have I already secured the job based on a crappy, two-inch napkin sketch?

I take inventory of my pencils and charcoal again before tucking them into the pocket of my leather portfolio. I hiss through my teeth when my finger slips along the edge. The leather is frayed and torn with a piece of sharp-edged plastic sticking out. I shake my hand and suck on the tip, catching the blood before it spills.

"Ow." I pull my finger away and study the edge of my favorite portfolio. It wasn't this damaged before.

Selene woke me up before daylight broke to tell me there was a pile of my belongings blocking the hallway.

Like a gremlin, I rolled out of bed, not believing her. Sure enough, though, she was right. Boxes of my belongings from my home with Heath in Boston were piled three feet high and two feet wide in the hallway. She'd helped me slide the first few boxes inside her apartment before needing to race to the subway in time to make it to open Charleigh's flower shop, complete with a laptop case swinging from her shoulder and coffee perched in her hand.

Although we've been living with each other, it feels as if we haven't really spent much time together, mostly talking to each other through our girls' group chat. I'm thankful Charleigh and Julianna came up with the idea of a planned hang out once a week. I've always been an introvert to my core, but these women are different. I've never had friends that genuinely cared like they do. Most have ulterior motives, but not them. Like me, they just want to find happiness in whatever form that might be.

"Assholes," I grumble, knowing it will have been Heath's henchman who damaged my belongings when they shipped them out from Boston and literally dropped them at Selene's doorstep without a care.

Once I finish taking inventory, gathering all the supplies I think I might need to bring to The Veiled Door, I finish getting dressed, opting for my favorite pair of skinny jeans, with my silk tank top and royal purple blazer. I figure if I end up working with charcoal, I can take off my blazer without worrying about ruining my clothes.

Normally, I work in torn jeans or shorts and an old T-shirt, but something tells me West wouldn't appreciate me showing up so casually.

After applying a thin layer of lip gloss, I wrap a Band-Aid around the tip of my finger, over the small cut. I laugh under my breath at the Disney Princess bandage, wondering why the hell my sister opted to buy them when she doesn't have kids. Then after leaving the bathroom, I stuff my tote bag with my supplies and tuck my portfolio under my arm, careful not to cut myself or my clothes on the exposed edge.

I decide to take the subway, telling myself I need to get used to it if I'm going to live in the city for the foreseeable future. Once I find an open seat, I stare at my reflection in the window across from me, taking note of my appearance. I run the tips of my fingers down the length of my face before twirling the end of my braid around my pointer finger.

Nerves hum in the base of my stomach. Not only for the job but at the idea of seeing West again. I still can't explain the sensation he gives me, like this nagging prick to the back of my head. Like knowing you left the oven on after you leave the house. Or realizing you've forgotten something when travelling.

When I arrive at The Veiled Door, I tug the door open, immediately looking for West, but the bar is empty. At first I think it's odd, but then I remember the time. It's just after eight thirty in the morning. The bar isn't open, and I'm early.

I glance around, slowly walking farther into the room. Soft music plays overhead, similar to what I heard the first time I came here. The bar is dark, save for a few sconces hanging on the dark forest green painted walls. It looks like a cave in here. I drop my bag on one of the wooden tables in the dining area and peek down the corridor behind the bar.

"West?" I call out.

I hear a crash and what sounds like boxes sliding across the floor from upstairs. I didn't even think about there being an upstairs. But this is New York. There's no such thing as a one-story building.

A shiver slinks down the length of my spine, and I swallow my nerves, not understanding where this reaction is coming from. I shake the feeling, forcing my breathing to calm, but the air I'm managing to pull in burns.

Tears sting the corners of my eyes, and a cloud of black feathers the edges of my vision.

This suffocating feeling catches me off guard, consuming me without warning.

I stop, bend forward, and catch myself on the bar counter.

Another crash upstairs, and I'm gasping for air again. The

scent of wet dirt fills my nostrils, the acrid smell souring my stomach.

"Stop," I whisper. "Stop." My voice rises, as a rhythmic pounding sound grows louder. "Stop. *Please*."

Panic slinks down my spine. My grip on the bar top tightens, and my legs nearly give out.

But then his hand is on my back, his voice in my ear.

"Hey, hey, hey. London," West soothes. "You're okay. Look at me." He places his hands on my face, pulling me up to look at him. "You're okay," he reassures, staring into my eyes, and I catch the hint of fear in his.

A tear slips down my cheek and falls to his thumb.

"I don't know," I say, shakily. "I don't know what happened."

"Here." His hands slips away from my face, and he reaches behind him to pull out a barstool. "Sit down."

West keeps his hand on my back as he guides me onto the stool. I rest my hands in my lap, staring at the slivers of lacquer and wood beneath my fingernails.

"I'm sorry," I breathe out.

"Don't say sorry." He hands me a napkin.

With a shaky hand, I lift it to my face and wipe my cheeks. "I just came in and I heard some noises upstairs, and... I don't know..." I can't even finish the sentence.

"I should be the one saying sorry. It was stupid of me to try and rearrange upstairs right when you were supposed to be meeting me here."

"You must think I'm crazy." I shake my head, unable to look him in the eye, my embarrassment replacing the panic.

"I don't."

"It's my first day, and I haven't even started," I say. "I don't want you to think this happens all the time."

"You think a little panic attack will make me question wanting to keep you around?"

"I don't know." I whisper, stunned with his honesty. Does he realize what he's saying?

"Does this happen often?" he asks, concern buried in his gaze. "You had one at the funeral, didn't you?"

"It used to happen more when I was younger. Not long after the accident. But as I've gotten older, it doesn't as much." I swallow thickly. "I never know what triggers it. It could be a sound or a smell."

I haven't officially started working for West yet, and the last thing I want to do is dwell on this. I don't want him to think I can't handle these moments or that I'm bat shit crazy.

"Anyway." I inhale an unsteady breath, lifting my eyes to his. "I'm okay now."

"Are you sure?" He hasn't removed his hand from my back, and all I can think about is his touch. My skin is on fire. I stare into his eyes, and I swear, every ounce of fear dissolves. I didn't even notice until now how fucking good he looks today. Heat swells across my entire body, and I start imagining what it might feel like to have his hand dip between my legs.

"I am." I slide off the stool.

Startled, he steps back.

Needing to move on from my little episode, I cross the room and grab my bag and portfolio.

"I brought my portfolio to show you some more of my work," I say over my shoulder. "These are better than a little napkin drawing." I spin on my heel as West watches me.

He's wearing a simple T-shirt and a pair of dark jeans torn at the knee—the complete opposite of the other times I've seen him—and I'm suddenly aware of how overdressed I am compared to him. He's even trimmed his beard, revealing a more chiseled jaw line that any woman would love to drag their finger along. I tighten my grip on my portfolio.

"Here." I carry it over to him and unzip it on the bar top, careful not to cut my finger again. Realizing he can see the princess bandage, I try to hide it the best I can, using my other hand to pull the zipper the rest of the way. I open up my portfolio to the first sketch lying on top. A charcoal drawing of one of the ports in Boston.

"I drew this one when I took a walk on the first warm spring day last year." I flip the page to the next one. "And this one was the building next to my apartment."

"But not your apartment?" he asks, not even looking down at my drawings. His eyes are on me, unwavering and unmoving. His gaze burns a hole in the left side of my face, and my body engulfs in unrelenting heat.

I keep my eyes on the sketch. "No."

"Why not?" he's quick to ask.

I clear my throat and finally flick my gaze up to his. I know what he's truly asking. He wants to know why I didn't bother drawing my home with Heath.

"It was never worth drawing," I admit.

"So, you only draw things you deem worthy?"

"I don't know if you want the answer to that question."

He cocks his head to the side. "I never ask questions I'm not prepared to have answered."

I release a weighted sigh. What the hell? How does West do this so effortlessly?

I look into his eyes, and that same familiarity comes over me. As if we've known each other for years. As if there are cosmic forces between us, constantly pulling us together.

It's terrifying how I already feel closer to West than I have with anyone in recent memory.

"Our house never felt like home," I admit. "All the way up until the very end."

"What do you mean?"

"Never mind." I look down at my drawings and slide one out from under the drawing of the building next to Heath's old apartment. The sketch is one I made when I first moved to Boston. Before I met Heath. It's of a leaf I'd found at the base of a tree in the park. Dry, cracked, and shaped like the birthmark imprinted on my left hand.

I trace the curve of the leaf. I remember thinking this dead leaf lived more of a life than I had.

"I'm sorry," West says beside me, pulling me back from my rabbit hole. "I got us off track. I'd love to see more of your drawings."

The corners of my mouth curl as I look up at him, relieved. Art is my safe space. The one bright place I can rely on in a world of black. "Okay."

I spend the next twenty minutes showing West every single one of my drawings, avoiding the ones tucked into the back pocket. The ones I keep for myself. The ones drawn from the few flashing memories that have haunted me since I came home from the hospital after the accident.

Keeping those concealed, I start with the few I have out. I tell him the story behind each one, explaining what compels me to draw certain things. He asks me what I did back in Boston, and I tell him how my art career evolved over the years. I tell him about art school and how my adoptive parents disapproved simply because they were afraid of my future financial security.

If they were still alive, I bet they would have loved Heath simply for the number of digits and commas in his bank account.

When I finish showing West the last drawing, I close my portfolio and leave the talk of the past I do remember behind. Without a word, he slips off his stool beside me and walks around the bar to dig through a drawer underneath the register. He stands with a small roll of black electrical tape and, from the other side of the bar, reaches over to grab my portfolio. He spins it around and tears off a piece, covering the exposed, sharp edge.

I study the tattoos covering his arms. He doesn't look like a typical billionaire. Usually, men of his status walk around dripping with arrogance. But West almost seems as if he doesn't want to flaunt his wealth. When I first met him, he let me believe he was just a regular bartender. Not the billionaire owner of bars all over the city.

I eye him skeptically. "I don't *need* this job."

"I know you don't."

"Then, why are you doing this?" I finally ask what has plagued me ever since he offered me the job at Heath's funeral. "I told you how miserable I was being married to Heath. I said horrible things about your brother."

"My brother was a horrible human being." He deadpans. "What you said was nothing in comparison to the person he was."

I'm taken aback by his brutal honesty.

I wasn't expecting that.

I want to press him on it, but he still hasn't looked at me, his eyes on the task at hand.

"Still." I shake my head. "You don't even know me and clearly, I'm not reliable."

"Reliable in what sense?"

"My panic attacks."

"You're human, London," he says, matter-of-factly, as if he knows I'll argue against his point. He finally lifts his head, looking directly at me. "You aren't the first person I've known to have a panic attack."

"No, but I'm almost certain I'm the first person you've known with amnesia."

"Amnesia doesn't scare me."

"Does anything scare you?" I tease.

"Only a few things." His mouth twitches.

Heat pools in my belly, and my legs tingle from the weight of his stare as he uses the tips of his fingers to spin my portfolio back around.

I run my bandaged finger over the tape. "Thank you."

"No problem."

His voice slips over my body like velvet. It warms me in places that have been left cold for I don't know how long. The heaviness and weight in the aftermath of my panic attack is left far behind us. Now, we're simply just us.

"You're talented, London. You may not need me, but I need you."

His words are like stones landing at the pit of my stomach.

Heart racing, I tamp down my adrenaline. "What are you looking for me to create?"

He pauses before looking over my shoulder. "My bartender Lewis said the art on these walls doesn't fit the theme of this bar. He mentioned needing artwork that spoke to the history of the city. Ones that tell a story."

I twist on my stool and look over my shoulder to take in each existing piece before turning back around. "I can do that."

"I didn't have any doubt."

I lick my lips. "What about pay?"

He lifts his hand and rests his finger on his chin. I can't help it, my mind wanders. He runs his finger across his chin, then his bottom lip, and all I can think about is wondering what it would feel like to have his finger run up the inside of my thigh, quickly finding my clit and pinching it.

London, stop.

He inhales a deep breath and swipes his tongue across his lip.

Ooh, what would it feel like to have his tongue lick my clit? Dammit, London. Cut. It. Out.

I shiver and rest my elbow on the edge of the bar to massage the back of my neck.

I chalk up my illicit imagination to the fact that I haven't been touched in months. Not since shortly after Heath and I got married. When your husband constantly threatens you and causes you to live in fear, you lose all desire for him. Over the months, my sense of safety around him deteriorated, my appetite to touch Heath becoming nonexistent.

West has reignited a feeling inside me, and that is terrifying to admit.

He drops his hand and bends, resting his forearms on the bar. His face is closer to me now, and his scent surrounds me: fresh leather and mint.

"What do you think I should pay you?" He raises his brows, eyes widening with playfulness.

I scrunch my nose. "I don't know. Feels kind of weird since we're sort of family."

"Are we?" He cocks his head. "Is that how you think of me?"

I don't take offense to it. I never considered myself a part of the Hall family. I think back to West's pool confession and remember he isn't a Hall, either. There's more to his story. The divide between Heath and West is massive. One that gives our feelings about the Halls credence.

My sense of never fitting in with them is as justified as West's.

"I guess not," I admit.

He pushes off the bar and walks around the end, crossing back over to my side. He stands beside the stool he was sitting in earlier and grips the edge. Lifting his gaze from my portfolio, he flicks his eyes to mine, staring into my soul. "Now that we have that settled..." His voice deepens. "Before we get to the matter of payment, I want to make something very, *very* clear."

A chill prickles down the back of my neck. My lips part as a sharp breath passes through them. West's scent is stronger, and the heat from his body wraps around me. I squeeze my thighs together.

"Heath was *never* my brother."

His stare is unwavering, and he may as well have cut me open. I'm vulnerable, and one would think I would bolt in the opposite direction.

But one truth remains.

I've never felt safer than I do with West. I've never felt more myself than around him. Like he sees a part of me I didn't know existed. Or one that I forgot existed.

It's impossible. But is it?

I lean into the feeling, reading between the lines of West's very pointed statement.

Heath was *never* his brother.

Just like my marriage to Heath wasn't a real marriage. Heath didn't love me. He didn't worship the ground I walked on. He didn't cherish me.

Not the way I deserved. And truthfully, it wasn't just me. It was West, too.

NINE

LONDON

We never settled on the matter of payment. I plan on bringing it up to West today, as soon as I show him my first completed piece for the bar.

I carry my weathered portfolio with me as I race down the stairs of Selene's apartment, then to the subway that takes me to the other side of the city to The Veiled Door.

Living here in New York has been an adjustment from Boston. The air is different. The people are different. The feel of it. The smell of it. Even the sounds. All overwhelming but growing on me. As if there's an invisible pull this city has had on me and it's satisfied, knowing this is where I was meant to be all along. Like my heart belongs here.

Selene was right. There was nothing and no one left for me in Boston, and the longer I stay here in New York, the further my marriage to Heath and my abusive past fades into the distance.

As usual, I show up to the bar right after the bartender unlocks the door for opening. West introduced me to the bar manager Piper and a few of the other bartenders during my first week here. Most work the same shifts, and sometimes I only ever see a handful of them more than the others, including Lewis, the one I see the most. But Piper is the one opening today.

She stops me before I make it to the base of the stairs, telling me all about the man who sat next to her wearing a hot dog costume on the subway. I laugh and nod along, aching to get upstairs to start working. She's sweet and kind, but ever since I've started working on these pieces for this bar, my motivation to begin my new life here in New York has been at an all-time high.

Once she's finished, I leave Piper to slice her lemons in peace and race upstairs.

The boards creak under my feet. The quiet music of the bar below my studio fades in the distance, muffled by floors that have probably been around for at least a century. I push my shoulder into the door of my studio. Once a storeroom for all the bar's supplies, West has done his best to make it my own. He's reorganized the liquor and cleaning supplies, stacking them on one side of the room. The other side is mine, filled with bits of charcoal and a fresh stack of sketchbooks. Even a few brushes and palettes of watercolor if the mood strikes. All of it set up just for me. There are probably a million other places in the city I could work, but I like it here. It's private, quiet, and though I know West has other bars to run, the chances of seeing him while here are better than if I were anywhere else.

The room is more like a closet. If I were to estimate it's size, I'd say probably only about six by six feet, but I've done my best to put the lack of space out of my mind. Normally tight spaces are a trigger for me, but they haven't been here.

Although there are boxes piled on one side of the room, blocking half the filled shelves, I decide to work on the floor today. Sometimes I can get a different perspective on a piece when I'm looking down on it.

Dropping to me knees, I place my portfolio on the wooden floorboards in front of me and open it up. I slip out a piece of charcoal and the piece I've been working on the past several weeks. I ignore the sheets tucked in the back, the ones more personal to me.

I'm thankful I decided to wear leggings today so the splinters from the aging wood don't cut into my skin. Popping my ear buds in, I unlock my phone, press play on my favorite playlist and open up the image I've been using as reference for my first piece: a photograph of an older New York City in the nineteen twenties, filled with T-model cars and women in fancy dresses and bowl hats. All the men are dressed in perfectly-tailored suits.

The charcoal tip meets the paper, and my mind doesn't immediately go blank like it usually does when I work on pieces that aren't close to the heart. I stop, my hand shaking just above the paper.

I'm thinking about West.

Again.

Maybe it's the men in suits. They're faceless strangers who could be anyone, but all I see is West's face on every single one.

We've spent the past few weeks getting closer to one another. I don't know if it's part of West's usual routine to spend as much time here as he does over his other bars, but almost every time I'm here, he is too.

Over that time, I've felt it building between us. What *it* is, I have no clue, but I do know it's electric. Not the kind that's jolting and startling. It's a quiet, unsuspecting constant buzz, humming beneath my skin, like we both know it's there but refuse to acknowledge its presence. And as the days have passed, with me up here in my studio and him below, I have nothing but him on my mind. At night, I think about West, anticipating seeing him again the next time he decides to show up at The Veiled Door.

Ridiculously, I find myself filled with more disappointment when he doesn't show up than the last time he wasn't there.

I add shading to the man's back, using my fingertip to smudge the delicate black powder across the faded yellow paper. My hands are covered in charcoal as I kneel on the floor on all fours. My back aches and my legs tremble, the day's work wearing on me already when my breath gets caught in my throat.

I glance over my shoulder to the propped-open door, expecting West to be standing there. He isn't. At least not yet.

It's stupid, and I shake my head, turning back to look at my drawing.

"You can't, London," I mutter under my breath.

I shouldn't want West.

I shouldn't be imagining him touching me. Kissing me in all the places an ex-brother-in-law has no business being.

And despite his reassurances that he was never close with Heath, I can't help resisting. Even if it means I'm only kidding myself.

I sit back on my heels, trading glances between my drawing and my phone, searching for what's missing. When I find it, I bend back down and add a little more detail to the man again, sharpening the edge of his hat.

One of my ear buds pops out and tumbles to the floor. It rolls on the hard wood, and I lean forward, stretching to catch it before it slips under the metal shelf. I crawl several feet before catching it, but I'm startled when I hear a loud grating sound coming from behind me.

Stunned and remaining on all fours, I glance over my shoulder.

This time West is standing in the doorway.

He fills the entire threshold. A tall, towering frame that sends chills along the length of my spine, his arms crossed over his chest. The peaks and valleys of his muscles are strained against his dark blue button-down shirt. A black tie is wrapped around his neck, concealing the necklace I know he's wearing and have yet to see fully.

The familiar feeling fills my heart, and seeing him does something to my insides. Heat pricks the insides of my thighs, and the electric buzz I get when near him comes at full force.

West's eyes shoot straight for my backside, and I swear I see his muscles twitch. A groan rumbles from his chest before his eyes dart back to mine.

"Oh." I stumble, realizing how I must look. Ass is in the air, pointed directly at him. Also, I'm wearing thin black leggings that when stretched, don't exactly leave much to the imagination. "I'm sorry. I, um, I dropped my ear bud." I scramble backward to my set up with my drawing. Then I sit on my heels, turning so I'm facing the wall. I turn my head to my left and look up at West, holding up my ear bud as I'm removing the other one.

My cheeks are flamed red, and I'm waiting for him to say something. Anything.

Anything to break this awkwardness.

I. Am. Mortified.

"It's a beautiful view," he finally says, his voice is deep and low.

"What?"

He flicks his gaze to my drawing on the floor. "The picture."

"Oh." I laugh nervously. "Right." I wipe my hands on my leggings and stand, picking up the piece on the way.

Why am I disappointed he wasn't talking about my practically bare ass staring directly up at his face?

Crossing the room, I meet West and hold the piece of parchment out to him. He studies it intently, his eyes roaming over the page.

"Truly." His eyes dart to mine. "It's beautiful."

"Thank you," I whisper, stepping back. I'm too close. We're always too close.

Watching West in front of me has me thinking thoughts one shouldn't have for their ex-brother-in-law. Boss. Whatever he is to me.

I keep my focus on the drawing, but all I feel is his heat on me. Warning signs blare inside my head. Is he feeling what I am, or is it just my imagination?

I need a distraction.

Work, London. Focus on work.

"I have a few questions."

West's blue eyes widen. "Questions?"

"We never talked about how many drawings you want me to create." I tuck my bottom lip under my teeth.

His gaze drops to my mouth. "That isn't exactly a question." I expect his statement to be followed up with a laugh or a chuckle, but it isn't. We're both keeping up conversation, but it seems our minds are clearly somewhere else.

Again, am I imagining this?

"Okay," I draw out. "How many drawings are you wanting me to create?"

Scratching at his chin, his mouth turns down into a frown as he studies my almost completed piece. "I'm not sure. You've been downstairs. What do you think is a good amount?"

"Julianna is the interior designer, not me. I could always ask her."

"It's okay. Why don't you just create whatever your mind comes up with?"

A slow smile creeps onto my face. "Sounds good."

His heated gaze falls to my mouth again. "Did you have another question?"

"I did." I pick my portfolio off the floor and glance over my shoulder as I'm bent at the hip.

West's eyes move to the shelf containing a dozen rolls of paper towels and toilet paper.

"We never figured out the payment," I state.

His jaw ticks as he absentmindedly runs his finger across each roll. "How much do you usually charge for your drawings?"

I shrug my shoulder, organizing my various pencils and pieces of charcoal. "It depends. Usually around fifty to sixty dollars for an eight by ten canvas."

"Your art is worth more than that," he blurts out.

I snap my head in his direction, caught off guard by his brazen opinion.

I turn back around, planting my feet firmly to the floor. "I want my art to be accessible to everyone. Why should custom pieces only be available to the rich and well off?"

He smiles slowly and chuckles under his breath.

His stare burns a hole straight through me.

"What?" I ask.

He frowns, shaking his head. "Nothing. I just like that you're strong willed."

"Well, when you're part of the top one percent, I guess it's easy and comfortable to stay in your bubble rather than think of others who are scraping by just to survive."

"Is that what you think of me?"

My chest caves in. "No. I didn't mean to insinuate I was talking about you."

"You were talking about Heath."

I wring my fingers in front of me. "Well, Heath traded more

money in a day than others could ever dream of making in a life-time. So, what do you think?"

He smirks. Then nothing. Several beats of silence weigh between us before he takes two steps away from the toilet paper. "I have an idea."

"For?"

He scratches at his chin, looks at the ceiling before dropping his gaze. "Twenty pieces. You create at least twenty pieces to be framed and displayed for The Veiled Door's reopening."

"Reopening?"

"Does twenty pieces sound reasonable?" he asks, ignoring me.

"I guess."

"Good. You create twenty pieces, and when you're finished, we can decide which ones we'd like to keep displayed here at The Veiled Door."

"What happens to the other ones that won't be displayed?"

"We'll put them up for auction at the reopening."

"Like the other night at Holt's place?" I ask, holding back a chuckle.

"Yes. Whatever we raise with the auction money will be donated to whichever charity of your choosing. As far as your payment, I'll match what is raised and pay you that amount."

"West, that's, um..." I can't help but smile.

"What?" he asks, his eyebrows pinching.

"That's amazing."

His face relaxes. "I thought you were going to say complicated."

I laugh. "Well, it kind of is."

"But we have a deal?"

"Yeah." I nod quickly. "Sounds good."

"I'm glad we finally have that figured out." He laughs under his breath and points to the floor. "Now, get back to work."

I chew on the inside of my cheek as I watch him turn toward the door. My drawing isn't even on the floor anymore, along with my portfolio.

Before he's made it out the door, I'm slipping a blank sheet of parchment out of my portfolio and kneeling to the floor.

And before he disappears down the small stairway, I swear I see him flex his fingers before curling them into a tight fist.

Yeah, working for West is definitely going to be interesting.

TEN

What the hell am I doing?

It's the question I should be asking myself, but I'm not.

I don't feel guilty for the way I'm feeling. I've searched for London for years, and now she's here, a terrorizing brother who I never considered mine won't stop me from giving in to my feelings. I've suppressed them for so long. Pent up frustration and regret have eaten me alive.

But now? London has given me reprieve. She's a breath of fresh air, bringing me back to life.

Although a few truths remain.

Technically, I'm now her boss, and she's now my employee. We've settled into a basic routine. A professional one, but I can't help feeling like there's more. The little teases. The constant texting. The back and forth of pretending to talk about work.

There's also the matter of me proposing the idea of a reopening of The Veiled Door in a few months, all for the purpose of unveiling London's work, but now I'm kicking myself for putting a deadline on working with her. The kicker is, I don't even know *when* that might be. For all I know, London could be finished working on her twentieth piece within a matter of days.

I've pigeonholed myself into giving her an easy out. Not that I would force her to stay if she didn't want to, but I'm not even certain putting a deadline on it would be any better. No amount of time with her will ever be enough.

Then there's the little fact that she doesn't remember me.

So, the pent-up frustration still lingers.

It's been nearly a month since I hired her. I've cleared the upstairs storage room for her to work in, but I know it's only temporary. I plan on finding her a bigger studio, one she's worthy of. I've even considered hitting up Asher and putting an obscene bid on any listing he might have that would work for London's studio. Money doesn't matter to me at this point, especially when it comes to her, but I don't want to scare her away. Especially after what she told me about the top one percent and how they feel entitled to living in their own bubble without any regard for giving back to the society that lifted them up in the first place.

Although her marriage to Heath wasn't a marriage at all, her life has been uprooted. She's in a new city and adjusting to working with me.

I keep the idea of finding her a bigger studio in my back pocket, seeing if I can come up with another solution. She hasn't complained about working in the storeroom, but I don't expect her to.

My mind wanders to that day, when she had the panic attack.

The sound of me moving the boxes and the crashing of my clumsy movements triggered her. Deep in my gut, I know it's from her past. The time she doesn't remember, even though I do.

I remember it all. The beauty and the pain.

I'm dying for London to remember me, but her memory also comes with tragedy.

It seems like her mind is toying with the darkest memories.

I hang my head, staring at the rushing water twenty feet below.

"I know we haven't known each other long, but I realized I never told you that I'm sorry." Holt offers kindly.

I look over my shoulder to the table where Holt and Asher are sitting.

"Sorry for what?" I ask, confused, rejoining them at the table. I think about the past month and can't think of a single thing Holt should be apologizing for. His face is pinched, focused on the five cards in his hand.

Our friendship started as business. A reporter working for Holt's magazine wanted to write an article focusing on local breweries. After the initial interview, I'd gone up to the magazine's office and met with Holt. From then on, we hit it off.

It's interesting because when I think back on it, Holt's the longest friend I've ever had. My life never afforded me the opportunity to hold relationships for long, platonic or romantic. When you have a childhood like mine, you learn to accept that no one ever stays.

But there was one exception to this life lesson.

I swallow down the regret I have for knowing I could have had that with London. I *did* have that. A least we *had* had the beginning of it before it was ripped away.

Over the years, I've realized forcing a dream is a fool's errand. But is it possible to have second chances at a dream you had when you were fifteen? With someone who only knows who you are now?

"I'm sorry for the loss of your brother," Holt elaborates, plucking a card from his hand and placing it face down on the table. He picks up another from the deck and adds it to his hand.

"It's been two months since his death." I roll my eyes,

picking up the cards Asher just dealt. "And I really wish people would stop saying that."

Holt's expression deflates. Asher nervously trades glances between Holt and me. I can tell they don't know what to say or what to do. They weren't expecting that response from me.

"I'm sorry, man." I groan, running my hand down the length of my face. "I know you were just trying to be a good friend. It's just my relationship with Heath was complicated."

Holt sighs, his nostrils flaring. "It seems it was that way with his wife, too."

"Yep." I take a swig of my beer as the breeze brushes over my skin.

"How is it working with London?" Asher asks, taking a sip of his seltzer and lime.

The steward brings us another round of drinks without us even asking.

I tell him thanks and glance down at the pier, waiting anxiously for London. Since we're in the middle of summer, Holt invited the entire group to spend the day on his yacht.

"It's good." I play it cool, not diving into the complexities of my relationship to London. "I think she's adjusting to it fine. She's already working on the first piece to hang at The Veiled Door."

If my ties with Heath were too complicated to share with my friends, I won't even bother going into it with London.

Asher nods. "I think it's great you're there for her after losing your brother. I'm sure it's comforting for her to feel like she still has family on her husband's side."

I curl my lip, my stomach souring. "It's strange. I never thought of London as my sister-in-law. Heath and I hadn't talked for years, and even before that, we never got along."

Asher nods again, and I can tell I've made the situation awkward again. Dammit.

"I was adopted." I give in and share a slice of my past. "I didn't meet Heath until we were fifteen, and he hated me from the start. We had a rocky relationship."

"Trust me," Asher says, his eyes softening. "I know what it's like to have complicated family relationships. It's why Charleigh and I will never move back to Connecticut."

I nod, remembering how he told me about his rough beginning back in Connecticut. Our childhoods aren't the same, but they are parallel.

Neither Holt nor I elaborate on Asher's comment. Holt breaks the tension when he tosses out a plastic chip, laying down his bet on this first round. Asher flicks his eyebrows and begrudgingly matches his bet.

I do the same, then check my phone under the table for a text from London, smiling when I have a new one. She texted me earlier asking if I planned on joining the group today, and there was no way I was going to miss out on an opportunity to spend time with her outside of our work capacity.

London: I don't think I've ever been on a boat before. Have a bucket ready, just in case.

I quickly type out a reply.

Me: Don't worry. If there isn't a bucket, you can lean over the railing. I'll even hold your hair back for you.

The rolling three dots practically kill me before her response finally hits.

London: Such a gentleman.

I'm about to type out a response when Julianna emerges down the pier, followed by Selene, Charleigh, and London.

Julianna holds onto her large sun hat and looks up as she crosses the bridge, stepping onto the yacht. "All right, boys, the girls are all here! The party can officially begin."

"Party already started an hour ago!" Holt shouts back, never looking up from his hand.

The four women make their way up the stairs to join us on the top deck. Selene barely looks up at the group before spinning and spotting the table of snacks and champagne. She makes herself a mimosa and downs half of it in one gulp. Charleigh makes a beeline for Asher and slips into his lap. They're quickly tied up in each other.

London gives me a closed-mouth smile, and she's fucking breathtaking. She sits in the cushioned bench along the outer edge of the deck and crosses her long legs, her black skirt splitting to reveal her smooth skin underneath. The ties of the bathing suit she's wearing peek out from under her loose knitted top.

Julianna stands behind Holt and glances around the table. "Well, this is exciting."

"No one said you have to play," Holt spouts back.

"Trust me, I'm not." She snorts. "I've been waiting to take this baby out on the river ever since you bought it, and today is the perfect day for it. I plan on lying out in the sun the whole day."

"Just make sure you don't get burned," Holt mutters. "Might ruin your day."

"Trust me." She taps her hand on her brother's shoulder. "The only thing that could ruin my day is if I find myself staring at Rome Montgomery's smug face."

"Oh." Holt lowers his cards into his lap and looks over his shoulder to Julianna. He gives her a mock wince. "Did you not want me to invite him? Shit."

Julianna's expression immediately shifts. Her eyebrows

slant, and her cheeks redden. "What?" The 't' at the end of her word ends with incredible sharpness.

"Yeah." He shrugs and shakes his head. "He's actually below deck changing right now."

"What the fuck, Holt?" Her nostrils flare. "Are you kidding me?"

She looks at me and Asher for clarification, but we don't give her any, even though we know Holt is just giving her shit. Rome isn't here.

"No," Holt says, continuing as if he's still playing our game of poker, but none of us have taken a turn. "Are *you* kidding me, Julianna? You nearly chopped my head off the last time I invited him somewhere. Do you honestly think I'm that stupid to do it again?"

Julianna's shoulders drop with relief. "Wow. Okay." A small smile plays on her lips as she turns around and joins Selene by the table. "That's a relief. You know, I wish luck to whatever woman you end up with."

"I don't plan on getting married any time soon. Leave that to these two horny teenagers," he mutters, nodding toward Charleigh and Asher.

I'm watching the whole scenario unfold when I hear London giggle while watching Charleigh and Asher.

Asher lifts his hand and tucks Charleigh's hair behind her ear. He whispers something that causes her grin to widen.

London is watching them with a tiny smile playing on her lips. Selene and Julianna aren't even paying attention to them, instead heading down to the lower deck. The bottom deck of the yacht stretches out to a large rope net to lay out on. Selene and Julianna slip out of their sandals and take off their bathing suit cover ups to stretch out in the sun.

Holt slams his hand down on the table. "Fuck this game." He stands and swallows down the rest of his beer, eyes trained on the two women below. He flicks his gaze to me. "I'm going to talk to the captain to get this ship sailed."

I laugh. "This isn't a ship, but all right."

Holt cracks a smile, finding humor in my joke.

He disappears to the upper deck, and I turn my attention to London. The midday sun shines down on her from where she's sitting on the bench. Its rays reflect off her golden bikini top. I chew on the inside of my cheek, wondering how I'm going to spend the rest of this day looking at her with restraint. She's different today.

She's watching her two best friends below, with her forearm resting on the metal railing.

Asher is showing something to Charleigh on his phone. They both seem to be in their own bubble, so I leave them and join London.

I sit beside her as the yacht pulls away from the pier, leaving the city behind, close enough to where my knee touches her thigh. Although the bench faces the opposite direction, we're both twisted to look out at the water.

London glances at me with a satisfied grin before turning her attention back to the water. The increasing breeze catches her black hair. She has it twisted into a high, messy bun piled on the top of her head, but I find myself jealous of the stray hairs dancing across the skin of her cheeks.

She leans forward and rests her chin on her forearm.

With stolen breath and a burning chest, I force myself not to stare too long. We're definitely crossing into territory outside of work. None of this is normal for the type of relationship we should be having, but that's all we've done these past weeks: pretend as though that's what we are. *Normal.*

Instead, I focus on the water as we continue to head toward the ocean.

We sit in silence until I finally decide to break it.

"Still think you might need that bucket?" I ask her, laughing under my breath. "I don't know if there's one on the boat, but I can search for one if you need it."

She doesn't look nauseous, just happy. She giggles and rolls her head to the side, never lifting her chin. The sun reflects off her gray eyes.

"No. I think we're safe. At least for now."

"Good." I grin so large, my cheeks hurt. Fuck, I don't think this woman has any clue how much she owns me.

One look. One laugh from her beautiful mouth. That's all it takes for me to fall to my knees. I love seeing her happy. Unlike the day of the funeral or the day she'd shown up at The Veiled Door with her torn portfolio.

"You know," she says, with her chin still pressed to her arm. "Seeing the ocean like this reminds me of my favorite artist."

I look out at the rippling water. The warm sun beats down on my back.

"Who is that?"

"Emily Rapture." Three lines crease the corners of her eyes. "She mostly paints landscapes, and almost all of them are of the forest. The detail she puts in to the dirt and the trees has always captivated me." She sighs. "But she has this one painting of the ocean. It's stunning."

She rolls her head back to me again, and I swallow the bile coming up from my throat. Not because I have any clue who Emily Rapture is—I don't—but the idea that London is drawn to an artist known for painting forests.

I wonder if London's inadvertent pull to those paintings has to do with our beginning. The one she doesn't remember.

The sickness subsides when she elaborates on the single ocean painting. "I always marveled at how she used watercolor to capture the glistening water." She picks up her phone and opens the search engine before typing Emily Rapture's name into the bar. When she finds the image she's searching for, she passes me her phone.

"This is the one. Isn't it incredible?"

I study the painting, focusing in on the water and the high-lights London is talking about. In the upper right, there is a large, red-brick lighthouse.

"Beautiful," I say, handing her phone back to her. Our fingers brush, and I'm taken a back when she doesn't immediately pull away.

She lifts her eyes from our joined hands holding her phone. Inhaling a shaky breath, she blinks then pulls away, clearing her throat. "Anyway, Emily has this new gallery opening soon in upstate New York. I'm dying to see it."

"Upstate New York?" I ask, and fuck me, the bile comes back like a torrential storm.

I ignore the prickling sensation creeping along the back of my neck. What are the fucking odds London's favorite artist is from the same fucking state as her and me?

"Yeah," she says, but when she looks back at me, her eyebrows dip in concern, and her hand is on my arm. "Are you okay? Looks like you might be the one who needs the bucket."

"Um." My mind is overcome with reality, silencing me.

"On the bright side," London adds. "If you throw up over the railing, you won't have hair for me to hold back. But I would if you had. Then there's the matter of your beard, but I'll leave that one up to you." She laughs under her breath, but when I don't laugh back, her smile falls.

"I'm fine," I force out, chalking all of this up to coincidence. I don't know a fucking thing about amnesia. At least I didn't until it all made sense to me. My mother telling me Heath's new wife had amnesia. Then finding out that wife was London at Julianna's birthday party.

It took a few days for the shock to wear off and reality to set in. I did some research, and nothing I found put me at ease. Every case is different. Some have only short-term memory loss. Some only remember certain aspects. Some never regain their memories.

It's been fourteen years since London's accident, and she has yet to regain hers, only receiving snapshots she can't make sense of.

Nodding, she accepts my answer and turns her attention back to the water.

Watching her now, staring out at the ocean, I'm not certain she ever will, and that reality tears me in two. I place my hand to my chest, willing the pain to disappear.

The wind picks up, and her hair flies from her face, revealing the shape of her cheekbones and the curl of her black lashes framing her gorgeous gray eyes.

"I'm almost done working on another piece," she confesses.

"That's great." I clear my throat and focus on the spot where my knee meets her thigh. London hasn't moved. If anything, she's leaned farther into me, and I've done the same.

"I should be finishing it up in a few days, so I can show you." She sits up, straightening her back as she twists on the bench to turn her back on the ocean. "Only if you planned on being at The Veiled Door, of course. I know you have other bars to run."

I crack a smile. "I think I can make the time."

"Okay." She sighs, gently slapping her bare thighs. Her black cover up has fallen to either side of her, revealing her smooth skin and the bottom of her bikini. My cock twitches, waking from a deep fucking sleep. I curl my fingers into a tight fist.

London falls back against the bench, and my eyes travel up her body, over her bare stomach and the small diamond piercing in her belly button, to the swell of her breasts peeking out from the top of the thin, gold top. Breasts I could easily sink my teeth into.

Fuuuuuck.

My dick jumps at the thought.

I should feel guilty, but I don't. If Heath was alive to know the fantasies I've played in my mind about London, he'd have soon discovered that, *technically*, she was mine first. And knowing how London felt about Heath, *technically*, they never shared a real marriage. Not the one she deserved.

If she were mine, I'd make sure she knew it every single fucking day.

London nods toward Charleigh and Asher, who are now standing by the table filled with champagne and orange juice. He's pouring her a glass, never taking his eyes off her.

"It should be sickening, but it's kind of sweet, isn't it?" she says. She grins as if she's envious of her friend's happiness.

"It is." But I'm not looking at them. I'm only looking at her.

"We deserve a love like that, don't you think?"

"Yes." I'm quick to answer.

She turns her head my way, finding my eyes. We stare at each other for several beats, our silent thoughts filtering into the void.

"I'm going to join the girls and get some sun myself." She stands and adjusts her black skirt before opening the gate at the top of the stairs that leads to the lower deck... but I don't miss how she stops with the gate open, hesitating as she glances over her shoulder in my direction before she continues down the stairs, turning her back to me.

I force myself to focus on the water, thinking about anything but London.

A location in Miami I've been scouting for a new bar.

Renovations to my bar on Long Island.

Increasing my donation to the foster homes in New York State.

But all thoughts lead back to the woman I can't tear my gaze away from. She's now removing her thin black skirt. I press my fingers to my mouth, stifling the groan clawing up my throat.

London's full, round ass cheeks jiggle as she kicks off her sandals. Her full tits are perfect and her gold bikini shimmers in the sunlight, a stark contrast to her raven hair. Tucking her fingers under the hem of her bikini bottom, she runs her hands from her waist to her cheeks. Her nails grate against her fragile skin. The elastic fabric snaps back, hugging her curves. She glances down, adjusting the bottom of her bikini top, ensuring all the important parts are covered.

Her hands are all... over... her... body.

"Fuck." I groan.

London quickly looks in my direction, and her eyes find me. My face erupts into flames, and I dart my gaze back out at the water. I'm still shielding my mouth with my hand, forcing my dick to calm the fuck down. It's begging to be set free, practically screaming under my swim shorts.

I'm still catching glimpses of London from the corner of my eye, even as I adjust myself the best I can.

"Are you all right, man?" Asher's question drags me out of the trance London has caught me in.

I look to my right, finding him staring at me. "I'm fine."

I glance back over my shoulder to see London slipping her sunglasses down to rest on the bridge of her nose. There's no mistaking the curl in the corner of her insatiable mouth.

I imagine it sucking the crown of my dick before she sticks her tongue out, dragging that silver ball along my length. Fuck.

Finally, she lays down beside Selene on the net and rests her hands on her stomach, trailing her fingers absentmindedly along the skin there.

I lied to Asher when I said I was fine. I'm not fine. The biggest lie I've ever told.

ELEVEN

LONDON

I'm falling.

Falling, falling, falling.

It isn't hard and fast. It's slow and methodical. Like the blow of the breeze over the surface of the water. Like a whisper over bare skin. Like the sound of my name coming from West's mouth as though he's said it a thousand times before.

I'm falling.

The blood rushes to my head, and I crack my eyes open. Charleigh and Julianna are sifting through the rack of dresses one of Julianna's designer friends brought over thirty minutes ago. I'm pretty sure some of them cost more than the average person will make in a lifetime, but what Julianna wastes in expensive taste, she makes up for with her charity work.

She gasps and pulls off a floral dress from the rack that's covered in glittering sequins—not one I would pick out for myself. But it will look stunning on Charleigh, even if Julianna's only holding it up to herself.

One thing I've noticed about my new best friend, Charleigh, is that she wears flowers at least six days of the week. Where she adores bright and obnoxious colors, I like fading into obscurity.

"Come on, London," Julianna says to me. From how I'm lying on her bed, she and Charleigh are upside down. Julianna bends at the waist and talks to me with her head cocked to the side. "I *know* you'll find something in Massimo's collection."

I sigh, lifting my head up and spinning around to sit on the edge of Julianna's oversized bed.

"Your place is beautiful." I glance around the large open space, noting the touches of white, beige, and green accents scattered throughout Julianna's new apartment. She is a well-known interior designer in the city, but seeing her work in her own space, I can tell how talented she is.

"Thank you." Julianna grins. "Asher got me a killer deal on this place. I hated the one on the other side of the city. The view is better from here."

She's right, it is. The view of the harbor isn't obstructed, reminding me of where Holt's yacht is parked, which brings me to being out on the water with West the other day.

I eye Charleigh as she studies herself in her reflection of Julianna's floor-length mirror, running her hand over the dress that's draped across her front.

"You seem to have an eye for picking out dresses that suit us," I tell Julianna. "Is there one on the rack that speaks of me?"

Julianna claps her hands gleefully and spins on the ball of her foot with a squeal. "Okay," She's already flicking through them as if she hasn't already looked at them a thousand times over. "You're a little more on the introverted side, but I can tell you aren't shy when it comes to your body." She gives me a cheeky grin. "I gathered that on the yacht."

"I loved that gold bikini," Charleigh gushes, her eyes finding me in the reflection. "You looked so hot in it."

I stifle a laugh and bite down on my lip.

"For sure," Julianna agrees, removing a red dress. She shakes her head and places it back on the rack. "I noticed West couldn't keep his eyes off you."

"Not true," I'm quick to dismiss.

I'm lying, though. It's all I felt the other day, his eyes on me, burning me from the inside out. I was a powder keg, ready and waiting to be lit.

I knew what I was doing when I wore that bikini. I wanted his eyes on me. My heart raced at the idea of what seeing me like that did to him, and it was obvious in the way he constantly cleared his throat or adjusted in his seat.

He couldn't sit still.

Mission accomplished.

I haven't pinpointed my feelings yet, but the thrill I get when thinking about West is addictive. Something I've never felt before.

"West was Heath's brother, though. Then again, I heard they weren't close. They didn't even talk to each other at Julianna's party," Charleigh says.

"Yeah," I agree. "I didn't even know West was there. Ironic how small the world can feel even in the largest city in the world."

"Do you know what happened between them?" Julianna asks. "Sounds like they were practically strangers, not brothers."

"Sort of." I look away, keeping West's secrets to myself. These women are two of my closest friends now, but I feel protective of what West has told me. He doesn't want everyone to know the depth of his past when I would give anything to know mine. "But Heath and I didn't have a good marriage. Not sure if Selene told you."

"She hasn't." Charleigh's sympathetic eyes find me in the reflection of the mirror.

I nod in appreciation for my sister's discretion. Charleigh and Julianna know about my amnesia, but they don't know the sordid details of my marriage. "He was abusive. More mentally than anything. At first, I felt awful he'd died, but it's funny because the more time passes, the more I learn about myself."

"Like what?" Julianna asks, tipping her head to the side, her brows furrowing deeper.

"That I've been spending the last year of my life with him pretending to be someone I wasn't. That my love for myself was greater than the love I had for him."

"Wow," Julianna whispers.

"You deserve someone better than that tool bag."

I stifle my laugh at Charleigh's comment. It sounds more like something Julianna would say than her.

"It's okay to want to move on," Charleigh adds. "You know, Holt was looking at you, too."

I'm surprised by her comment. I never thought much of Holt. He's usually quiet around me, and whenever Selene is around him, she doesn't have much to say.

"Ugh." Julianna rolls her eyes. "We're all adults, and I obviously can't tell you who to date, but there are better men than my brother."

"Why do you say that?" I ask.

She shrugs, pausing at looking at a dress. "He's just consumed with his magazine, and there's this matter of him trying to get close to the Montgomerys all of a sudden."

"Are you saying you don't trust your brother?" Charleigh asks.

"No." Julianna inhales a breath. "It isn't that. I just don't know what his angle is. He's just being secretive." She pauses. "More so than usual."

"Huh." Charleigh looks at me, raising her brows with a shrug of her shoulders.

I shrug back.

"Anyway..." Julianna blinks her thoughts away. "I have

enough going on in my dating life, or lack thereof, to pay attention to what my brother is doing."

I see the war in Charleigh's eyes, wanting to ask Julianna to elaborate on her dating life, but she clamps her mouth shut. I've been around them enough to know Julianna is constantly finding the worst men, and this rivalry with Rome Montgomery is curious.

"Selene asked me to set this one aside for her." Julianna twists her mouth in thought, moving the dark blue dress to the end of the rack. It's stunning, with a slit driven straight up the thigh and a deep v-cut neckline.

I check my messages for one from Selene but find none. Instead, I find myself wandering to her Instagram account. There's a new post of her open laptop at a coffee shop. Her caption reads: *The work never stops. News coming soon.*

I'm closing out my screen when Julianna gasps.

"Yes!" She rips one of the hangers off the rack and crosses the room to meet me. Stopping in front of me, she holds the dress out, staring at the back of it.

"With your dark hair and those golden rings you always wear, this will be perfect for our girls' night at the club." Julianna giggles.

I'm wondering why Julianna picked a club for our first girls' night. All four of us are in at least our late twenties to early thirties. Never being a club goer myself, even when I was in my early twenties, I'm nervous. Mostly because of other people and tight spaces.

But this is *New York City.* Ever since my newfound freedom from my controlling mistake of a marriage, I'm telling myself to break out of the box I've placed myself in, despite the anxiety I might get from it.

I reach out and slide my hand along the black sequins. The bottom portion of the dress is covered in them. From the waist up it is all thin, black lace. Although the dress has long sleeves, it's incredibly revealing. And short. At least shorter and more revealing than I would typically gravitate toward.

The neckline is similar to the dress set aside for Selene.

"It is beautiful," I say quietly.

"Try it on." She holds it out for me, but I know I need to get going. I promised West I would meet him at The Veiled Door.

"I actually need to head out." I sit up from Julianna's bed. "I finished my first piece for the bar and need to show it to West."

"Oh." She frowns, then spins on her heel. "Take the dress home and try it on. See if you like it."

"No, no, no." I hold my hand up. "I can't do that, Julianna."

"Yes, you can." She slips the short dress into an equally short, protective bag. Like it was made specifically for it. She crosses the room and hands it to me, draping it over my arm. "I need to get these other dresses back to Massimo tonight, so if it doesn't work then just let me know."

"I don't know." I'm still hesitant. I don't have time to drop the dress off at Selene's apartment before heading to The Veiled Door. They're in opposite directions. And I don't want to be late meeting West. He always sticks to his word when it comes to meeting me. I want to return the favor.

"London." Julianna places her hand over mine, forcing me to look into her gorgeous eyes. Her gaze brings me comfort and reassurance. "You're like a sister to us. Well, you're already sisters with Selene, but you know what I mean. To Charleigh and me. Take the dress."

Emotion is thick in my throat, and I look down at the bag hanging over my arm before looking back up Julianna. "Thank you."

She smiles. "Of course."

TWELVE

WEST

I tell myself to think of anyone else while I'm jerking myself off in the shower, but my mind constantly swings back to London.

Raven hair. Golden rings. That goddamn fucking gold bikini.

She knew what she was doing, testing the boundaries placed on us by unfortunate circumstances. Another thing to add to my list of reasons why I hate Heath.

I slap my palm against the cold tile as hot water streams down my back. I'm angrily stroking myself, thinking of her with him. I shouldn't be thinking of him with her, especially not with my hand wrapped around my dick, but I can't help it.

I'm jealous of my dead brother. I have been since I saw him wrap his goddamn arms around London at Julianna's birthday party. I'm jealous of how he stole her and took her for granted. London deserves to be worshipped. She always has been. I think about my promise to her all those years ago and how I've failed at every turn to keep it. I've tried to make it up to her this past month and am determined not to fail again.

Even if she doesn't remember me.

It makes me angry how she remembers him, not me.

I close my eyes and think about her in her gold bikini. The way the sun shimmered against her black hair. Her fingers running along the backside of her bikini bottoms. The way the curves of her breasts bounced as she adjusted her top. How her fingers danced up and down the curves of her stomach, taunting me.

Heat explodes in my lower belly, and my cock swells. I stroke myself until I hang my head between my shoulders and watch the cum spill from the end of my dick.

"Fuck," I breathe, watching it swirl down the drain until the last bit is gone and all that's left is clear water.

I squeeze my eyes shut, shame filling my gut. Not because I've just jerked off to the thought of London, but for every day that's passed since I was fifteen.

My knees pressed into the cold, wet dirt. The leaves that had fallen from the tree last fall were still on the ground, surrounding me as I lifted my hands to cradle London's terrified face.

Her gray eyes were panic stricken, spread wide with fear. Dirt covered our skin, her cheeks, my hands. Blood spilled from my knuckles, but I didn't care. I only cared about the blood spilling from her nose.

"I'm here, London. I'm here."

"Is he..." She quivered, unable to look at the body lying beside us, keeping her eyes trained on the cold, hard dirt. "Is he dead?"

I snap my eyes open, breathing as if I've just completed the Boston Marathon. I curl my fingers against the cold tile and force the memory of the last time I'd seen London before she returned from my mind.

I'd much rather remember her as the last time I actually saw her, with sun glistening off her skin, and that goddamn gold bikini.

Although I thought I was taking a shower to release some of

my tension, when I rinse off and step out, I'm more wound up. My muscles feel tight, and the frustration grows.

All I want is for London to remember.

But all that does is make me selfish because along with me comes the nightmare we lived through in foster care.

I step into my walk-in closet to get dressed in a daze. A cloud hangs over my head as I button my shirt and tuck it in to my dark forest green slacks. Once I've adjusted my tie, I drape my suit jacket over my arm and stride out to the main living area of my apartment.

I'm clasping my watch when I find my driver Alden standing in my kitchen with a cup of coffee. "Good morning, sir."

"Morning, Alden." I eye him over my mug and look at him apprehensively.

Besides Holt and Asher, Alden's the closest thing I have to a friend. In all honesty, he was the first friend I made when I decided to open my first bar, and the real money—money that didn't get handed to me for simply being adopted into the right family—started pouring in.

"Have you ever been into art, Alden?"

His eyebrows arch across his forehead before they furrow in thought. "In what sense, sir?"

"Do you follow any big-name artists? Modern ones, not the classics like Van Gogh or Picasso."

"Hmm. I can't say I do. But you know who might be able to help?"

"Who?"

"Your friend, Holt Capuleti. A man like that who runs one of the top editorial magazines in the country knows practically everything about everyone."

"You're right." I clear my throat and shoot Holt a quick text, asking if he has a minute to talk. He must find it strange yet intriguing, considering I'm not usually the one to reach out first, because he's quick to call me.

I'm swallowing a sip of my coffee when I answer.

"Hey, man," he says.

"You were quick to call." I suddenly feel weird for reaching out to him at such an odd time. "We can talk later if it's better for you."

"No. I'm in the middle of my workout, but I could use the distraction. I've been up in my head lately."

"Okay." I scratch at my chin, then run my fingers through my hair, resting my elbow on the kitchen counter.

"What's going on?" he asks.

"Do you happen to know any big artists in the New York area?"

"Of course," he answers casually. "I know plenty. Is there one in particular you think I might know?"

"Um, Emily Rapture?" I ask, diving straight in while I massage the back of my neck.

"Oh." Holt scoffs. "I know her. Emily is huge in the art scene. My magazine wrote an article on her a few years back. This was before she blew up and became a household name, but she's incredible. Her art, I mean. She has this incredible gallery in Upstate New York that's supposed to be opening sometime this year. I can't recall when, though."

"Would you be able to find out for me?" I ask, checking the time on my watch before checking my phone. I've already done a search on Emily Rapture and know she's opening her new gallery in New York in the next six months, but I don't know the specifics.

"What's all this about? If you don't mind me asking."

"London mentioned her being one of her favorite artists, so I thought I'd see if I could get more details on when it opened."

"Of course. You know, if you want, I can see if Emily can get you an early showing."

"What? Really?"

"Definitely," Holt answers. "I like to follow up with people we've covered in the past. See if there are any fresh stories we can write about them. This will give me the perfect opportunity to do that."

"Awesome, man." I sigh. "Thanks."

"No problem. We should grab a drink this week. When you're not working, of course."

"Sounds good," I tell him, and I mean it. I could use a night with my relatively new friend. I don't have many, and while I like to keep it that way, I don't want to stay a recluse.

It might be a good distraction from London, anyway.

I hang up with Holt just in time to catch Alden slipping off the stool in the kitchen. He leaves his mug on the counter and says he'll be waiting for me downstairs. I give him a nod, but my mind quickly falls back to London in her gold bikini. My dick jerks, and *fuck me*, how am I going to spend the rest of the day like this?

My housekeeper makes her way down the expansive hallway of my high-rise apartment in Brooklyn, picking up Alden's empty mug and loading it into the dishwasher. Alden is already out the door when she asks if I'd like her to make me breakfast. I tell her no. I'm hungry, but I know it isn't food that will satisfy me.

I'm ready to walk out the door and race to The Veiled Door. London said she wouldn't be showing up until later this afternoon, but I try to eliminate any chance of missing her. It's starting to become problematic for me when it comes to the other bars. I've ignored my bar manager's suspicions as to why I don't visit their locations as often anymore, but I can't help it.

London has stolen all my attention. To the point that I'm

now jerking off in the shower like some fucking teenager, fantasizing about her in a way I've never done before. Remembering the old London is one thing. Back then they were sweet and innocent thoughts. It was about protection and laughter. About finding friendship and solace in a place of complete utter darkness.

But now? Now my feelings have transformed to an instinctual, hungry need. I imagine my teeth sinking into her flesh. My dick sinking between her thighs. How her voice would sound screaming my name.

It's a clusterfuck of emotions I hadn't been expecting. Incredible... but also terrifying.

My feelings for London aren't simple, and they never have been.

And every day I see her I leave with a little more hope that she'll remember me. Maybe I'm foolish for believing she might one day. But I hold out hope, despite knowing what comes with the memory of me.

I finish the last bit of my coffee when my housekeeper answers the ring of the doorbell.

I'm slipping into the sleeves of my suit jacket when my mother walks in. Her black and gold sunglasses are perched on the bridge of her nose, despite the fact the sun isn't shining today. Her heels click on the tiles as she pushes past my housekeeper, not bothering to wait for an invitation before barreling in here. I can tell she's already angry with me as she lifts her glasses and slides them to the top of her head.

Her eyes are narrowed into two slits, her daggers aiming straight for me.

"Well, good morning, Mother." I sigh, not in the mood for playing her games.

A piece of my heart has always softened for her. She cared for me when no one else did. She took me in and gave me a life full of possibility. If it weren't for her and my adoptive father's financial stability, I wouldn't have had the starting point I had to get to where I am today. Their bit of wealth blossomed into the level of wealth I have today.

Over the years, I've repaid them for what they've done, and ever since my father's death I've ensured my mother hasn't gone without. He'd left her a sizeable sum, but I've never shied away from offering her any additional support to maintain her comfortable lifestyle.

But it seems the little bit of the hatred Heath held for me has spilled over to my mother in the wake of his death.

We haven't spoken since the day of the funeral. I haven't had the energy to speak to her, knowing it will only end the way it did the last time.

She grabs the fur stole she has wrapped around her arms and tosses it onto the large marble table in my entryway, meeting me at the end of the hall. Bypassing my morning greeting, she places her hand on her hip, a pointed stare aimed my way. "Is it true?"

"Is what true, Mother?" I don't care that I'm using the name she dislikes. I'm frustrated. Emotionally and sexually. The last thing I need is my mother barging into my apartment and scolding me like I'm fifteen again.

"Stop playing games, Weston. Tell me the truth."

"I have no idea what you're insinuating." I move past her. "Can we talk about this later? I have to travel to several of my locations today, and I'd rather not spend half my day stuck in traffic."

"You hired her?"

I come to a screeching halt, my body turning cold and rigid. She hasn't even said her name, but I know exactly who she means.

It isn't my mother is talking about London that has the hair standing on the back of my neck. It's the way she allowed the three words to fall from her mouth as if she's just caught her husband cheating on her. With disgust. With suspicion. With anger and fury.

I spin around, finding her body just as rigid as her words. With pursed lips, she keeps her hands planted on her hips.

"I'm assuming by that shocked look on your face that it is true," she chides.

"I have businesses to run," I say casually. "I do hire people from time to time. I needed an artist to create works for my bars, and London is insanely talented."

"But she's different, West."

I won't argue with her there. London is different.

Mom takes a few steps forward, her pencil skirt restraining her steps. "If he were still alive, how do you think Heath would feel if he knew you hired his wife to work for you?"

"London is a strong woman, Mother. She's capable of making her own decisions."

She rolls her eyes. "That's not the point."

"Then, what is your point?" I ask, not hiding the edge in my voice.

She marches toward me, keeping one hand on her hip. With her other, she lifts it and sweeps my hair from my forehead, studying my face. Her eyes roam over me as if she's holding back a secret she has yet to share. The corner of her mouth lifts into a reminiscent smile. "You know, your father wasn't sure we were doing the right thing when I told him I wanted to adopt a teenager. He said teenagers were unpredictable, especially one who had never been in a stable home."

My mother has never shared her feelings about why she and my father adopted me. They never offered it up, and I was never brave enough to ask.

She runs her manicured fingers through my hair, meeting my eyes with hers. "But I fell in love with your eyes when the adoption agency showed us your picture. They were the brightest shade of blue. Like staring at the ocean." Her reminiscent smile deflates and her gaze falls. "I wanted my Heath to have a brother, and when we adopted you, we were able to give him that."

The idea that I was in a sick, twisted way a gift for Heath rather than my parents makes me ill. A crack forms in my heart, realizing the change in Glenna since Heath's death. I can see the vacancy growing in her eyes.

"But you two never could get along, could you?" She steps back, allowing her hand to fall away.

"It wasn't for lack of trying on my part." I grind my teeth as my temple pulsates. "What does any of this have to do with London?"

I study my mother, wondering if she knows London and I were raised in the same foster home. It was only for a few short years, so I doubt she knows, but I don't know how detailed my records were.

She backs away and spins around, trailing her fingers over the marble entryway table. She runs her hand over her white stole, the strands of fur collapsing under her touch. Glancing over her shoulder, she inhales heavily.

"I spoke with your brother's lawyers."

My face pales, and my heart jolts. "Okay..." I narrow my eyes.

My mother waves her hand flippantly. "Are you familiar with Mercedes Rhodes?"

"No. Why would I know who Mercedes Rhodes is?"

"Right." She purses her lips. "You and Heath hadn't talked in, what was it? Ten years?"

I huff and my nostrils flare. Suddenly, my mother feels cold and distant. Completely different from the woman admiring my eyes only seconds earlier.

"Who the fuck is Mercedes Rhodes?" I sigh. "Get to the point, Mother."

A flip is switched, and I see the true reason for her visit. We've reached the point where the finish line is in sight. The one she's been dragging me toward since she opened her lipstick-painted lips. What was once love and admiration for me has completely evaporated. It's now replaced with anger and indignation.

"Mercedes Rhodes has been handling all of your brother's financial accounts, investments, and interests in the wake of his death." Her voice is entirely too cheerful to match the words coming out of her mouth. "I spoke with her because I was curious to know whether London would be staying in the apartment in Boston. According to his will, your brother requested that once she were to speak at his funeral, she was never to return."

"Return?"

"To Boston." She shrugs a shoulder. "Days after the funeral, Mercedes told London she wasn't to return to her home—the one she shared with Heath. He instructed the locks to be changed and all London's belongings to be shipped away to wherever it was she decided to stay."

She says it as if she assumes London would have somewhere to stay when being kicked out of her own home. Either that or she doesn't care.

Most likely the latter.

Though I'm still not fully understanding what Heath's end goal would be. I know the truth about Heath. London told me the day she stumbled into my bar, and even if I did question the validity of her claims, which I never did, I definitely wouldn't be questioning them now.

White-hot anger floods my veins. What the fuck kind of husband kicks their wife out after their death and leaves them with absolutely nothing? I thought what London told me about Heath was awful, but this is next level.

"Sounds fucked up if you ask me." I try to tamp down my anger, but it's increasingly more difficult the more I think about what Heath has done to London.

Impatience boils over in Glenna's expression. Her already pink-dusted cheeks redden even further. "If your brother wanted her expelled from every aspect of his life in his death, he clearly wanted her as far away from our family as possible. Now, I'm curious to know his reason why, but I knew my son well enough to never question his intentions." Her lips are tight. "If he didn't want London to receive any financial support or otherwise after his death, there must be a reason. And if he was cutting her off, then we have no reason to keep her around."

"Right." I nod, grinding my jaw so tight it feels like I've cracked my teeth. "Because everything Heath did was for a reason, Mother." I close the gap, my protective nature for London clawing its way up through my neck and out of my mouth. "Did you ever think Heath was just a fucking asshole? Did you ever think that he was, quite possibly, a terrible husband who never did anything unless it served him and only him?"

Widening her eyes, she takes a step back. Her arms are now at her sides, hands curled into two tight fists. "I knew it," her venomous voice draws out.

"Knew what?"

"You would take her side over your family's." Tears line her lashes, but she never lets them spill. She puffs her chest out, and the scent of her overpriced perfume stings my nose. "Whatever she said about Heath is a lie. For all we know, she could have been lying to us all along. Maybe Heath found out the truth about her past. Maybe she was faking all this amnesia so she could sneak her way into our family and steal all his money. What if it's a story she made up in her head?" She stabs her red-painted, pointy nail to her temple.

What the fuck?

I curl my lip, barring my teeth. I can't help it. My vision turns red. My mother seems to forget I was raised in a dozen different foster homes, and I've dealt with manipulative, arrogant people like her before. I'm no stranger to what people can do when they feel they have all the power or think anyone who is an outsider has other intentions.

I'm thankful for the boost Glenna gave me to get where I am today, but no amount of manipulation will get me to take her side over London's. I won't put up with it.

"Let's get one thing straight." I growl. "If you think for one second I would ever defend Heath for the way he chose to live his life, you're sorely mistaken. He squandered the life he was given. Not all of us had the luxury of being born into a wealthy, stable home, and Heath did nothing but shit all over you and Richard. He took advantage, manipulated, and used his way to the top. Then he manipulated London into marrying him, using her and controlling her until he got what he wanted out of her. So, no, *Mother*. I will never take his side over hers. And I sure as fuck am not going to leave her just because it's what Heath wanted."

Her entire demeanor shifts the second the last sentence leaves my mouth. It hangs heavily in the air between us. My mother's eyes soften, and her bottom lip peels away from her top.

"Oh," she breathes, realization dawning on her. Her shoulders drop, and she blinks her tears away. "Leave her?"

I swallow, snapping my mouth shut. Fuck.

A sickness brews in my stomach. There's no denying what I

feel for London, what I've always felt. But knowing my mother has a sneaking suspicion of why I'm truly keeping London around doesn't sit well with me. I still don't know if she'll ever discover the truth of what happened at my last foster home.

My mother smirks like she's a dog with a bone, as if she's cracked the code to a safe she's been trying to open her entire life. She's looking at me as if I've betrayed her and her family.

Like I said, I've never been a Hall.

Fear of what this means creeps into the back of my mind.

"I see now." She presses her lips firmly together and nods, picking up her stole. She folds it over her arm and slings her purse over her shoulder. She stands in front of me with a stiff spine and pointed stare. "I fell in love with you when you came to live with us, and I never spent a day regretting my decision. I always felt like you were part of this family. I always felt you belonged with us." She tips her chin higher, squaring her shoulders. "That is until today."

The air is punched out of my lungs as she removes the sunglasses perched on top of her perfectly-styled, silver hair, and slips them back onto her face, shielding her eyes from me before spinning on her heel and walking back toward the front door.

My housekeeper holds it open for her, and I watch her turn the corner without a single breath.

I don't regret what I said about London. I meant it. I won't leave her for a family I never considered mine.

My only regret in this moment is that I've allowed the only mother I've ever known to walk out the door thinking I never loved her.

Because it wasn't only London who was saved the day she was adopted.

I was, too.

THIRTEEN

By the time I make it to The Veiled Door, the sun has nearly set. Darkness is about to take over the city, with only the artificial light keeping things bright.

I'm still carrying the dress Julianna gave me when I pull open the door. Alden, West's driver, is sitting in his usual spot at the end of the bar, sipping his usual seltzer water. He immediately spots me and greets me with a small smile and a nod.

It's funny how he's always here, hiding in plain sight. To others, he's just another customer. I thought he was the first time I stumbled into The Veiled Door.

Tonight, the bar is packed, wall-to-wall. Crowds of people are gathered near the counter, hoping for the chance to catch Lewis's attention behind the bar. Him and another bartender are working away like a well-oiled machine. They glide back and forth like ducks in water, never missing a step. Lewis moves from one end to the other, reaching for a vodka bottle set on the green-lit shelf on the back wall. Spinning around to face the crowd again, he flings the bottle into the air, making it fly from behind his back and over his shoulder before he looks up and catches it. Tipping it upside down, he pours a steady stream of the clear liquid into the metal mixer set on the edge of the counter, not bothering to acknowledge the people who gasp and clap in awe of his incredible talent.

I force my anxiety down and push my way through the crowd to the back of the bar.

"Hello, Miss Walker," Alden greets, stopping me in my tracks.

I haven't heard anyone call me by my adoptive name in a long time.

"Alden." I crack a smile. "I didn't know you knew my maiden name."

"Mr. Knight told me."

Hearing West's name reignites my anticipation at seeing him. My stomach flutters. I begin looking around, behind Alden and toward the narrow staircase leading to my studio.

"He stepped out back to take a call," Alden says, pulling my attention away. "He'll probably be back in a few minutes."

"Oh. Do you mind telling him I'm upstairs then?"

"Of course."

I move past Alden and duck my head as I push my way through another group of people near the opening in the bar, leading to the open doorway to the stairs.

I always keep the door propped open, and I pop my ear buds in to drown out the darkness that plays at the edges of my mind. Although I'm supposed to be working on sketches for the bar, I keep wandering to the sheets tucked into the back of my portfolio. I hang the dress Julianna gave me on the shelf to my right—the one filled with toilet paper and paper towels.

I don't know how long West will take before he comes up here, but I need to look at the drawing I abandoned yesterday. The pull it has on me is suffocating.

I keep my playlist low so I can still hear what's going on in the bar below. The music playing is a little more upbeat than usual, the deeper bass and the beating of drums vibrating into the soles of my black and white chucks. I pinch the paper between my fingers and slide it out from the back of my portfolio.

The second my eyes land on the palm covered in specks of dirt sketched on my sheet of paper, I close them. The memory flashes in my mind. Cold, wet hands touching warm skin. The soft grating of dirt, and the scent of wet earth surrounding me.

Comfort and safety wrap around me, but then it's quickly replaced with panic. My neck prickles with fear, and I shiver.

I'm here, London. I'm here.

His light, cracked voice is a whisper in the back of my mind. Not the voice of a man, but a boy. A teenager, maybe. What once was the smell of fresh earth is now laced with the metallic, acrid scent of blood. Another puzzle piece I have yet to put together.

I open my eyes to focus on the drawing of hands. Do they belong to the voice in my head?

Grabbing a piece of charcoal, I add a few more dots of dirt and add the detail under his fingernails that suggests he's been digging in the ground for days.

They're beautiful, I think, as I add the final touch.

The mixture of smells dissipates, and all I'm left with is the scent of mint, wood, and charcoal.

I'm lost in smudging the charcoal over the fingers, adding shadows, when I know I'm no longer alone. The hairs on the back of my neck stand up as I feel footsteps inside the closet of a room. I drop the piece of charcoal quickly and flip the sheet of paper over.

"I'm sorry I'm late," West's muffled voice says behind me.

These earbuds really aren't that great at drowning out outside noise.

I already feel his body heat behind me. Not like there is

much space for him to move with the door shut. I scramble to tuck my drawing in the back of my portfolio, and I slam it shut before spinning around to face him. I'm met with his broad chest. My eyes fall to his shirt, open at the top, revealing hardened muscle.

He's smells good. Too good.

My thighs clench and heat expands in my belly.

We've never been this close, not even in here.

Somehow the room feels impossibly smaller. West's towering frame takes up nearly all the wiggle room, and his growingly familiar scent of mint and leather is overwhelming. I can practically taste it.

"What was that?" I ask him, plucking one of the buds from my ear.

"I'm sorry I'm late," he repeats. "I was on a call I couldn't pull away from."

"It's okay. Doesn't surprise me."

"No?" he asks playfully.

"You're a billionaire bar owner. Aren't you always talking to someone?"

He chuckles, his eyes flashing with amusement. "Would it bother you if I was always on calls?"

"No." My heart flutters. "Why would I care what calls you're on?"

"You may. You may not." He shrugs.

"From the look on your face, it was pretty important."

"No." He frowns, shaking his head. "I just needed to get some facts straight and get a better understanding of something concerning a conversation I had earlier."

Conversation with who? I wonder.

His expression relaxes, no longer teasing. It's then I notice the weight of today in his body. I shouldn't care who he talks to or what calls he makes and takes. But curiosity digs at me, and I do care. I decide not to ask though, since it really isn't my business.

Silence swells inside the tiny space, and his heat surrounds me.

Realizing how close we are, I take a step back, but it's of no use. I'm met with the open shelf behind me that my portfolio sits on. I reach behind me and grip onto the shelf's metal edge.

"What's in the bag?" He nods toward the dress hanging off the shelf, but his eyes catch my attention, tormented and weighted by the thoughts going on in his mind.

"Oh." Heat fills my cheeks as I nervously glance toward the bag. "It's a dress Julianna lent me for girls' night this weekend. I didn't have time to try it on or stop by Selene's apartment to drop it off."

His jaw twitches as he stares at the bag before he finally tears his eyes away.

"Here," I say, wanting to change the subject. "I'll show you what I've been working on." I move to turn around but can't with how close he is.

His eyes flash under the dim lighting as he looks around. "We need to find another solution for your studio."

"It's fine, really," I brush him off. "I've worked under worse conditions."

"Oh, really?" He raises his eyebrows, revealing more of his blue eyes. His beard is noticeably shorter than every other time I've seen him. With every day that passes, he's sharing more and more of his face with me, and that thought makes my heart leap in my chest.

"Yes." I suck in a breath.

His eyes fall to my mouth.

"Is that supposed to make me feel better?" He lowers his voice.

"It's the truth. In college, I once drew all of my assignments under my bed for nearly the whole semester."

"Why?"

"Because my roommate was never shy about bringing over her boyfriends, and she had a lot of them."

"Huh. Why didn't you just tell her it made you uncomfortable?"

"I did, but she didn't care. For a while, I would just escape and draw somewhere else, but I refused to give up my side of the room just so she could have sex. I thought if I hung around enough, she would get the hint and stop."

"And did she?" He's standing so close to me, his chest is only inches from mine, that his heat pours into me, and my eyes fall to his necklace. The flash of the memory of dirt-covered hands flickers in my mind. I blink it away.

"At first," I answer. "But then she stopped caring whether I was there or not."

He laughs as the corners of his mouth lift. "What did you do then?"

"I put in my ear buds." I point to my ear still filled with music. My playlist is still going, playing barely above a whisper.

"I'm curious." He raises his hand. His fingertips graze the shell of my ear, and I practically melt. My entire body tingles, and my nipples harden under my thin Nirvana T-shirt. Suddenly, I'm aware of how I look. My long hair is piled loosely on top of my head, barely held together by my favorite green silk scrunchie. Having only taken the time this morning to put on one coat of mascara and a miniscule eyeliner wing, my face is practically bare. I know it looks like I've rolled out of bed, but West doesn't seem to mind.

I'm frozen, knowing we're crossing into new territory. We're testing the boundaries. The teasing thrill burning in his eyes tells me as much. Then again, I think we already crossed into it the other day on the yacht. I teased him. I pushed the boundaries because I crave his touch. I've never been touched by him, but it feels as if I'm missing it. How do you miss something you never had? How do you crave someone you've never been with?

Everything I'm feeling is thrilling and new, like I'm suddenly eighteen and losing my virginity all over again.

"What do you listen to when you work?" West's smile never wavers as he plucks the bud from my ear before placing it into his.

I hold my breath. No one has ever cared to know what I listen to when I work.

I place the bud resting in my hand back into my other ear.

"Pretty Slowly" by Benson Boone plays quietly, and we stare at each other for a few beats, listening.

West's smile fades, and he closes his mouth. His neck bobbles as the chorus starts back up. Benson's raw voice rings in my right ear, but West's breath floats in my other.

Intense heat runs through my veins when he lifts his hand again, this time grabbing mine. He slips the other around my waist, pulling my hips against his. I gasp, not doing anything to stop this.

"What are you doing?" I whisper, searching his face for answers I know he won't give.

The steady, heavy beat of the music playing downstairs vibrates through the creaking floorboards as I follow West's lead. He takes a step to his right, then the left.

We're dancing.

His hand on my lower back is a branding iron. My body hums, electricity crackling across my skin as he moves us back and forth. With each sway, we're close to bumping into the shelves on either side of us. We bounce between the stacks of boxes and kegs, but West doesn't seem to notice or care. His eyes don't leave my face.

The song is a mixture of slow and fast beats, and West doesn't miss a single one, keeping up with the fast-changing rhythm. I giggle as he moves gently when the song slows, then quickens when the beat picks up.

My cheeks grow sore from smiling, but as the song comes to an end, the reality of this moment kicks in. West's hands are on me, and I don't want them to leave. I feel safe and cared for. The hopelessness I often feel is gone. West has given me all the clarity without ever helping put anything together. Again, how is this possible?

Looking at West now, he's no longer my dead husband's brother. He's simply West.

My hand is wrapped across his shoulder, and I slide it down the front of his chest. His muscles harden beneath my touch, and I move lower, trailing my fingers over the curves of his abs.

We stop dancing, and I can't make sense of what I'm doing anymore. I can't stop the pull he has on me.

The song changes to "Fade" by Lewis Capaldi.

West's hand moves from my lower back to the front of my jean shorts. His fingers slip down my hip and over the torn fabric. Leaning forward, he brings his mouth close to mine.

"West." His name falls from my mouth with what little sanity I have left in me.

"I need to tell you something," he says, his lips torturingly teasing. If he were to lean forward even just a fraction of an inch, he'd be on my mouth.

I stick my tongue out and sweep it across my lips. My nerves are all over the place. So are my eyes. I don't know where to look or what to think. "What is it?"

"I haven't stopped thinking about you."

His confession rocks me to my core. Brazen and bold. I don't know what to do with this information. I should correct him. Tell him this isn't right, but I don't want to.

Because it doesn't feel wrong.

It feels right.

It feels *so* right.

"What do you mean?" I squeak out. "Since the day on Holt's yacht?"

"No," he hums. "Before then."

It's a vague answer that does something to my insides. A fuse sparks inside my stomach, my chest, between my legs. It's impossible for it not to when we're in a tight space like this one.

"You're beautiful, London."

"I'm not." It's a bit of a lie. I've always thought I've been beautiful, but as far as others are concerned, that's another story. A knee jerk reaction for someone who always seems to attract men who never take the time to appreciate.

"You are," he muses with wandering hands. "You're beautiful in the way that makes my heart ache. The way your eyes light up when you're talking about something you love. The way you smile, and suddenly two dimples appear out of nowhere on those smooth cheeks of yours."

"West..." I didn't realize how much he'd noticed about me.

"It's impossible to think straight when I'm around you, and when you walk away from me, I can't help but stumble over finding the words to try make you stay. Anything to make you stay."

I grasp onto his shirt, clutching onto the expensive fabric, using it as an anchor.

"Do you want me to stop?" he asks, his fingers grazing my bare skin, below the torn hem of my shorts. He's teasing my inner thigh, and I can't bring myself to look up. I focus on his chest and my breathing, his confession still ringing in my ears.

I can't think straight with his hands on me.

"Yes," I say. "No."

"Which is it, London?" His voice is husky and weighted. Every word is laborious, pained, and ravenous. "Yes... or no?"

I lean back against the shelf and let his hand wander. He slips it under one of the legs of my shorts and flits his fingertips over the front of my lace panties.

The sensation makes me weak in the knees, and I can't help the moan that passes my lips. I sag, but West catches me by the back of my neck. His fingers clamp around it, digging into my flesh, sending a jolt of excitement down my spine.

The song playing in our ear changes to "One of The Girls" by The Weeknd.

"We shouldn't," I tell him, betraying my body. I don't understand what I'm saying, but it doesn't feel right. That's how I should be feeling. At least not here, right now. Not in this cramped space. Not when West is technically my boss.

"You're right." He growls. "We shouldn't."

"Okay." My eyes flutter. "Then, stop."

His hand abruptly stops moving, frozen under the bottom of my shorts.

My eyes snap open. "What are you doing?" I breathe.

"You told me to stop." His eyes narrow, hardening with every agonizing second that passes without him touching me.

"I'm not sure I want you to stop." I roll my hips, urging him to press his finger closer. Harder.

He does, taking my signal.

"You said we shouldn't." He slips his fingers deeper, his entire hand now pressed between my thighs.

"I know," I moan, rolling my hips again. "We shouldn't."

"Give me one good reason this shouldn't happen."

He isn't moving fast enough. I'm hungry for his touch, and he's too cautious. Too methodical. There's a painful need growing between my thighs.

Heath. Heath should be a good reason, but he isn't. I've

known West for less than two months, but I know what I feel for him is infinitely more than what I felt for Heath. Where Heath was cold, West feels as if I'm barreling toward the sun with no way to stop.

"I can't," I tell him confidently.

"You can't?" he asks, his brow deepening.

My mind is foggy, and I have to ask him to repeat the question.

"You can't think of one reason?" he asks again, running his forefinger along my slit, over the mesh fabric. He's already coated in my wetness.

I'm going to fucking explode already.

I tip my head back and breath heavily as his chest rumbles with a hungry grunt. "No," I clip. "Absolutely none."

Tucking his fingers under the bottom of my panties, he slips his fingers along my wet slit.

"Jesus, fuck. Your cunt is already weeping for me." He buries two fingers inside me, and I'm gasping for air. I reach behind me to the shelves above my head. My fingernails scratch into the metal, and I roll onto the balls of my feet, rocking my hips with West's touch.

I look at him with hooded eyes as he pumps his fingers into me.

"I have a confession," he whispers, leaning into my ear.

Another one? How many of these has West been keeping from me?

His lips brush against the shell of my ear when he says, "I can't give you any, either."

I want him to kiss me. I want his mouth on mine. I want more of this feeling. Not knowing what it is or where it's coming from, I welcome it with open arms.

West was a stranger to me less than two months ago, though

he's never felt like one. I've never felt more myself in any part of my life than I do with him.

"Tell me what you want," he says, groaning into my ear.

I can tell it's difficult for him to not completely let loose. He's like a caged animal, waiting for his moment of freedom.

"I want you to kiss me."

"Where?"

"Everywhere."

"Tell me *where*," he orders.

I swallow the fire burning in my throat. I'm not lying. I want him to kiss me everywhere. My mind scrambles to pick just one place. One I know I need touched by his lips. More than just my mouth, even though we haven't kissed yet.

His hot breath brushes my ear again, and I squirm with his fingers pumping inside me.

"I want you to kiss me down there."

"Where? Say it, London. I want to hear you say it." He jerks his hips forward, pressing his hardened erection against my thigh, his hand still moving inside me. He hooks his fingers, and I quiver when he reaches deeper.

My jaw drops, and my mouth falls open.

"Here?" he asks, placing his lips to the spot underneath my ear. He breathes in through his nose, and my skin breaks out in a shiver.

"No," I tell him.

Fire sparks in my chest with anticipation.

He chuckles, and I feel him smirk against my skin. He brings his mouth lower to my collarbone. "Here?"

I swallow again, frantically licking my lips. I'm thirsty. Thirsty for West. My need is painful.

"No." My voice strains.

West lowers himself, bringing his mouth down to my hardened nipple poking through my T-shirt. I'm wearing a bra, but the thin, mesh fabric does nothing to conceal what's underneath. I hate bulky thick bras, and for the first time, I'm really fucking thankful there isn't much between my breast and West's mouth.

He flicks his devious eyes to mine as his mouth pops open. "Here?"

His fingers move quickly inside me and I'm already quivering, nearing my orgasm. His palm cups me, rubbing just above my clit. There isn't enough pressure. I want more.

"West." His name drips from my mouth on a moan. "Harder."

He does as I wish. His palm presses against me, and I'm riding his hand hard. My legs quake, and I'm shivering.

But it feels so fucking good.

Reality taunts the back of my mind, reminding me that I haven't felt this free in a long time, if ever. Somehow, having West touch me this way makes me feel powerful. In control. Free.

All the things Heath or any other man have never given me.

Heat spreads across and down my legs, and I know I'm close.

"West," I breathe into his ear, driving my pussy over his hand. "I'm going to—"

Knock. Knock. Knock.

"Mr. Knight?" Lewis's muffled voice shouts from the other side.

West rips his hand from between my thighs, and I'm left gasping. Cold air meets my heated skin, and I whimper, feeling West's absence immediately.

Clearing his throat, he runs his other hand through his hair and down his face, catching his breath. He takes two steps to his left and leans on the shelf, hanging his head, and keeping his back to the door.

I absentmindedly stare at the rows of liquor bottles on the opposite shelf, reality crashing down around me as I catch my breath.

Lewis jiggles the door handle, then tugs it open.

I keep my eyes fixated on the bottles, but from the corners of my eyes, I see West push off the shelf and face Lewis. He plants his hands on his hips.

"I'm sorry, Mr. Knight," Lewis pants.

My cheeks flame with heat. I don't think Lewis has a clue what we were just doing up here, but I refuse to face him in fear that he might be able to read every single thought in my mind. Does he realize West was about to give me the most mind-blowing orgasm of my life, all from the touch of his hand?

"Sorry if I interrupted your meeting."

Meeting. That's what you want to call it?

West lets out a small chuckle, but I press my lips together and hold my breath, twisting my charcoal-dusted fingers. They're noticeably less black now, and I know there are most likely gray streaks across West's shirt—evidence of where my hands have been. A flashing red light for everyone to see.

I feel West's eyes on me for two beats. "What is it, Lewis?"

"There's a fight between two customers downstairs," Lewis pants. "Alden and a few others have pulled them off one another, but apparently someone called the police. They're on their way."

West's body turns rigid, and he brushes his hair away from his forehead. "Fuck."

Finally, I lift my eyes to see Lewis standing in the doorway. His are widened in fear, hoping West will come to his rescue.

I pull the single ear bud from my ear, listening to the sounds coming from below. Screams and shouts echo up the stairs and through the floor. The faint sound of one of the songs on my playlist is still streaming from the ear bud pinched between my fingers.

"I'm sorry." Lewis lifts his fist and gently knocks it against the doorframe, sucking his teeth. He looks over at me, then at West. "I'll meet you downstairs."

Lewis has barely made it down the first step when West starts to follow him. But before he leaves the storeroom, he stops, spins around, and plucks my other ear bud from his ear. He grabs my hand and drops it into my palm, closing my fingers around it.

I look into his eyes and swallow the lump in my throat.

His fiery gaze delivers electricity straight for my heart. It's a jarring sensation I try to wrap my head around. Just like the near orgasm I had less than sixty seconds ago.

A conflicting ball of emotions weaves itself through my chest. The puzzle pieces are scattered already, and these moments with West are only adding to the mess.

I've never felt freer than when I'm with him. The feeling of his hands on me tells me this isn't as simple as it appears, though. I can't see through all the smoke and mirrors, distracting me from the truth.

It's not that West is Heath's brother on paper. I honestly couldn't care what Heath or his family would think if they knew I was falling for West.

Fear sinks its teeth into that single fact.

I'm falling for West.

And I've never been more terrified in my life.

The feelings I have for him are cataclysmic. Earth shifting and soul shattering. It isn't the ear bud we're cradling in the palm of my hand. It's my heart. My fragile, lost, broken heart. The one that, up until it knew West, couldn't function. Now it's been jolted awake, and I don't know how to sort through it all. We're free falling over the edge of a cliff at a thousand miles an hour.

I look down at his hand over mine and study the lines of his knuckles, and I shove down the dull, aching sensation that I've seen them before.

It's odd. When I'm with him, I've never felt safer, and his feelings for me are almost as bright as the sun on the first day of summer. But then there are moments, like right now, where my mind registers every line of his hand over mine, then it switches to the drawing I've made. Hands littered with dirt. The smell of freshly shed blood. The scent of cold, wet dirt. The safety morphs into fear.

"I'm sorry. I don't know how long this will take but I'll get it sorted," West softly says.

"It's okay." I swallow the heat in my throat. "I'll see you later downstairs. I need to finish up here anyway."

He lifts his other hand and traces the tip of his finger along my cheek.

The corner of my mouth lifts gently as his finger finds my dimple.

He studies me as if he's waiting for an answer or permission. I can tell he wants to kiss me, but I'm afraid of what it'll mean if I do.

Worry seeps into his expression as though he doesn't want to leave my standing here, alone. But when I still don't say anything, he swallows and looks down before reluctantly dropping his hands.

All I'm left with when he bounds down the stairs is the mess of puzzle pieces and my body engulfed in flames, clearly angry for the orgasm it's been denied.

When West disappears, I bury my face into my hands and groan.

Half of me wants to say fuck it, open my arms, and welcome the imminent fall.

The other half?

That wants to cling to the edge of the cliff for dear life.

Dammit.

FOURTEEN

Reality is a fucking bitch.

Always has been.

I haven't thought of anything else but what happened with London upstairs. I still feel her. The way her pussy clenched around my fingers and her clit throbbed against the inside of my hand. I can still feel her slick, warm flesh even as I load the last glass into the dishwasher.

Lewis watches me as if I have a third eye or an extra arm growing out of my head.

"Seriously," he says, cutting in and tearing the glass from my hand. "I can do this."

"Seriously," I bite back, frustration getting the better of me. "I can, too. I'm fully capable of loading a dishwasher, Lewis."

Honestly, I'm just trying to stay distracted.

"You're the owner." Lewis shrugs. "You don't need to be doing my job for me. When you do, it makes me think I'm slacking or that you're second guessing why you hired me in the first place."

"You aren't slacking, and that's sort of dramatic." I swing my eyes up to the stairs for the thousandth time in the past hour.

The police left about thirty minutes ago, after I'd showed them the surveillance video of what went down between the two men. Fists broke out after one of them caught the other flirting with his girlfriend. Multiple statements and two citations later, the bar is finally nearing closing time. There are still a few customers sitting around the bar and in the dining room. Lewis sent our other bartender home and has insisted he can finish the rest of the night on his own.

"I didn't think you came to work tonight," Lewis says, closing the lid to the dishwasher and starting the wash.

"I'm always working," I tell him, my eyes lifting to the staircase again.

I want to see London.

"I meant not to bartend," Lewis argues. "I know you came for London."

I bite back a barking laugh.

I wish.

My face heats and my heart races. Does Lewis know the depth of my feelings for London? Am I that obvious? I eye the ceiling, knowing she's still upstairs, most likely getting lost in her artwork. Just like she used to in the foster home. It's her escape from reality. I look back down at the stack of receipts next to the register, pretending to read the countless numbers stamped onto them.

I want to get back upstairs and finish what we started. Instead, I overhear a customer sitting at the bar order a mojito. Before Lewis has a chance, I snatch a tall cocktail glass and muddler, and begin stuffing a few mint leaves into the bottom of it. I crush the leaves, the scent of mint filling my nostrils almost immediately. I grip the wooden muddler stick, twisting and pounding it into the glass with more force than is probably necessary. I feel Lewis's uneasy gaze on me, but I don't give a fuck. I need to channel this frustration somewhere.

I don't think I've ever had such a large case of blue balls as I do right now, but fuck, I can't get the last look in London's eyes out of my mind. The look of regret.

The thought brings a sickening feeling to my stomach that I shove aside, remembering the feeling of her against my skin and the way she quivered for me instead. She was close, painstakingly close to falling apart for me.

It was a feeling I've only ever dreamed about for the past decade. A feeling I never thought I'd have.

Despite the assurance I have from her reaction to my touch, I can't get those last crucial seconds out of my head.

Like reality was crashing down around her.

See, reality is a fucking bitch.

"Yeah, I think that's enough of that," Lewis mutters, snatching the glass from my hand. At first, I resist but, snapping out of my thoughts, I let it go. I've turned the mint into jam at this point.

Lewis eyes me curiously as he grabs the rest of the mojito ingredients, and this time, I let him.

I sift through the stack of receipts for absolutely no other reason than to buy me time before racing back to London, when I hear the floorboards creak upstairs. My eyes immediately dart to the staircase, and London appears. First, her black and white chucks, then her long legs. Then her long, black hair flowing behind her as she bounds down the stairs. She's unraveled her hair from her silk green scrunchie.

The dress Julianna lent her is draped over one arm, her portfolio tucked under the other.

I'm forcing myself to remain calm as I watch her move through the opening of the bar, already making her way toward the front.

She's leaving.

She catches my and Lewis's attention, and he quickly

glances at me over his shoulder. I'm not paying attention to him, though. I drop the receipts and race around the end of the bar, stopping her before she makes it to the front door.

"London, wait," I say, jogging after her like the fucking idiot I am. I wrap my hand around hers.

London stops, but doesn't immediately turn around. Her head rolls back before she spins on her heel to face me.

"You're leaving?" I blurt out.

She won't look me in the eye. She focuses on the back of the bar, the wall behind me, the customers in the back. Anywhere but on me.

Her hand slips from mine, and she places it on the top of the dress bag still draped over her arm. She tugs her bottom lip under her teeth before finally looking at me. "I should go home."

Distance. I don't only see it in her gray eyes. It's in all of her, her body curling in on itself, closing me off.

Seeing her this way toward me feels like a lead weight is dragging me under water. We took a million steps forward, and now we're taking half those back.

"Why?" I ask her.

She moistens her lips and shakes her head, looking down at her feet. "I'm sorry if I distracted you tonight."

"You didn't distract me." I take a step forward, forcing her to look up. "Why would you think that?"

"I insisted you meet me tonight to look at my drawing, but I don't want you to stop what you're doing around here for me." She stares vacantly over my shoulder. "You were on a call earlier and I could tell it was still weighing on you."

Oh, that.

I rake my fingers through my hair. "It was nothing."

Her shoulders sag. She's growing more distant with every word that spills from my mouth. I sigh, knowing I need to tell the truth. That's all London ever wants. I just wish I could give her all of mine.

"I was on the phone with some contacts I have in Boston."

"Boston?" she asks, her gorgeous eyes widening, swinging back to me.

I see the pieces fall into place for her. Boston equals Heath.

"Is it true what he did to you?" I ask, blurting out the one question that's been weighing on my mind since my mother told me this afternoon, even though I already know the answer. My call earlier confirmed it.

"What do you mean?" Her eyebrows pull together.

"My mother came by my apartment earlier," I explain, the knot in my chest tightening. "She said..."

Fuck, her entire body tenses. She wrings her charcoal-stained hands.

"I never told your mom about Heath's abuse," she stammers. "How could I when I didn't even talk to her until the day of his funeral?" She won't look at me. "Did she find out what I told you and now she doesn't believe me?" She finally shifts her attention to me.

I grip the back of the chair to keep myself from falling to my knees.

She thinks *I* don't believe her.

"I'm not questioning the abuse, London. I wouldn't. I'm asking you if it's true what Heath did to you *after* his death. Did he truly kick you out and that's why you're staying in New York?"

Her silence is enough of an answer for me.

Not that I needed it anyway. After I got to the bar, before London showed up, I reached out to a few contacts I have in Boston and asked if it was true what my mother had said. That Heath had told his lawyers to order her to never return to their home and had all her belongings shipped here to Boston.

I thought I was angry when they confirmed it was true, but seeing London's broken heart takes it to another level. Rage consumes me.

The fucker can rot in Hell for what he's done.

"It's not right what he did, London."

"I'm fine." She isn't cold or angry with me. She's firm, strong. But, fuck, if she only knew that I already know how strong she is. If only *she* remembered how strong she was. "I considered fighting back against Heath's lawyers, but I'd rather not waste my time or money. Even if he were alive, I wouldn't have fought him on it."

"Di—" The name I've fought to keep locked away nearly breaks free. I clear my throat as blood drains from my face. I know the feeling of regret. It's a demon I've become all too familiar with over the years. "London." My voice cracks. "Are you already regretting what we did up there?"

Her eyes soften, and tears line her black lashes. When one slips down her cheek, I not only want to wipe it away, I want to lick it away, too.

"I don't know," she confesses, her chin wobbling.

"I'm not." I say it so fast, it takes her several seconds to register what I've said. "I meant every word I said. If this is about Heath—"

"It's not about Heath." She sighs.

"Then, what is it?"

"I don't know." She shakes her head, avoiding me again. "I like you, West. More than I should, but it's hard to explain."

"You know you can talk to me, right? About anything."

An arrow aiming straight for my heart severs me and splits my chest in two when her eyes dart to mine.

"That's what I'm afraid of." She inhales another shaky breath, her bottom lip quivering.

I wonder if there's more to what she's saying than she's

letting on. Is she afraid because she's remembering? Even just a little bit? Is she afraid of me?

I hope to fucking hell she isn't. I meant every word upstairs. This moment is a prime example. I'm stumbling to find the words to keep her here. I know I can't forever, and I can't shake the fear of her disappearing again. A fear I've held on to for far too many years. Old habits die hard, I guess.

I want nothing more than to wrap my arms around London and never let her go, willing her to remember me. Call me selfish; I don't fucking care. I want her memories to come flooding back because I know in the midst of it all, I'd catch her. Just like I'm willing to catch her now.

But the truth sits at the edge of my tongue, refusing to leave, despite how fragile my soul has become these last few weeks with her. I thought it was torture living in a world without her, but living in a world with her, with no memory of me, is a new kind of ache. A slow, torturous one, like living in an endless black tunnel with no sign of light.

Is this how London feels?

She may be the one with amnesia, but it seems we're both lost in the dark just the same.

I'm a fool if I think I can confess something like that without rocking her entire world.

Would she even believe me? Would that help jog her memory? If I told her about our ugly yet beautiful past?

Probably not.

The past isn't easy to overcome. Even if you've forgotten it. Even if you haven't.

Now wouldn't be the best time to tell her, anyway. Not when she's clearly wondering if she regrets what happened with us upstairs.

"I, um," she says, shifting on her feet. "I completed this one, and there's another upstairs that I'll come back to finish after the weekend." She removes her portfolio from under her arm and lays it on the top of the bag draped over it. Tugging on the zipper, she opens it, slipping out the top sheet of paper. She hands it to me, and I take it, careful not to smudge the charcoal.

My stomach flips when I see trees and a park bench with city buildings in the background.

"Central Park."

"It's beautiful, London." *Like you,* I want to tell her. Again.

I lift my gaze.

"Thank you." She brushes a few strands of her dark hair away from her face, then closes her portfolio. "We should stick to work, West. I think that's best for now."

"Tell me I didn't imagine what happened up there," I beg her. "Tell me it's what you wanted as well."

There's hesitance in her eyes. She's standing on the other side of the line drawn between us, too afraid to cross it.

"One thing I've learned over the years, living with half of my memories, is that it doesn't matter how bad I want something, West. The real world doesn't give a shit about feelings." She sighs, and her gray eyes soften, still lined with tears. "I'll see you on Monday."

The words get caught somewhere between my head and my heart as I watch her leave my bar. My hand shakes as it holds onto her drawing. The echo of her against my skin, her voice moaning my name in my ear... I want it all.

And her last response tells me she does, too.

She doesn't regret it. She doesn't regret *me.*

LONDON

I wake with a start. My heart is pounding. My body is frozen and stiff.

Squeezing my eyes shut, I will my muscles to move like my therapist told me to do. I count my breaths and sort through what is reality and fiction. Finally, when I'm able to, I check the time on my phone, massaging away the ache in my chest with my fingertips.

Two thirty-eight in the morning.

Dropping my phone back onto the nightstand, I clutch the bedsheet, pulling it up under my chin as I stare through the small window of Selene's bedroom. The view from here isn't great, with nothing but a brick wall on the opposite side of the glass that belongs to the apartment building next door.

My fingers dig into the sheet as I struggle to catch my breath, curling in on myself. My stomach curdles as I stare at the brick wall still shrouded in darkness from the night.

All I see is West.

Not as when we first met. Not wearing the silver chain around his neck or the expensive watch around his tattooed wrist. Not with his overgrown beard.

This West is a younger version of the one I know.

While the dream is still fresh, the image of him is unfocused. But I can still feel him, his warmth, his touch as he reached out and pressed his finger to my cheek. Even though I've only known West for a short time, I know it was him in my dream. He had the same crooked smile, the same laugh as he tilted his head, telling me I was beautiful.

The setting was somewhere we'd never been before, featuring a red plastic tablecloth and metal chairs that smelled of rust. Then there was the rapid beating of little feet racing through the kitchen.

All of it designed in my mind, coming together. But even as I stare at the brick wall, the vision of West fading from memory, I can't shake the feeling that it wasn't a dream at all. I've been there before.

I think.

It's like unlocking a childhood memory. A smell. A sound. Or so I've heard. It's never happened to me before.

My stomach curdles again. Needing to shake the feeling, I toss the blanket aside and slip into my sweatpants. I pile my hair high on my head and tiptoe around the bed, but as I head toward the kitchen, I realize the bed is empty, so I make my way out of the bedroom, following the blue light coming from our tiny living room.

I make a beeline for the cabinet and pull a glass from the bottom shelf. I fill it halfway with water, downing it in one go. I quickly refill it, eyeing Selene settled on the small, plush chair situated in the corner of the room. Her laptop sits open in her lap, her head resting against the cushion.

"What are you doing out here?" I ask her.

She shifts, lifting her head and sighing. "I couldn't sleep. You?" She runs her hand down her face as she yawns.

"Dream."

"A bad one?"

I frown, swallowing down another gulp of cold water. It offers momentary relief from the heat in my throat. "I'm not sure."

Setting the glass down, I grip onto the edge of the counter, thinking of the best way to answer.

As my dream begins to fade in the rearview, my mind wanders back to a few short hours ago. The way West pleaded with me not to leave, watching me slip through his fingers. But in all honesty, I haven't stopped thinking about all of it. The echo of the orgasm I was denied is still fresh. My thighs ache with a painful need. I need relief, and living and sleeping with my sister isn't exactly the best situation for someone like me. Someone who has been denied any real satisfaction for years.

But I know what I'm feeling now is a self-inflicted wound.

I push down my regret from walking away from West earlier. Fear has taken hold, sinking its claws into every knee jerk reaction I've instilled over the years.

I ran from West because the truth was staring straight at me.

When I first met Heath the day he saved me from being crushed by a Porsche barreling down Newbury Street in Boston, he'd asked me out on a date. He took me to the fanciest restaurant—one well-known to the richest names in Boston. I felt out of place there, but Heath comforted me. I fell for his charm, thankful he'd saved me. Later that night, as he sat across from me with that charming smirk, I'd spilled my entire back-story to him. At least the parts I'd remembered. I told him about my amnesia, and he listened on with fascination. For several weeks after we officially became a couple, he pretended to care about helping me regain my memory. He'd constantly ask me if any memories had risen to the surface. At times, he would even force me to watch an old movie or listen to an old song, asking me if it triggered any memories. Then, I suppose, after a while, he'd given up on being the one to help regain my memory.

Looking back, that's when he'd started to change. He'd lost his charm and with it, his ability to truly care about me.

However, in the few weeks I've known West, he's managed to do what Heath tried so hard to do in those first weeks.

I don't know if what I'm seeing and feeling are memories, or if my imagination is playing tricks on me—the mind is notoriously unreliable—but I do know they mean *something*.

My *feelings* toward him mean something, and it's a terrifying realization.

"It's been a long time since I've had a dream." Selene yawns, pulling me from my thoughts. "It sucks when you wake up and don't know how you feel about it, though." She uncrosses her legs and places her fuzzy, sock-covered feet on the faded carpet.

"Yeah," I croak. I'm still tired and want to go back to bed, but when I close my eyes, will I have the same dream?

Several beats of silence descend upon the apartment. I'm setting my glass in the sink when Selene breaks it.

"I think I'm finished." She slams her laptop shut.

"Really?" I move around the counter and stand at the edge of the living room.

"Yeah." Her lips crack into a small smile. "It's just the first draft and still needs work, but it's done."

"Selene." I bounce on my heels. "That's amazing. Congratulations!"

"Thank you." She slides her laptop onto the coffee table and crosses her arms over her chest. "I'm thinking about self-publishing it, like you said. I just have to find a way to come up with the money."

"I know you can do it," I reassure her.

She nods once, then leaves me with nothing.

My sister has always kept her thoughts and secrets to

herself. Growing up, she kept a journal with a tiny gold lock and key, refusing to tell me where she hid the key. One day, I snuck into her room and searched everywhere for it, to no avail.

Now she keeps the lock and key around her heart.

I guess the same could be said for me. I want to open up to my sister, but I still haven't worked out my feelings. I want to tell her that I have feelings for West, but that there's something inside me preventing me from giving in completely. How can I tell her that when I barely understand it myself?

The longer the silence lingers, the tighter I wring my fingers. The dream is still there, but the events that unfolded in the storeroom of The Veiled Door come rushing back.

I think I'm falling for West.

That's what I want to tell my sister.

Well, I didn't mean to say I think I've fallen for him. I know I have.

Is what I would clarify to her if I spoke my truth out loud.

It isn't that I don't want to tell her what's going on with me, but just like it is with West, it's impossible to explain when you don't understand the meaning yourself.

Selene crosses the living room, surprising me when she wraps her arms around me as if she's reading my mind. She knows I want to tell her everything but doesn't beg for an explanation. She simply wants me to know she's here for me. I wrap my arms around her, relishing her embrace. When the world feels so lost, I at least know I have my sister.

"I'm here for you, London," she mutters against my shoulder.

"Same here." I bury my face against her shoulder and into her blonde hair. She smells of vanilla and warmth. "I'm proud of you," I tell her, breathing her in. Even if I can't wrap my mind around my feelings for West right now, I allow my sister's love to wrap around me. "My sister wrote a book!" I gush, shoving my restless, haunting thoughts aside.

"Thank you." She chuckles, pulling away. She tilts her head and grins softly. "Let's go back to bed."

"Sounds good."

We link arms and walk back down the hallway toward the tiny bedroom we share. Although I know this isn't permanent, I wonder how long I'll be staying here. I've been saving the money I've set aside in my separate bank account—the one Heath didn't have access to—slowly adding to it over these past couple of weeks. West and I still haven't settled on payment for my works, though that's the last thing on my mind when it comes to him.

One day soon, I plan on moving out of here.

My sister and I climb into her bed, and we turn our backs to one another.

"Goodnight, London," Selene whispers. "I love you."

"Love you, too," I gently say over my shoulder.

I tuck my hands under my head and stare at the brick wall again. It's still shrouded in darkness, but West's face is no longer there.

Real West, nor dream West.

My eyes grow heavy, but nerves still flutter in my stomach at the memory of my dream reeling in my mind.

I reach for my phone and unlock my screen. It's almost three in the morning, and even though my eyes felt heavy before I laid back down, I can't shut off my thoughts.

Opening Instagram, I immediately search West's name. His correct name.

Weston Knight.

His account is the first to pop up, and I scroll through his posts. There aren't many, and most are of his bars throughout the city. Some I have yet to visit.

My thumb stops over a single picture of him. The one he did for the cover of Holt's magazine, when he was featured for being a rising star in the nightlife community.

Heat climbs up my throat, and every drop of water from earlier is gone.

In the picture, West is sitting back, relaxed in a wooden chair, his arm draped over the back. The sleeves of his black button-down shirt are rolled up to his elbows, displaying his corded muscles and tattoos. A watch that probably costs more than three months of Selene's rent is wrapped around his wrist, and he's wearing rings on three of his fingers. I study each of them, remembering how they were between my thighs only hours ago, bringing me to the edge of a tall precipice.

His blue eyes stare straight at me, which is a ridiculous thought because he's on the cover of a magazine. He was simply looking at a camera lens. But the emotion is still there, evident on his face, like he's lived a life full of regret. I'm lost in his eyes when the necklace wrapped around his neck catches my attention. The air is lodged in my throat seeing it for the first time. It isn't tucked under his shirt like it always is when I'm with him.

I click on the picture and try to zoom in to get a better look at what I'm sure is a charm resting against his chest. The balloon in my chest pops when the details are too difficult to make out. All I can see is that it's a long, pointed piece of metal. Maybe one to two inches in length.

I sigh, scrolling back up to the top, and I tap my finger on the blue follow button before closing out the app and practically tossing my phone back onto my nightstand as though it's on fire.

Forcing myself to close my eyes, images of West on the cover of Holt's magazine, then the younger version of him in my dream, immediately come to life.

West breathing in my ear.

Telling me I'm beautiful.

His finger.

My cheek.

Moments both real and imaginary blending and turning to memories.

I don't know what any of it means.

Are all these moments real?

Or do they only exist in my dreams?

Is my mind playing tricks on me?

The mind is a notorious liar.

Sleep drags me further into the darkness, taking with it the unanswered questions and one simple fact:

I am, without a doubt, down bad for Weston Knight.

SIXTEEN

"I'm Stephanie, and I'll be your personal bartender tonight!" the woman in a skimpy black cocktail dress shouts over the music. She turns to the side and gestures to the table set up in the corner of our VIP section. "If you need anything at all, please let me know. I can make you any drink you'd like."

"Oh!" Julianna claps gleefully. "Let's start with a bottle of champagne."

Stephanie is quick to disappear to her drinks table, moving fast to get working on Julianna's request.

"Are we celebrating something other than it just being our first girls' night?" Selene asks. Her blonde hair is weaved into a beautiful Dutch braid, resting over her shoulder. She's wearing the slinky number Julianna set aside for her yesterday, and she looks absolutely stunning. As do all of us.

"Are you kidding, Selene?" Julianna runs her hands down the front of her dress, glancing around the club before settling her bright eyes on the three of us standing in front of her. "We have a shit ton to celebrate. Charleigh's wedding plans will finally begin, I finished up a remodel for a massive client out in

Paris, London landed a massive job drawing I don't even know how many sketches for West's bars."

I can't deny the way my heart jumps at the mention of West's name. I haven't stopped thinking about him since, well, since we first met. But the frequency of my thoughts has increased, especially since he's now had his fingers buried deep inside me. I'm trying to slow it down, forcing myself not to text or call him until I'm required to see him again on Monday.

Julianna continues her praise on our groups accomplishments, when she lifts her arm and points directly at my sister. "And to my girl Selene, for finally, *finally* finishing the first draft of her very first book like the badass she is."

"Hell, yeah!" Charleigh shouts, clapping enthusiastically.

Julianna and I join her before I lean to my right and give my sister a tight squeeze.

I release Selene as Stephanie returns with four champagne flutes resting on top of her black serving tray. Each one is filled with a beige-colored, fizzy liquid.

The four of us take a glass and clink them together in a toast. After I take a drink, I sit in the booth beside Selene, with Julianna on the other side of me.

Club Verona is the hottest new spot here in the city. According to Julianna, that is. I wouldn't know otherwise. It's massive, with multiple levels, and several different bar stations. Julianna reserved an exclusive VIP section for the four of us, complete with our own personal bartender. AKA Stephanie.

Red curtains line the outer walls of our cornered section, with an opening overlooking the dance floor below.

I adjust the bottom of the dress Julianna let me borrow as I cross one leg over the other. She was right; this dress fits me like a dream, and it screams London. Although it's probably the slinkiest dress I've ever worn, I've never felt more confident and comfortable in something than I do now.

It's like the pseudo family I've had around me has brought out the true me. The one afraid to come out of her shell.

"If Stephanie keeps bringing these over, Asher might have to come and carry me out of here." Charleigh laughs, setting her glass on the small, square table in front of us.

"Watch," Julianna cuts in. "If he does, he'll probably bring Holt and West to help drag us out of here."

"Probably," Charleigh agrees.

A groan makes its way out of my throat, and I scoff against my glass. Just what I need. West carrying me out of here. I'm certain if West were to touch me again, my body would burst into flames. Admittedly, it would be a good way to go.

Silence.

I look over the group. I've caught their full attention by my sudden outburst. All eyes are on me.

"What was that groan about?" Julianna's mouth splits into a gleeful grin.

"Nothing." I sigh.

If I'm going to have this conversation, I need more champagne at a faster pace. Thinking and talking about West not only makes my pussy clench with need, but it makes my heart race too. An intoxicating combination I can't decide what to do with.

"Oh, this isn't nothing," Charleigh chimes in, flipping her long hair over her shoulder and leaning forward. She crosses her arms over her crossed legs.

Another groan vibrates up my throat as I twist in my seat to steal the bottle of champagne Stephanie left on the bar cart behind me. Our personal bartender stares at me in horror as I pour myself another glass. If she's worried our table won't leave her a massive tip, she must not know that half the people at this table make an obscene amount of money.

I open my mouth wide and guzzle down my entire glass. The bubbles fizz and sting their way down my throat.

"So, what?" Selene asks beside me. "You don't want to see West?"

"It isn't that."

This time, our personal bartender is already cracking open another bottle of champagne, rushing to refill my glass. I give her a smile of appreciation.

"Oh, wait." Julianna crosses her legs, her tan skin shimmering under the club's lights as she smooths a hand over her knee. She drapes her other arm across the back of the leather booth. "I know what this is. You're in the denial stage."

I scoff, laughing off her comment.

"It's true." She gestures toward Charleigh, then me. "Little Charleigh here was the same when Asher came back into her life. Pretended not to have feelings for him, but eventually confessed it was all a ruse."

"Sort of like me, huh?"

Julianna's eyes spread wide with shock, but then her face falls with recognition at the voice meeting her ear. The man behind her is bent at the hip, standing so close to Julianna, you'd think they were a couple.

Rome Montgomery. I remember meeting him the night of Julianna's party.

He's the one she can't stand.

"Is that how you feel about me, Lark?" he teases close to Julianna's ear.

"Rome," she grinds out, the muscles in her temple twitching.

Rome's mouth curl deviously. "Your hatred from me is just for show, isn't it?"

If I wasn't sitting directly beside Julianna, I wouldn't have been able to hear Rome's teasing. His use of a pet name 'Lark' has me feeling as though I'm witness to something private.

"Absolutely not. You know exactly why." Julianna's jaw clenches before she's popping up and out of her seat. She spins around and kneels on the bench where she was just sitting. She leans forward, delivering her ire directly at Rome. "How do you keep showing up when you are the absolute last face I want to be looking at?" She narrows her eyes. "Are you stalking me?"

"Stalking you?" Rome tips his head back and roars with laughter, pressing his hand to his chest. "This is my club, Lark." He leans forward, over the top of the bench, and brings his face closer to Julianna's. She instinctively jerks her head back in disgust, stumbling back off the bench. Her feet land on the floor. "Seems you're the one stalking me."

"Right." She scoffs, trailing her tongue across her lips. "You wish I was stalking you, if only to inflate that fragile little ego of yours."

His eyes roam over Julianna, drinking her in with his heated gaze.

Julianna snaps her fingers. "Eyes up here, Montgomery."

Rome's expression turns cold, and his mouth curls. "Who's the one with the fragile ego now, Julianna?"

Her mouth falls open as she stands stunned with his comment.

Rome turns to the rest of us. "I hope you ladies have a wonderful night and enjoy yourselves." Without another word, he leaves our VIP section.

"Of course, he fucking owns this club." Julianna swirls around and sits back down with a huff. "I don't know if I can stay here knowing Rome owns it. I should have known or looked it up or something."

"Seriously?" Charleigh asks, looking around the room. "This

place is great so far, and you've already paid to reserve this section."

"Fine." Julianna groans, leaning forward and resting her elbows on her legs. "I just hate him. I don't think there's ever been anyone else in my life I haven't been able to stand as much as that man."

"What's the story with you two?" I dare to ask, hiccupping from the sips of champagne already settling in my stomach. The alcohol is bringing out my more courageous side—the one risking asking my new friend the details of her past with her mortal enemy.

Sensing the tension, Stephanie is quick to drop a drink in front of her. Julianna tips it back, but not without muttering, "I'd rather not talk about it," beforehand.

When she's done drinking another glass, Julianna pulls out her phone, and her face lights from the screen, highlighting her mischievous grin.

"What are you doing?" Charleigh asks suspiciously.

Julianna simply shakes her head, then slides her phone back onto the table with a satisfied grin. "Nothing but a little harmless fun."

We don't ask for any more details.

As the hour ticks by, Rome's brief visit fades away, and so do my thoughts of West. He's still there in the back of my mind, but I'm at least able to enjoy this moment without allowing the memories to swallow me whole.

The girls don't mention him again, dropping the subject of my hidden feelings for my ex-husband's adopted brother.

Another hour passes, then another. Julianna and I have paced our drinks, but it appears Selene and Charleigh haven't.

Selene's eyes are glassier than usual now, and Charleigh's forced herself to stay where she is on the booth, no longer dancing.

I feel relaxed as I take sips of water between my champagne, but my attention is pulled to the entrance of our section when Asher appears with Holt.

Then West.

Asher greets the three of us before meeting Charleigh.

"Had a bit of fun, did you?" he asks her.

Charleigh laughs, wrapping her arms around Asher's neck. "A little." Her grin widens. "Does this mean you get to carry me home?"

There's a twinkle in Asher's eye, as if it's an inside joke between them.

Holt asks Stephanie for a drink before he makes his way inside the booth to sit beside Selene. "I heard you finished your book," he says to her.

She tilts her head and gives him a small ghost of a smile. Her cheeks blush with red. "I did."

"Well…" Holt clears his throat. "I guess I owe you a congratulations."

"Thank you." Selene swallows. "I need to use the bathroom." She pops up from her seat and corrects her dress before walking in the direction of the bathroom, a slight sway in her steps.

I turn back to Holt, but he hasn't looked away from Selene. He eyes her the entire way until she disappears around the corner. The smile he had when congratulating her fades.

"I'll go make sure she's okay," he mutters, then follows her.

I look over my shoulder and find West still standing in the entrance to the club. We don't speak a word to one another as his gaze rakes over me, taking in my outfit.

His beautiful, towering frame fills the opening to the club below. The room grows smaller with every passing second between us. Air squeezes through my lungs and the image of West in my dreams comes back to me at full force.

"I need some air," I say to no one in particular.

Asher is already lifting Charleigh into his arms, and Julianna is dancing with herself.

I make my way around the table and head toward the entrance where West is standing. I avoid looking at him as my shoulder brushes the smooth fabric of his sport coat, which is dark blue with black lapels over his black collared shirt. Like the one on the cover of Holt's magazine.

I immediately smell him: mint and leather. The heat I've ignored for the past twenty-four hours is back between my thighs. Memories of his hands on me and his breath in my ear come roaring back. Every muscle I have aches for him.

I avoid looking at West as I move past him and head for the stairwell leading to the dance floor below. The open area of the club is as dark as the VIP section, though different as bright lights flash across the entire room. The DJ at the front of the dance floor holds his headphones to one ear as he bobs his head to the steady beat.

"London, wait," West says behind me.

"I need air, West," I rasp, desperate for relief.

"Talk to me, please," he begs, and the pain in his voice forces me to stop at the edge of the dance floor. The sea of dancers threaten to suck me in, but I turn my back on them, staring at the man I know I'm falling in love with.

The man in my dreams.

He's breathing heavy with that same look of panic I've already seen on his face a million times. Like I'm suddenly going to evaporate into thin air or fade before his very eyes.

"I need to talk to you about what happened yesterday," he says over the music. "It's killed me not texting or calling you. I want to give you space, but—" He struggles to finish his sentence, raking a frustrated hand through his dark hair. His rings and watch glint under the white strobe lights.

"I can't do this."

"Why?" He asks, desperate. "Tell me why you can't."

"It's too complicated."

"Because of Heath?" He shouts. "Or is it something else?"

"All of it." My confession steels us both. I get lost in his eyes, wishing we were having this conversation somewhere else. The alcohol swimming in my body is starting to hit me.

"So, you do feel something for me?"

A lump swells in my throat.

Bodies press into my back around me, and I allow them to swallow me up before I turn and push my way through the crowd, even though I know West is quick to follow. The crowd parts, giving West and me the space to make our way toward the center of the dance floor.

"Can you honestly tell me you feel nothing for me?" he pleads behind me.

"Let it go, West!" I yell over my shoulder, continuing to shoulder my way through.

"I can't let you go."

I stop, spinning on my heel. Lights flash across his face in rhythm with the pounding music vibrating through the floor. One second, I see him. The other, he's gone.

But then he's back, his eyes shining under the strobe lights again.

I can't let you go.

We're standing chest to chest. The dancers surrounding us slowly push us together, and within moments, I find myself looking up at West.

"What are you afraid of, London?" he shouts over the music. "Falling for me?"

"Yes!" I shout back, not caring if he knows my truth. I've kept it safely locked inside a vault, not even telling my sister. Now I've cracked the code, opening the safe door wide open. I stiffen my arms at my sides, balling my hands into fists. "I already *am* falling for you West."

He blinks, shocked by my answer.

"But we shouldn't, and I can't," I continue. He opens his mouth, but I stop him, grinding my teeth until they crack. "And I swear, if you try to argue that this is about Heath... I'm only going to tell you one last time that it isn't. If you suggest it again, I might just lose my mind."

"Then, what is it? Because I'll be damned if I'll let you walk out of here like you walked out of my bar last night without you knowing exactly how I feel about you."

A knot twists in my stomach, and I feel nauseous. Nauseous in a good way. If that makes any fucking sense. West makes me feel whole and complete. Like puzzles pieces falling into place without me even trying. He's familiar, but how can I tell him that? How can I tell him I have memories of him when I know it's impossible? Right?

I remember his hands and his voice, even before he touched me the other night. It's as though I'm looking through a kaleido-scope. The image of him is there, but the picture doesn't make any sense. He's a Picasso painting to me, blocks of colors not quite lined up. They make a picture, but they don't quite make sense at first glance.

"West, I—"

"Hey there, gorgeous." A deep voice comes up behind me, loud and clear straight for my ear. "How about I take you out of here and you can dance all over my cock instead of on this dance floor?"

West's attention immediately lifts to whoever is over my shoulder. His eyes have darkened, transforming to a full deep shade of black. His nostrils flare, and his neck swells. I can see the muscles in his jaw ticking with pulsating fury.

The man behind me leans closer, and his hand slinks around my hip, down to the top of my thigh.

I freeze, my skin turning as cold as ice.

My mind is screaming for my body to move but it doesn't listen.

But the next several moments happen in a flash.

I gasp as West pushes me behind him, stumbling and catching myself before spinning around. An ear-splitting crack pierces the music as West's fist connects with the face of the man who touched me. He drops to the floor with a thud, and West is quick to stand over him.

"Stay the fuck away from her," he seethes, venom dripping from him as he leans down and fists the man's shirt. He lifts him up effortlessly before he rears his free arm back in the air and drives his fist into the man's face again. Then again. Then again. Blood sprays from the guy's face as he's jerked to his right, the crowd jumping back as crimson hits the floor around them.

The stranger's eyes roll to the back of his head, but West doesn't relent, delivering another blow. The music hasn't stopped, and neither have the lights. The club descends into chaos. Some people move away from the fight while others stand and watch in shock.

I leap forward, trying to stop West from delivering another blow to the man before he kills him. "West!" I shout, grabbing at his shoulders. "Stop."

He doesn't listen, instead punching the man again. He lifts him up with a single hand again, inches from the dance floor. Snarling, he presses his nose to the man's. "You motherfucking pussy. Say shit like that again to my girl and I'll snap that tiny dick of yours and shove it right down your throat until you fucking choke on it."

"*West*," I cry out. "Please, stop."

The man's eyes slowly roll to me over West's shoulder.

"Don't you fucking look at her, you piece of shit," West threatens, snarling. He shakes him as if he doesn't already have his attention. "Do it again, and I won't think twice about killing you."

The man eyes roll to the back of his head, and West unravels his fist. The stranger drops to the floor like a sack of potatoes.

The feathers of darkness return as I watch him lying there, lifeless, head to the side, blood pouring from his face. Lights dance across his body, and I watch his chest, waiting to see if it rises.

"London," West says in my ear, his voice warbled and distorted, like I'm trapped underwater.

"Dimples, look at me!" West shouts.

At least I think it's him. It could be the cacophony of voices around us. Or the champagne still lingering in my blood and swimming in my head.

The man on the floor doesn't move. He just lies there, lifeless.

I'm watching his chest move just an inch when West steps in front of me, blocking my view.

"London, are you okay? Look at me." His warm hands press against my face, forcing me to look into his eyes.

Blue eyes. Kind blue eyes. Eyes that are no longer black.

I swallow and look at West with tears ready to fall.

"Look at me, London," he begs. "We need to get out of here. *Right now.*"

I've barely given him a nod before he's wrapping my hand up in his and leading me out of the nightclub.

WEST

I may have killed him, but I couldn't stick around long enough to figure out if I had or not. All I know is that I needed to get London out of there as fast as possible.

She's as pale as a ghost when we stumble out the back door of the club. My feet hit the pavement, and I take a few steps forward to stand in the middle of the alleyway, deciding which way to go.

"West," London whispers behind me.

I frantically fish my phone out of my front pocket. I want to check on her, but I need to secure us a way home first.

"I rode over here with Holt," I pant, unlocking my phone. "I'm texting Alden to pick us up at the end of the alleyway. He's not far."

"Alden?" she whispers again.

I snap my head up and drop my phone back in my pocket. "He's never that far away unless I drive somewhere myself."

A small, dim security light hangs above the back door of the club we just walked out of. London's skin is even paler now, and she's shivering, her vacant eyes spread wide with fear or confusion. Probably both.

I wrap my arms around her and hold her head against my chest.

Music from inside the club hasn't stopped, but neither has the shouting and screaming. I pull London away and press my hands to her face again, trying to steady her. I can see it in her eyes, the panic and sheer terror. A trauma response, I think. Seeing her this way makes me wonder if her lost memories have anything to do with her behavior right now, because even if I beat that man within an inch of his life, she wouldn't have this bad of a response.

Same could be said for me.

Seeing the man come up behind her and hearing him say vile shit into her ear instantly took me back to that day. For me, it's impossible to forget the last day I saw London. Muscle memory took over.

"Are you okay?" I ask her.

She inhales an unsteady breath, and I want nothing more than to be her anchor, pulling her fear away from her. "I don't know."

After pressing my lips to her forehead, I close my eyes and count to ten. London shivers against me.

Pulling back, I shrug out of my sport coat and drape it over her shoulders. She slips her arms inside and brings her closed fists to her chest.

Two seconds later, Alden sharply turns down the alleyway.

The headlights of my car are spotlights on us as he races toward us. The tires screech as he slams on the brakes. Wrapping my hand around London's, I pull her toward the car and help her into the back seat before sliding in behind her, telling Alden to drive us home.

We ride in silence, but I can't help staring at London. I haven't stopped looking at her. Not when I showed up to Club Verona and saw her sitting on the couch in this fucking dress that made me weak in the knees. The moment we shared yesterday had clearly been in her glassy, champagne-filled eyes as she stared back at me.

The room was suffocating, and when I watched her walk away, the need inside me to follow her was just as smothering.

Perhaps it's the same damn foolish hope I have in believing she's remembering me, but I could have sworn she'd recognized me then. She was looking at me the same way she used to when we were kids. Like I was her safe space. Back when we promised to be each other's first in everything. The days we used to lay in the woods, before they were tainted by what happened, and we would dream of building a house on the lake surrounded by a white picket fence, and we'd adopt a black kitten.

I still clung to that hope even as she told me to let it go. Even as fear of the unknown took control.

But I can't let her go. Ever.

London's smooth legs are still covered in goosebumps, and I want nothing more than to reach out and rub my hands all over them. Heat blasts from the air vents, stifling what little oxygen there is, but it does nothing to break the chill over her. She clings to the side of the door, staring out at the city, leaving the club and the man I nearly killed behind.

The words I want to say sting the tip of my tongue.

"London." I swallow my goddamn nerves and reach out to her, my knuckles swollen and red from the fight. "Are you okay?"

Her eyelids slowly close. "Please stop asking me that, West."

"I won't," I argue back. "Your wellbeing is all I'm concerned about, and I can't help feeling like you're not okay."

Her eyes open, and all she does is stare out the window with the tip of her black-painted thumbnail between her teeth. She shakes her head and a bitter chuckle passes her beautiful lips before she snaps her head in my direction. "Even if I wasn't, I always find a way to be okay. My life is messy, West. That much hasn't changed."

Her words are a hammer to the chest.

Alden eyes us in the rearview mirror, and I fucking hope we get home soon. I hate having this conversation with London while he's in the car. Alden already knows more than he probably should for someone who works for me, though I know he won't intervene when it comes to personal matters.

"Talk to me." I beg. "Tell me what's going on in that beautiful head of yours."

Her mouth curls. "Where do I even begin?"

"I don't know." I run a frustrated hand through my hair, ignoring the searing pain. Alden takes a sharp turn, and I have no clue how close we are to my place. I've lost all sense of time and space. Judging the brief stop-and-go movements of the car a few seconds ago, I'm guessing we're at least across Brooklyn Bridge.

"Start with tonight," I tell London.

"You nearly killed that man, West."

"If you think I regret the way I responded to that fucking asshole, you're mistaken. He deserved it."

"You can't just beat someone up because he said some stupid shit to me."

"I absolutely can and I would do far worse to someone for far less."

Seconds pass by in painstaking silence. My muscles tense, and the pain in my knuckles intensifies, but it isn't from the fight. It's from the need to touch London. I want more than what we did yesterday.

She inhales a sharp breath. "You'd kill someone for me?"

Oh, you have no idea.

"I think you already know the answer to that question." I growl.

Her chest is rising and falling with every laborious breath she takes in and pushes out. Her eyes are the shade of cold steel until they soften just for me.

Her chin wobbles, and my coat slips away from her shoulders. She scoots closer to me though barely. With one hand, she grips the back of the passenger seat, the other planted against the back between us.

"I'm hanging on by a thread, West," she breathes, her shoulders dropping. "Cut it."

Then my hands are in her hair, and I'm stealing what remaining breaths she has left in her lungs.

EIGHTEEN

LONDON

Finally.

Fucking finally.

We collide, his hands in my hair, my mouth starving for his. West's kiss is exactly how I hoped it would be, hungry and frantic, yet still measured. I should have asked him to kiss me last night. I was a fool for not because damn, he's a good kisser. His soft lips press firmly to mine, drinking me in. I've never been kissed like this. An explosion bursts in my chest, and I'm worried I'm caught in another dream—one that has me questioning what's reality and what isn't.

Not breaking our mouths apart, I shrug the rest of my arms out of his sport coat, allowing it to fall to the footwell as I lift my leg up and over him to straddle his lap. Fresh goosebumps slither across my skin from West's touch. He grips my ass as I lower myself over him, immediately feeling his stiff cock rub against me, making me moan. His tongue slips between my lips, tasting and teasing me. My heart bursts with every lap of it against mine.

I don't know when, but at some point the car stops, and Alden's door is slamming shut, leaving us alone.

"You almost killed that man," I pant against West's mouth.

"I did and it would have been worth it." His voice is dark and full of unwavering conviction.

The scruff lining his jaw grates against my skin, sending electricity shooting straight between my legs. I know I'm already dripping wet for him. I rock my hips against his hardened length, straining against the zipper of his pants. It twitches beneath me, begging to be set free.

West groans as he squeezes my ass before sliding his hands up my back. "You have no idea what I would do to protect you, London." His hand stops at the base of my neck, and he pulls me down to look at him. "You make me feel something no one else ever has."

I feel his words. Feel them to my core. Suddenly everything makes sense. In my heart and deep in my bones, I know not *everything* makes sense—my memories are still a jumbled mess —but some puzzle pieces click together seamlessly.

I'm tired of holding back the way I feel in fear of what all of it means, so I give in to my feelings for him, trusting my fragile heart.

"Same for me." I kiss him. "Every day, I wake up looking forward to seeing you." I kiss him again. "My heart jumps at the thought of what you might be feeling for me, too."

"Then, why have you been running away?"

I rock my hips. "I haven't been running away. I've been right here all along." I tell him, pressing my palms against his thick neck. The tips of my fingers slide across the silver chain, and I fight the urge to pull it up and finally see the charm for myself. "I've just been afraid to step off the edge of the cliff."

He tucks my hair behind my ear and presses his finger to my cheek. "Oh, baby, we're already driving over a thousand miles an hour off this cliff."

The corner of my mouth lifts, but West is quick to catch it.

My hands are soon in his thick, dark hair, and I roll my hips against him once more.

West claws at my back as he tears the dress from my body, ripping the fabric.

"This dress isn't mine." I stifle a giggle, my skin buzzing with heated anticipation. "I was only borrowing it from Julianna."

"I'll pay her back for it."

I laugh and tilt my head back, sinking into this feeling with West. "She'll hold you to it."

My now-torn dress pools around my waist. The warm air hits my breasts, and I'm already tingling under West's touch. My nipples harden into two peaks as he pinches them between his fingers. I hiss as his hands explore my body. Steam coats the windows, blocking what view we have. Thankfully, the car windows are tinted, nearly black.

I have no fucking clue where we are. Are we at West's place? Are we even still in the city?

"I want to finish what we started yesterday." He growls.

My thighs quiver with painstaking need. I'm already past the point of wondering if this is what I want. Despite the fear I have in not knowing if my dreams of West are somehow reality, I know what I'm feeling isn't wrong. I'm tired of convincing myself it is.

I need to trust myself. I need to trust that this feels right in a way it never has before with anyone else I've been with.

"Tell me where you want me," he begs, heat searing his kind blue eyes. It's amazing how they transform for every situation. They're kind when they want to be, protective when they need to be, and now completely under my spell.

I smirk, a firecracker sparking to life inside my chest. I grab his hand and place it over my cheek, all the while continuing to roll my hips over his hard-as-stone cock. Every few breaths, he lets out an impatient growl.

"Here," I whisper.

The corners of his beautiful mouth twitch, and his hungry eyes fall to my cheek. He places his lips gently to my cheek, and I hold my breath as he pulls away.

I move our hands, placing the tips of his fingers over my collarbone. I roll my hips again. "And here."

He follows my lead, and his mouth presses against my skin with a little more pressure. With a deeper hunger.

I trail his fingers down and over the swell of my breasts, dragging them over one nipple, then the next. "Here," I breathe.

Sticking his tongue out, he laps it around the tightened bud. I squeeze my thighs around him, whimpering with the sensation. Heat pools in my belly, and I know I won't last long like this.

"Fuck," I breathe out. "Your mouth feels so good."

With his other arm, he holds me against him. "Stay right where you are, London. Surrender to it. Surrender to this feeling."

"I'm going to fall apart."

"You won't. I won't let you."

Well, damn. Now I'm not thinking I'm going to fall apart. I'm going to fucking melt into a puddle right here in his car.

West pinches my nipple between his teeth, and a sharp jolt of delicious pain slithers down my spine. I whimper again, needing him inside me more than ever.

"Tell me where next." His voice is deep. It vibrates against my skin, and I lift myself up enough to slip my hand between us.

I begin to unbuckle his belt. Once I have it free, I start for his zipper, but he shakes his head, clicking his tongue in disapproval.

"Not yet."

"Please," I beg.

"Your turn first. I want to watch your reaction to what I do to you first. So, *tell me where you want my mouth*, London."

My thighs hum in anticipation. I slide West's hands down from my breast to my clit, and I gasp when I press it to the already swollen bud.

"Here." I quiver, tingles breaking out across my body.

He quirks a smile, and his eyes flash with hunger. "That's my girl." He growls. I gasp when he rips his hand from my clit and places both hands on my ass roughly to lift me up. Quickly, he lowers me down until my back is lying against the center console.

Thank God I was right in assuming we're alone. Alden is no longer in the car. I can't tell where we're parked. I know we're no longer in the center of the city, at least. Trees dance above us in the wind as I lean back, pressing my hands on either seat beside me. The moonroof of West's car stretches from the front to the back, making up the entire ceiling. Here, it's just West and me beneath the stars.

The leather console digs into my lower back as I sit up, staring at West sitting back in the middle of the back seat.

I have no idea what he wants to do with me, but I put all my trust in him. Seeing his protectiveness in the club earlier has rebuilt the armor around my heart. This time, though, it isn't to keep others out. This armor is a sign of strength. I've never been more certain or comfortable with someone than I am now.

He's now reclined back in the seat, staring at me as if he's trying to decide which part of me to devour first. His legs are spread as he strokes himself with one hand.

"Do you know how hard I am for you right now?"

"Yes." My throat is dry, and my need for West is cresting. "I felt every inch."

He chuckles, and his jaw twitches. "Do you know how beautiful you are?"

I hum in response.

"Not good enough," he grunts, stroking himself harder. "Do. You. Know. How. Beautiful. You. Are?"

My eyes fall to his hand working his cock.

He leans forward, resting his elbows on his knees as he pops an eyebrow. "Well?"

My chest rises and falls with every heated, wanting breath. "Yes."

"Say it."

"Say what?"

"Say you're beautiful."

I moisten my lips and whisper, "I'm beautiful."

"Fucking right you are." His voice is silk as he presses his fingertips to my knees, pulling them apart. "Now, spread those gorgeous legs for me like a good girl."

His hands glide down the length of my legs, around to the back of my calves before stopping on my heels. He lifts each of my feet and places them on either side of him. I'm still wearing my black strappy heels, but West doesn't seem to care.

"Leave the heels on," he orders, as if reading my mind. "You look sexy in anything, but seeing you *just like this*, bare for me, spread open and ready in just your heels does something different to me."

My heart is racing as he leans forward and slides his hands along the insides of my thighs. I'm quivering under his touch. My dress is still bunched around my waist, but it doesn't matter. My skin is on fire, and I shift against the console, the leather rubbing against the small of my back as he grips onto the waist of my black lace thong.

With a snarl and a flash in his heated gaze, he clicks his tongue against the back of his teeth in disapproval. "Such an inconvenience, these things."

Slowly and torturously, he slips it over my ass and down

each leg, cradling each of my feet in his large hands. Smiling, he stuffs my lace thong into the pocket of his pants.

"Seriously?" I giggle, but it's quickly stifled when he leans forward and blows on my wet slit.

Holy shit.

"Oh, my God, West." I dig my heels into the edge of the seat, but West is quick to pull me back.

"We've barely started." He grins wickedly.

"Please." My mind falls back to last night when I'd almost reached my orgasm. The first orgasm I would have felt in way too long. At least one that wasn't of my making. Still, even though it's been months and months since I've been touched, I've never felt anything close to the way I do when West touches or kisses me.

Leaning forward, he keeps his eyes on me as he lowers his face between my thighs. His fingertips play at the edge of my crease, and I feel my wetness dripping down my center. I watch in wanting fascination as he sticks his tongue out and licks me from the back to the front.

Overwhelmed with the sensation, I tilt my head back and close my eyes. My mouth falls open and, holy shit, I've never felt anything like it before.

Leather. Sweat. Heat. Mint. The mixture of scents override my senses, and I find myself slipping forward, pressing my clit harder against West's mouth. He holds me steady, dipping his arms under my legs. Pressing his fingers into the flesh of each of my cheeks, he rests my legs on his shoulders.

"Oh, God, yes," I whimper, feeling myself reaching the edge faster than intended. Suddenly, I'm not wanting this to stop. Reality hits, and I wonder if this will be it. Will this be the moment we share before we go back to the way it was? Pretending as if there isn't this spark between us? Will we both spend our lives living with this as a memory until we die?

West is quick to pull me back when he plunges two fingers inside me. He keeps his mouth pressed to my swollen clit. His tongue dances across it, over and over and, holy shit. He doesn't pump his fingers in and out of me the way I expect him to. I've been finger-fucked before, but not like this.

Hooking both his fingers, he moves them only slightly, finding the one spot inside me that turns me completely inside out. The one place no one else has ever found.

Fuck, he's good.

"Don't stop. Right there..." I sob, but quickly clamp my hand over my mouth to stifle my cries.

I'm panting so hard, I know I'm going to reach my orgasm soon. I remove my hand from my mouth and press it to the back of West's head, keeping him as close as possible. He bites and sucks and pulls. His fingers hook upward, then again. He works me expertly, as if he knows exactly what to do to make me come in practically no time at all.

"Come." His heavy voice vibrates against my wet and swollen pussy. "Come for me like the good girl I know you are."

My thighs squeeze around his head, and I'm rocking my hips as tiny explosions burst across my skin. My fingers are deep in his hair when I finally reach my orgasm. I'm falling off the cliff, soaring.

West keeps one hand wrapped around my thigh, pressing his finger deep into my flesh to keep me steady. My stomach tightens, and I'm squeezing my eyes shut, writhing as I surrender to every feeling I'm experiencing.

I'm still quivering when I loosen my grip around his head. He pulls away and looks up at me with a heavy, heated gaze, his eyes an intense shade of blue. Like the scorching-hot, blue flickering flame in a fire.

I'm still working to catch my breath when he sweeps his tongue across his glistening mouth. Then he sits up and kisses me. My lips. My jaw. My forehead. He's tender and soft, soothing me after what his mouth and fingers have made between my legs.

When he finishes kissing me, he sits back on the seat and finally undoes his pants. He pulls the zipper down and pulls his cock free. Stroking it, he keeps his eyes focused on me.

Pre-cum spills from the tip, and I don't know what to focus on: him, or his hand on himself, clearly turned on by the state I'm in. I know I'm a complete mess. My dress is torn, and my hair is completely tangled, but I don't care.

I'm still coming down from my orgasm when my stomach heats at the idea of having West inside me.

"Well, London." West grunts with a wicked grin. "That was the hottest fucking thing I've ever seen."

"Was it?" I tease.

"Yes. I need that sweet pussy wrapped around me before I fucking explode." He stops stroking himself and grips my ankles, sliding them from the seat. My feet hit the flooring, and I sit up. My ass presses into the center console, but it doesn't stay there long. West leans forward and tugs on my hand, wrapping the other around my waist.

"You want my cock inside you, don't you?"

"Yes," I whisper.

I feel exhilarated. Excited. Safe. I'm scared to say the 'L' word right now, but if it isn't, it's a feeling like it.

West is looking at me, begging for me like I'm the air he breathes.

"Yes, what?"

"Yes, please."

"Good girl." His eyes flash with satisfaction.

I follow his lead as I straddle his lap the way I had earlier. My wet crease sets right over his stone-hard length. He grunts, and I moan, rubbing myself over him. Pressing my hands to his neck, I hover my mouth over his.

"Tell me how bad you want me," I whisper, lifting the corners of my mouth.

He drags his finger down the length of my cheek, pressing it into my dimple again. My heart leaps at the memory of my dream. And him, here in front of me.

"You have no fucking clue how badly I want you." Slipping his hand between us, he wraps it around his cock and teases the tip of it at my entrance, then he guides me in place, lowering me down onto him. "Let me show you. Normally, I'd want to take my time, but I think I've been patient enough."

I take every inch. My mouth falls open, my body adjusting to having his thick cock inside me.

When I've taken all of him, he lifts me again before I've had a chance to catch my breath.

It's a different sensation than before when I'd been laid out for him.

We're closer. More intimate. Vulnerable. Hungry.

I'm just catching my breath when he slams me down again. I tilt my head back, and West's mouth meets my neck. He sucks hard on my skin. His teeth graze against me, and I come even faster than before. I tighten around him, clutching his head to my bare chest as I moan his name. Grunting, he slams me down several more times, guiding me up and down his length, thrusting, burying himself deep inside me. He bites at my breast, sucking on the hardened nipple. I cry out, my orgasm ripping through me. He was right.

He didn't intend on taking his time.

Three more thrusts, and he's spilling inside me, digging his teeth into my collarbone and gripping me tightly.

My fingers are threaded through his sweaty hair, and once

we've caught our breaths, he pulls back to look at me and hooks his fingers under my chin. His eyes meet mine, and we look at each other in utter silence, allowing reality to crash down around us and settle in the steamy, heat-filled car.

Then he kisses me.

NINETEEN

LONDON

I'm standing in West's enormous bathroom wearing nothing but his sport coat. I look down at myself, thinking I look like one of those models on the runway, dressed in men's clothes fit and altered for a woman's smaller frame. I'm swimming in it, completely naked underneath. The thought is exhilarating as I look around.

I bring my hands to my face and breathe in West's scent buried in the sleeves: leather and mint.

I've lost all concept of time. It feels like Club Verona and the chaos we left behind after West beat the shit out of that creep was ages ago.

My body aches in the best way. I'm tired, but if West were to touch me the way he did earlier, I wouldn't stop him.

After we finished in the car, I wrapped West's sport coat around me, and he brought us up to his apartment. From what I could see in the darkness, the building is a modest brick one. But once I stepped inside his place, I gasped in awe at the vastness of something that seems so normal on the outside.

I'd barely had a chance to look around before West scooped me up and whisked us off to his bathroom.

The rushing sound of water fills the room now as water pours into the clawfoot tub in front of me. Steam lifts from the surface, evaporating within seconds. The entire bathroom is covered in wood and steel, with an exposed ceiling, large black pipes, and golden lights running from one side to the other. There is lush, dark green cabinets with copper trim, as well as black slate tile flooring. It's warm and comforting yet luxurious at the same time.

It reminds me of The Veiled Door. And West.

Insanely wealthy but surrounded by warmth and... normalcy.

The complete opposite of the home I had with Heath.

I'm wiggling my toes against the heated tile when I feel West come up behind me. He turns off the water once it's filled, then his tall, hard frame presses against my back, and a flurry of flutters rage in my stomach.

I'm grinning stupidly as he slips his hands around my waist, slowly undoing each button of my makeshift coat-dress.

His mouth hits the shell of my ear, and my legs immediately become Jell-O. "I have a truth to tell you." He pops one button, then drifts his hands to the next.

I shiver, closing my eyes and resting my head back against his hard chest. I hum. "I love your truths."

He smiles against my ear. "I like you in this better than that dress you were wearing."

"You didn't like the dress?"

He chuckles, and the heat from his breath makes my heart pound erratically. "Oh, that dress took my breath away. But this..." Another button pops free. "Seeing you in something that is mine, makes me feral for you."

"Feral?" I laugh, unable to control the giggling coming from my chest. I cover my mouth, stifling my outburst.

West's hand wraps around mine, pulling it down. Cold air

hits my stomach as his fingers trail down my skin and over my belly button ring.

"I love your laugh. Don't ever feel like you need to hold it back for me."

West's confession hits me hard. I love how his compliments spark what I thought were dormant nerves throughout my entire body. With every praise and comment he makes, my chest crackles with electricity. Heath hated my laugh. As far back as the day I woke up in the hospital, with no memory of my past, I was convinced I was born with a broken heart. But West makes me feel like I'm not as broken as I thought I was. He's the glue filling in the creases and gaps now.

I spin in his arms as he slips his sport coat over my shoulders, so I'm standing in front of him completely exposed, though he doesn't make a move to take me.

His eyes simply search my face.

I reach up and begin unbuttoning his shirt. My gaze falls to his neck, and I feel a twinge of disappointment.

"Where's your necklace?" I ask, running my hand over his collarbone and chest where the silver chain usually rests.

"I never wear my jewelry when I bathe."

"Oh." I hold back my frown. I can't explain the pull I have toward his necklace.

Once I have all his buttons free, I slip my hands over his chest, shoving his shirt off his torso. My palms graze over the curves and ridges of his muscles, and I drag my nails over the black ink, taking in every tattoo. Moving to his buckle, I remove his pants and black boxer briefs. He steps out of them, never breaking eye contact.

"I was disappointed I didn't get to see you in the car." My attention dips to his body, but he lifts my chin back up with his fingers.

"You'll have plenty of chances to see me." He presses his

lips to mine. Warm, soft lips send warmth down to my center. I'm sore from the assault West gave to the space between my legs. The bath will give it much needed relief, but I can't help wanting West between them again.

I yelp when he breaks away and lifts me into his arms.

Water splashes over the top of the tub when he steps inside, his grin making me melt.

He sets me down into the water. The heat stings my skin, but it feels amazing.

I stand nearly knee-deep in the water when West sits down, sliding backward until his back hits the far end of the tub. He reaches up and holds his hand out for me. I take it, and he spins me around. Placing his hands on my hips, he pulls me down to sit in front of him, between his legs. The water is now up to my shoulders as I lean against West's chest. His erection presses into my back as I rest my head back on his chest. We sit like this for several moments before he grabs a washcloth draped over the edge of the tub. He gestures for me to sit up as he submerges the cloth beneath the water. I feel the absence of our skin-to-skin contact, but he's quick to remedy that when he begins cleaning me, starting with my aching shoulders.

I run my hands over the surface of the water, like I did in the pool at Holt's apartment. I feel the swelling, pounding ache between my legs evaporate, and I moan, letting West know what he's doing is soothing not only my body, but my soul. Then I crack my eyes open and look around his bathroom again.

"Your apartment isn't what I was expecting. Then again, it is."

West chuckles. "I'm not sure if I should take that as a compliment."

"You should." I smile, raising my legs to bring my knees to my chest.

West runs the washcloth over my back, following his path

with his hand, like he doesn't want to stop touching me for a single second.

"I just meant that it's like when we first met. I wouldn't have pegged you for a billionaire... or to be living in Brooklyn."

"Why?" I imagine his brows pulling together over his stunning blue eyes. "Holt lives in Brooklyn."

"You're right. But he lives in a different area, and you aren't Holt."

"True." He laughs under his breath.

"So, why Brooklyn?"

"I was drawn to the old charm of it, I guess. Sort of reminds me of where I came from."

"It does have a certain charm that's missing in Manhattan, doesn't it?"

I rest my cheek on my knee, staring at the forest-green-painted wall. "You have all these nice, expensive things, but they aren't obvious. You don't really see them until you look hard."

"So, what you're saying is, I'm hiding in plain sight?"

"Sort of," I say softly. "You aren't cold like you would expect form someone with your wealth." I'm hinting at Heath and we both know it. West's hand hesitates for a moment, but he's quick to recover. I clear my throat. "What I mean is that you're warm and inviting. You make people feel comfortable and safe, like you could be anyone's friend."

West's hand dips beneath the water as he runs the washcloth over my lower back.

"But still not take anyone's shit," I add, lifting my head and glancing over my shoulder with a smirk.

West smiles back, a close-lipped one, though there's a sadness in his eyes I can't pin down. Like the topic of our conversation is somehow heavier than either of us were expecting.

"Do you remember much about your life before you were adopted by the Halls?" I ask.

West doesn't immediately answer me. I've never asked him questions about his past. The only bit of information I do have is from what little bits he's been willing to give me.

"I do."

I turn back to look straight ahead again, catching our reflection in the full-length, mahogany-framed mirror propped against the wall. I watch West through the reflection. His eyes meet mine, but his hands continue to run over my body.

"From the day I was born, my mother wasn't stable. She'd float in and out of prison and jail. She'd be arrested for all sorts of things: drugs, evading police, domestic disputes with my father. Nothing was off limits for her, but she refused to give me up, despite every reason she had to. Until I was three, I was constantly bounced between my mom, my grandmother, and my father. Then when I turned four, everything changed."

I hold my breath, listening to West share his dark past with me. Something tells me this isn't a story he's shared more than a handful of times, if that.

His blue eyes soften, staring blankly at my back. "My grandmother suddenly died, and the next day, my mother was arrested for drug distribution. My father wasn't addicted to drugs the same way my mother was, but he couldn't hold down a stable job. He could barely afford to pay for his own shitty apartment or to feed himself. So, he surrendered me to Child Protective Services, and I was placed into foster care."

A tingly sensation slithers down my spine, following West's finger.

I open my mouth to let air fill my lungs. The familiar feeling I've had when I'm around West hits me up again, like I've known him longer than a few months. Like I've heard this story before. Or that it's similar to mine.

I don't remember my past, but I do know I was adopted from a foster home. Maybe that's why his story is familiar.

"The first foster home was rough. I was only four, so I don't really remember it that well," he continues. "After a while, the people who fostered me no longer wanted to take care of kids, then I moved to another." He pauses. "Then another."

I tilt my head and swallow back the tears stinging the corner of my eyes. I picture a small version of West. An innocent boy dealt a shitty hand in life, all at the fault of the adults who were supposed to care and protect him. "How many did you live in?"

"In total, six before my last one." He lifts his eyes to mine.

"Were they here in the city?" I ask him, raising my eyebrows.

I gnaw on the inside of my cheek. I'm getting the sense I'm pushing West too far, asking him to share too much. He's right, we're driving right off the edge of this cliff, and there's nothing below to catch us.

My stomach swarms with nerves... until he clears his throat and answers my question.

"I grew up in Upstate New York, near Albany."

I stare at West through the reflection. He lifts his hand out from the water and brushes his hair back, away from his fore-head. The water holds it in place, and drops slip down the side of his face.

"Have you ever been?" West asks me.

I consider my answer. Twisting my tongue, I slip the silver ball between my teeth before inhaling a deep breath. "I haven't. I don't think." I shrug. "Maybe I could have. In my life before..."

I look down at the surface of the water, and I wiggle each toe. For some reason a wooden sign, set out front of an old Victorian-style home flashes in my mind. I recognize it as a puzzle piece I've locked away. I've seen it before. Darkness edges my vision, and what was once happy fluttering in my stomach is now tainted with sickness. Forcing the feeling down, I bury it, refusing to let it take hold. I think back to the few times I did therapy directly after the accident. I flex my fingers, hold them, then release. I bend my foot, stretching my calf, hold it, then release.

"Hey," West says softly, placing his hands on my back. He turns me around to face him.

I spin in the tub, keeping my knees close to my chest, and my head down, wondering why this keeps happening. Why I feel the puzzle pieces starting to come to the forefront of my mind the longer I'm with West.

Slipping his large palm over my cheek, he lifts my head to look up. "Are you okay? I didn't mean to—"

"No, it's okay." I swallow the lump in my throat, not wanting to ruin tonight. It's already been a rollercoaster, and now that I'm looking through West's kind blue eyes, sitting in his clawfoot tub, feeling the hot water kissing my skin, reality hits.

West and I have crossed the line we've both been afraid to cross.

I don't want to let this feeling go just yet, either. I don't want the dark tunnels of my past to drag me out of the daylight.

"I'm good. I was just thinking about how coincidental it is that you're from the same area as the artist I was telling you about, Emily Rapture."

It's a lie, but one West accepts.

"Is she from Albany?" he asks. "You never said where in Upstate New York."

"Somewhere outside of there," I say, my mind still wandering.

"Quantum entanglement." He works his fingers at the edge of my hairline.

"What's quantum entanglement?" I ask, curiosity tugging at me.

"I'm totally going to sound like a nerd." He chuckles, falling against the back of the tub. I miss his hand the second it falls away from my face. "When I was in college, I took a physics class. It was only one day of class, but the professor gave a lecture on quantum entanglement. When two particles become entangled, they remain connected even when they are separated by vast distances. It's the idea that particles are somehow tethered across space and time."

I hold my breath and swallow thickly.

"Basically," West chuckles. "It's a fancy way of explaining coincidences."

"Right." My mouth twitches into a small smile. "Quantum entanglement sounds like something I can get behind."

"Oh, yeah?"

I nod, tucking my bottom lip under my teeth. "Do you think it was quantum entanglement the day I walked into your bar and drew on your napkin?"

Without a word, his eyes darken, hungry for me. His jaw twitches, and his corded muscles swell when he pulls me forward and I slip my legs on either side of him. His cock rubs against my crease, and the delightful fluttering returns. I find myself smiling. The soreness has already evaporated, and I'm wanting West inside me again.

"It was definitely quantum entanglement," he says, confidently.

I hold West's injured hand in mine and run my fingers over each knuckle. The lines look familiar, and my mind wanders to my drawing hidden in my portfolio. West's is different than the one trapped in my head, though similar. I turn it over, running my finger over his palm. West's cock jerks under me, and I smile as a growl rumbles from his chest.

With his large arms wrapped tightly around my waist, he pulls me up, then lowers me down over his length.

"I want you to fuck me." Honesty and lust spill from me as fast as the wetness between my legs, now coating his cock. "I want you to fuck me in your bed, where you can take all of me."

"In time." His voice lowers, slipping over my skin. "I like feeling you like this first. Besides, I don't want to wait until then."

Cupping the side of his face, the stubble along his jaw grates against my skin like fine sandpaper, but the shape of his prominent jawline fits perfectly into my palm as I lean down and capture his mouth with mine. Soft and full, his lips mold to mine before I slip my tongue between them.

My insides stretch as he fills me, and I sigh with his mouth still on mine, relishing in the way it feels.

His warm hands slip down my back. We move slowly to not make the water splash over the edge, but with every rock and roll of my hips, it does so anyway.

Our slow pace allows me to focus on the small details: our heated breaths, the way the veins in West's neck bulge as he moves me over him, the way his eyes soften and look at me as if he still can't believe I'm here, in his arms.

It's different than it was in the car. Here, in the warm lighting of West's bathroom, a thin veil in the dark of night isn't over us. Here, we're stripped down, raw and bare. Every angle and imperfection is visible. We're seeing each other in a new light.

I drape my arms over his shoulders and lift myself up his length before driving back down, and soon, it becomes difficult to hold back. His large hands move from my waist to my chest. He palms each breast, flicking and pinching each of my hardened nipples. Electricity crackles along my skin, sending heat to my core. I move faster, rolling my hips harder and deeper as more water splashes over the edge.

By the time we're finished, and West has spilled himself inside me, nearly half the water is puddled outside of the tub.

"I'm sorry," I pant, biting back a laugh. "Looks like I made a mess."

"A beautiful mess." West tucks my hair behind my ear before he kisses me gently, then winks. "I don't mind a little mess every now and then."

TWENTY

All I want is to stay in bed with London, burying my cock inside her so deep, I'd convince her to never leave. I spent years pining for her, running a fool's errand, searching for her among the millions of faces in New York City. I'd almost given up hope.

Especially the day we crossed paths, about a year and a half after we'd been forced apart by the adoption.

I was seventeen, and she was fifteen. I'd remembered our age difference. In fact, I'd remembered everything about her: the birthmark on her hand, her long black hair, the way her eyes shined whenever she'd show me a new drawing.

But that day at Coney Island, all my hope of reuniting with her shattered within seconds.

I meant what I told her about quantum entanglement. It's always been around us.

I nearly broke when I saw her that day. The sun glistened off her black hair. She stood in front of the bumper cars, watching them going around in circles. Holding a large ball of cotton candy on a stick, she used her other hand to point and yell at whoever was out on the track. She wasn't tipping her head back in laughter, but I couldn't help noticing the smile on her face and the dimple in her cheek.

She was happy.

Free.

I stood several feet down from her then, against the fence. It had been over a year since I'd last seen her. Since our circumstances ripped us apart. But I knew she would recognize me. She had to.

I didn't look much different. My muscles had grown, and my jaw had become more defined, but she would recognize. My eyes hadn't changed, and they were her favorite. She never went a day without telling me.

I'd promised her I would find her again, and I had.

She was there, within reach.

I watched her nervously, gathering up the courage to speak to her. To tell her I found her like I always promised I would.

In a cruel twist of fate, the words got lodged in my throat when she looked at me.

I'd caught the attention of her gray eyes. The ones I'd stared at for days in our foster home. The ones I fell in love with long before I even understood the depth of what it meant to love someone.

Reality had punched me in the gut when she looked at me with no expression. No recognition. I'd opened my mouth to speak. There was less than ten feet between us, but I knew she was further away than that.

My mother's voice called for me in the distance, and a chill hit the back of my neck when London looked away. Not even hearing my name pulled her back to me. I was a ghost, a stranger, a blank face.

I was heartbroken that day, wondering how London could have forgotten me so easily. How could she have let me go and pretend I no longer existed? My teenage mind and heart were at war that day. I couldn't wrap my head around the idea of her forgetting what we'd been through, even if it had been over a year before.

Trauma like ours wasn't easily forgotten.

Then, years later, when my mother told me my brother's new wife had amnesia, then seeing her and Heath at Julianna's birthday party, it all clicked into place.

London hadn't forgotten me by choice. I was stolen from her, just like all her other memories before she was fourteen.

Now, when I press my lips to her forehead as she sleeps, I wonder what memories have come back to her. If any.

She moans and moves underneath me. I've stirred her awake, and a flash of guilt washes over me. That is until I hear her moan and watch the dimple in her cheek deepen.

"Good morning," I hum across her skin, dragging my nose along her collarbone. I slip my hand over her breast, pinching her nipple.

She hums, too, constantly shifting beneath me. I know I've already driven her wild. My suspicion is confirmed when I slip my hand between her legs and am met with wetness. I start to circle her swollen bud, and her head jerks back, digging into my pillow. Her jaw falls slack as a loud moan escapes her.

"It is a good morning." I growl. "Isn't it?"

"It is." She raises her hands and wraps them around my neck.

Her fingers touch the metal chain and then her eyes snap open as if a blaring alarm is sounding off.

Fuck.

I forgot that I put the necklace back on when I woke up an hour ago, or maybe it was two. However long ago it was, I woke up long enough to use the bathroom and grab myself a glass of water while London stayed in my bed, sleeping deeply and peacefully. I pull my hand from between her legs and move over her, resting my arms on either side of her head.

It isn't that I don't want London to see the necklace I've worn since my fourteenth birthday. I've thought about this moment since seeing her again. Would she remember it? Would it stir up a memory for her?

It has to, right? Considering the drawing she did on the napkin?

Either way, I hold my breath and try as hard as I fucking can not to freak out as she delicately grabs the chain. She holds it between her fingers, using both hands to smooth down the length before her eyes fall to the tiny charm at the end.

I watch her with bated breath, terrified, naively believing this could be it. This could be the moment her memories are triggered. I feel nauseous. My stomach wobbles, and I can't figure out what to say or do.

Deciding on saying absolutely nothing, I wait and watch, shaking like a leaf with anticipation.

Her brows pull together, and she pulls her chin back. She doesn't say anything, turning the charm over in her hands.

I'm aware of every breath, and every second of waiting is spent in agony.

"Is this...?" She never looks away from the charm.

Holy shit. This is it.

I swear, I see the memories falling into place for her.

The three lines between her pinched eyebrows disappear as they settle back into their natural place, then she finally looks up at me.

"Big Ben?"

I swallow, loudly. "Yeah."

"Why?" she asks, confused, her gaze dropping back to the tiny clock tower.

I'm wrong. This isn't it. This isn't the moment she remembers.

Disappointment floods my gut, but I try my best to keep breathing and not let it show.

"A birthday gift from a friend," I tell her plainly. It's the truth. A vague one, but true.

"Were they from London?" she asks, her mouth tilting into a ghost of a smile.

"No." I clear my throat.

"Oh." She frowns. This time, she's the one who looks disappointed. "What's the story behind it, then?"

She lifts her chin, staring straight at me. The words stick like glue to the back of my throat, refusing to budge.

"It's a long, complicated one." I smirk, letting out a sigh.

I can't be the one to tell her. Either she won't believe me, or if she heard me out, what would happen then? Would I run the risk of losing her again? Because she'll not only remember me, but everything else that comes along with it?

Her face relaxes. "Maybe for another time, then."

"Another time." I nod.

She looks at the necklace longingly for a moment before wrapping one hand around the charm. With her other, she drags her black-painted nail down the length of my jaw.

"Kiss me," she whispers, her eyes falling to my mouth as she tugs on the charm.

I do so without hesitation. My lips press to hers, and I'm transported back to the day she gave me this necklace. The memory plays in my mind, and for a moment, I imagine a world in which she remembers it just like I do.

"Touch me again," she says against my mouth.

"Are you sure?" I ask, leaning on my left arm while using my free hand to explore her body.

She wiggles beneath me, the heaviness around the topic of

my necklace dissolving with every breath. Sadness tugs at the barbed wire wrapped around my wounded heart, but it subsides long enough to allow the happiness I feel wrapped up in London to take over.

My fingers find her swollen clit again.

"You aren't too sore, are you? I didn't hurt you last night?" I ask, fighting back a smirk. I don't ever want London to be in pain or hurt, especially because of me, but there's a flutter of satisfaction in knowing it's only because we haven't been able to stop since last night.

"No." She shakes her head. "You could never hurt me."

I grin wickedly. "Do you want me to kiss and make it better?" I start to lower myself down her body, but she stops me, spreading her legs wide.

She lifts her hips to meet me.

My dick is wide awake, our conversation about the necklace now long gone.

She bites down on her bottom lip, and for a moment, I catch a glimpse of her tongue piercing, the silver ball sitting on top of her tongue.

She hums as she shakes her head, then pushes against my chest. Fire rages in her eyes as she straddles me as soon as my back hits the mattress. We both laugh, only to stop abruptly when she slides herself over my dick.

Fuck, I'm going to come if she does that again.

Leaning down to meet me, she brushes her nose to mine as she holds back her curtain of raven-colored hair.

"It's my turn to kiss and make it better," she whispers.

And holy motherfucking shit.

I'm in love with London Walker.

Her nails scratch the front of my hardened pecs, and my entire body stiffens. Each of her kisses against my muscles is a silent bandage to the pain we've been through. The years of silence. London hasn't regained her memory, but I know she's in there.

Because the London I fell in love with at fifteen is the same as the one in my bed right now. Only she's now a twenty-eight-year-old woman. Fucking beautiful.

She lowers herself until her mouth is in line with my cock. She grips onto the base, each of her gold rings glistening in the morning sun. "Tell me what you want me to do, Mr. Knight."

I sit up and scoot back until my back hits my headboard. London stays on all fours, crawling to catch up to where I am. Her full breasts sway as she moves, the curve of her hips on full display with her actions. She grabs onto my base again, and I hook my finger under her jaw, tilting her face up to me.

"Open that pretty mouth of yours," I tell her, deepening my voice.

Goddamn, this woman has all of me.

She does as I command. Her pouty lips part, and her jaw drops.

"Let me see your tongue."

She sticks it out, and my dick jumps. I'm pretty sure I'm already oozing pre-cum. Heat builds in my belly, and my legs start to tingle.

"This." I tap my finger on the delightful little silver ball. "I've been aching to have this sweep across my cock."

When I pull my finger away, she slips her tongue back into her mouth.

"You've been fantasizing about this?"

"You have no fucking idea."

She doesn't waste any more time. Opening her mouth, she takes my cock, driving it all the way back until my tip meets the back of her throat. She gags slightly, but that doesn't stop her. Since I'm sitting up, I have better access to her. I gather her long, black locks around my hand and fist her hair, holding it against the back of her head, guiding her with every thrust.

Heaven. I've died and gone to fucking Heaven.

Pressing both hands to the base of my stomach, she moves over my cock, allowing me to guide her. I gently lift myself off the mattress with every hard thrust, meeting the back of her throat. The little ball pierced into her tongue is a completely new sensation and adds to the buildup. I've never had a woman suck my cock who had a tongue piercing before.

London is the one and only, and I know from this day forward, she'll be the *only* one.

She sucks and puckers her cheeks, her dimple deepening. I try not to close my eyes or tilt my head back against the headboard. I want to watch her. I want to watch her tits swinging under her, her eyes widening as she watches my face to see what she's doing to me. She licks the tip and drags her tongue up and down the length. Then she cups my balls as she takes me all in again.

"Holy shit, London," I grunt.

She moves faster. Or I move her faster. I'm not exactly sure who is doing what. It doesn't matter. The blood shoots straight for my cock, and two more pumps of her mouth on mine, and my cum is exploding into the back of her throat. My legs shake as I ride out my orgasm.

She swallows my cum and licks the corner of her mouth as she sits up and falls back on her heels.

"Fuck." I tilt my head back and push my hair off my forehead, catching my breath for only a beat.

Seeing London sitting between my legs, on her heels, bare, and with my cum inside her both ways, does something to me. A switch is flicked. Catapulting myself forward, I wrap my arm around her and spin her around before dropping her down onto the bed.

She yelps, but when she falls back, with her arms above her head, and her hair spread out maniacally around her, I lift her leg until her knee meets her chest.

She's spread wide and open for me.

I lean down and give her a gentle kiss on her forehead, then her mouth.

"You're right," I tell her. "This is a good morning."

Lifting her hand, she trails it down the side of my face. For a moment, I see her eyes change. It's brief and fast, almost as if she recognizes something. I've learned it's a sign for when she remembers something or is thinking about those puzzle pieces she talks about. False hope, probably. Another fool's errand.

Though I can't help the flicker of hope sparking in my chest that maybe she's starting to remember. We'd never been together like this until last night, or even the night before, but maybe it is possible she's starting to remember me.

"Don't you have a ton of bars to run or something?" she teases. "I would feel terrible if you started neglecting your businesses for me."

"Oh, trust me." I bare my teeth, pull back my hips, and drive my cock inside her. She stills, tipping her head back on a gasp. I hold still where I am and stare into her eyes before I bring my mouth down to her ear and pull my hips back once more. "If you were the reason my business empire crumbled"—I slam back into her—"it would all be worth it."

TWENTY-ONE

LONDON

West asked Alden if he could give me a ride home so I could change before heading over to Charleigh's flower shop.

Neither West nor I wanted to leave his bed, but when one of the managers at West's beer garden called to tell him a brewer was there waiting for his scheduled meeting, we quickly cleaned up and raced out the door. West wanted to be the one to drive me home, but I told him no, I didn't want him to keep his client waiting.

Besides, I don't mind Alden's company.

He doesn't say much on the ride over, barely looking at me in the rearview mirror. I'm glad because I know I can't wipe the stupid smile off my face the whole ride over from Brooklyn to Manhattan. Every inch of my body is alive with the memories of West's touch, his kisses, his cock in my mouth earlier. Inside me. Last night and this morning.

It's surreal, like being inside a dream.

I also finally got to see the necklace. The one tugging on my memory like the end of an invisible string. I stared at it, hoping it would tell me something. Anything. I hoped it would tell me that I wasn't just making up that feeling I got every time I looked at it.

But nothing came.

Other than the coincidence of it being Big Ben; the same clock tower I find myself sketching time and time again. The same clock tower that shares the same home as my name.

I want to believe there's something deeper to all of this. I want to connect all the dots, but as hard as I try, I can't. Every piece is still a jumbled mess, and the more I try to fit them together, the tighter I feel the walls closing in around my mind. Like it isn't ready for whatever is hiding on the other side of the curtain.

Tears prick at the back of my eyes as the same disappointment I've felt time and time again since the accident settles in my fractured heart.

I shove the small setback aside and focus on the good.

West.

After stepping out of the back of West's car, I say goodbye to Alden and take the steps up to Selene's apartment two at a time.

I need to brush my teeth and change into clothes that are mine. I wouldn't mind spending the day in West's entirely too large sweatpants and T-shirt if I wouldn't end up looking like I was drowning in cotton.

After jiggling my key in the doorknob, my phone rings from the small handbag I took with me to the club last night. It's about a quarter of the size of my regular everyday purse, so my phone isn't difficult to find. Hoping it's West, excitement bubbles in my chest, inflating like a balloon. It's ridiculous, but I already can't wait to be with him again.

Thinking back on the reasons I was pushing him away seems so ridiculous now that we've crossed the line we set. Ridiculous because, deep in my bones, *in my soul*, everything about him feels right and in place.

Being with West feels as natural as breathing.

My chest deflates when I see it isn't West calling, though. Instead, it's an unknown number. Annoyance digs at me, figuring it's probably one of those scam companies calling to tell me I've been preapproved for some fifty-thousand-dollar loan or some insane number like that. I ignore the call and drop my phone and handbag onto the tiny kitchen counter once I step inside the apartment.

"Selene?" I call out. "I'm home." I stand between the kitchen and hallway, waiting for Selene to poke her head out from her bedroom, but she doesn't.

Other than a quick check in text last night, letting me know she made it home, I haven't spoken to her. At least not fully since watching her walk out of our VIP section, Holt following after her.

I let her know I was staying with West and would explain it all to her today.

After telling me it was fine as long as I spilled every single detail to her, Selene had dropped the conversation, promising to talk with me at home. I was expecting her to be here. Especially with how adamant she'd been about finding out about all the sordid details of West and me.

Glancing around the apartment, I find a small, pink note on our coffee table.

> *Had to pop into the flower shop for a few hours.*
> *Meet me there. Since we're talking men, bring some*
> *coffee, with extra espresso.*
> *P.S. Oh, Charleigh's first shop, not her new*
> *one. xoxo*

I drop Selene's note with a small smile and make my way to

the bathroom. I crank the shower faucet all the way and strip out of West's clothes. I fold them neatly before stuffing them into one of my artist canvas bags to give them back to him when I get to The Veiled Door later. I wait nearly five minutes for the water to reach a tolerable temperature, then welcome its soothing warmth.

I think about all that's changed in the past few days.

My hands are aching to work, aching to create. As I'm scrubbing shampoo into my hair, I think about the pair of hands I've been slowly working on over the past several months. The lines and creases. They remind me of West's hands, now that they've explored my body.

I'm lost in every memory of the past twenty-four hours when the realization dawns on me. I'm tired of running from my past. I'm tired of sifting through the puzzle pieces, forcing myself to not pick them up willingly.

I know my panic attacks are caused by the flickers of my past. There's tragedy weaved into it, and the thought is fucking terrifying, but I know if I don't lean into my memories and remember, I'll never feel complete. I'll forever feel half-myself, with nothing but unanswered questions.

Being with West has breathed new life into *my* life, and I want to start living it.

I'm rinsing the shampoo from my hair when it feels as if the stars are beginning to align. I've stepped out into the daylight and let go of everything I've ever let hold me back.

Closing my eyes, I run the water over my hair, sifting through every flash of memory I can think of.

The sign reading Albany.

The hands covered in dirt.

Someone's voice telling me I'm alive.

Then another.

I squeeze my eyes shut, forcing down the sense of panic

trying to take over. The feeling is similar to the one I got in the club last night when the stranger came up behind me.

It's vile, and my stomach sours.

Make one peep out of that pretty little mouth, and I swear to God, I'll slit your fucking throat right here.

My eyes snap open. I bend over, gasping for air, sputtering and coughing. My hand flies to my throat, and I swear I feel the sharp edge of cold metal. I run my fingers over my taut skin, but there's nothing. No scar, no evidence of anything. My body wracks and spasms as I grip the edge of the tub with my other hand, struggling to breathe.

The water is freezing cold as it slides down my back. Though it could just be from the memory. The darkest memory I've yet to pull.

Panic builds inside me, and I second guess whether this is a good idea. Should I lean into the memories? Or is this a mistake? At this point, I'm not even sure I have a choice. Every single one comes without warning, happening when I least expect it.

The saying usually goes 'the heart wants what the heart wants', but for me, it's my mind. My mind wants me to remember, and now that I'm slowly getting them back, I'm absolutely terrified down to my bones.

I shut the water off with shaking fingers and wrap a warm towel around me. Concentrating on my breathing, I force the darkness away, and focus on the good.

The light.

Meeting my sister.

My art.

West.

The feeling I had when I walked into Selene's apartment slowly edges its way back in, and I'm thankful for the relief. Maybe the voice has something to do with the sign I envisioned last night when West and I were talking about Albany.

Quantum entanglement.

A tiny, barely-there smile finds the corners of my mouth. No, it must be coincidence that West is from Albany when I swear I've seen a wooden sign painted with the word Albany on it.

I get dressed under a haze of the memories I've conjured, and when I leave Selene's apartment, I'm trying as hard as I can to leave the memory I experienced in the shower behind.

With my canvas bag of West's clothes and Julianna's ripped dress slung over my shoulder, I take the subway to the Upper West Side. To Charleigh's flower shop. I've only ever been there a few times, but of those times, I've always enjoyed it.

The shop is small and intimate. Although I've never been to Paris, it reminds me of a flower shop you'd find there, covered from front to back with flourishing bouquets and plants. The scent when stepping through the wooden door is overwhelming, and one I welcome. It's refreshing when coming from the streets of the city and people on the subway.

I find my sister finishing up with a customer. She hands the woman her freshly wrapped bouquet with a smile, and her eyes find mine.

"Oh, good. You got my note." She sighs.

Clutching her flowers to her chest, the customer gives me a smile before leaving.

I stop at the counter and pass my sister her coffee.

"I didn't think you had work today."

"The other girl who works this shift got sick, and Charleigh was already scheduled to work at her second location." She tucks her blonde hair behind her ear. Her large, gold earrings sway as she tips her head back, taking a sip of her triple espresso. Despite having to wake up early today, after a night like last night, she appears surprisingly restful.

"Thank you for bringing this."

"You could have just sent me a text." I giggle, setting my bag on the counter. "Risky leaving a note. You could have been waiting for me all day."

"I know, but I knew you would find me." She shrugs and sighs. "I've been trying to stay off my phone. Social media has been a little much lately. After months of pouring over my manuscript, I'm giving myself a break from technology."

"I get that." I nod, playing with a single flower on display near the register.

"I saw Grandma the other day." Selene's mouth dips into a frown. "She misses you."

"I want to see her." I didn't realize until now how I've put everyone at a distance, caught up with my own problems. "Next time you go, I'll come with you."

Selene reaches out and squeezes my hand, her mouth tilting into a smile. "She'll love that. Okay..." She thrums her fingers on the counter. "It's been entirely too long since we've talked." She lifts her hands in surrender. "I know you aren't exactly an open book, so if you don't want to tell me everything, you don't have to. I don't want to push you."

"No." I straighten my back. "I want to." I stare blankly at the single flower again. "It's hard to explain, but I think only living with half my memories, and with my marriage to Heath, it's held me back from being myself. Living here in the city with you and making friends with Charleigh and Julianna has helped. Working on these pieces for West's bars has done..."

"Oh, yeah." Selene dips her head, pulling for my attention. "About that."

"About what?" I crack a smile.

"West." Her shaped eyebrows rise. "I may have been a bit drunk last night, but the girls told me about how West beat the shit out of some guy before the both of you left. What happened?"

Biting back the feeling I had last night when the man was at my back, or the vision of his blood spurting across the club dancer's legs, I think about all the good parts. How West protected me without hesitation. How he confessed his feelings for me, leading the way for me to confess mine.

I fill Selene in on every detail. How I wanted to get away from him because I couldn't breathe and how I melted when he told me he'd kill for me as if it's something completely normal to say. Telling her about that moment leads me to tell her about the night before in my makeshift studio closet, too.

By the time I'm done telling her everything, up until the second I walked in here with our triple espressos, her jaw is practically on the floor.

"Holy shit, London." She clamps her mouth shut and swallows before breathing out. "I don't know whether to be excited or angry with you."

"Angry with me?"

"Yeah." She scoffs. "This is insane, and I can't believe all of this has been going on without you telling me any of it."

"You haven't exactly been open with me, either," I argue back. Then I remember her note. "Your note. You said in your note we were talking men. Plural. So, this isn't just about West, is it?"

The only response I get from my sister is a coy smile.

"Who?" I ask her. God, it feels like it's been forever since Selene and I talked about men. "Is it Holt?" I whisper, glancing around as though Julianna or Holt might overhear.

Selene's eyes spread wide, then she frowns, shaking her head. "No, it isn't Holt. I met someone through a book blogging account. He's also a writer and editor. We met for coffee one time but that's it." She shrugs. "I think I like him. I don't know yet. I kind of want to keep this to myself. For now."

I can't help but smile, thankful my sister is no longer in the writing cave like she has been over the past several months.

"Anyway." She lifts her shoulders and blows out a dramatic breath. "That's all I'm going to say about it right now because it's not nearly as serious as everything you're telling me."

"Well." I breathe deeply, the heaviness of the conversation quickly shifting back to me. "It isn't everything."

"What?" She chuckles sarcastically. "How could there possibly be more?"

I nervously play with my tongue piercing. "I can't explain it, but I think some of my memories are starting to come back."

"Oh, my God." Selene gasps, covering her mouth. Her pink-glossed lips disappear, and her eyes spread wide again. Then she's shuffling around the counter to meet me. She clips the edge, and it hits her gut, but it doesn't faze her. She stops in front of me. "How do you know?"

I wrap my hand around the base of my neck. "They've been coming back to me really since Heath's death. More so since I've been living here and working with West."

"Are you okay?" Selene grabs my arm. I don't miss the worried expression etched into her gorgeous face. She's worried about me because she knows the ones I had before always sent me spiraling into a panic attack.

"I'm fine," I tell her, dropping my gaze, knowing I'm not ready to share how dark some of them are. "I just haven't made sense of them yet. I know they're ones I've never remembered before or seen until recently. I'm also having these dreams…" I lift my gaze back to hers. "But I swear they aren't dreams. They feel too real to be."

"Dreams about what?"

"West."

Selene cocks her head to the side, her brows pinching. "West?"

"Yeah. Maybe it's because I've been around him a lot lately. Maybe it's because I've developed these feelings for him. Right?"

She considers answering me, but I can tell she isn't positive about her response. "Maybe." My sister lifts her hand and lovingly tucks my hair behind my ear.

"I need to apologize to you."

"For what?" she asks.

"For being distant. For not letting you in."

"Don't be sorry." She wraps her arms around me, and she smells just like the shop as she rests her chin on my shoulder. "We're both guilty."

"Oh, yeah." I gape, ripping her away from my arms. "What happened with you last night?"

Selene's eyes shoot up and over my shoulder. Following what's caught her attention, I look over my shoulder to see Julianna enter Charleigh's shop. She's gorgeous, even in her leggings and off-the-shoulder, oversized T-shirt.

"Hey, girls." Julianna's grin stretches from ear to ear. "What's going on?"

"Selene was just about to tell me what happened last night after I left." I grin, anticipating my sister's story.

"Oh." Julianna moves closer. "You mean after West beat the shit out of that guy, and you two split?"

My face falls. Is Julianna mad that we ruined her night?

"Because that was fucking awesome." She laughs.

"What?" I ask, giggling.

"The thought of Rome being pissed that West started a fight in the middle of his brand-new club only places the cherry on top of the mountain of icing on this cake." Her cheeks redden with her enthusiastic grin. "Because trust me, nothing gives me greater pleasure than seeing Rome's reputation get tarnished.

The man needs a good smack on the beautiful ass every now and then."

Selene snorts, covering her mouth and nose to stifle it. I laugh, catching onto her unintentional joke. Does she realize what she's saying right now? Probably too many glasses of champagne still floating around in that beautiful brain of hers.

Julianna's phone rings in her pocket. She ignores it and stares at Selene and me, her attention drifting between us.

"Um." Selene clears her throat. "Are you going to get that?"

"No," she clips, still smiling. "What happened to you last night, London? Was West okay after beating that guy up? Some people in the club were saying that guy just came up behind you and started touching you, and that West looked like he was going to kill him."

The ringing stops.

"Yeah." I lean against the counter, resting my elbow on the wooden top. "The guy was a total creep. I'm glad West was there. When we got back to his place, his hand didn't look too bad."

"His place, huh?" Julianna wags her eyebrows and clicks her tongue with delight.

I nod, heat spreading in my cheeks.

Her phone rings again. She still doesn't answer. Selene looks at Julianna with piqued curiosity, and I do the same.

"What is going on?" she asks, drawing her words out.

Julianna tugs her phone from her pocket and groans, rolling her eyes. She stuffs it back inside. "Remember how Rome was a complete dick last night at the club?"

Neither Selene nor I answer her.

"Well..." She clears her throat and grins, bouncing on her heels. "I signed him up for an erectile dysfunction support group newsletter last night after he left. I think he figured out it was me." She scrunches her nose, holding her breath for our reactions.

The three of us burst into laughter.

"Julianna." Selene gapes.

She shrugs, unable to wipe the smug grin of satisfaction on her face when she turns her attention back to me, arching a single eyebrow. "Enough about me."

"About last night." I sigh and avoid her gaze as I'm pulling the dress she let me borrow out of the bag. I frown as I hand it to her. "I'm so sorry the dress got ruined, Jules."

Julianna takes it, turning it over in her hands, finding the damage done to the back. "Was this from the creep at the club or from West?"

Embarrassment and shame overtake me. I know my friends won't judge me for being with West, but I don't like feeling like my whole life is on display. My private life, at least. That, and I feel guilty for ruining a dress that isn't even mine. Especially when that dress is probably worth more than a month's worth of art sales for me.

I slowly look up at Julianna. "He said he would pay you back whatever the dress was worth."

"I'm just glad you chose West and not my brother." Julianna cracks a devious, knowing grin. "Because this... this is hot."

Selene's is slower to start, but it's there.

I find myself smiling, too. My cheeks grow sore, and I don't think I've ever been this happy. At least not that I can remember. Though Julianna's words echo in my mind.

I didn't choose West, and he didn't choose me.

Our connection was already mapped out in the stars.

TWENTY-TWO

WEST

Holt is sitting at the end of my bar, with a half-drunk beer, staring blankly up at the TV hanging above the door that leads to the upstairs closet, which now serves as London's studio.

Wearing a simple, white button-down shirt, he has the sleeves rolled up to his elbows, and I can't help laughing under my breath as I make my way toward him. He looks out of place sitting here casually with a beer, especially focused on the basketball game playing.

The Veiled Door isn't as casual as some of my other bars, but during the day we play sports before switching them off for the nighttime crowd, focusing the attention on conversation or any live performers we might host instead.

Holt is too clean cut, more like my nighttime crowd. Neatly shaven, corporate elites, with perfect hair, dripping with arrogance.

"Feel like a bit of day drinking?" I ask my friend, laughing as I slip into the stool beside him.

"I took the day off today," Holt mutters, playing with his half-empty glass. He spins it over the black coaster, staring at it blankly. "Just wasn't feeling the hectic environment of the office after last night. You know?"

I nod. "Sorry I bailed." I look down at my hand, running my fingers over my bruised knuckles. Surprisingly, they aren't as bad as I expected them to be, considering the way I left the asshole bleeding and unconscious.

"Did the guy deserve it?" Holt asks, catching my attention.

I look up and chuckle. "I never threaten to kill someone unless they deserve it."

He nods once. "Good."

"So, what's up?" I sigh, glancing around the bar. It's a busy lunchtime. Slowly, more and more people are pouring in from the street. Piper and Lewis start moving faster behind the bar, darting from one end to the other.

"Hey, boss," Piper interrupts, giving me a smile. "Can I get you something to drink while you're sitting here?"

"No. I'm all set."

"Okay." She grins, then nods toward the staircase. "She's already upstairs, working." I'm pretty sure Piper has already had her ears up that something's going on between me and London, just like Lewis. She has ever since London started working here, and I've been showing up more in the past few months than I have in the past year of owning this spot.

Piper leaves Holt and me to tend to the customer on the opposite side of Holt.

"Was she talking about London?" Holt asks.

I grin like a fucking lovesick teenager. "Yeah."

Holt doesn't ask any more questions, and I'm glad for it, because I wouldn't even know where to begin. Instead, he leans forward, resting his arms on the edge of the bar top. He turns his head on a swivel and looks at me. "I came to tell you I got in touch with Emily Rapture."

I sit up in my seat. I'd almost forgotten I'd asked him to look into getting in touch with her.

"You did?"

"Yep." He smiles, scratching at his chin. "She agreed to do an interview for the magazine again. I was going to put one of my reporters on it, but she told me she would only do it if it were me."

"Really?" I can't help but laugh. What does that mean if she's refusing anyone else but Holt?

"Anyway." He waves me off. "I told her I had a friend who admired her work, asked if she'd get you into an early showing, and she agreed."

"Seriously?" I feel like I'm going to jump out of my seat, but I contain my excitement because I don't want to look like a fucking idiot. Or scare customers away.

Holt nods and finishes the last of his beer. He slides out of his stool and slips back into his suit jacket hanging on the back. "The gallery opens in a few months, but Emily said she'd be willing to get you in next month. I gave her your email, so keep an eye out for it." He flicks his wrist and looks down at his watch. "I've got to meet someone for lunch, but I just wanted to give you that info in person." He looks up. "And to make sure you were all right after last night. I'll see you later."

I can't fucking wait to tell London.

"Hey," I say, slipping out of my own stool. "Thanks, man."

Holt's smile meets his eyes. "No problem."

Excitement builds inside me after Holt leaves, and I spin on my heel to head upstairs to meet London. It's only been a few short hours since leaving her, and I already want to bury myself inside her again, just to make sure I didn't dream up the past twenty-four hours.

"Weston Knight!"

A chill skates down my spine at the shrill voice screaming my name.

Frozen, I don't immediately turn around. Customers seated at the dining room tables in front of me eye the person behind me. The sharp clicking of heels fills the silence of the bar, mingling with the music playing overhead.

Closing my eyes, I sigh heavily and pinch the bridge of my nose before I spin around.

My mother's sharp, daggered eyes are zeroed in on me as she marches down the length of the bar. She tosses her handbag on the counter, points with demand at Piper. "Vodka soda on the rocks, hold the lemon."

Piper's eyes spread wide with fear. She puts her head down and immediately gets to work.

"If you're going to barge into my bar, screaming my name, you'll treat my staff with respect." I grind my teeth.

"Fine." My mother groans, rolling her black-lined eyes. She twists at the hip and places her hands on the back of the barstool. "*Please.*"

Piper only glances up quickly and gives her a curt nod before grabbing my most expensive bottle of vodka.

"See," my mother muses, sweeping her hands down the front of her blouse, pretending to pick off a stray speck of dust. "I'm polite."

"Why are you here, Mother?" I ask her, the memory of our last conversation still eliciting white hot anger within me. That doesn't even begin to touch the hurt portion of my frustration with her.

"Oh, Weston." She softens her voice, stepping forward. She lifts her hands and straightens my tie. "I came to tell you that all you needed to do was ask for it, and I would have agreed. No need to take it behind my back."

"Take what?" I ask, confused.

She stops fussing with my tie and looks up at me with her hands pressed flat to my chest. Despite her bitterness, she's still beautiful. Her hair is perfectly styled, and the lines embedded in the corners of her eyes are evidence of years of happiness and laughter. But ever since Heath's death, I haven't heard her laugh or seen her happy.

"The money." She blinks.

I take a step back, and her hands fall away from my chest. "What money, Mom? I have no clue what you're talking about."

"In our account."

Again, no fucking clue.

I begin to mentally sift through all the bank accounts in my name and any that can be tied to my mother, but none come to mind. I only have my business ones and my personal accounts.

"The account I opened after you were adopted, West." My mother scoffs, already exhausted with having to explain. "I opened a single savings account for you and Heath after you joined our family."

"Seriously?" I ask her, the veins popping in my neck with anger. "You opened an account with my name on it and never even told me? Now you're accusing me of stealing money from it?"

Her patience wears thin. In fact, it completely disappears. Her once simple, kind expression is now filled with indignation and hatred that's being directed at me.

"Your brother is dead, so it couldn't have possibly been him. I know you touched it," she spits out, her lips curled, barring her porcelain veneers. "All of it is gone."

I'm losing my shit. I curl my fingers into a tight fist, and suddenly I'm wishing I could drive it right into the fucking wall. But I'm not my brother, and I don't want to scare my mother, no matter how unreasonable she's being.

"How could I possibly touch it when I didn't even know about it? I'm literally just finding out about this now."

"Where is the money?" She grinds out, stepping closer to me.

"Asking the same question over and over won't magically change the answer. Why don't you just ask the bank where the money went? Someone who works there must know where it went." I state as calmly and rationally as possible, forcing my blood to stop boiling. "Berating me isn't going to get you anywhere, because I don't know what the fuck you're talking about."

Patrons at the bar glance over their shoulders, and I feel eyes looking up at me from the tables surrounding us. From the corner of my eye, Lewis is filling a draft beer, and he's close to letting it spill over with how hard he's staring at us. Piper is nowhere to be found.

"Did you give it to her?" Mom asks, nodding toward upstairs.

What the actual fuck?

"What?" I ask, not recognizing the woman in front of me. "Seriously?"

"Heath made it pretty clear she isn't to be trusted, Weston." She sneers. "If I find out you took our money and gave it to her" —she points an angry finger over my shoulder—"that slut –"

"Get out."

"What did you just say to me?" Her stiff eyebrows slant dramatically.

"I said get out. This is my bar, and I won't have you talking this way in front of my customers. I won't allow you to talk about London that way either." The oxygen gets lodged somewhere in my throat over the fact that the woman I'm kicking out of my bar has been the only mother figure to ever give me a true life. But like I said, I don't recognize her anymore.

Her mouth falls open, and her chin trembles. "I'm your mother."

"That's right. You are," I tell her. "But that doesn't excuse the horrible things you've said about me and London. Now, get out." This time, I'm the one pointing.

Tears well in her eyes, and it takes everything in me not to cave. I *want* to give in, but I can't unhear her accusations and *that* word that spilled from her mouth. The name she easily called London.

"I know you took it, and I'm going to find out why," she snaps, spinning on her sharp heel. She swipes her handbag from where she tossed it on the counter and forces her way out the front door.

I stand frozen, the muscles in my arms tense as my nails cut into the inside of my palms. I clench my teeth so hard, I'm certain they're going to crack. My skin is hot and filled with anger. I think about my childhood. The constant bullying from Heath. The constant hatred spewed toward me. The competition and need to prove he was the better, more legitimate son. I was the extra. The unwanted. The spare.

My vision turns hazy, and I think I might pass out. Forcing myself to breathe, the air sears my lungs, burning every inch of flesh.

I look around. The entire bar has fallen silent. All eyes are on me, bouncing between me and the front door.

Then I remember London.

She's still upstairs. Waiting for me.

I leave everyone downstairs, as well as the remnants of my argument with my mother. Her accusations. Her hatred. All of it.

I race up the stairs two at a time, my feet beating against the loosening floorboards. My hand slaps against the wooden door, and it flies open, catching the attention of London.

She spins around on her toes and leans back against the shelf. Glass bottles clink and wobble as she steadies herself.

First, she's excited to see me, then her eyebrows pull together in concern.

I don't speak a word before closing the distance between us. I capture her face in my hands and crash my mouth against hers. I breathe her in, pulling her until she stumbles forward, leaning into me.

"I missed you today," she says against my mouth.

"I missed you, too," I say back, forcing the words to come out without me falling apart.

It's painfully true. She's the balm to my wounded soul. She always has been. She doesn't even know it yet.

Our teeth click against each other's, and I capture her top lip between mine. I bite down, then slip my tongue into her mouth, finding hers. She moans, and all I can think about is burying myself in her so deep, I forget everything. I get lost in this world we've made. Not the one of our past. The one only I remember. But this one, where we want nothing more than each other.

I'm hungry for her love. I've missed it.

Breaking our kiss, I pull back, cupping her gorgeous face in my hands. "I need you."

Her mouth is red, her pink lip gloss smeared across her mouth. Hot, trembling breaths pass through the small gap between her full lips, and the look in her eyes is all I need before I'm grabbing her hips roughly, spinning her around, then bending her over.

She catches herself on the edge of the metal shelf, sticking her beautiful round ass in my face. Fisting the edge of her leggings I tug them over her two round cheeks, then I remove her thong.

"I'm sorry," I tell her, unbuckling my belt. "This time, I

won't be gentle. I need you, and I need you *now*." The metal clinks in the heated air as I'm slipping down my pants and my boxer briefs. My cock springs free, and I tease her crease, rubbing against the wetness already dripping down her legs.

She looks over her shoulder and presses her beautiful ass against me. "I'm yours."

Grabbing onto her hips like my life depends on it, I rear back and drive my cock inside her, listening to the sweet moan that falls from her mouth.

It's then that I realize I hadn't truly taken a breath until now.

TWENTY-THREE

LONDON

West: Good morning. Don't head to The Veiled
Door for work. Meet me at my place instead.
Be sure to bring your portfolio. With love, W.

I'm re-reading the text West sent me this morning as the elevator takes me to his floor, focusing on the four-letter word beside his initial.

He hasn't outright told me he's in love with me, but I know we're already there. I've caught myself nearly saying it several times only to stop with fear. Not because I don't think he'll say it back, but because I've never felt more certain of anything in my life. Which is saying a lot for someone with only half her memories.

Over these past several weeks, the memories of my past are still alive and breathing in my mind. I still remember the cold metal against my neck. The scent of blood in the air, mingling with cold dirt. West sitting at a kitchen table, pressing his finger to my cheek.

That last one still has me wondering whether it's a memory or just a dream. I've had the same dream twice more since the first time, and it still feels just as real as it did then. Even more so with each one. It's clearer now, and I know it's West looking at me with love in his eyes. Just like he does now.

My heart vibrates with an echo, and I smile to myself. It wasn't broken after all. It was just lost.

The doors open to the hallway of West's apartment, and I step out, immediately searching for him. Seeing his apartment never gets old, even after two months of coming here nearly every day. I still step inside, in awe at the size and décor, the enormous ceilings, the brick-covered walls, as well as the shiny, stainless-steel appliances. He really leaned into the industrial look, but it suits him.

Unsuspecting and sophisticated.

"West?" I call out, setting my bag and portfolio on the counter. I shrug out of my black cardigan and set it beside them. I cross my arms over my chest and walk across West's living room. Staring out of his black-framed windows, I watch the city below and the life breathing through it. With every person that passes by, I think about what lives they lead. Who they could be and the memories they hold. How far back to they go? Do they remember the bulk of their lives?

I'm envious of them.

I leave the intrusive thoughts behind, continuing my search for West.

"West?" I call out again. I slowly make my way to the living room again before wandering down another hallway—the one leading to a full bar West had custom built when he moved in. It's where he spends most of his free time at home when he isn't at his office or any of his locations. It's the place where he experiments with new drinks and where he can get lost in his own thoughts, leaving the outside world behind. Much like me when I get lost in my sketches.

I emerge from the hallway and find West behind the bar. I

break in to a full smile watching him stuff a handful of mint into the bottom of a tall glass.

Hearing me, he looks up.

"About time you showed up." He smiles. "I was about to race over to Selene's apartment myself and force you out of bed."

A shiver slinks down the back of my neck, and my legs tingle, knowing once he'd found me in bed, he wouldn't have been able to stop himself and would have found a million reasons to keep me in bed versus pulling me out of it.

Stepping farther into the room, I stop several feet from the long bar stretching across the space.

I laugh under my breath. "I came as fast as I could."

"Hmm." He picks up a long thick, wooden device. "Are you coming without me, Dimples? Tell me you're at least thinking about me when you do."

I jerk my chin back. "Dimples?"

His face falls, and the air gets caught in my throat.

My mind reels, and a piece of a memory clicks in my brain. I've heard that name before.

I think.

I get the same feeling I did at Club Verona months ago. When he was calling after me.

I could have sworn I'd heard him use that name before, but I wasn't certain with the music flooding my ears.

But this time, there's no music. Just West's voice.

I tilt my head, frowning in thought. "Have you called me that before? Dimples?"

His face twitches, and he clears his throat. "No, I don't think so."

I stare at him, swearing I've heard it echoing in my mind.

"I don't know why I said it just now." He waves me off, his

attention falling back to his drink. He sticks a long, thick stick into the glass, pressing the end of it into the mint.

"It's okay," I breathe out, the nickname forcing the twist in my chest to soften. "I like it."

"You do?" He abruptly stops and looks back up, but I can't miss the twinge of sadness in his eyes. Or regret? Or fear, maybe? I can't place it.

"Yeah. I just wasn't expecting it."

The memory of the same dream I've had several times comes to me. A young West sitting at the kitchen table, his finger pressed to my cheek, laughter filtering through the air.

Dimples.

"Well..." His eyes darken. "I guess it just spilled out because I was thinking about how these dimples do something to me."

I crack a smile. "Like what?"

"They make my heart melt," he says, staring directly at me. "Among other things."

I giggle, when my phone starts to vibrate in my pocket. I pull it out, just in case it's my sister or one of the girls. When I read the name across the screen, I can't help shoving it back into my pocket with a groan.

"Who is it?" West asks, concerned.

"No one." I sigh, not wanting to waste the moment we just shared. "Just this unknown number that keeps calling me. Probably a scam caller."

"Damn," West grumbles. "Those are so annoying. They are relentless and leave you a million voicemails, too."

I tuck my lip under my teeth. This unknown caller has never left me a voicemail, only calling incessantly over the past two months, but I keep that part to myself.

I brush off the change in conversation, wanting to get back to being here with West.

"Now, what were you saying?" I ask him.

He lifts his hand again and presses his finger to my cheek. "There's something I want to show you... Dimples."

Butterflies rage inside my stomach. I'm liking this new nickname. "Show me."

"Well, I think I'd like to finish this drink first," he says, his voice deep and low. His eyes lower, taking in my short black dress and bare legs.

"Thirsty?" I ask him playfully.

His eyes have darkened again. He's back to focusing on quenching his thirst, and not just with the drink he's making.

Still holding onto the long thick piece of wood and glass, he walks around the counter and leans back against it, crossing his legs at his ankles. He's only three feet closer to me, yet still too far away. Even with six feet of distance between us, though, I feel him everywhere.

He sets the glass on the counter beside him, then lifts his chin, staring at me through hooded eyes. "Crawl to me."

"What?" I ask, the blood in my veins draining. Heart racing, I swallow thickly.

Crossing his arms over his chest, he tips his chin up again, raising his voice a bit louder. "Crawl. To. Me."

The corner of my mouth lifts, and I fall to my knees. Leaning forward, I press my hands to the hardwood. The floor is cold against my heated body. I flip my hair over my shoulder and look up at him as I start to crawl to him.

"Good girl," he says, rubbing his hand over the front of his pants. The outline of his growing erection is evident beneath his smooth, black slacks. He's already stiff and ready for me. Seeing the size of his cock makes my insides tighten with an ache to have him inside me.

I make sure to emphasize the sway in my hips. His eyes constantly move from my ass to my breasts, spilling from the top of my dress. When my fingertips reach the toes of his shiny, black shoes, I look up.

"You're so goddamn fucking beautiful on your knees for me."

"Do you want me to stay on my knees?" I ask.

He reaches out and runs his hand through my hair, pushing it off the side of my face. His long fingers rake through my black strands, landing on the base of my neck. "As much as I would love for you to stay on your knees, I don't think I'm that patient."

Hooking his fingers under my chin, he pulls me up. I follow his lead, moving to my feet. He leans forward, and I stand on my toes, thinking he's going to kiss me. His mouth is dangerously close to mine, and I think he's going to give in, but he doesn't give me the satisfaction I'm craving.

He pulls away, but quickly wraps his arm around my waist, lifting me up and turning me around. My ass slams against the counter, and I wrap my legs around him, pulling him close. He rolls his hips, rubbing his stiff cock against my slit. I moan, allowing my eyes to roll back.

"I want you now, West."

"Patience, Dimples."

I lower my gaze to his, my lips parting. "You said yourself you can't be patient, yet you're asking me to be?" I moan, letting him know exactly how badly I want him.

He chuckles. "Not patient in that way."

"Then, in what way?" I feather my mouth against his. "Until you finish making your drink?" I grab the wooden stick he was using to mash the mint and hold it between us. "What's this thing called again?"

It's less than two inches thick, but about eight inches long. The end is covered in tiny raised points used to mash and bruise any fruit or herb.

His heavy breath brushes my lips when he grabs onto it. "A muddler."

"Muddler." I repeat the word, allowing it to roll off my tongue. "Huh."

With a heated gaze, he presses the end of it to my bottom lip. "Stick out your tongue."

I do as he says.

The taste of mint immediately fills my mouth, and I close my eyes. It tastes good.

West moves the muddler across my tongue, then slowly moves it farther back into my mouth. The tip rests again the back of my tongue, nearly hitting the back of my throat. I open my eyes and fight back the gagging sensation crawling up my throat. Tears sting the backs of my eyes. I'm about to gag when he pulls it back toward the front of my mouth.

"Wrap your lips around it," West orders, grinding his cock against me. He grunts, and his mouth falls open as he watches me wrap my lips around it, puckering against the tingling mint.

"Now, suck on it. Suck on it like you're sucking on my cock."

I tighten my lips around the end, my cheeks sinking in.

West rolls his hips against me again and unzips his pants. He lowers his boxer briefs until his erection springs free. Lifting his hand, he presses his finger into my dimple. "That's my girl."

Then he moves his hand low between us to stroke himself, but I stop him, shaking my head in disapproval.

He freezes, and his eyes light with amusement.

I pull the muddler out of my mouth and lower it to my entrance, slipping it along my wet folds. The mint immediately hits my soft, slick flesh, a cooling sensation spreading across me.

Grabbing West's hand, I guide him to the muddler while I grab onto his thick length, tugging him forward. He grunts, his cock twitching in my grip.

"Fuck me," I tell him, lifting my chin. "I want you to fuck me."

He drives the muddler inside me, and I gasp at the feeling. It's rock hard and cold. Completely opposite to the feeling of having West's cock or fingers inside me.

I grab his length, but he grunts with the friction against it. He moves the muddler in and out of me, fucking me with it. It's hard to concentrate when every second I feel closer to coming. Coming all over a drink muddler. He uses his thumb to press against my clit, tilting the muddler at just the right angle, hitting the perfect spot.

My eyes flutter with every motion, and I try to move my hand against him, but I pause when he says in a low voice, "Spit on it."

I widen my eyes. I've never had sex like this before, so bold and adventurous. Being with West is different. *I* feel different when I'm with him.

I do as he says and gather a pool of spit in my mouth before letting it drip onto his erection. His mouth falls open, and his eyes follow the trail all the way down until it hits his flesh. I'm quick to grab onto his length, smearing it all over. I screw my hand around his incredibly hard, thick cock, stroking him slowly at first, but I'm quick to pick up the speed, matching what's he's doing to me with the muddler.

"Fuck," I moan, tilting my head back. "I'm going to come, West." My muscles tighten around the muddler, and the tingling echo of the mint still lingering on the muddler nearly pushes me over the edge.

"Same." West growls. He rips the muddler out of me. "Fuck patience."

The muddler falls to the floor, clattering against the hardwood, and West slams himself inside me, filling me all the way. He immediately feels better than the muddler. Warm and hard yet still soft. Pulling back, he slams into me again, and I wrap my legs around him tighter, gripping onto his back. I claw at his shirt, driving my nails across his tense muscles.

"Yes, West," I moan. "Right there."

He steals my mouth, clashing our teeth together in a frenzy. He bites my lip, pulling and tugging on it, grunting and groaning with every thrust.

Heat pools in my lower stomach, and it only takes him a few more thrusts before I'm exploding around him. My body quivers. I can't control myself. I fall apart around him and then it's only a few more seconds before he's doing the same. He stills, twitching against me as his cum spills inside me. Pulling away from my mouth, he rests his forehead on my shoulder. We're both panting, taking a moment to catch our breath, and I lift my hands to run my fingers through his hair, feeling his heart beating against mine.

"You're incredible, Dimples," he mutters against me. His voice vibrates against my still-humming skin. "You're incredible."

Then my eyes fall to the muddler sitting on the floor, covered in my wetness. All remnants of the mint are gone. My cheeks heat, realizing I've never done anything like this before.

I'm someone else when I'm with Weston Knight, and I fucking love it.

***

AFTER WEST and I clean ourselves up, and the bar, he leads me out of the bar and through the living room, toward the open staircase set in the middle of the room. I've never ventured up the stairs before. West's place is larger than expected and most of the time when I'm here, we stay either in his bedroom or out on the balcony.

I follow his lead, never letting his hand slip from mine. I could hold his hand forever and never tire of it.

Once we reach the top of the stairs, he leads me to a door at the far end of the hallway. Pushing down on the handle, he holds it open for me, waiting for me to walk in first.

My jaw drops, and I stop just beyond the threshold.

Floor to ceiling windows cover half of the room, the city on full display from here. Even more so than the main living area downstairs. My eyes dance around the room, taking in every easel propped in each corner. Stacks of parchment line the tables set against the far walls. Unopened packages of charcoal, pens, and pencils litters the tabletops. All brands I use.

Tears line my eyes, and my vision is distorted. A tear slips from my eye, spilling over as I inhale an unsteady breath.

"Do you like it?"

"West," I whisper. "What is this?"

"It's your studio." He steps farther into the room. He wanders past me, admiring the view before moving in front of the table. He runs his fingers over the unopened packs of charcoal, then lifts his gaze to mine. "If you want it to be yours, of course."

"I don't..." I quiver, unable to comprehend that he did all of this for me.

His brows pinch with worry.

"No, no, I didn't mean that. I just meant I don't know what to say. This is..."

His thick shoulders sag with relief.

"I was tired of watching you in that little closet," he says. "You deserve better. A studio where you can thrive and create. I don't know if this one is worthy of you." He massages the back of his neck. "You have no idea how difficult it was not to pick up the phone and tell Asher I wanted to buy whatever building he had available so you had all the space you could ever need.

Other than the fact that I knew you wouldn't want that, doing this was also a little selfish of me."

"How?"

"If you want to use this as your studio, you'll be closer to me. I'll get more time with you this way."

I look around in awe, not knowing what to look at first or second. It's all too much, yet perfect at the same time. No one has ever done anything like this for me. It's a grand gesture in a beautiful space, and I already know I'll be able to get so much more work done here. Surrounded by the city and West all at once.

"I don't deserve this, West," I croak, tears still streaming down my face.

"You deserve the world, London."

I cross the room as fast as my feet will carry me and leap into his arms. I wrap my legs around his waist and drape my arms around his neck. He catches me, wrapping his arms tightly around me. He inhales a sharp breath, and I stare into his blue eyes. Those kind blue eyes that I'm absolutely head over heels in love with.

"Thank you," I whisper just above his mouth before claiming it.

Removing one hand from under me, he grips the back of my head, holding me to him.

His kiss consumes me, like pouring kerosene on an already raging fire. The feeling is vast, and while there are so many things still unclear, one constant remains:

West.

Everything about him feels right: my feelings, him, the bits and pieces of dreams. Fragments of what I think are memories that all lead to him: the necklace, the dirt-covered hands, the nickname that caused the spark of a flame in my mind like a piece of flint.

It feels like free falling. I open my arms and let it swallow me up.

I pull away from West's mouth and search his face, steeling myself for the words I want to say.

"I'm falling for you, Weston Knight."

I already know I'm in love with him, but something keeps me from committing to saying it out loud. As if saying it will throw some bad karma out into the world, and all of this will just fade away, like the memories I've lost.

"I've already fallen for you. A million times over," he muses, and my heart explodes.

I look around the room, still in West's arms, and if I ever thought I was happy before, I was wrong.

So wrong.

This is much, much more.

TWENTY-FOUR

LONDON

Hours later, I'm caught up in finishing my nineteenth piece for The Veiled Door.

West ran out a while ago to check on a few of his bars and stop by his office, promising he'd be back with lunch to spend the rest of the day wrapped up in me.

Part of me must admit that while I love the amount of space West has given me and being here in his place, surrounded by everything that makes up who he is, I miss the noise and company of the bar. I've grown close to Alden, Lewis, and Piper, among some of the other frequent customers. It's an adjustment, and I know it will only take some time.

I'm jamming out to Dua Lipa when West comes back.

I remove my ear buds as he sets two bags of takeout on the large table. He crosses the room to where I am on the floor, looking down at the drawing I've made. He sits beside me, bending his legs, resting his forearms on his knees, facing the opposite direction.

"How are you liking the studio?"

I grin and sit back on my heels, giving him a quick kiss. "I'm loving it."

"Good." He gives me an ear-reaching grin, one that adds life to his blue eyes. He rests his chin on his shoulder as he gazes down at my work. "What number is this one?"

"Nineteen." I study it, falling in love with it even more. It's a path in Central Park. Although it's charcoal on parchment, I imagine the changing colors of the leaves falling to the ground. The black shine of the wrought iron fence overlooking the pond. The sun's rays peeking through the branches.

"Almost finished," West points out, his eyes darting up to mine.

"Yeah." I sigh.

The moment settles between us. I'm almost complete with my twenty pieces, then comes the reopening of The Veiled Door. Followed by uncertainty.

I don't know what's going to happen once I've finished working for West. This was never meant to be a permanent situation, but so many things have changed since we first met. Will he want me to keep working for him, designing pieces for his other countless bars? Or is this it? The Veiled Door and then I'm finished, going back to selling pieces online?

I put the worry aside as he shifts himself and plants one hand to the floor, straightening his arm. He's wearing another well-tailored suit. This time, his suit jacket and pants are a deep emerald color. I love them because they bring out the intensity of his blue eyes.

"At this point, we'll be hosting The Veiled Door's grand reopening next week." I laugh, not wanting to make any of that true, but if it's what West would want, then I would try to finish the last piece this coming week.

"Possibly." West's grin twitches. "Though next weekend won't be any good, considering we won't be here."

I pull my brows together. "What do you mean?"

Pulling his phone from the inside pocket of his jacket, he taps the screen a few times before handing it to me.

It's open on an email.

Hello Mr. Knight,

I first want to apologize for emailing you later than I had originally anticipated. It's been a busy time for me and my team as we prepare for the opening of my new gallery at the end of the month. Your friend, Holt Capuleti, reached out to me a while back and told me your situation. He explained that not only does your girlfriend admire my work, but that she's also an artist herself. I must admit that when he told me her name, I couldn't help myself, so I looked her up online and, wow, her work is phenomenal! You are one lucky man, Mr. Knight.

I would absolutely love the opportunity to meet her and hope you will both accept my offer to preview my gallery this next coming weekend.

I will have my team forward you the address, along with the date and time in a follow up email once I receive your reply.

I'm looking forward to hearing from you and London!

Warmest regards,

Emily Rapture

"Holy shit." I gasp, covering my mouth and looking up at West, wide-eyed, tears welling in them.

West grimaces. "I hope those are happy tears."

"Yes." I nod enthusiastically, bursting with disbelief. "Of course, they are." I drop West's phone and reach for his arm. "You've got to be kidding me. This can't be real."

He chuckles, the lines in the corners of his eyes deepening. "You just read the email yourself. It's all there in black and white."

"I can't believe you did this for me," I gush.

West shrugs. "With a little help from Holt."

"I'll have to thank him later." I grin. Then I lean forward and kiss West, because that's all I can think to do. That's all I want to do.

"Is this you thanking me?" he asks, wrapping his hand around the back of my head.

"Not yet." I smile against his mouth and gently push him back onto the floor.

Straddling him, I tuck my long, black hair behind my ear and lower my face until it's just above his. I roll my hips, rubbing myself over his already swelling cock.

"This is my way of saying thank you," I tell him, feeling the groan rumbling from his chest vibrate through my body.

His hands move to the bottom of my shirt. I raise my arms up over my head as he pulls it off. I'm sitting on top of him, bare from the waist up. Holding onto my hips, he flips us over until it's my back against the floor instead of his.

"You're welcome." He shrugs out of his suit jacket, then loosens his tie.

Raising my arms above my head, he wraps his tie around my wrists, tying my hands together.

I'm writhing for him, unable to lie still. "I want you, West."

"I want you, Dimples." His voice is low, slithering over my

skin like velvet. "You have no idea how bad I want to sink my cock into that sweet pussy of yours. Tell me you're mine."

"I'm yours."

After picking up a piece of my charcoal, his heated gaze travels down the length of my body before stopping on my stomach. He flicks his eyes up to me with a mischievous, devious grin that makes my heart flutter. Pressing the tip of the charcoal to my stomach, he draws a line from the top of my belly button before sliding over to my breast. My mouth falls open. I've never felt anything like it. I'm tugging at the restraints around my wrists, arching my back off the floor. Wearing nothing but my leggings, I know I'm already soaking wet.

"You're absolutely beautiful, London." He admires his hand creating circles around my breast.

He's drawing me, paying delicate attention to every detail, outlining my curves with precise measure. He circles the charcoal around the bottom swell of my breast before gliding it up over the mound and circling my already-peaked nipple. It's tantalizing, sending shivers down the length of my body.

I let out a moan. "Oh, God, West. *Please.*"

Gasping for air, I look down as he drags the charcoal from my nipple to my chest, directly over my heart. Once there, he draws his initials.

W. K.

Then he draws a simple heart around it.

"I tell you you're mine all the time," he says, lifting his gaze to mine. He tosses the charcoal aside, climbs over my body, parting my legs with his knee. "But the truth is I'm yours."

"West," I breathe, unable to control my movements. "I am yours."

My words catch him for a moment, stealing two beats of breaths he should be taking, then he starts moving again. He's already lowering himself, grazing his chin between my breasts and down my stomach. His eyes have transformed, filled with hunger and need.

He presses his mouth over my center, kissing it, then licking it, and my eyes flutter shut as I tilt my head back into the hardwood floor.

"Eyes on me, Dimples." West growls against my heated skin, fisting the top of my leggings before tugging them down. "Eyes on me."

Yes, sir.

WEST

I don't think I've ever seen London this happy. At least not since we were kids.

We're surrounded by Emily Rapture's art, but all I can look at is London and the permanent smile she's carrying with her around the gallery.

My girl.

She's always been mine.

The bottom of her black sundress flares away from her body at the hip, swaying to the rhythm of her steps. I stay a few feet behind her, watching and admiring as she follows Emily throughout her gallery, who is explaining the inspiration behind each piece and the medium used. I don't understand either of them half the time, but I see the beauty in Emily's work. Although, I must admit, I love London's more. What can I say? I'm biased.

The scent of fresh paint lingers in the air, and undisturbed furniture is placed throughout the room. It's interesting how Emily has used nature throughout even those pieces. Stools and tables look like sawed off trees. The walls and ceilings are draped in artificial leaves and vines. It looks like we've stepped into the forest.

When I point out the sawed-off tree stumps, Emily explains how she wanted to showcase the beauty of nature and how man easily destroys it with no regard.

London nods in agreement, and I fall in love with her even more. If I thought that was possible.

Her gold rings glint in the subtle lighting of the gallery as she tucks her pin-straight, black hair behind her ear. Her lips are painted a deep purple-red, and fuck me, I want to kiss her, absorbing the happiness she's feeling in this moment. I can see her dream of meeting Emily Rapture glowing in her eyes now she's realized it's her reality.

London is so fucking happy. Just like I'd seen her that day at Coney Island. Only this time, she's with me.

It's hard to explain, but being out here, surrounded by nature, stirs our souls. I can see it in London's entire body. The way she carries herself. Like the air is lighter and she can breathe easier.

I was nervous, considering we're in Upstate New York, but Emily's new gallery isn't as close as I thought it was to where London and I grew up.

Taking the weekend off, I'd decided to drive us up here ourselves, away from the stress of my bars and the city. Away from the knowledge that London has almost completed her twentieth piece, and I've already hired an event coordinator to plan the grand reopening of The Veiled Door.

After seeing the last piece of Emily's work, the three of us saunter back to the entrance of the gallery.

"I don't even know what to say, Emily," London gushes. "This gallery is next level."

The attendant standing at the front door hands us our coats. Aside from the three of us, there are only two others here. One man following about ten feet behind Emily, who I'm assuming is a member of her security team. And the attendant, who must work for the gallery in some capacity.

I hold London's black coat out for her, and she slips her arms into it, still talking to Emily.

"Thank you. I wanted this gallery to be an immersive experience." Emily grins, placing her hand over her chest. "I hope the both of you will return when we're officially open."

"Of course." London beams, turning to me and slipping her hand in mine. "We would love to."

"Absolutely," I agree, looking between London and Emily. "Since you've been so gracious with letting us preview your gallery, I'd love to extend the invite to the reopening of my bar, The Veiled Door." I gesture toward London. "We'll be unveiling London's pieces that she's curated for it and auctioning off a few others."

Emily's jaw drops. "I would love to."

"Really?" London gapes in disbelief.

"Of course." Emily laughs. "From the work I've seen of yours, I would love to see them in person. Just email over the details, and you can count me in."

London blushes. "I can't believe you're coming."

Emily reaches out and gives London's arm a reassuring squeeze. "I'm glad your friend Holt got in touch. It's always nice to meet a fellow artist that shares the same passion for their work as you do. Makes us feel less alone."

"Agreed." London nods. "Thank you."

With that, London and I say our goodbyes and leave Emily's gallery. I keep my hand wrapped around London's the entire walk back to the car parked in the lot down the street.

It's midafternoon, and unfortunately overcast. Heavy fog hangs low, hovering just above the dead leaves coating the ground. The trees of Albany are nearly bare, the promise of the coming winter evident with every day that passes, and the temperature drops.

But that doesn't detract from London's mood.

Even in the misty air, she hasn't stopped smiling.

"I know I've said this a million times," London says, squeezing my hand, "but I can't believe we're here and that just happened."

"This might be a foolish question," I start, unable to contain myself. "But I need to ask. Was it worth the drive up here?"

London screeches to a halt. Her heel scrapes against the pavement as she spins to face me. Emily's gallery is located on the outskirts of Albany, set in a small town wedged between the city and the more rural parts of New York. Although we're outside of the city, we're pretty isolated out here.

She tips her chin up. Although she's wearing heels, she's still a head shorter than me.

"Are you fucking kidding me, West?" Her eyes spread wide, full of happiness and awe. "This was incredible."

I laugh, tucking her hair behind her ear before leaning down to kiss her. "I knew the answer, I just wanted to hear you say it again."

She playfully slaps my chest, ghosting my mouth with hers. "Why?"

"Because I will never tire of hearing how happy you are." I say, lowly. "Especially when I'm the cause."

"Oh, I think you're mistaken," she teases. "Meeting Emily made me happy. Not you."

I jerk back, pretending to be offended. "Are you saying I don't make you happy?"

"You don't." Her gray eyes narrow, coyly. "You make me so much more than that." She wraps her hand around my necklace, cradling it in her palm, protecting it as if, deep down, she knows its significance. From the first time she saw it, she hasn't indicated that she remembers it, but sometimes I think she does, subconsciously. She's drawn to it without even knowing why, anchoring herself to the small piece of metal.

I hold my breath, never taking my eyes off London when I pull off the necklace. I slip it over her head, and my eyes drop to the charm resting against her chest. She fingers the tiny metal, then lifts her gaze to mine.

"Same here, Dimples," I confess. I smirk when tears well in her eyes. Maybe I'm a fool for thinking her wearing it might trigger a memory. No, scratch that. I am a fool.

She doesn't let go of the charm even when I pull her toward me, claiming her mouth with my own. My hands smooth down her backside and I palm each of her ass cheeks, tugging her upward, showing her exactly how she's making me feel. She moans against my mouth as my partially hardened dick presses against her thigh. I'm slipping my tongue between London's full, gorgeous, painted lips when her phone rings in her pocket. The moment quickly fades. I reluctantly pull away, and she tugs it from her coat. She barely looks at it before shoving it back into her pocket, but I already read the screen.

"They're still calling you?"

"Yeah. They haven't been that bad this week. In fact, this is the first call I've gotten all day."

"Huh." I look around, a sudden chill slinking down the back of my neck. My stomach sinks, and I can't figure out why this unsettling sensation washes over me.

We're alone here. Right?

I look down at London, who is looking up at me, wide-eyed. The joy from our day is quickly sucked out of her.

"Come on," I say, sniffing. "Let's go home." I drape my arm around her, pulling her into my side as we head back to the car.

Once inside, she buckles herself into the passenger seat, and I start the engine. It roars to life, and my headlights don't reach nearly as far as they did on the drive over here. I can only see about ten feet in front of the car.

"Well, shit." I sigh, rubbing my fingers over my stubble. "This drive will be fun."

London leans forward, narrowing her eyes as she looks through the windshield. "Hopefully, it'll clear up the closer we get to the city."

I agree and shift my car into drive before pulling out onto the road. I opted to take a different car than the one Alden usually drives for me, this one small, with black interior. I fell in love with this car as soon as I saw it. The seats are a rich, black leather, trimmed with bright red stitching. It's sportier than any car I've owned, but when I glance over to London and place my hand on her knee, I know it's perfect. This car suits her.

I'm following the directions from the GPS, noting this time, it's taking us on a different path. The trip is about twenty minutes longer, but I don't mind. Not when I'm with London.

"I know it sounds crazy," she says, resting her arm against the car door, gazing at the endless trees we pass by as we pull out of the town onto the back roads. She pinches her thumb nail between her teeth and glances over at me. "But I kind of like it here. I can't explain it, but I feel like I've already been here before. Or somewhere like it."

I grip the steering wheel tighter, rubbing my hand over the sharp leather.

I was worried taking London this close to the foster home we grew up in would trigger something for her. Then again, she has triggers all over the place, and none of them have caused her to regain her memory.

Besides, I don't even think we're close to that house, anyway.

"You like it?" I ask, checking the rearview mirror.

There's a black car following us out of town. The last traffic light turns red, forcing us to a stop. I keep my eye on the car, wondering if it's going to take a turn at some point before following us down the back road. I recognize it from when we pulled out of the parking lot down the street from Emily's gallery.

My heart pounds, and the same feeling slithers down my spine that I got when we were walking to the car.

"I do." London gently smiles. "I wonder if I grew up somewhere similar to this."

"What makes you say that?" The blood slowly drains from my face. I take a left onto a smaller, residential road, lifting my eyes to the rearview mirror again. The car is still tailing us. I try to weave from one lane to the next, but it's quick to mimic my moves.

"I don't know," London continues, scratching her head. I nearly forgot I'd asked her a question. "When you told me you grew up around here, I swear something in my head clicked. I got this flash of a memory. Or what I think is a memory."

"Seriously?"

"Yeah." She lowers her arm from the side of the door and rests it in her lap, turning her beautiful face in my direction. "I couldn't make sense of it like all the rest, so I didn't say anything."

"What was it?"

I turn down another small, winding road. One the GPS tells me to stay on for the next eighteen miles. Glancing in the rearview mirror again, I see the car is quick to follow. It's growing closer, the headlights clearer than they were before. I try to get a read on what type of car it is but can't make the emblem out with the fog obstructing its view. By my guess, it's an expensive car, especially if it can keep up with mine.

The dense fog hovering above the ground has grown heavier now that we're no longer in town. The car gains on me. Close enough that if I were to slam on my brakes, he'd crash right into us. My adrenaline kicks in. Spotting a split in the road several hundred feet ahead, I lay on the gas and stiffen my arms, readying myself.

"Oh..." London mumbles, twisting her fingers in her lap. "It was a sign—"

I cut the steering wheel, and the tires screech against the asphalt.

"West!" London yells. "What are you doing?"

My hands shake as I straighten the steering wheel and glare into the rearview mirror. "Someone's following us."

"What?" She gasps, twisting in her seat to look behind us. She grips onto her seat before whipping back around. "Who is it?"

"I don't know," I say, lowering my voice. My adrenaline is racing, but I try to remain calm for London's sake. I don't know who is following us or why. We're far from home, or anywhere really. There's nothing but back roads and trees for what seems like miles.

My foot leans into the gas a little harder, and I watch the dial rise faster and faster, going up to ninety. Then one hundred.

The GPS hasn't caught up with my sudden shift in direction. We must be getting a weak signal where we are.

"How long have they been following us?" London squeaks out, constantly glancing between the road, then to the car behind us.

"Since we pulled out of the parking lot."

"Are you kidding? And you didn't say anything?" she asks, panic stricken.

The air in the car has grown tenser. Clenching her hands into fists, her chest rises faster with every breath.

She's having a panic attack.

"I couldn't be sure," I tell her, grinding my jaw. "But now I am." Although I'm driving faster than I've ever driven before, not to mention on a road I've never fucking driven down in my life, I reach out and squeeze London's thigh. "I'll get us home safely. I promise."

"What if he follows us the whole way? Where are we?"

"I don't know." I swallow, uncertainty settling in my veins. "Don't worry. I'll lose him."

Seeing another split in the road, I take it. Leaves and dirt kick behind my tires, and I'm fishtailing.

London tries to stifle her screams, but she fails, clutching onto the side of the door. She slaps her hand on the dash to steady herself when we reach the edge of a cliff. I slam on the brakes, quickly whipping the steering wheel back in the opposite direction. My foot grinds on the gas, and I pull back onto the small road.

I take another turn when I see another road. The farther we travel down the back roads, deeper into the woods, the more dangerous the turns become. It feels like we're driving on the side of a fucking mountain.

If I take a turn too soon or too fast, we'll roll hundreds of feet into the valley below. Just like we did almost a few minutes ago.

It feels like forever that the car follows us, and it seems like every turn I make, he has the chance to catch back up. Between the fog and the overcast skies, night begins to settle in. The sun sets behind the tree line, and it's harder to see the roads or which direction I'm going.

"West?" London asks, still panicked. "He's still behind us."

I grind my jaw, taking another turn. "I know."

Finally, another chance to lose him reveals itself around a sharp curve. Once we round the corner, I see an opportunity to turn down a private road. I have no clue if it'll connect to another route, but I take it anyway.

It's a narrow dirt road, uneven and bumpy. I hit a million potholes, and I'm bottoming out all over the place. My sweaty palm grips the steering wheel as I drive us farther into the cover of trees.

"Did we lose him?" London asks, turning in her seat to look behind her while I glance in the rearview.

"I think so," I breathe out.

London slowly turns back in her seat and grips the leather edge beside her legs. I reach out and squeeze her thigh again. "Hey," I urge her.

She doesn't answer. She lifts her hand and fingers the Big Ben charm again, vacantly staring at the dash in front of her.

"Hey, Dimples," I repeat, this time catching her attention. "We're safe."

Her bottom lip quivers, and she inhales an unsteady breath. "Okay." Her eyebrows slant into concern. "Who was that?"

"I don't know."

I drive us down a private road for what feels like several miles before coming out to a main road. There are farmhouses and what looks like a small, abandoned town in the distance. Rolling hills covered in trees for miles.

Once I reach the end of the private road, I type in the address to my house in Brooklyn. I immediately take a right, but when I recognize the sign for the gas station at the next intersection, the air is sucked from my lungs.

Oh, shit. I recognize this place.

How the fuck did we end up here?

Giving London the side-eye, I watch for her reaction. She's still anxiously fingering my necklace, her glassy eyes frantically looking through the windshield and passenger window. She examines every building and landmark we pass, and the longer we stay here, the harder the pull is on me.

The pull to get the fuck out of here and away from this place. I haven't been here since I was fifteen years old.

I press my foot into the gas pedal, knowing what we need to pass to get to the highway.

We leave the center of the town behind, and I find myself looking in the rearview more times than I should, just to make sure I really did lose the asshole who was following us.

"Wait, stop," London says beside me. Her eyes roam across the countless trees, and she sits forward.

I snap my head to the right. "What?"

"I've been here before," she breathes. Her seatbelt strains against her shoulder as she leans forward. "I've been here before."

"London." My stomach swims with nausea.

Her fingers spin the charm, and she presses her hand to the dash. "I've been here, West. I recognize these houses. I know it."

I drive us past the houses I've been to a million times. The yards I used to play in. The woods London and I used to chase each other through.

Panic settles in. Fear makes a home in my bones.

Is she finally remembering?

My mind screams at me not to stop the car. I feel like I'm standing in the middle of a train track, watching it barrel toward me. It's blaring its horn, screaming at me to move, but I don't.

I don't know what to do.

I press on the gas a little harder, hoping I can drive straight past the house and get us out of here.

"Stop the car, West," she cries, digging her nails into the dashboard.

"London. We're almost to the highway."

"No." She shifts to clutch the door. She follows every single building and tree, watching as they pass us by. "We need to stop."

"We can't."

"Stop the car."

"No. I can't do that, London."

"Stop the car."

"I can't." I don't know what I'm saying anymore.

But my heart shatters when she whips her head in my direction, tears streaming from her wild eyes. *"Stop the car, West!"*

TWENTY-SIX

LONDON

West slams on the brakes, and the tires screech against the road.

Tears are streaming down my cheeks, and my vision wobbles. My entire body is shaking.

I can't breathe.

I can't. Breathe.

My hands shake uncontrollably as I scramble to unbuckle my seat belt. After the third attempt, I finally break free and jump from the passenger seat.

My feet hit the road, and I stand in the middle of it, still holding onto West's necklace as I look around.

We're in the center of a neighborhood. Old, Victorian-style houses are situated along each side of the road, but it's the sign in front of the one three houses down that caught my attention. I know I've been here before. Since I was fourteen years old, I've never been certain of anything. I couldn't be. Memories are unreliable. Distorted. Fact turned to fiction.

But this. This place I know for certain holds the key. I feel it in my soul.

"London, wait," West's calls out for me, but my feet are already carrying me toward the house.

I jog down the road, my heels clicking against the pavement. I hear the pounding of West's feet following me, and when I reach the abandoned house with the sign out front, a sob breaks free.

The scent of fresh pancakes, and the feel of West's finger against my cheek. The plastic tablecloth, sticky with dried maple syrup. I reach out and run my shivering fingers across the faded paint.

Sunlight Foster Care
Albany, New York

Snapping my head to the right, I look up at the house.

Peeling gray and purple paint.

Broken windows.

A lawn that looks like it hasn't been mowed in years. It's completely abandoned.

West catches up to me. His leathery scent immediately surrounds me, pulling my attention away.

"London." His voice is shaky, and when I turn to look at him, the memory of being at the kitchen table comes back to me.

"I remember," I whisper, unsteadily. "The kitchen table. The first day I came to the house. We sat and ate blueberry pancakes, and you touched my cheek."

"What?" His eyes widen, and his hand flies to his chest. Tears line his gorgeous blue eyes.

"You called me dimples," I sob. "You said it was because they made your heart melt every time I smiled, and you'd never felt that before. I was twelve. You were fourteen."

"London." His voice strains, and he can't breathe. "You remember me?"

"Yes," I try to say but the word crumbles when it spills from my mouth. "But..." The memories are still fragmented, coming to my mind in pieces. A large chunk of the puzzle is coming together. The happier parts. The ones where I knew I fell in love with West. It was the innocent kind. The kind where we never did anything but spend every possible minute together, holding each other's hand. We'd never kissed or done anything other than be each other's best friend. Even at twelve, I knew he was my soulmate.

"But what?" he asks, reaching out.

I take a step back, my body growing cold.

An older kid runs by as West presses his finger to my cheek. He tugs on my hair, laughing and taunting when he passes us. His cackling laughter sours my stomach.

I look up at the house again, then my attention moves to the dilapidated, detached garage beside it and the trees behind it.

I start walking. My feet carry me through the front yard, then to the side, where I find myself heading straight for the woods.

With every step I take, the less I smell the crisp, warm scent of West's cologne, and the more I smell blood.

Blood and tears and dirt.

"London, wait!" West calls. "Don't go back there."

I'm breathing heavy. Every breath that passes through my lungs is painful. My feet are unsteady as I tread over the tree roots and dead leaves. Twigs snap under my weight. My ankle rolls, and I hiss, shoving aside the pain. I stop momentarily, willing the memory to keep playing out.

It's dark and ugly and full of pain.

This isn't like the memory I had out front. It's taken a turn, and darkness edges my vision as I walk farther back until I spot the broken-down tree house. It's nothing but a floor of planks, twenty feet above the ground, but it's the backside of the tree that tugs on my chest.

"London," West says, running up behind me. "Please, stop."

I'm struggling to breathe as I round the large trunk. My

fingers grip into the peeling, aging bark, and it crumbles under my touch.

So do I.

I fall to my knees and lean forward.

My hands press into the wet dirt, clutching onto the dead leaves as the memory slams into me at full force.

I feel his body on mine. The sickening sound of his zipper opening. The cold metal pressing against my throat. His dirty fingers pressed to my mouth.

"Make one peep out of that pretty little mouth, and I swear to God, I'll slit your fucking throat right here."

"No, stop," I sob, crying out. Tears stream down my face, and everything hurts.

But it's what I said back then, too, when he attacked me. When he woke me from a deep sleep, held a knife to my throat and forced me outside and into the woods.

"No, stop!" I cried out, but it was no use with his hand clamped tightly over my mouth.

"You think I'd let you leave with that new beautiful family you're getting without taking what's mine first?"

I wanted to vomit.

I felt his knee between my legs, forcing them open, and it was then I looked up at the night sky. Tree branches swayed in the breeze against a backdrop of twinkling stars. It was a warm, autumn night. I closed my eyes and imagined myself somewhere else. Anywhere else that wasn't with him on top of me, touching me in places I'd never been touched. I pounded my fists against the hard ground. I kicked and flailed, but it was no use. He was too heavy. Too big. Too overpowering. He tore at my shirt, exposing my chest. I tasted my own blood as it dripped from my nose.

"Please, stop...." I cried again, uselessly.

"London. Baby." West's hands are suddenly pressed against

my face, urging me to look at him. "I'm here." But the memory pulls at me again.

"Get the fuck off her."

Panic had overtaken my body. I was frozen, afraid that if I moved even a single inch, he'd kill me. Surely, he was going to kill me. Use me, then kill me. I was ready to surrender. To let the star-studded sky swallow me up, wrapping its warm arms around me.

But even then, surrounded by the shadows, I recognized his voice. The one who always swore to protect me, and did.

"I said get the fuck off her."

Then the sound of crunching bone. The sharp metallic scent of freshly spilled blood filled the air. He was no longer on top of me. Instead, he was now the one with his back on the ground.

I was gasping for air when I shot up and saw him towering over him, beating him without even a second of hesitation.

"I'll fucking kill you, you worthless piece of shit," he seethed.

He beat him until he stopped resisting. He beat him in the dead of night before crawling toward me. His hands were covered in blood and dirt as he cupped my face. The Big Ben charm I'd given to him for his birthday glinted in the moonlight.

My attackers body laid still beside me.

"Is he..." I gasped. "Is he dead?"

"I don't know," West said, his warm hands cupping my cheeks. "But I'm here, London. I'm here. You're safe."

My fingers dig into the ground now, clutching fistfuls of leaves. The dirt slips under my nails, and I let out a scream. A tight, painful scream that sucks all the life out of me. My lungs burn and my muscles contract. Every single fucking memory comes flooding back to me. It's as if every memory, a flash in time, has been stored in neat little boxes, but now I've found the skeleton key, and I'm unlocking every door. They swing open, flooding my brain.

My knees are pressed into the cold dirt as the memories are now alive, back from the dead. They're unrelenting, a flurry of bitterness mixed with sweetness. Dark twisted with light.

"London. Please talk to me." West kneels beside me and wraps his arm around my shaking body as I remember all of it.

The pain. The beauty. The love. The hatred.

"I remember what he did. The other foster kid. He woke me up, forced me out of the house while everyone slept. He tried to..." I can't get the words out. "He didn't die, but you almost killed him," I sob, sniffing. Steeling my chest, I look up at West. My hair clings to my wet cheeks as I look at the man I've loved longer than I've realized. The one who promised he would find me again. "I remember it all."

"Oh, my God." West's eyes widen, and his mouth falls open as he rocks back. His feet slip out from under him as he sits on the cold, wet ground. Then he's back on his knees again, sobbing. I've never seen him this way. Even when he saved me that day, he's always been the strong one.

He crawls toward me, pressing his hands to my cheeks again, cradling my face.

"Being here," I choke out, shivering. "Something about this place brought all of it back."

"I didn't mean to drive through here," he pants, tears streaming down his face. "I was just trying to get away from that asshole. I didn't realize how close we were to this town or neighborhood."

I nod as the weight of everything tears me apart. I'm looking at West now, at thirty, but remembering it all. Him at thirteen. Then him at fifteen. The last day when I'd walked away from him. His kiss on my cheek lingering long after I'd driven away from this place with my new family.

"You promised me," I say, my voice shaky as fresh tears spill.

"I know." He nods, his own voice breaking. His gorgeous blue eyes are wide, glassy with tears.

Then reality hits. My marriage to Heath. The day of the funeral, when West had seen me at The Veiled Door, drawing the charm on the napkin.

"The whole time," I cry, unable to stop the words spilling from my mouth. "You knew the whole time and you didn't tell me. Oh, God." I press my hands to the side of my head. "The *whole* time."

"What?"

I back away from him, moving to a stand. My palms and knees are sore. My throat is scratchy and pained as I struggle to compartmentalize my thoughts.

"This whole time we've been together." I point to the ground, then grab onto the necklace. "Every time I had a glimpse of a memory, this necklace or when you told me about Albany, you were acting as if we'd never met until the funeral." I grind my jaw, a bit of anger and resentment simmering under my skin.

I can't be angry with West for the past few months, but knowing he didn't speak a word of it this whole time, knowing the truth, doesn't sit well for some reason.

He pulls himself to a stand, moving closer to me. He takes a few steps forward, and my heart swells. It swells, more alive than it's ever been, but then the cracks appear, fracturing my full heart, feeling this sense of betrayal.

"Why didn't you say anything?"

"What was I supposed to do? I *couldn't* say anything. I wanted to, but I couldn't."

"Why?" I cry. I'm tired. *So* tired.

"Because!" he sobs. "If I had and you still didn't remember, would you have believed me? You would have run away and then I'd be left with another disgusting layer of regret all over again. I've spent the past fifteen years living with this immense guilt."

Seeing him broken breaks me.

"You promised you would find me again," I rasp, holding my hand to my chest, over West's necklace. Sadness eats away at me for all the years stolen from us. "Right here, in this place, you promised. You swore you'd find me after the Walkers adopted me. Then when you did find me, you still didn't say anything. What was your plan? To just live our lives together never mentioning our past? Letting me believe we didn't start until these past few months?"

"I don't know." He pushes his hair off his forehead and narrows his teary eyes as he takes a large step forward to reach out for my hand. "I didn't have a plan. All I knew was that I'd found you again. I'd let you slip through my fingers that day at Coney Island, and I've regretted it ever since. Every single day of the past fifteen years I've been living in regret, drowning in it."

"Coney Island?" I ask him, jerking back. "You saw me at Coney Island?"

"Middle of summer. I was seventeen. You were fifteen. You wore a worn pair of black and white chucks. Jean shorts and a blue shirt that read NYU in faded letters." His neck bobs as he swallows. "You were wearing five gold rings, one on each finger, just like you wear now. Your nails were painted this light blue glitter color that shimmered in the sunlight, matching the ball of cotton candy you were holding."

"West." God, the earth is slipping out from under my feet. It's shifting, not waiting for me to hold onto it.

He lifts his hand and traces his finger along the side of my face, leaving a trail of warmth on my cold, damp skin.

"You looked at me but didn't recognize me," he whispers. "I couldn't speak. I didn't know what to say, thinking I would only embarrass myself. I was heartbroken that day, thinking you'd forgotten me."

"I...I..." I try to say, but he cuts me off.

"I didn't know what had happened to you until my mother told me Heath's new wife had amnesia. I didn't think anything of it until Julianna's birthday party when I saw you with him. It was then I knew you hadn't forgotten me by choice. Your memories were stolen from you." He runs his finger along my cheek again, where my dimple rests when I smile. "From us."

I haven't moved, allowing his words to settle into my broken heart and my now pieced-together memories. The puzzle pieces all fit, clicking into place with ease. The whispered promises he made to me after saving me, telling me to go live my life with a safe, loving family but still swearing he'd come find me. I'd done that, but in the trade, I'd lost all memories of him.

"I regretted walking away from you that day," he confesses, filling the eerie silence. "Then again when I watched you walk out of my bar. But you left this behind." He reaches inside his pocket and pulls out a folded napkin. My napkin. My empty eulogy.

My shoulders rack with new tears. Chest caving in, I fall more and more in love with West.

"I had hope that one day you would come back to me, and you did," he says, dropping it into my hand.

I unfold it, revealing my sketch of Big Ben.

"You don't understand the depth of my love for you, Dimples," he says, pulling my attention back up to him. "I would have done whatever it took to keep you. I couldn't stand the thought of losing you again. Even if it meant you would never remember our history together. Because with the memory of my love for you also came with the pain of what happened here. It hurt me to know that if you remembered me, you also remembered the worst part of your past, and the thought of you being hurt tears me up inside. You are the air I breathe, London. Without you, I'm nothing but a ghost wandering through this life that I won't have, *can't have*, without you."

With tear-filled eyes, I look up at West. God, seeing him now as the man he's turned into from the young man I now remember is an arrow aiming straight for my heart.

"I love you, West."

My confession rocks him. He stumbles, shifting on his feet, and he lifts his hand to his mouth to stifle his sob. It's as if our entire world has come crashing down around us, but somehow, it's being pieced together at the same time.

"Look at me, West," I beg, grabbing his hand. "You found me." I tip my chin up, pressing his hand to my chest, over the Big Ben charm resting above my heart. "You saved me, then you found me."

He breaks. His mouth opens as he exhales, tears slipping from the corners of his kind blue eyes. With fevered hands, he cups my face. "I love you, London." He crashes his mouth against mine, breathing me in. A sob escapes both our chests as our mouths meet. "God, how I fucking love you."

TWENTY-SEVEN

LONDON

I used to lie awake at night, staring at the ceiling, wondering what it would feel like to regain my memories.

I always imagined it clearly, everything slipping into its rightful place. Each memory compartmentalized into neat, tiny boxes. All of them are connected yet still organized, as if I'd been spending my life blindly searching for the light switch to the room that is my life, and once I found it, the room would light up and I'd feel right at home again.

I imagined living a happy life—one where I had two loving parents who only gave me up for reasons out of their control. I imagined a life of sunshine and rainbows. Other than the blip of me ending up in a foster home, my life was perfect.

Oh, how I wish that were true.

"Are you okay, Dimples?" West asks me for the millionth time.

"Yes." I sigh, giving him the same exact answer. I try to give him a small smile of reassurance. He accepts it with a twitch of his mouth before focusing back on the gate that leads into the parking garage below his apartment building.

I don't tell him to stop asking me, though. I get it. He's

worried about me. We're both wandering through uncharted territory, and I know the dam breaking on my memories isn't as perfect as I'd always imagined it to be.

Over the past few months, West and I have lived a separate life from our pasts. Now our pasts have collided with our present, the future is more uncertain than ever.

We haven't spoken much since we left our old foster home behind. I know he's giving me space, and I need it. I constantly twist my fingers in my lap, trying to focus on the good memories. The ones with West. But then the flash of the star-speckled sky comes to mind, and I feel his hand over my mouth, starving me of oxygen.

I go from warm and happy, to cold and terrified. Calm and still, to frozen, shaking with fear.

West parks his car in his designated spot and flips off the engine. Without a word, he steps out of the car, and within three seconds, he's opening my door and scooping me up into his arms.

I can't stop my teeth from chattering or the chill that's embedded itself in my bones. My whole body hurts. I don't know why when I haven't physically exerted myself other than sprinting down the road and into the woods in high heels, but all the energy has been sucked out of me. Physically, my mind is all over the place.

I drape my arms around his neck and rest my head on his sturdy chest, listening to the steady beat of his heart. He rests the side of his face against the top of my head, and I can hear every word he's saying without him ever speaking.

He holds me tightly. His large hands mold to my body and I'm aware of every touch point, like connecting stars to a constellation. He carries me all the way to the elevator and up to his floor. When he steps over the threshold, he loosens his grip and lowers me.

We're home.

My feet have barely touched the floor when I fall against him, collapsing in his arms.

Sobbing uncontrollably, I clutch onto his shoulders. He's no longer wearing his suit jacket. The soft fabric of his button-down shirt slips across my skin. I hang my head low, unable to lift it long enough to look into his eyes.

Then I fall to the floor. My knees slam against the hardwood before I catch myself from face planting the mahogany. Tears slip from my tired eyes, splashing to the carpet/tiling beneath me.

"London." The broken tone in West's voice causes another wrack of sobs to escape my fractured ribcage. "I don't know what to do, baby. Tell me what you need."

I shake my head, squeezing my eyes shut. Why does my past have to be so ugly? Why are the horrifying memories tearing apart the new, good ones?

When I think about it, I'm not only crying over the memory of my attack. I'm crying over all my memories of West. Every single one beautiful in its own way only to be left stranded and abandoned for fifteen years.

It's all too much, and guiltily, for a moment, I wish I hadn't regained my memories. I wish this sense of dread and emptiness would go away.

Clawing at the floor, I want to scream, but nothing comes out. Only silence. I open my mouth wide and force air in, focusing on my lungs, picturing them expanding, filling with life.

"What do you need?" he asks again, running his hand over my back. "Baby, please, tell me."

I sniff as tears stream to the floor, then I close my eyes and breathe in the memory of West kissing my cheek before the last time I'd seen him. Standing in the doorway to his bedroom of the foster home.

I strain my neck to lift my head, meeting West's gaze. He's crying again the way he was out in the woods with me earlier.

"I... I don't know."

He lifts his free hand and massages the back of his neck. He's drowning, and so am I.

I find his kind blue eyes, clinging to them like a life raft bobbing aimlessly in the middle of an open ocean.

"Just love me," I whisper. "I just need you to love me."

And he does.

Slowly, he reaches out, slipping my coat over my shoulders. He's gentle and precise, never once taking his eyes off mine as he scoots closer to me, running his hands down the length of my arms as the coat falls to the floor. My shoulders are exposed, but I don't shiver. His touch warms me from the outside in. He's reaching deep in my bones and into my soul, breaking the cold festering inside.

Then his hands meet my jaw. Then my nose. My cheekbone, just below my eye. He's studying me. Admiring me.

"I love you," he says, softly, as gentle as an afternoon breeze. He kisses my forehead.

I reach up and loosen his tie. It unravels beneath my dirt-laced fingernails. I shove the memory of what happened in the woods aside and focus on West. His touch and his voice. I wrap myself up in the only comfort I've ever truly known: him.

"I love you," he says, tugging on the ends of the bows of my dress straps; two thin pieces of fabric tied together on my shoulders. They fall when they come undone, and his hands graze over my collarbones before he slips the top of my dress down, revealing my bare chest.

"I love you," I say, my voice hoarse. I'm no longer sobbing, but my tears are still fresh, welling in my eyes. I can't stop crying. It's an overwhelming mix of emotions. Ones I haven't yet taken control of.

I unbutton his shirt, then slip it down his arms. I press my hand to his hardened muscle, just over his heart, and look in his eyes. "I love you," I repeat, this time a little stronger than the last.

Shifting to our knees, we kneel in front of each other. I run my hands over West's face. My fingers trace his eyes, then the stubble lining his jaw. My chest sparks, recognizing the curve of that jaw. It's more prominent than it was at fifteen, the last time I'd seen him. I've looked at it many times over the past few months, but I'm seeing it differently now.

"Our past is ugly." I tremble, admiring his face. My nail grates against his stubble, then I flick my gaze to his. "But looking at you now, with my memories of you then and what we had..." I swallow. "It's something I didn't have before, and it's beautiful."

A tear slips from his eye, and he inhales a sharp breath before claiming my mouth with his. He slips the rest of my dress over my hips. We both move to a stand, still locked in a kiss, and I kick off my heels. I'm standing in front of him in nothing but my thong. He's already working to remove it when I start unbuckling his belt. When we're both free of our remaining clothes, he wraps his hands around the back of my thighs and lifts me.

I curl my arms and legs around him. I think he's going to carry us to the bathroom, but he surprises me when he walks over to the plush, leather chair set in the middle of his living room. I fall against it, with my back against one arm, my legs over the other.

The chair smells exactly like West, and I'm overcome with love for him.

The apartment is dark. Apparently, it's still nighttime. The room is covered in shadows, and when West looks down at me, all I see is the hint of light in his blue eyes.

Wrapping both hands around my ankles, he pulls me until my ass lifts onto the arm. The warm air of his place breezes across my nipples. I hold my breath.

West is healing me, doing exactly as I asked him to.

He's loving me.

Holding onto the back of my knee, he drives himself inside me. I tilt my head back, overwhelmed with the feeling of being wrapped around him.

When he pulls back, I look up at the ceiling.

"Look at me, Dimples."

He wraps a hand around my face, pulling my gaze to his beautiful face above me.

A tear streams from the corner of my eye, and my chest expands before it finally explodes with love for West and all he's given me. I think about the years he spent searching for me, and the two times when he did, I'd treated him like a stranger. Like a ghost.

Clasping my legs around West tighter, I hold him against me as he drives himself in deeper. We move in sync effortlessly. His hand falls to my hip, and as I stare into his eyes, I come undone, gasping for air. Then he's bending, stealing my mouth, breathing air back into me.

He's bringing me back to life one breath at a time, and when he stills, with his cum spilling into me, he falls forward and rests his head on my chest.

He lifts his shaky hand and traces an invisible heart over the swell of my breast, complete with a large 'W'. "I've always been in here, Dimples. I've always been yours."

I HOLD me knees close to my chest, staring at the opaque water in West's bathtub.

"Tell me what you're thinking," West says, running his fingers through my hair. He's rinsing the rest of the shampoo out, taking his time, and I let him. I think at this point, we're both caught in a daze.

I lift my hands out of the water and turn them over. The dirt that accumulated under them has dissolved, so I dip them back under.

"A lot of things." I frown, biting the inside of my cheek to keep me from falling apart again. I don't want to cry anymore. I'm so tired of crying.

West smirks behind me in the reflection of the floor-length mirror in front of the tub. "I figured."

"For years, I thought if I was able to put all the puzzle pieces together, I'd get a good idea of the entire picture of my life, but it's massive and messy. Somehow, the puzzle is even more confusing now that it's pieced together."

"It'll take time, Dimples."

I sniff and nod before looking down at the water again. I run my hands over my knees. "I only want to ask you this one time, and once I have my answer, I never want to talk about it again."

West shifts behind me, straightening his back against the tub. I lift my eyes and find his in the mirror.

"What happened to him?" I whisper. "After I left..."

Pressing his lips together, he averts his gaze to the side, then he's back to me. "You remember what we said that night, when he was still lying there?"

I sift through the memories that have come back to me of that night.

West had told me I was safe, then when he made sure, he slowly walked over to Ryan, the older foster kid who'd bullied me for three years since the day I moved in. West lightly kicked his shoulder. Ryan moaned but wouldn't wake. He was still alive, and I couldn't look at him for long or else I was certain I was going to vomit. I covered my exposed chest with my arms, and West walked back over to me, kneeling in front of me. He asked me what I wanted to do, and I felt like my world was crashing down around me. I was attacked on my last day there. Nearly raped. But West saved me, and then I was losing him, too. My eyes fell to West's hands covered in blood.

I told him I didn't want him to jeopardize his chances of being adopted, because there was a possibility West could be charged with assault. Knowing Ryan, he would twist the story to turn himself into the victim. He'd claim West attacked him. Then I told him not to tell anyone about what Ryan tried to do to me. I knew I needed to leave the past behind me the second the Walkers signed on the dotted line that I was theirs. I needed to live my new, beautiful life, trusting West would follow through on his promise to find me.

I made West not only promise to find me, but that he wouldn't tell anyone what happened that night.

"I remember," I tell West as I spin around and slip both of my legs on either side of him.

He pulls me close, wrapping his arms around me.

I press my hands to his bare chest, then remove his necklace from around my neck, returning it to its rightful home. "We promised to never speak of it again."

"I did as you asked," he chokes out. "But only until after you left."

"What?" I ask, looking up from the Big Ben charm below his neck.

"I waited until I was certain you were far away from the foster home when I made the anonymous call to the police. I couldn't let him get away with it, London. I just couldn't. They showed up the next day, arrested Ryan on all sorts of charges, including drug possession. They never investigated your attempted rape because I never gave them your name, only that I'd witnessed him attacking someone in the home. Apparently, there were a whole litany of charges that were more solid than my anonymous tip, but after Ryan was arrested, the foster home lost their credibility and reputation. All the children still there were either placed into another foster home, an orphanage, or adopted out."

"What happened to you?"

West's neck bobs as he looks down, his gaze heavy, and I run my hand along his sharp jaw, forcing him to look up at me again.

"Glenna Hall showed up and saved me."

I press my fingers to the side of West's face, pulling him in for a kiss. We stay like that wrapped up in each other until the night sky starts to lighten.

Closing my eyes, I remember the day of the accident before it happened.

I pedaled down the street as fast as my legs could take me, soaking up the warm autumn air. Leaves were falling all around me, and I'd spread my arms wide. I felt like I was flying. Then I smiled, finally feeling free for the first time.

I'm filled with immense sadness for that hopeful fourteen-year-old girl I left behind.

I crack my eyes open, looking at the man I love. I study his face, taking note of every lash and every imperfection. His blue eyes brighten, like the sun glistening off the ocean.

"So, what do we do now?" I ask him, holding back my tears.

He pulls me closer, feathering his mouth over mine. "We breathe, Dimples," he whispers. "We breathe, and we start living."

TWENTY-EIGHT

WEST

Besides grief, regret is the only emotion to stretch on forever.

London regaining her memory has turned my world upside down. We've spent the past several weeks exploring, relearning, and wrapped up in each other. Not as who we were since Heath's death, but as who we would have been had we never separated the day she was adopted by the Walkers.

I've told London about my time in high school, the vacations the Halls took across the world, and how that sparked my passion to start my own business. I'd experienced more cultures in a few short years than I had my entire life before them.

London shared her love for the family that adopted her, and how they were what she clung to during the darkest of times. Then how she met my brother, fell for him, and married him.

It hurt to hear her tell that story, but I knew her love for him wasn't true love. Not like the love we have. Heath lied, offered her a false sense of security, then took her for granted. He used her.

She felt she had no way out. His death opened the door to freedom, and she stepped through it.

There are no more secrets between us. No more gaps of lost

time. We can't change the past, and I can't take back the regret I feel for letting London slip through my fingers time and time again, but we have forever to try.

Now, she's here where she belongs, and I'm coming home to her.

We still haven't figured out who it was that was following us after leaving Emily's gallery. After the first few nights of London regaining her memory, we tried to think of who it could possibly be but with no luck. I asked Alden to investigate, telling him any details I could remember about the car that night, but he's come up just as empty as I did.

Considering I haven't seen the car since, I've let it go. For now.

My jet lands later in the afternoon than I expect, but my body is buzzing with impatience the entire drive home. I tell Alden to step on the gas as hard as he can. Spending one whole day in Texas was entirely too long and too far of a distance from her. I'd asked London to go with me, but she wanted to spend time with her sister and her ailing grandmother, which I understood.

Alden manages to get us there sooner than I expect, then I'm racing out of the parking garage and up into the elevator. Before the lift has even reached my level, I hear London's music.

Heart racing and dick jumping, I gnaw on the inside of my cheek and curl my fingers into a fist. My hands are aching to touch her. My mouth aching to taste her.

Once inside, I immediately search for my raven-haired girl.

"Dimples?" I yell, shrugging off my suit jacket. I toss it aside, then start working on my tie. Unbuttoning my collar, I step into the kitchen. My personal chef must have left a plate of fruit out for London to grab whenever she takes a break from work.

I grab a handful of grapes from the charcuterie board and

carry them with me, following the music pouring from London's studio upstairs.

Popping one into my mouth, I can't help smiling as I grow closer, knowing when I step into the room, she'll turn and look at me.

Not the me she met months ago.

The me she left that day at the foster home.

She'll be looking at me as the Weston Knight she knew she loved, even at thirteen. Our love was innocent back then, more a friendship than anything else, though I believe our love is stronger for it. Through all the regret, the grief, and profound sense of never-ending loss, our love has transcended what I ever imagined possible. Our love is greater than one experience in a lifetime. It's infinite. Transcending even past our lives here on earth.

London will be looking at me with all the memories of our love story alive in her eyes.

The door to her studio is cracked open, allowing the music to filter throughout my entire penthouse apartment. The breath is knocked from my lungs when I stop in the doorway, watching her.

Dancing. She's dancing.

Leaning against the doorframe, I can't help smiling as London stands in front of her large, wooden worktable. Sheets of paper and art supplies are strewn about. When shimmying her hips, her ass shakes to the beat. I have no fucking clue what the song is or who sings it, but I'm silently thanking the artist for bringing joy to my girl's life. It's a live version, the chants of the crowd heard loud behind the singer's voices.

Stifling a chuckle, I press my fist to my mouth, sucking in my teeth.

The curves of London's full ass peek out from the bottom of her torn jeans. They're covered in streaks of charcoal. If I didn't already know what caused them, you'd think she'd been digging in the dirt all day.

It's funny how I only just saw her this morning, but it feels like it's been ages. I flew halfway across the country and back in time to be home for dinner.

Her long hair sways across her back, fanning out as she spins around.

She shrieks and stumbles when she sees me. Falling backward, she catches herself on the edge of her worktable, and her mouth pulls into a wide grin.

Then she's giving me the gift I've been waiting all day to see.

The look in her eyes alive with her memories of me.

I fight the urge to fall to me knees, and pop another grape into my mouth. It bursts, filling my mouth with sweetness.

"Like this song?" I ask her, smirking. She used to only listen to her music through her ear buds. Now, she hardly ever uses them. I like it because I get an inside peek into London's music taste.

She grins. "You're home."

Fuck. I swallow, then pop another grape into my mouth before crossing the large studio. Wrapping my arm around her waist, I crash my mouth to hers and lift her up, setting her down on the table. I drop the few grapes I have left beside her.

Her arms and legs are immediately around me, pulling me close.

Rolling my hips, I push my stiff cock against her. I cradle the side of her face and pull back.

"How was Texas?" she asks, still smiling.

"Terrible." I growl, against her ear. I breathe her in, and she tightens around me, goosebumps breaking out across her skin.

"Terrible?" She giggles. "Why?"

"You weren't there."

"West." She sighs, pushing me gently away from her. Her gray eyes meet mine. "I'm always with you."

"It isn't the same, Dimples. But I'm here now, so that's all that matters." I kiss her again before glancing over my shoulders at her work area. "How's the last drawing coming?"

She cracks another small smile, unraveling her legs from around me. I back away, and she hops off the edge of the table. I have half a mind to stop her and bend her over the edge of the table right now, sinking my cock into her, but I bite the tip of my tongue instead.

She walks over to her easel and unclips the drawing held to it by a small metal clip. After handing it to me, she plants her hands on her hips. "It's finished."

It's a sketch of Brooklyn. Specifically, my neighborhood. Recognizing the top of my building, I point to it. "Is that our place?"

Her cheeks redden, probably because I called it *our* place.

She nods. "Yeah." Then she clears her throat. "I told you I only draw places that have meaning to me."

I grin, thinking back to that day she'd first shown me her work. "You did."

"It's my home." She lifts one shoulder. "Our home."

Tears sting the back of my eyes, but I force them back. She never drew Heath's place because she said it never felt like hers.

Now, she feels at home here. With me.

"This is the last piece, then?"

"Yep." She pops the 'p' and points to the new portfolio she bought to store all the pieces she plans on displaying at the opening. "I would say, now that I'm finished, we can start planning the event, but Julianna and Charleigh might have already started taking over in that regard."

I raise my eyebrows. "Oh, yeah?"

A beautiful laugh escapes her. "You'd think Julianna would

have gone into event planning more than interior design. Our group chat has been blowing up the past several days with her ideas."

"I'm not surprised. I was going to hire an event cooridinator, but Julianna seems to have it covered. As long as you're happy, then whatever you want is fine with me." I eat another grape, never taking my eyes off London.

"I know. We're thinking another month or so until the re-opening of The Veiled Door."

I nod my agreement.

Her smile fades, then she looks around. "I guess that means we're almost done here then, huh? My job creating pieces for your bar is finished."

I narrow my gaze and take a step toward her. She steps back. The corner of her mouth lifts, and I want to steal the smirk from her with my own mouth.

"What was that?" I ask, swallowing my grape. I eat another one and take another step closer while she takes one back, testing me.

She giggles, tucking her long hair behind her ear. Her gold rings glint under the bright studio lights, revealing her heart-shaped birthmark.

"I don't see a need to stay here any longer," she jests. "I'm not needed anymore, so I can just head back to Boston once the reopening is finished, right?"

I know she's teasing, but the idea of her leaving me injects urgency into my veins. The thought of her returning to Boston, in the shadows of her life as my brother's wife, makes me physically ill.

Her teasing grin fades, and her chest stills as I close the gap between us. She's no longer backing away from me.

"You aren't going anywhere, Dimples," I growl, slipping my

arm around her again. I walk her backward until her back lands against the brick wall.

"No?" She tips her chin up, drunk on the love I'm giving her.

I shake my head and lean in, dragging my nose across her face, breathing her in like the starved man I am. Starving for her love. "No." I feather my mouth over hers. "You're mine forever."

TWENTY-NINE

HOLT

It's the quiet ones you need to watch out for. Or in my case, the one *I* watch.

Call me obsessed or whatever, it's in my fucking nature.

Work.

Fuck.

Eat.

Sleep.

Repeat.

Did I forget to mention obsessing over Selene gorgeous-as-sin Walker?

She's there somewhere, between working, eating, and fucking. Fucking women who, notably, aren't Selene Walker.

It's insane that my little sister's best friend consumes my every thought, but it's fact. Maybe it's that she drives me crazy with her quiet, reserved nature. Like she's always there lurking in the background, like a fucking wallflower when she should be the one who's center stage. Though I've learned over the years, Selene likes it that way, as though she has something to protect behind that guarded heart of hers.

She revels in not being the center of attention, descending

into the shadows, but from the first moment I caught a glimpse of her blonde hair and green eyes, I knew I wanted her more than any other woman I've ever had.

I shouldn't, though.

But there's one thing she doesn't know: I'm a wallflower just like her.

I stay quiet with almost everyone in my life. They think I'm this organized, overworked, professional rich prick, when deep down, I'm not. I'm more like Selene.

But no one likes that version.

They prefer this one.

"Fuck! I forgot the wonders your cock can do to me when I'm stressed." Emily sighs, climbing off me. She keeps her neck bent, trying not to bump her head against the ceiling of my car. Streams of my cum slip down the inside of her thighs as she moves to sit beside me. She spreads her legs and steals the handkerchief from the front pocket of my suit, wiping it up like it's spilled milk. "Here." She slaps the ball of now-sticky fabric into the palm of my hand. "Thanks."

I roll my eyes, toss the napkin aside, and tuck my dick back inside my pants.

"You didn't need to pull out you know." She breathes heavily, practically still moaning as if her orgasm is still humming inside her. "I'm on birth control."

Emily adjusts her breasts back into her dress, shielding the bite marks I've left around the outside of her right nipple. Once she's satisfied with the way they look, she begins fixing her hair, looking at her reflection through the tinted window.

We're parked out front of The Veiled Door, and there are a shit ton of guests filtering inside, walking along the red carpet like it's some Hollywood movie premiere.

Good. I'm glad.

West and London deserve this success.

But I needed a moment before walking inside and facing everyone. Especially when I know I'll be seeing Selene.

Emily Rapture just so happened to ask if I could give her a ride, and I wasn't going to turn her down when her definition of a ride meant more than sitting in the back of my car from one side of Manhattan to the other. I needed to purge the hunger my dick gets every time I'm around the one woman I know I shouldn't be obsessed with, and I wasn't going to let the lack of preparation get the better of me.

"I didn't have a condom on me." I tilt my head back as a bead of sweat slips down my forehead. "Though I remember you telling me you were on birth control the last time."

Her eyes slide to mine. "Maybe we could do this again sometime." She turns her attention back to her reflection, brushing her finger over her lip. "Preferably not outside of a gallery opening, and with less risk of an audience."

"I thought that's what you liked." I'm still catching my breath as I lift my chin and adjust my tie through the tiny rearview mirror. "An audience."

"Not always. But it is kind of thrilling, isn't it?" She smiles, revealing her perfectly straight, white teeth. She's beautiful, but nothing inside me shifts. I feel nothing for Emily. And despite knowing this isn't the first time we've fucked, I have a feeling this time will be the last.

It's a shame, too, because she is a good fuck.

"It's whatever." I clear my throat and sit on the edge of the leather seat.

Her hands fall into her lap, and we just sit there, looking at each other.

Well, this is fucking awkward.

"So." She inhales a deep breath, and her shoulders rise. "Do you want to do this again? I'm only in the city two more days before heading back to Albany."

"I don't think so."

She hums, twisting her tongue in her mouth with pursed lips, but her irritation is momentary. She brushes me off, her expression shifting as she gestures in my direction. "I get it. Good luck with everything. You know, the magazine and all that. Oh, and thank you for the second article. It'll look good for the new gallery." She twists in her seat and opens the car door. She steps one leg out as the valet stationed out front holds his hand out for her.

I watch as she stands and adjusts the bottom of her silver dress. It sways as she turns around, bends at the waist, bringing her face in line with mine through the open door.

"Oh, and Holt?" She lifts her eyebrows, giving me a sickly-sweet smile. "Next time you fuck someone for the fun of it, make sure you aren't moaning another woman's name. Selene, was it?" She scrunches her nose. "Even if she's just using you to get off, too, it's still a bad look."

She slams the door in my face.

Falling back against the seat, I rake a hand through my hair. Sweat sticks to the back of my neck, and the ends of my brown strands. Fuck. My palm slowly slides down my face as I look in the mirror.

I did it again.

Dammit. I shouldn't care what Emily Rapture thinks or what she said. We've never been more than business acquaintances, using each other for an occasional fuck. But her pointing out my one weakness does something to my insides. Frustration simmers beneath my skin, and my suit suffocates me with sick pleasure.

I pour a quick shot of whiskey from the small shelf built into the back of my car and toss it back before sliding across the back seat of my car.

I hold my breath, preparing myself for tonight. To mix and

mingle with anyone who would be beneficial to me or my magazine. My hand freezes on the doorhandle when I see her.

Blonde hair, full, bright-red painted lips. She glances over her shoulder, laughing at my sister as she leads the way, which is strange for a wallflower such as her. Her laughter sings, breaking through the sounds of the city around us.

She's fucking breathtaking.

My stomach does that fucking thing where it somersaults, watching her hips sway beneath her baby pink, silken gown, but then it screeches to a halt when someone grabs her hand. He slinks his fingers down the length of her arm, then hooks it onto his before escorting her inside.

Who the fuck is that?

Grinding my teeth, I run my fingers through my hair one more time before opening the door and stepping outside to find out who the asshole is that Selene brought with her.

While making my way out front, I'm closing the single button on my suit jacket, watching Selene and her date disappear inside.

"Holt Capuleti? CEO of Scribe Magazine?" the beady-eyed man in a generic brown suit asks, standing directly in front of me. He looks out of place for this type of event.

I stuff my hands into my pockets. "Who's asking?"

He reaches inside his briefcase and pulls out a manila folder, slapping it against my chest. "You've been served."

"What the fuck?" The words tumble from my mouth on a single breath.

Then the man disappears in the opposite direction.

Turning the folder over, I scramble to tear it open and slip the paper out from inside, reading the name of the asshole who has the fucking nerve to sue me.

Rome Montgomery.

Mother fucker.

LONDON

Living my life with all my memories is something I'm still getting used to. I've never felt more certain of myself.

I stand close to the end of the bar, talking with Kingsten Capuleti, beloved former mayor of New York City, and Julianna's dad.

"Your display here, London, will make a great asset to the city," Kingsten boasts, gesturing around the room.

"Thank you, sir." My cheeks heat, and I look down at my half-drunk mint julep. West made it quickly, adding extra mint, just the way I like it. Ever since that day in his apartment, I haven't been able to dispel the heat that consumes my cheeks when watching him mash the mint with the muddler.

"I placed a sizeable bid on one of them myself," Kingston adds, lifting his hand in the air. "Let's hope I win." He finishes off the rest of the cocktail Lewis made him.

"Not so fast, Mr. Capuleti," Asher says, holding Charleigh close to him. "I put my name behind yours, so you may want to keep an eye out. I'm not afraid of a little competition."

"Well, shit." Kingsten hisses, turning toward the auction

area. Not a single hair on his head moves, practically glued together with the amount of gel he's used.

"Did you forget Asher is a real estate CEO, Mr. Capuleti? He's a master negotiator and never backs down from a good bidding war." Charleigh laughs and lightly taps Asher, looking up at him with a smile. With their wedding planned for next summer, Asher and Charleigh have spent most of their summer and fall travelling around the world. It feels like it's been forever since we've talked outside of our girls' group chat or even had a girls' night out. I'm just glad she's happy. *They're* happy.

Asher looks sharp in his black tux, the perfect complement to Charleigh's bright, flowered, sequin dress.

"You're right, Ms. Keeler. I guess I shouldn't get too comfortable, then." Kingsten turns his attention back to us. "The auctioned pieces add a nice touch to this unveiling of the bar, Ms. Walker. What charity organization are the proceeds going to again?"

"Foster Alliance. It helps children in foster care receive proper clothing items and beds, as well as personal care items."

"Admirable cause," he praises, the wrinkles in the corners of his eyes deepening. "You know when I was running my campaign for mayor—"

"Dad!" Julianna groans, appearing from behind Kingsten, flipping her long, brown hair. "You aren't boring my girl London, are you?" She stands beside him and nudges his shoulder.

"Of course not, Jules." Kingsten frowns, elbowing her back, his mouth morphing into a face-splitting grin.

Julianna laughs, wrapping her hand around her father's arm. She leans forward and scrunches her nose in my direction, teasing. "Sorry if he was. He hasn't been mayor in years, but sometimes I still catch him talking politics. I think it's in his DNA."

I giggle, my eyes shifting to West standing close the row of drawings up for auction. Including the one of our home in Brooklyn. I was hesitant to put it up, but I wanted to raise as much money as possible for the foster charity.

West is wearing my favorite suit of his. The deep green with black lapels does something to my insides, and every time I look at him, I still can't believe he's mine. He's breathtaking.

We found each other again and came out the other side of what was an ugly period in our lives.

I am absolutely head over heels, madly in love with Weston Knight.

The Veiled Door looks completely different from the day of Heath's funeral. Unlike the sad, quiet vibe I felt then, now it is vibrant and full of life. It's living and breathing, surrounded by *my* artwork.

All four walls are decorated with my sketches of the city, professionally framed and preserved, matching the vibe of the bar, celebrating the city that's become my new home. Situated against the farthest wall, toward the back, is a long table with each piece on display behind it. Clipboards are set in front of each one, open for guests to place their best bids.

I've barely taken the time to walk around the room and admire my own work, to really let it sink in. I've never seen The Veiled Door as packed as it is tonight.

There's a red carpet running down the length of the pavement outside the front door. West hired an entire security team to handle admissions and flow of traffic. Last I heard, the line stretches to at least the end of the block.

West is busy talking with Selene and the man she has her arm hooked around, when their attention is pulled away by Emily Rapture. I smile, excited to see all of them together.

"Would you excuse me?" I ask, turning to the group I'm standing with.

All four shift their attention to me. They nod, and Julianna reaches out, squeezing my hand before I turn away. I leave them, anxious to not only be with West again, but to meet the man my sister is seeing. I'm nearly halfway to them when my phone vibrates in my hand. I turn it over and read the screen, my stomach dropping.

Unknown Number. Again.

I haven't told West that the number has continued to call me. At first, it was just a few times a week. After the car followed us from Emily's private gallery showing, the calls stopped.

I didn't think much of it after they stopped and decided to not let it take space in my head. The caller never leaves a voice-mail, and they don't do anything other than let it ring until they decide to hang up. I shut my phone screen off, and West is immediately pulling me into his side when I reach him, dissolving the icy chill at the back of my neck.

He gives me a warm kiss. "Enjoying your night?" he asks, bringing his mouth to my ear. His lips graze my earrings.

I shiver, heat pooling between my thighs. I clear my throat and pull away. "This is just as much your night as it is mine. Without you and this bar, my pieces wouldn't have a place to hang."

"She has a point, West," Selene chimes in.

"I agree," Emily says, admiring the walls. "Your work is just as exceptional as I thought it would be." Her silver dress shimmers under the bright lights of the bar. She's different than the first time we met. I guess Emily adapts to fit into every situation she's in.

The man beside my sister catches my attention.

"Hi," I say to the man with Selene. "I'm London, Selene's sister."

"Adam," the man says, giving me a small smile. "It's nice to finally meet you. Selene has told me so much about you. Congratulations on your gallery." His eyes shift to West. "To you as well."

"Thank you," we both say in unison.

"Adam is one of the editors for the New York Times," Selene adds, but her smile doesn't reach her eyes.

I tilt my head, unsure why it doesn't sit well with me.

"No shit," West blurts out, his mouth pulling into a smile under his short beard. He's growing it out again, and I can't say I'm disappointed.

"Yeah." Adam laughs.

"Excuse me?" A shout from the other side of the bar causes the four of us to snap our heads up. "Are you seriously trying to charge me for a drink? Do you even know who I am?" the woman shouts again from the area of the bar.

The room is packed wall-to-wall with guests, making it nearly impossible to see more than several feet ahead of me. I roll onto the balls of my feet, trying to get a better view of the person shouting. The voice sounds familiar, and when I catch sight of her brown hair, I know exactly who it is.

I fall back onto my heels, feeling like a heavy bag of sand is sinking into the pit of my stomach.

"Your mom is here," I tell West.

He lifts his chin, looking over the heads of the guests.

"Would you excuse us?" he says to Emily, Selene, and Adam.

His hand is already wrapped around mine, pulling me through the crowd and toward the bar.

When we reach his mom, she immediately turns around, spotting us.

Her hair is swept up into a French twist, bits of her brown hair framing her face. She's still just as pretty as the last time I saw her at Heath's funeral, but the light in her eyes is gone. She only looks at me with indignation now.

Her eyes narrow with scrutiny before she's looking up at West.

"Congratulations, son," she clips. "Why are you charging for drinks tonight? This is a charity event."

"I didn't think you were coming," he says quietly, ignoring her question.

She casually shrugs a shoulder and looks around. "Of course, I would." Then she lifts her eyes to his. "I've always celebrated my children's successes. Why would tonight be any different?"

"Oh, I don't know," West says, clenching his jaw. "Maybe because the last time we saw each other you accused me of stealing money from an account I didn't even know existed."

His hand tightens around mine, and I wrap my free hand over his, steadying him.

Glenna's eyes fall to our joined hands. She has yet to look at me again.

Pursing her lips, she vacantly looks over West's shoulder. "I still have no idea where that money went, but I've decided to move on."

Now she finally looks at me.

Her eyes harden, but I can see the tears building in them. "Seems you have as well."

I don't know whether she's talking to me or to West. Maybe both.

"You don't understand," he starts.

Glenna's hand shoots up, cutting West off.

"I don't want to hear it." Her eyes close. "I don't want to hear about you and your brother's wife."

My jaw drops, and tears prick behind my eyes. I don't know why I care what Glenna Hall thinks. I never did before. I accepted it when Heath kept me from his family. But now that I'm with West, suddenly, I find myself caring.

"Mom..." West breathes, and I know he's hurting, too.

Deep down in my bones, I know Glenna is a good person. She took West in when he had nowhere else to go. She saved him from a life that could have taken a completely different turn from the one he has now, but the grief of losing her first born has blinded her.

"Sorry to interrupt." Lewis appears from the other side of the bar. He trades nervous glances between West and me. "Do you know if we have any more of this whiskey?" He holds up the empty bottle. "We're pretty swamped here, and I haven't had time to check upstairs in the storeroom."

"I'll go check," I tell him. I turn to West and stand on my toes to give him a kiss.

Glenna rolls her eyes.

I look at her with sadness and regret. Regret only for knowing she's hurting. I'm hoping one day she'll understand when West tells her about our history together.

I turn my attention back to West, giving his hand a gentle squeeze. "I'll be right back."

"Don't take too long," he says, his eyes softening with longing.

It jumpstarts my already revved-up heart.

I reluctantly leave West and his mom, hoping somehow that the time it takes for me to run this errand for Lewis will give them the opportunity to repair the damage Glenna's put between them.

I'm weaving my way through the crowd when my phone vibrates again in my hand. I ignore it, knowing it's the unknown caller. Several guests offer me their congratulations. I nod and continue through, finally taking a breath once I reach the bottom of the stairwell.

I take the stairs slowly, lifting the bottom of my floor-length, black satin gown. My heels clank against the weathered boards, and my mind wanders to the countless days I came up here to work, secluded from everyone downstairs. I was in my own world up here, lost in the memories of West's hands and the necklace I'd given to him for his birthday. Before our world came crashing down.

The price we paid to get here has been worth it.

I'm smiling to myself, thinking of West's mouth against my ear when I reach the top landing. The door to the storeroom is propped open. I push it open and immediately start scanning the shelves for the whiskey Lewis needs, but the blood drains from my face when I see the man standing in front of the opposite shelf.

Crisp and clean, he's unmistakable, wearing a freshly-pressed suit. His blonde hair is neatly styled, pushed back, revealing his crystal blue eyes. Unsteady on his feet, he sways as he holds a small piece of paper between his fingers, and the thick, black diamond wedding band on his fourth finger causes my stomach to somersault with nausea. How? How is he possibly standing here in front of me when I'd seen his coffin. I'd seen the hole dug into the ground, ready and waiting to be his final resting place.

"Heath?" I whisper, my voice already shaking.

"London." He sighs, his shoulders dropping as if he's relieved to see me. "Finally."

His arms sag in front of him, and he takes a wobbly step forward. His eyes are bloodshot, the dim light of the closet casting shadows across the sharp planes of his face.

"You're, um..." I swallow the bile in my throat. "You're alive?"

Ten agonizing seconds of silence pass.

"You know," Heath finally says, slurring. "It's a shame I cut my brother out of my life. I didn't realize I'd have all the liquor I could ever want at my disposal." He swallows thickly, then lifts his angered eyes toward me. "And an unobstructed view of my wife's heart."

The breath catches in my throat when he holds up the piece of paper pinched between his clenched fingers.

"Heath." I close my eyes. In fact, I squeeze them tight, trying to wrap my head around the fact he isn't actually dead. "Heath, listen to me..."

"Don't," he booms, causing my eyes to snap open, my heart leaping at the sound.

The memories of being Heath's wife come back full force. It's amazing how the mind can spend months pushing aside the trauma, but once you find yourself faced with it again, you're transported back to feeling as little and insignificant as humanly possible.

Instinct and a year's worth of conditioning myself to create as few waves as possible when it comes to Heath's outbursts settles in like muscle memory. I wring my fingers and take a step back, reaching for the doorknob behind me, but Heath is quick to stop me.

He stomps across the room, the boards creaking beneath him. My back falls against the door, slamming it shut.

A small whimper escapes me as he slaps his hand against the door behind my head. I wince, turning my face away from him.

"Don't you fucking say a word," he seethes. His breath reeks of alcohol. "You always opened that mouth of yours when you should have kept it shut. Seems my sweet London hasn't learned her lesson."

Forcing the tears back, I stare up at Heath with as much anger and hatred as I can muster. "I'm not your wife anymore."

He slams his hand against the door again, this time with a

clenched fist. I jump again, but Heath forces me to look at him when he grabs my chin and presses the base of his hand to my throat. "I'm alive and breathing, my love, so you are very much still my wife."

"Why are you here?" I bite through the growing pain from his tight grip. I stretch my neck, attempting to release the pressure he's placing on it, but it's no use. "How?"

"No, no, no. I get answers first." He clicks his tongue in disapproval, then carries me over to the shelf, never letting up on his hold on me. His hand is a vise, tightening around my throat with minimal effort. Each finger presses into my neck like thick strands of rope, slowly and mercilessly strangling me.

Fear grips me as he drags me to the other corner of the closet. It's a small space, but it's too much when trapped with Heath. Still gripping my neck, he bends down and picks up the sheet of paper.

The drawing of West's necklace.

"What is this?" he asks, spit flying from his curled lips.

My eyes feel like they're going to pop out of their sockets. I claw at his wrist, tugging and pulling on it. My nails scratch against his skin. I wedge my fingers under his, hoping to pry them off, but again, I fail.

"Tell me!" he booms, shaking me.

"It's a necklace," I grind out, gasping for breath, black spots feathering the corners of my eyes.

Heath smirks devilishly. "Whose necklace?"

I look straight into his eyes. The ones I thought I loved before I remembered what true love felt like. I'd already loved before, and if I knew then, if I'd have kept my memories, I would have known what I felt for Heath was nothing compared to what I've always felt for West.

Tears well in my eyes, and my throat burns. I may never see him again after tonight. I think back to seconds earlier, the way he kissed me before I said I'd be right back. His kind blue eyes full of love for me.

Then I get a flash of the day I left with the Walkers. The way he kissed my cheek, whispering he wouldn't stop searching for me, promising we'd be together again. Even if I were to die by Heath's hand, I'm thankful West was able to fulfill his promise. He won't have to live with the regret.

I feel my body going limp, my arms and legs turning to lead. The strength I have is quickly fading. Metal digs into my back, but it doesn't matter. It won't matter when I'm no longer breathing.

"Whose necklace, London?" Heath booms, his face turning cherry red, the veins popping in his neck.

"Your brother's."

His eyes darken. "I always wondered why he wore this. What it meant. Where he got it. He was always so goddamn protective of it, and always so disgustingly secretive." He looks down at the drawing, then shoots me a glare. "But now I understand it. Now it makes sense."

"West..." I start, but Heath stops me.

"West has always tried to take what's mine. He inserted himself into my family and tried to fit in where he didn't belong. The asshole always thought he was so fucking special because he was dealt a shitty hand in life. Boo-fucking-who." He mock frowns and rubs under his eye, wiping away invisible tears.

"Now that motherfucker thinks he can steal my wife from me. But you're mine." He pulls me forward by my neck, then slams me against the shelf. "Mine!"

I cry out, a loud yelp squeaking from my throat.

A searing pain shoots across my back, and I want to give in. I want to surrender like I did the night Ryan attacked me. I want to surrender like all the other times Heath lashed out.

"Tell me you're mine, London. Tell me you're mine, or else I'll make sure West can never steal you from me again."

I don't answer him. I'm not even certain what his threat means. I'm too focused on the black spots creeping into my vision. Too focused on simply trying to breathe.

Heath leans in, his whiskey-scented breath stinging my nose, surrounding me like an invisible cloud. "Say it," he hisses. "Say you're mine."

A tear slips from the corner of my eye and down my cheek.

I look Heath straight in the eye before the stars swallow me up. "I was his," I squeak out, my throat searing with pain. "I was his before I ever became yours."

Then the stars call me home.

THIRTY-ONE

WEST

I barely heard the crashing sound coming from the closet upstairs before I was running. I shouldn't have been able to hear it. Not when there are hundreds of people chatting downstairs and music playing. But my heart is always tied to hers, calling me.

"London!" I yell, racing up the steps. Panic overtakes me when I hear a heavy sound coming from the closet. I reach the landing, force the door open, then I'm struggling to catch my breath and understand what I'm seeing.

Heath standing over London's lifeless body.

Ignoring the fact my brother is here and alive, I fall to the floor and crawl the two feet to her.

"London, baby," I softly say, cradling her head in my hands. "Come on, London. Breathe." Her neck is red, but her face is pale. A strong sensation of dread washes over me. I push her black hair aside, revealing her soft cheek, continuing to stroke my hand against her skin.

"Oh, no," Heath mocks behind me. "Are you going to cry over the loss of *my* wife?"

I ignore him, despite the instinct to fucking kill him. "You aren't gone. You're okay," I tell London.

Fear creeps in, and every moment of the past fifteen years crashes into me. The sleepless nights, wondering how I'd let London slip through my fingers. I'd watched her disappear in the distance, and with time, I was convinced I'd never see her again. And now that I have her back, *all of her*, I'm losing her all over again.

"West." Her beautiful mouth falls open on a small gasp.

Holy shit.

Relief hits me, and I cup London's face. She hasn't opened her eyes, but I see her breathing. I hear the air she's pulling in and letting out.

She's alive.

I'm almost distracted by her proof of life until I remember why we're here in the first place. My vision quickly turns red, and every muscle in me fights to control itself.

"What the fuck did you do?" I snap my head up to Heath.

He's swaying, switching between using either shelf on either side of him to keep himself steady. With half-closed eyes, he glares at me lazily. "I only gave you what you deserve."

"You could have killed her." I pull myself to a stand in front of London. If Heath attempts to touch her again, there wouldn't be any question as to whether he's truly dead this time.

"I was dead," he slurs in a somber tone. He frowns, then sluggishly lifts his arm, gesturing toward London. "But that didn't stop you from fucking my wife."

I grind my teeth. "She isn't your wife."

"The fuck she isn't!" Heath straightens his arms at his sides, his body stiffening.

"You were dead, Heath! She was free the moment your casket was lowered into that fucking hole in the ground."

"Doesn't count when I'm not in it." He laughs. No, in fact, he cackles, like he finds all this so fucking funny.

"You treated her like shit. You abused her and treated her as if she were anything but your wife. So, don't stand there acting all high and mighty, as if you have any argument to stand on."

"West," London croaks behind me. I fall to the floor again, holding her head as she tries to sit up. Her eyes roll as she tries to open them. She sits up, curling in as she starts coughing, her hand flying to her neck.

"I'm here, London," I soothe.

She nods, then looks up at me with bloodshot eyes.

"See?" Heath releases a cynical laugh. "She's fine."

"How?" London asks, looking up at Heath. "How are you here?"

"Oh." Heath swipes the open bottle of whiskey sitting on one of the shelves. It's practically empty, with less than a quarter of it left. "My brother here hired some shitty security, that's for sure." He looks at me. "One of your guys took a cigarette break down the alley, so I strolled in through the back door. I came up here hoping to find my wife, since this was her workspace before you let her move into your place. Then I found these." He picks up a handful of papers and tosses them to me, followed by him guzzling down the remaining bit of liquor left in the bottle he stole.

My Big Ben charm. Dirt-covered hands. *My* hands.

"Seems she left them behind when you built her an entire studio at your place," he mocks. "I guess she's an easier fuck when she stays at your apartment instead of this shithole."

I'm on my feet and crossing the room before I can take my next breath. I close in on Heath, pushing him back against the shelf, pressing my forearm to his chest, hoping it'll keep him from going anywhere near London.

"You have ten seconds to explain how the fuck you are alive before I—"

"Before you, what?" Heath raises his chin defiantly. "Before you kill me? Like you threatened everyone else who harms your precious London."

He's challenging me, daring me to kill him. Eyes the exact replicas of Glenna's stare up at me, narrowed and menacing. Everything and everyone is a game to Heath.

"How do you know all of this?" I ask him, ignoring the twist of sickness in my stomach. I don't know how the fuck my brother is still alive, but I know whatever answer he's about to give won't be a good or reasonable one.

The corner of Heath's mouth tilts into a sinister smirk. He chuckles despite the hold I have on him.

"I had a plan," he says, his eyes shifting to London. I don't take a chance by taking my attention off him for even a second.

"A plan?"

"I had to." His evil eyes shift back to mine. "I had to fake my death."

"Are you serious?" I jerk my arm against him again. I knew his answer would be fucking stupid. It makes my blood boil.

"Yes. I *had* to."

Silence, then...

"The helicopter pilot," London croaks behind me.

"Unfortunate, really. Nice man." Heath scrunches his nose, shrugging off his pilot's death as insignificant. "But I had to do what I had to do."

"You murdered him," she adds.

Heath brushes her comment off again, the alcohol settling deep in his bones. That, or the man no longer has any fucking feelings whatsoever.

"Why?" London asks, her voice sounding stronger now. I

don't know whether she's had a moment to catch her breath, but she sounds closer to me than before.

"What possible reason could have for faking your own death, Heath?" I seethe. "Who fucking does that?"

"You have no right to judge me. Not when you've been fucking my wife behind my back, but I should have known."

"What? That I would betray you?" White-hot anger causes my fingers to coil. My muscles strain, holding back the inherent need to beat the shit out of him.

"It was only supposed to be for a short while," he starts to explain. "Just long enough to convince Rhys O'Connell that I was gone. Then I was going to come back."

"Who the hell is Rhys O'Connell?" London asks.

"He's an associate of someone I used to work with," Heath slurs, but his anger hasn't let up. His chest is still hard as stone under my arm. "I might have given him a heads up on an investment in the stock market." He sniffs, narrowing his blue eyes. "But it didn't exactly pan out how I thought, and, well..."

He has got to be fucking kidding.

This time, I'm the one narrowing my eyes.

"This is insane. You know that, right, Heath?"

"You don't understand." His nostrils flare. "Rhys's family has operatives everywhere. They were tracking me and waiting for the moment to snub me for the poor advice I gave them. I tried to reason with them that any market investment advice I gave wasn't guaranteed to be successful, but let's just say the O'Connells don't exactly give a shit when it comes to those sorts of details. So, I did what I had to do."

I pull off him. The longer we stand here, the more drunk he seems. The alcohol is settling into his veins with every second. His eyes are bloodshot and lined red.

Fuck, how much has he had?

"What changed, then?" London asks, moving behind me. "If you're supposed to be dead, why are you here?"

His expression shifts. Drunk, blue eyes darken, and the muscles in his jaw swell as he clenches them. There's anger and fury aimed toward London. He take a step forward, jutting his chin out. "Because I found out you were fucking my brother!" he shouts. "I tried to get answers, but you've ignored every single one of my calls. I've been watching you, London. I had my suspicions. Ever since the day of my funeral."

"You were there?" she asks.

"Of course, I was." Heath laughs maniacally. "I needed to see how my family mourned me and what my wife had to say when she realized she was going to live without me."

"Heath..." London's voice is quiet, caught in disbelief. She isn't alone.

He frowns and shakes his head in disbelief. "Not one thing." Holding up a single finger, he wags it in the air. "Not one single sentiment fell from that pretty mouth of yours. You couldn't say one fucking thing!"

London shudders, blinking with Heath's increasing fury.

I look at my adoptive brother—the one who's hated me from day one—with repulsion.

"Anyway," he sniffs, raking his hand through his disheveled hair. "I forgave you. Chalked it up to you accepting your life as a widow in mourning. But then..." He dramatically inhales a deep breath.

"I kept watch over you, staying in the shadows like I was supposed to. It was difficult to hold back and stay hidden, but I knew I couldn't show myself until I knew for certain. Then I saw you at Club Verona. I knew you were fucking each other then. After that, I made a plan. I followed you out to Albany and—"

"That was you?" London cuts him off.

"You know, babe, I'm surprised your pretty little head didn't catch on to that earlier. You may have lost your memory, but I thought you'd at least kept your intelligence. I guess I was wrong, huh?"

"Our marriage was over long before you faked your own death, Heath," London says.

Though that doesn't seem to faze my brother.

I grind my teeth, certain they're going to crack. If this is the way Heath is talking to London now, I can only imagine how it was when they were married. The thought makes my blood fucking boil.

Heath shrugs a shoulder, swaying on his feet as if he's on the deck of a ship at sea. "I had hoped forcing you two off a cliff and to your deaths would be considered an accident."

Fevered anger sizzles in my veins, and I clench my hands into fists.

"Asshole," I practically hiss. "You almost killed us."

Heath's eyes dart to mine. "That was the point, West. You stole what was mine, and you needed to pay the price." His eyelids flutter, and he leans to one side, unstable on his feet. I take several steps back, landing on the creaking floorboards, and before I know it, we're standing at the top of the stairs, outside of the closet.

"You've always stolen what was mine!" Heath shouts, spitting in my face. "Now you've stolen my slut of a wife, and for that I'm going to do what I should have done when we were kids. Kill you." He raises his fist in the air, rearing his arm back to deliver a blow, but I duck before he gets the chance. Wrapping my arms around his waist, I try to push him back into the closet, but I'm unsuccessful. The fucker is stronger than I anticipate, and my foot is already hanging over the edge of the staircase.

Heath and I are wrapped up in each other, but I'm unable

to push him back. The alcohol has somehow made him stronger. My feet are hanging too far over the edge for me to gain my footing. Out of nowhere, his body stiffens against mine, and we're tumbling. London shrieks in the background, but she's quickly drowned out by the sound of breaking wood, the music downstairs, and Heath's grunts in my ear.

My back hits the wall, and my ass lands on one of the steps. I try to let go of Heath, but his grip around me is relentless, and he pulls me until I'm flying over him. I brace myself for the blow surely coming to my head. Squeezing my eyes shut, I wait for the pain. The edge of the step slams into my spine, and I can't figure out what's up and what's down. We just keep rolling.

At some point, Heath and I come to a stop. My head pounds, and my body aches, but I'm quick to my feet.

Heath's fist is the first thing I see when I gather the strength to look up. It connects with my jaw, and I stumble backward. I grab onto a chair in the dining room and slump over. Blood spills from my mouth onto the rich, dark wood, a sickness washing over me. The bar is quiet now. The live band has stopped playing, and when I look around, the entire crowd has fallen back, creating a circle around us. Every single person is frozen, staring at us.

I try to catch my breath. I spit, letting the blood spray to the floor. A sharp pain stabs at my ribs from the inside, the sensation even more intense when I try to take a breath.

London races down the stairs, pushing through the outer edge of the crowd to get to me. Her eyes are wide with shock, bouncing between Heath and me.

Heath stands on the opposite end of the circle the crowd has made, close to the front door. Blood spills from the top of his head, down the side of his face.

When London reaches me, she places her hand on my back, urging me to focus on her. But I don't trust Heath. I don't trust him as long as he's near London. His mission is to kill the both of us, and I have no reason to believe he won't follow through on that promise, even if there are hundreds of witnesses.

I wipe the back of my hand across my mouth when someone emerges from the crowd, standing between Heath and me.

My mother steps back unsteadily, her mouth agape. "Heath?" She glances back and forth between her two sons. At first, I think she's looking at me with just as much surprise and unanswered questions swimming in her mind. Then I recognize her expression. The one of suspicion, as if I somehow knew Heath has been alive this whole time. As if I knew about Heath's insane scheme to fake his own death. Like I *must* be involved in some way.

"Mom," Heath slurs, unable to make eye contact with her. He sways again, stumbling on his own feet. Falling back on his heels, he crashes into a group of people near the middle of the dining room. No one catches him, gasping as they step back, allowing him to fall to the floor in a heap.

Groaning, he rolls onto his side and attempts to stand. He squeezes his eyes shut, staying on his hands and knees as he attempts to regain his bearings.

"What are you doing here?" my mother asks. "How are you alive?" Tears well her black-lined eyes. She blinks, allowing them to spill over, leaving trails of white across her pink-dusted cheeks.

Alden, Holt, and Asher appear at the edges of the crowd. When they see my face, they immediately turn their attention to my brother, ready to pounce on him, but I raise my hand and shake my head. I don't want to make this a bigger scene than it already is. I just want my brother to leave.

"How are you here?" my mother asks Heath again.

Dots flicker in my vision, and I swear, London's hand on my back is the only thing keeping me anchored to the floor, holding me to this earth, saving me from being swallowed up by the darkness.

Heath's once-blue eyes have now turned completely dark. Pools of black cloud his vision as he stares at our mother. He points directly at me with a shaking, angering finger.

"My so-called brother is fucking my wife!" he booms, filling the eerily silent bar.

I immediately feel everyone's eyes move to me. Including my mother's.

"What?" she gasps.

"I'm not fucking her, Heath." I snarl, anger getting the best of me. I feel lightheaded, and I think the pain from the blows to the head and falling down the stairs are starting to catch up to me, but I don't lose focus. "I'm in love with her, and I've been in love with her since we were kids."

"Kids?" my mother asks, her penciled brows pulling together. "What do you mean, West?"

Heath lets out a bitter laugh. "Oh, this is a story I've learned while following them over the past several months. One you won't want to miss hearing, Mom. Old-fashioned love story right there."

My mother turns her attention back to Heath. He begins making his way over to me, shoving chairs aside and bumping into tables along the way. The wood creaks against the marble floor.

"West and London came from the same shithole foster home," Heath continues. "And it seems my wife's little memory loss wasn't so little after all. She'd forgotten all about how she was in love with West before."

My mother covers her mouth with her hand. With teary eyes, she slowly turns to look at London, then me.

"Glenna," London says, stepping closer. "I—"

"I don't understand." Glenna turns back to Heath, ignoring London and me.

"Heath faked his own death," I say with as little emotion as possible. "He's been stalking us for months. He tried to kill us when we took our trip up to Albany."

Heath's now standing a table length's distance away from me, and I swear, I can still smell the whiskey on his breath. Though it could be the blood still pooling in my mouth. I can't differentiate anything anymore.

"Is that true?" Mom asks, her eyes bulging out of her head. "Heath?"

"Yes." He whips his head her way, staring coldly in her direction.

"How?" Her face transforms from confusion to realization. "Is that where the money went? *You* took it?"

"I needed it," Heath spews, spit spraying from his lips. "I needed it to survive, and my connections at the bank assured me they wouldn't reveal it was me."

When my mother doesn't respond to Heath's confession, his bloodshot eyes search the room before landing on me. I shudder when Heath tips his head back as another sinister, bitter laugh escapes him. Swaying some more, he presses his hand to his chest and tips his head back, squeezing his eyes shut, his mouth wide open. Then he lurches forward, moving around the last table separating us.

From the corners of my eyes, I see Alden and a security guard growing closer. Even if they were to jump in and intervene, though, Heath would still get to me first.

With his shoulders slumped, my brother looks up at me with hooded eyes. "Do you know what I find ironic about this whole situation, *brother*?" His mouth curls, his tongue laced with poison.

"What is that, Heath?" I ask, sniffing. Whiskey and blood. It's all I can smell and taste.

"That even as I'm finally revealing the truth to an entire room of people about how you've always tried to steal what's mine, like the dirty little thief you are, you still come out looking like the hero."

"I'm not a hero, Heath." A cold drop of blood slides down the length of my jaw to my neck. "You're just the fucking coward who felt the need to beat his wife to make himself look like an even bigger asshole. I didn't have to do a fucking thing."

"Fuck you." Heath growls, lunging for me.

I've barely taken a painstaking breath when his arms wrap around me again. He slams me onto the table. Shrieks and cries from the crowd vibrate across the bar as the force he's used on me snaps the fragile table in half. Splinters and shards of wood dig into my back. The lightheaded feeling expands. Flickers of black dots pepper the edges of my vision. I squeeze my eyes shut, trying to inhale a breath, starving for oxygen.

When I manage to crack my eyes open, I see Heath on top of me, rearing his fist back. He tries to hit me but fails, his fist missing and slipping past my shoulder. I take the opportunity to fist his shirt and pull myself up, then I slam my head to his, forcing him back.

I grit my teeth through the pain, the echoing agony expanding in my brain. It feels like it's going to explode. More blood spills down the side of my head, and I can feel my hair sticking to my skin.

But I don't stop. Once I pull myself to a half stand, I grab Heath by the shirt and hit him again. Anger overtakes me, and I think of all the times he treated me like shit growing up. I think about what London told me that first day, the truth about her marriage to Heath. How he'd abuse her in every way he could.

I hit Heath again, forcing him to his knees in front of me.

His eyes roll back before his head falls forward, his neck going limp, unable to hold it up anymore. Blood drips from his face, spilling into his lap. With what little strength I have left, I wrap my hand around his arm and lift him up, thrusting him toward the front door. The crowd clears out around him.

He stumbles back as Alden and the security guard quickly grab hold of him.

"Get out!" I shout. The bitter, metallic taste of blood is impossibly stronger. One of my eyes is already swelling shut, but my vision of my brother is still clear. "Get the fuck out."

He resists the security guard and Alden's hold, but they don't let up.

"Fuck you! You can't order me to do shit." Heath shouts, still trying to jerk away from Alden.

I have half a mind to call the police and turn him in for faking his own death. But when I see Glenna standing on the edges of the crowd, tears streaming down her face, something inside me cracks. Her shoulders are wracking with sobs. All Glenna ever wanted was two boys. Two boys to love, and while Heath doesn't deserve her, he's still her son. He's her flesh and blood. I'm thankful for the gift of a stable life she was able to give me, and while I've always thought of her as my own mother, that's one fact I've never been able to understand. A fact I've always been envious of.

Glenna looks at Heath the way I'd always wished my own mother would have been able to look at me.

Her obvious heartbreak causes me to make a split-second decision—one I'm not certain Heath deserves—because all I want to do is move on. To live my life with London, hoping my brother will take his second chance and slip back into the shadows. We can each live our own lives without interfering with the other.

"It's over Heath," I tell him, sticking out my chin. I clutch onto my side, another sharp pain like a dagger to the ribs. "Leave before I come to my senses and turn you in."

"Fuck you." He huffs, still defiant. I know part of his stubbornness is from how drunk he is, but not all of it. It's in Heath's nature not to let go and admit defeat. "Always so disgustingly soft. Something that will always be your downfall."

I nod my head toward Alden, silently telling him to take Heath outside. He nods in acknowledgement.

Walking backward, they lead Heath through the front door and don't let go until they've reached the sidewalk, which is still crowded, filled with the line of guests waiting to gain entry. All of them have now turned their attention to the scene that's continuing to play on outside.

"I'll be back for her," Heath says, staring blankly at me before shifting his attention to London beside me. He narrows his eyes, wiping the back of his hand under his bleeding nose. "I'll be back for you, my sweet little cunt."

She slips her hand in mine, and only then do Heath's bloodshot eyes fall.

The corner of his mouth tilts as he continues walking backward. The streets of New York City are alive. Bright neon lights flash, and traffic whizzes by, everyone out there oblivious to what's happening.

Heath continues stepping back, his foot wobbling on the edge of the curb. He slips between two parked cars, stumbling onto the street.

London's hand falls away from mine as my blood grows cold.

"Heath." Her voice is unsteady. "Heath, stop."

My stomach lurches with sickness, watching him continue to step backward, never taking his eyes off us. He's sloppy and lazy, unaware of how far he's wandered. His feet scrape against the rain-soaked street. The reflection of the surrounding lights brighten his skin, highlighting the blood and bruises from our fight. But they also highlight the sheer bitterness and anger engrained in his expression.

"I'll come back for you," he calls. "And I'll take you down with me."

He takes another unsteady step backward into the street, into the traffic lane, past the cars parallel parked along the edge.

I follow London as she moves forward, but we barely make it to the point where the sidewalk meets the street before I hear her bone-chilling scream and feel my face splatter with blood I know isn't mine.

THIRTY-TWO

LONDON

I figured I would be accustomed to the taste of blood by now, but it's different when it isn't your own.

West's arms had just wrapped around me, dragging me toward the front of The Veiled Door, trying to pull me back from seeing Heath's ravaged body smeared across the concrete.

He was too late.

I'd witnessed all of it. Heard it. Felt it.

The large New York City tour bus is splattered with Heath's blood, but so are we.

It screeched to a halt, stopping as soon as it hit him.

Heath is dead. Officially.

Taking all his lies, deceit, and vengeance with him.

Snapping my mouth shut, I get a true taste of Heath's blood. Bitter and sour. Pungent.

I vomit all over the wet pavement.

It's only a matter of minutes before the crowd both gathers and disperses, all at the same time. It moves like a current to where Heath's crushed body is smeared across the city street.

My hands shake uncontrollably, and when I finally gather

the courage to look up and see West staring directly at me, reality sets in.

Blood is sprayed across my hands, like the splatter of spray paint I'd once used on a commissioned piece I'd done back in college for a friend of mine. I frantically try to wipe it away, but the dots just spread into streaks, coating my skin like faded ink.

"London." West's bloodied, bruised hands cradle my face, imploring me to look up at him. His face is covered with cuts, and I can't tell which drops of blood are his, and which are Heath's. He's covered in it.

"West," my voice quivers. "I tried—"

"I know. It wasn't your fault. It wasn't your fault."

"I tried to stop him but—" Heath has spent months stalking me, nearly killing us in the process, and although my love for him no longer exists, still, witnessing the death of your ex-husband, watching as his body turns to mush on the pavement, is something I would have never wished for Heath.

"There was nothing you could have done, London," West says, blood dripping from his chin.

"No!" Glenna emerges from the front of the bar, racing across the sidewalk to try and reach her son, screaming at the top of her lungs, but Alden and the security guard posted at the front entrance of The Veiled Door stop her. "Heath!" she shouts, trying her best to fight against their hold, but she quickly gives up, collapsing onto the wet pavement. Her shoulders wrack with sobs and she rocks back and forth, clutching her chest. "My son!" she wails. "My son."

I bite down on my bottom lip, trying to wrap my head around how the best night of my life turned into one of the worst.

Turning my attention back to West, I look up at him with watery eyes. Tears spill down my cheeks, and when I see the large gash to his temple, I gasp. Reaching up, I press my hand to it, trying to stop the bleeding.

The red splatter of blood has turned an unnatural shade of black, soaking into West's green suit. I've never seen blood like this before.

Forcing myself out of the shock inside me feels like I'm being yanked back down to earth. West is my entire world, and he doesn't look the same. He stumbles forward.

I catch him. "West, what's wrong?" I ask, panic stricken.

"My ribs hurt and my head," he mutters.

I look up at the spot where my hand meets his temple. Blood leaks between my fingertips. "West." I chew on the inside of my cheek, frantically searching for an ambulance or for anyone who can help.

"I'm okay, Dimples," he croaks, his voice too light.

He doesn't look okay.

He slumps forward again, and I catch him a second time, cradling his head against my chest.

Flashing red and blue lights flicker against the front of West's bar, and relief trickles down my spine. "An ambulance is here, West. Just hang on."

I wave my free arm frantically in the air, calling them over.

The paramedics rush to the spot where the bus crashed into Heath, but one runs over to me, noticing West slumped against me.

"What's going on here?" the paramedic asks.

"He has an injury to his head." I remove my hand and show him the wound. "He's also complaining about his ribs."

"Seriously, Dimples," West breathes, exhausted. "I'm okay. It's just a scratch."

"Stop, West." I run my hand along the back of his head. The thought of losing him is unimaginable. I already spent fifteen years without him.

The paramedic leaves to grab a gurney, pulling it up behind him.

West lifts his gaze long enough to look me in the eye. Fresh tears fall from me as he raises his hand and brushes my cheek. "If you think I'm leaving you now, London, after all this time, you have another thing coming. My love for you is endless, and I won't let a fucking scratch to the head or bruise to the ribs take me from you."

I sob harder, his words hitting me.

"I love you." I lean down and press my lips to his before he's sitting back onto the gurney.

"I love you, too." Tilting his head back, he squeezes his eyes shut and grunts in pain, still clutching his side. Then his eyes crack open to find his mother still crumpled on the sidewalk. "Make sure my mom is okay. *Please.*"

I tremble and suck in a quick breath. "I will, but I'm going with you to the hospital."

There's no fucking way I'm leaving West.

"Were you a witness to what happened here?" The paramedic nods his head toward the grisly scene.

"Yes." My voice is weak and uncertain.

"The police will need a statement from you."

I open my mouth to protest, but West stops me. "I'll be okay, London. We'll find each other afterward. We always do."

His words hit me like an arrow aimed straight for my heart. "Fine." I whisper, not arguing.

"I love you." West kisses the back of my hand before surrendering to allow the paramedics to do their work.

Once they start to wheel West toward the ambulance, I meet Glenna where she is on the pavement.

Julianna and Selene are kneeling beside her, and when they see me, they stand. Glenna looks up with her tear-stained cheeks.

"London," she sobs.

I kneel beside her and look at her with sympathy. Despite how horrible her son was and the pain he caused not just me, but to everyone around him, I feel for her.

Although I felt the love from my adoptive mother, I never felt this type of love. The kind where they would do absolutely anything for their child. Cut from the same cloth, walking around with the same blood coursing through their veins. The kind of motherly love where they wouldn't willingly leave this world while their child was still in it.

My mother's love wasn't that deep, but I know Glenna's was for Heath.

"Glenna." My chin trembles. "I'm so sorry."

I'm not just sorry for Heath's death. I'm sorry he lied to her, keeping his true colors hidden.

Her eyes soften, and for the first time since we met, she's looking at me with love and kindness, no more bitterness. Only understanding. While I could also be angry at her for all she's accused me and West of these past few months, I'm not. I only feel sympathy for a woman who has nearly lost everyone she's ever loved and been betrayed by her first born.

"He was my son." Her brows pull together, her eyes softening with tears.

"I know." Opening my arms, I pull her to me. I hold her and allow her to cry into my shoulder for what feels like forever until a police officer is standing above us.

"Excuse me, ma'am," she says, holding a notepad in her hand. "Are you the wife of the victim?"

I let go of Glenna, pull myself to a stand. "I was."

The police officer's brows knit before she tips her head back. "May I speak with you about what happened here?"

I nod once, then turn back to look down at Glenna.

She reaches up and grabs my hand, shifting her attention to

the back of the ambulance before she turns back to me and gives my hand a reassuring squeeze. "Take care of my son."

My chest warms, despite the cold, darkness of tonight. I squeeze Glenna's hand back. "Always."

After she lets me go, I follow the police officer over to her vehicle parked along the curb. We pass the ambulance, where West was taken to moments earlier. The back doors are open, and there are at least two paramedics hooking him up to various machines. They've removed his suit jacket and tie, leaving his button-down shirt open, revealing his tattooed chest. One of the paramedics is hunched over, examining his side. Torrential waves of emotion fill me.

My love for West.

The betrayal of Heath faking his own death.

Him on a mission to kill both of us.

My memories coming back to me after all these years.

Everything crashes into me as I follow the policewoman and take in the scene outside of The Veiled Door.

The bus that killed Heath is in the middle of the lane, and the crowd surrounding it has dispersed. Police caution tape now blocks off its perimeter, preventing onlookers from getting too close. A chill slinks down my spine from the memory of Heath's hand around my neck, promising me I would forever be his.

Then I remember the strength in my voice when I fought back and spoke my truth without any fear.

Taking in a deep breath, I look away from the evolving crime scene and toward the still-open ambulance to find West's kind, blue eyes staring directly at me. A familiar sense of calm wraps around me, the same as it was the day I walked into The Veiled Door for the very first time. When West was behind the bar. I may not have had my memory then, but I think, looking back on it now, I loved him at first sight.

When the ambulance doors shut, and I turn to the policewoman, with her pen poised to take my statement, I decide to leave my past behind.

This time, for good.

THIRTY-THREE

WEST

Five Days Later

A fractured skull, four broken ribs, and a splintered tibia.

Apparently, I hit every corner and sharp edge of the stairs on my way down, and my body paid the price for it. The doctors said they wouldn't normally keep me in the hospital this long, but considering all three injuries together, they thought it would be best to observe me for a few days before discharging me.

The physical injuries are nothing compared to the mental, though.

Watching your brother die before your very eyes is traumatic, even if you had hated each other.

It's been five days since the accident, and it's going to take years to recover from the distress of it all. I may have been spared from Heath's attempts to kill me, but I know my injuries are nothing compared to what Heath suffered: death.

Over the past few nights, I've had nightmares about that night.

Seeing Heath disappear right in front of my very eyes. His body disintegrating before me. The shrill sound of London's screams. What I thought was her lifeless body lying on the floor of the storage closet. The hollow sensation that immediately filled my chest thinking I'd lost her for good, and by the hands of my adoptive brother—the one who faked his own death. I've tried to wrap my head around the lengths Heath must have gone to to fake his own death. The people he must have paid in exchange for their silence. The helicopter pilot who lost his life was merely collateral damage.

All of it has weighed heavily on me these past few days, and I know it's done the same for London, even if she hasn't told me as much out loud.

Like all traumas, it's something I know will take time to heal.

For now, I try to focus on the good.

I take comfort in knowing I have London, and that we're safe. *She's* safe.

Every cut, bruise, and broken bone was worth protecting her for. And being here with her, with every memory of me alive in her mind, was worth all the pain it took to get here.

"Oh, wow." London giggles, covering her mouth with her delicate hand. "I'm sorry, I don't mean to laugh."

"Oh, yeah?" I pop an eyebrow.

"Yes." She laughs again, tucking her bottom lip under her teeth as she reaches out and touches my arm. "I really don't mean to." She tries to hide her grin. "I mean, it's only temporary, right?"

I sigh, pressing my lips together as I look down at the large, black boot on my left leg. I'm thankful to finally be going home today, but I wish I didn't have to leave with this monstrosity on my leg.

"They say I have to keep it on for a few weeks," I mutter, resting the heel on the faded tile of my hospital room. "Which means no working at the bars and a lot of desk work."

I hate the idea of not working. Behind the bar, at least. My life and businesses have been put on hold. The Veiled Door has officially become a crime scene, and from what everyone has told me, the police have just released it back to me this morning, completing their investigation. Considering there were hundreds of witnesses to Heath's sudden death, and the toxicology report found an incredibly high level of drugs and alcohol in his system, they concluded there was no foul play. Heath died from an unfortunate set of choices and circumstances.

Aside from the disruption to business, I worry about London. I don't doubt her resiliency, but I wonder how much this will affect her. If it has, she hasn't shown it yet.

I look back up at her. She's stunning, standing in front of me with her black sweatpants and faded gray T-shirt. They cling to all my favorite parts of her.

My dick twitches, aching for her touch.

"Come here." I growl, hooking my fingers under the hem of her T-shirt. I tug her forward until her legs slip between mine. She looks down at me, raking her fingers through my hair before she leans down, her mouth hovering over mine.

"No strenuous activity for six weeks, Mr. Knight," she whispers. "Doctor's orders."

I chuckle, lifting my mouth into a smirk, biting back the echo of pain in my side. "If you think I'm going to take orders from a doctor—"

"Don't," she stops me, lifting her finger to my lips, shutting me up. "Don't finish that sentence."

She isn't helping matters.

I wrap my arms around her waist, slamming the front of her thighs against my swelling cock, showing her exactly what she's doing to me.

"You are the worst when it comes to listening to instructions. You could aggravate your injuries and then we'll end up right back here." She gives me a quick kiss, but I don't miss how she rubs her legs against me. Her smile widens, her dimples deepening.

Such a little tease.

"The doctor didn't say anything about you, though, did he, Dimples?" I palm her sweet pussy. She's warm and, fuck me, what I wouldn't give to be able to sink my cock into her flesh.

"No," she breathes, rolling her hips and rubbing against my hand. "Not here." She pushes away, stumbling over her own feet, trying to put some distance between us. Her cheeks are blushed a faint red, and I bite back a laugh.

"Oh, fine," I grumble. "Well, let's get home, so we can get this going." She snaps her head in my direction, and this time, I let out my laughter. "I mean to get going with my healing. Well, and you. I want to finish what we've started here. On your end of course."

My heart turns to molten mush around my girl. I may not be able to have sex, but watching her react to my touch in all the best ways is satisfying enough. For six weeks, at least. Thank fuck it isn't forever.

"Okay." She walks toward me again with a smile.

Her phone pings in her pocket, and she pulls it free, reading a message on the screen.

"What is it?"

"Girls' chat." She holds her phone up. "They were asking if you'd been discharged yet."

"Oh."

"And to let me know they're finished."

"Finished with what?"

She scrunches her nose, then smiles. "I think they did a little welcome home decorating and what not. I believe Holt and Asher were dragged into it, too."

"Nice, but I'm surprised they convinced Holt into helping. Considering he's been a little quiet these past few days."

"I noticed that, too." She frowns. "Do you know what that's about?"

I shrug. "No. He's messaged to ask how I'm doing but otherwise hasn't said much. Maybe the other night fucked him up like the rest of us."

"Could be." She nods as she types out a quick reply, then drops her phone back into her pocket. "So, are you ready?"

She grabs my hands and helps me stand. I'm careful not to put too much pressure on my foot. She hands me the single crutch I'm supposed to use for the first two weeks of my six-week healing journey. I stick it under my armpit and lean on it.

"Are you good?" She hooks her arm under mine, and her eyes spread wide with worry. Her hand rests gently at my side, steadying me as though she thinks I might topple over at any moment.

I'm more than good.

I stare into her gray eyes, seeing every memory playing out in her mind. The bad. The good. The agony. The beauty.

I tuck her long, black hair behind her ear. "Have I ever told you how gorgeous you are?"

She rolls her eyes.

"I mean it, London." I lower my voice. "You aren't just gorgeous on the outside. Every inch of you is beautiful. Your soul. All of it."

Her bottom lip quivers as she sucks in a breath of air.

"You once told me that losing your memories felt like you were wandering in the darkness alone." I continue. "Losing you made me feel the same way. Regaining your memories brought you into the light. Finding you brought me out of my darkness."

My heart skips a beat, and I can't wait. I can't wait to give her the life I always promised her. I can't wait to live the rest of my life with London.

My girl. She's always been my girl.

I press my lips to her mouth before placing a kiss to her forehead, where I breathe her in, lingering for a few moments. Then I reluctantly pull away.

"Let's go home, Dimples."

THIRTY-FOUR

LONDON

The Next Day

"We don't have to do this today," West offers, grunting as he stabs the tip of his crutch onto the curb, lifting himself up and out of the car while trying to put as little pressure on his broken leg as possible.

I roll my eyes and hook my hand under his arm to steady him. "I know, my love."

His blue eyes shoot up. I've never called him that before, but I think I like the sound of it. So does West, apparently. His face lights up and he gives me that panty-melting grin I've fallen for a million times over.

We've spent nearly all our lives feeling like outsiders, navigating life alone, never belonging. Others have caused us pain, never allowing us into their worlds. But now we have friends that treat us like family, and we have each other.

West is the love of my life. He always has been. Ever since that day in the foster home, when he pressed his finger to my cheek. He's fought for me every second since, even when I had no memory of him.

"So, why are we here?" he asks, closing the car door behind

him. Alden moves around the front of the car and stands along the curb.

I don't bring myself to look at the lane where the bus hit Heath. I don't think I'm quite ready to look at it just yet.

"You gave me this idea last night," I tell him, turning to face The Veiled Door. "At dinner, when you were talking about how we didn't really get a chance to enjoy the reopening of this place."

We'd also talked about other things. Like how we know we want to get married someday soon, and how we want children of our own. Though not before looking into adopting a child from a foster home, giving them the life our adoptive parents gave us.

Talking about a future with West, unplagued by darkness, is a feeling I'll hold onto forever.

"I did?" West asks me.

"Yep." I cross my hands in front of me, fingering each of my rings, then I turn to face West. "The last time we were here, a nightmare unfolded. Our last memory of this place is dark and ugly. I want to take all that back. I want to walk through and look at what we created here."

"London..."

Tears sting the corners of my eyes as I turn back and look at the man I love. "Seeing the foster home in Albany brought back my memories. For years, that house held them captive until I faced it, forcing it to give them back. It brought me back to you." A tear slips from my eye, and I'm quick to wipe it away, my mouth lifting into a soft smile. "We deserve ownership of our memories, West. We deserve to give them a proper space where they belong, or else what's the point of it all?"

He doesn't speak a word.

I clear my throat, thinking back to the past two years of my life. "It wasn't just the house that held my memories hostage. It was Heath, too."

I've tried not to think about my ex-husband these past few days. While his death was tragic, it doesn't erase the pain he caused West and me. How he tried to kill us, lurking in the shadows, stalking us. My marriage to Heath was failed the moment I said, "*I do,*" and Heath was willing to do whatever it took to keep me, all the way down to his stupid fucking plan of faking his own death. He expected me to mourn him until the time was right to show me it was all an illusion to put off the threat he'd faced from the Irish mafia. The Irish fucking mafia.

West lifts his hand to my cheek, and I place mine over his. I feel his warmth wrap around me. "Heath's power came from making me feel as little as possible. He'd clipped my wings and made me feel like I couldn't survive without him. Maybe part of him was afraid that I would regain my memories if he gave me freedom... but it isn't like that with you." I move my hand to West's brow, where I trace the dark hairs arching over his blue eye. I study him like a painting I have yet to create. "You allow me to fly, West."

The corner of his mouth curls under his growing beard. I love that he's growing it out again. "Always." He leans in and presses his soft lips to mine.

I moan against it, pressing against West with my whole body. I grip his shirt, pulling him closer to me.

When he grunts against me, I pull away.

"I'm sorry." My eyes wander over his body, falling to his foot. "Did I hurt you?"

"No," he chuckles under his breath. "My ribs are still sensitive, but that just shows the affect you have on me, London Walker."

My stomach flutters. "Come on." I laugh, wrapping my hand around his bicep and turning on my heel to face the front of The Veiled Door. "Let's see this grand reopening the way we should have seen it last week."

ONCE WE STEP INSIDE, all our friends are gathered near the back of the bar. The group turns around, Julianna, Charleigh, and Selene lifting their arms enthusiastically in the air, shouting congratulations like we've stumbled into a surprise birthday party. We all laugh, and I keep my hand wrapped around West's thick bicep as we make our way over to join them, loving how they came here to show their support for us, ensuring we gain new memories of this place.

After grabbing a few drinks for ourselves, the group walks around the bar and looks at every piece of art I completed, even discussing the new pieces of furniture and flooring Lewis helped West pick out. The Veiled Door hasn't opened back up since the night of the reopening event, but seeing it the way it is now, eerily quiet and void of life, aside from our friends, I feel like not only are we ready to move on, but the bar is as well.

Decked out in a mix of black, gold, and rich, dark shades of green, it's the perfect homage to old town New York City and deserves to be celebrated.

I take a moment to listen as Julianna tells me about the new prank she's pulled on Rome, and Charleigh asks me to be her bridesmaid. I happily tell her yes, knowing there was no other answer I could have given her. Selene is mostly quiet. She doesn't mention her relationship with the date she brought to the reopening the other night. She's always held her relationships close to her chest that way.

Afterward, I find West talking with Holt behind the bar. Holt's expression is nearly vacant, and when I drag West away, I can't help but feeling like I interrupted a serious conversation. I decide not to pry or ask questions, though.

When we're finished walking around the bar, the group leaves the two of us to enjoy the place we've poured our work into the past several months. I tell West I'm going to pop in the bathroom before we head out ourselves, but when I step out, I hear him working his way up the stairs leading to the storage room.

My old workspace.

An ice-cold chill slithers down my spine. I round the corner to the base of the stairs to find West hopping from one step to the next. His crutch is propped under one arm while he grips the rail. The wood creaks beneath him, and when I look down at the steps, I'm thankful the splattered blood has been cleaned up. The memory of watching West and Heath tumbling down these stairs causes my stomach to sour.

"What are you doing?" I ask, rushing up the stairs to catch him.

But he's already made it to the top and is pushing through the door.

When I reach the landing, he's standing in the middle of the room, looking down at the pieces of crumpled-up parchment lying on the floor.

I clear my throat, my stomach suddenly performing somersaults. I cross the room and bend down to pick up my drawing. "These are..." I shake my head and begin to fold the papers.

"Wait," he says, placing his hand over mine, stopping me.

I slowly open them back up, and West takes them. The top paper is of his necklace, but he shifts them, revealing the drawing underneath. He ghosts his finger along the sketched lines of his own hand, recognizing each curve and line. I don't know why, but I feel nervous. Exposed and raw. They represent the most vulnerable parts of my brain.

Heath found this piece the other night, and West was too wrapped up in the chaos to focus on my drawing or the meaning.

His hands.

His necks bobs as he swallows, taking it in. "London..." My name tumbles out of his mouth, and my gaze drops.

We're suspended in time, letting the heaviness of this moment weigh down on us.

"When..." he chokes out, his voice thick with emotion. He clears his throat, then looks up at me with glassy, blue eyes. "When did you draw this?"

"This one?" I raise my eyebrows. My pulse is racing, but a blanket of comfort wraps its arms around my heart. "A few months ago, but it wasn't the first."

"It wasn't?"

I shake my head, biting on the inside of my cheek.

"How long?" he asks, searching my face for answers. "How long were you drawing my hands?"

I shrug, despite knowing the answer, and I look away, unable to tell him the full truth. It's amazing how my mind was trying to give me clues to my memories, using my art to help me remember. But in the end, it didn't matter.

I was drawing my memories of West without knowing they were him.

"Since I could start drawing again after the accident." A tear slips from my eye. "After I lost my memory of you."

"Hey," he hushes, resting his hand on his crutch. He uses his free hand to crane my head back up to face him, and I wrap mine around his, using him as an anchor. There's worry deep in his cobalt blue eyes. "Why are you crying?"

I blow a heavy breath through my lips. "I drew you for fifteen years, and I never remembered. How, when I our love is so strong? How could I have possibly forgotten you?"

The guilt and shame swells inside me, thinking back to that day at Coney Island. I'd looked right at him. He'd had hope in his eyes, holding his breath as he waited for me, but I gave him nothing. I forced him to walk away, heartbroken.

Realizing where I'm going, he drops my drawings on the floor and closes the small gap between us.

"My art didn't bring my memories back," I confess, my lip trembling. "My art didn't bring *you* back to me."

"No." He frowns, then traces his free finger against my soft cheek, pressing it into the space where he knows my dimple will form when I smile. The corner of his mouth lifts, despite my sadness. "It didn't bring you back to me."

I close my eyes, shame filling my gut. I shouldn't feel it, but I can't stop the torrent of waves coming. With how strong my love for West is, I still can't comprehend how easily he was stolen from my mind, and how it took this long to get him back. I'm caught up in my spiraling thoughts when he ghosts his thumb across my bottom lip, causing me to open my eyes again. This time, I'm looking directly into his that always bring me back.

"Your art didn't bring you back to me, London," he whispers. "It couldn't bring me back because I never left."

Emotion overtakes me, and I shudder in his grip.

"I've always been with you," he adds. "I love you, London, and I will give you the life you deserve. I will spend every minute reminding you that you are worthy of someone's love. I will always be your light when you feel lost in the dark. I will love the fucking hell out of you for the rest of our lives."

"I love you." My mouth pulls into a smile, and everything clicks into place.

I may have spent years trapped in the dark, but West has always been my light.

He was my past. He is my present. And now he's my future.

"You promised you would find me again, but you've always been here." I point to my temple, then I move his hand to my heart, placing my hand over his. "And here."

West leans in, letting his crutch clatter to the broken floorboards of the storage room, the memories of all the drawings I created in here alive and breathing in these four walls.

"I found you," West whispers against my mouth. "Now, I get to keep you."

He twists around and picks up a small piece of charcoal I'd left on one of the shelves. Rolls of toilet paper now cover the shelf, and I wonder, even after all these months and the clean up after Heath destroyed this room, how my piece of charcoal remained here.

Holding my left hand in his, West singles out my ring finger.

Tears build behind my eyes, and I look up at West. His gaze is gripped on me as he holds the tip of the charcoal to the end of my finger, just above my gold ring. He has the same look in his blue eyes as he did that day at the funeral when he'd written his phone number on the inside of my forearm.

"I know we talked about this last night, but I want to officially ask you." His voice drops, and heat pools in my belly as he drags the charcoal across my skin. He draws a thin line, then flicks his gaze back up. "Will you marry me, Dimples?"

I look down at my hand, at the ring he's drawn on me. I've never felt more at peace or more whole than I do today. I've barely nodded my head and uttered the word "Yes" when he wraps his hand around the back of my head and crashes his mouth against mine, sealing my answer to his.

"Yes," I breathe.

Then he kisses me like he knows he gets to kiss me this way forever.

And he does.

It seems my heart wasn't broken after all.

CAN'T GET ENOUGH **of West and London?**

Use this link to read a bonus chapter that includes some special surprise appearances! - https://dl.bookfunnel.com/5qluz i2ob6

WANT **to know more about Holt and his secret obsession with his sister's best friend, Selene? Not to mention what happens now that his enemy, Rome Montgomery, has just drawn a line in the sand between the Capuleti and Montgomery family feud?**

You can preorder Holt and Selene's Book Now!!! - http://mybook.to/fhwp

- "Wonderland (Taylor's Version) by Taylor Swift
- "Good News" by Shaboozey
- "Dancing in the Flames" by The Weeknd
- "Can't Let Go" by Will Swinton
- "Scared of Loving You" by Selena Gomez
- "I Will Follow You into the Dark" by Death Cab for Cutie
- "Pretty Slowly" by Benson Boone
- "Daylight" by Taylor Swift
- "Fade" by Lewis Capaldi
- "One of the girls" by The Weeknd
- This Love (Taylor's Version) by Taylor Swift
- 28 (with Dean Lewis) by Ruth B.
- "Think I'm In Love With You by Chris Stapleton
- "Physical" by Dua Lipa
- "It's All Coming Back" by Celine Dion
- "Hello Love" by Benson Boone

ACKNOWLEDGMENTS

The NYC Billionaires Series has been something I've been excited about for quite some time. When I set out to write this series, West and London's love story was the first that came to mind. Theirs was different than any I'd written before. Ex's brother. Foster home background. *Amnesia.* All tropes that spoke to me, crying out to have their story written. I think as I was writing West and London's love, I fell in *love* with their love. It's like West said, his love for London wasn't just measured in their time on earth... it would exist past their lifetimes. It was cosmic and infinite. The kind of love that could only be explained by quantum entanglement. *sigh* I sincerely hope you loved reading their story.

First and foremost, for this book, I need to acknowledge someone very important to me.

My step-mom. My *second* mom. Who had every reason to leave but chose to stay. You deserved only the best. And you deserved more. You deserved better. I hope you knew how much I loved you and appreciated the love you showed me over the years. Thank you for following through on the promise you made to my mom before she passed. Thank you for loving me as your own and for protecting me. I miss you every day.

And of course...

My husband, the love of my life. You're the only person I ever imagine doing life with and I couldn't be more in love with you than I am today. At least I don't think so. Our love is cosmically infinite.

My two boys, Jase and Connor. I love you both SO much and I hope you know I do all of this for you. You're the best boys I could have ever hoped for. I love being your mom.

To my assistant/alpha reader/best friend/proofreader/PR Team, April Pallett. Wow, April, it seems I keep adding more titles for you with every book I publish! You are absolutely incredible and sincerely... none of these books would be what they are if I didn't have your support and friendship. The time you put in to helping me achieve the success I desire is unmatched. I could probably write a whole book with how much you do for me and the ways I can't tell you enough of how much it means to me. Thank you and I love youuuu!

Major shoutout to my agent, Nikki Groom. For all your support and encouragement. I'm truly grateful to always have your back.

My editor, Vicki James. I know, I know. This one was rough. *insert the nervous face emoji* But I can't thank you enough for your work and dedication to West and London's story, not to mention your honesty. Thank you for loving my work and wanting it to be the best it can be. My appreciation for you is immeasurable!

My designer Amanda for always creating beautiful works of arts with your covers and graphics. I love you.

My beta readers Amy and Lori. As always, I appreciate your honest input and for help making my stories better.

To Lori Keenom for helping run my reader group and building up my community.

And to every single book blogger, bookstagrammer, booktoker, and reviewer. I know authors always say we wouldn't be able to do what we do without you. But it's absolutely true. Every share and every word of encouragement is LITERALLY what keeps me going some days. I've met some incredible new friends in the book community since the start of this series and

your love has made the harder days a little easier to tackle. So
THANK YOU!

And to you the reader. Thank you for loving love stories as much as me. I hope you enjoyed reading this one and are looking forward to the next. Love to you all!

NYC Billionaires

From Asher, With Love

Harding Brothers Series

Gorgeous Lies

Sweet Nothings

Pretty Heartache

The Heartbreak Series

The Rules of Heartbreak

The Secrets to Heartbreak

The Troubles with Heartbreak

Standalones

See Through

Paper Hearts

The Wrong Pitch

What are the Chances

The Back to Me Series

Dissipate

Mine

Back to Me

ABOUT BRITTANY

Brittany Taylor grew up all over the world including places such as California and England. Her love of reading started at a young age. Finally deciding to fulfill her lifelong dream, she took the plunge into the writing world and published her first book when she was twenty-eight. Today she resides in Maine with her husband, two sons, two cats and one dog.

www.brittanytaylorbooks.com